KIT McBRIDE GETS A WIFE

Kit McBride

GETS A WIFE

AMY BARRY

JOVE
NEW YORK

A JOVE BOOK
Published by Berkley
An imprint of Penguin Random House LLC
penguinrandomhouse.com

Library of Congress Cataloging-in-Publication Data

Names: Barry, Amy, author.
Title: Kit Mcbride gets a wife / Amy Barry.
Description: First edition. | New York: Jove, 2022.
Identifiers: LCCN 2022001078 (print) | LCCN 2022001079 (ebook) |
ISBN 9780593335574 (trade paperback) | ISBN 9780593335581 (ebook)
Subjects: LCGFT: Romance fiction. | Western fiction. | Novels.
Classification: LCC PR9619.4.B3746 K58 2022 (print) |
LCC PR9619.4.B3746 (ebook) | DDC 823/.92—dc23/eng/20220211
LC record available at https://lccn.loc.gov/2022001078
LC ebook record available at https://lccn.loc.gov/2022001079

First Edition: August 2022

Printed in the United States of America
1st Printing

Book design by George Towne

For my brother,
who is both littler and bigger than me.
I love you, G.

One

Well, spit. How was Junebug to know flour was flammable? It was *flour.* You cooked the stuff, for Pete's sake. It wasn't gunpowder. Only somehow that great big sack of flour had blown the belly out of the cookhouse, she marveled as she watched her older brothers try to save the outbuilding.

"You could have killed yourself!" Morgan raged as he threw buckets of creek water at the snapping flames.

She *was* rather singed. And her rear end sure did hurt from where she'd landed in the woodpile. But she was fine. And what a thing to see. All that flour floating about in the air and then *wham*, no cookhouse.

"You ought to be tarred and feathered for this," Beau grumped, sloshing water on Junebug's bare feet as he jogged up from the creek.

"Well, *spit*," Junebug said, "it ain't like I set fire to the cook-house on purpose. Not this time *or* the last time." If this was any-one's fault, it was Morgan's. He'd been the one to dump that great big sack of flour in front of her and shut her up in the cookhouse to bake, rather than let her go fishing. If it had been up to *her*, she'd be stretched out in the meadow, pulling a few fat bull trout from the creek, and their cookhouse would still be standing. But no, *Morgan* had to go force her into an apron and lock her in the dark little hut for the afternoon. If anyone was to blame for this, it was definitely him. Not that she was game to tell him that yet; she'd wait till he cooled off some. She'd at least wait until the fire was out. Morgan was worse than a grizzly coming out of hibernation when he was in a mood. And he was pretty much always in a mood.

"How do you burn a *stove* down?" Jonah asked as they watched the remains of the cookhouse smolder. "Surely the whole point of a stove is that it's fireproof."

"Junebug could burn down hell itself," Kit sighed. He and Morgan had that mountainous look they got when she was in trouble. They went all immovable and stony, and she knew there was no way around them.

"It wasn't my *fault*," she reminded them.

"It never is." Morgan looked madder than usual.

"But this time it *really* wasn't."

They weren't listening. They never did. Not for the first time, Junebug wished she had a sister. A proper live one. Technically she had three of them, but they were all bundled up under the choke-cherry tree, no use to her at all. *Sleeping with the angels* was written on their gravestones, but Junebug never believed it. Why would you sleep if you got to see angels? No, she was certain those three little girls were having a time of it, flying about, instead of being here to help Junebug deal with their brothers. And she sure did need some help.

With the cooking, for a start. Those four could eat more than a herd of buffalo. And they were fussy as hell, always complaining that she'd burned this, or put too much salt in that. Where was it written that she knew how to cook just because she was a girl? Nowhere, that was where. And she *hated* cooking. Almost as much as she hated doing their laundry, and she hated *that* something fierce. Those boys *stank*. After winter, their long underwear was fit for burning rather than cleaning. And did they thank her when she took the trouble to burn it? No. Morgan just shouted at her about the cost of new underwear.

"They were *unwashable*," she'd tried to explain, but that had been another prime example of a time when he didn't listen to her.

"Don't just stand there." Kit thrust a pail at Junebug. "You made this mess; you help clean it up."

Junebug followed him down to the creek. "I told you, it was Morgan's fault."

"You're just lucky we were smart enough to build the cook-house close to the water and away from the woods. The last thing we need is a wildfire." Kit scooped up creek water.

"It was *my* idea to build it close to the water," she reminded him, filling her own pail. "So I wouldn't have to haul water so far."

"I swear, Junebug, you're as lazy as a house cat."

"*Lazy!*" Oh, Junebug could have dumped the whole pail over his head, and she would have if he wasn't already halfway back to the smoking cookhouse. Lazy! She did nothing *but* work. She scrubbed and cooked and mended and fed the animals and gathered eggs and did the work of seven women. At least. Maybe *ten* women.

But did they give her any credit?

No!

Instead, it was *you can't pick blackberries, you have to milk the cow; you can't go wandering, you have to darn some stinky socks; you can't go fishing, you have to bake bread with all this stupid flour.* And when Morgan's deadly flour blew itself up, it was somehow *her* fault. And she was also to blame for how slow they were to put out the fire.

Well, she wasn't taking that.

"No!" Kit said flatly as she stalked up behind him. "I don't want to hear it."

"But—"

"*No*." He kept his back turned on her, like she was nothing more than an irritating mayfly. "You know the rule. You got something to say to me, you write it in your book," Kit told her shortly.

"I will," she promised his great big slab of a retreating back. "You just wait."

As soon as the fire was out and Morgan was done growling at her, she marched straight down to the trading post. It was a ramshackle log building down by the creek, older and more substantial than the cabin they lived in. The trading post was the chief reason the McBrides were in Buck's Creek at all; their father had been sure he'd make his fortune trading with the trappers, and with the Nez Percé, Blackfeet, Bitterroot Salish and Crow, who took a well-established trade route right through the mountains. The McBrides' wide mountain meadow was a pleasant camp spot for travelers, with fresh flowing water and abundant game. And it did good business in fair-weather years. Good enough that the McBrides had settled in, building a cabin farther upriver, on the rise near the tree line, and a barn and forge. In the beginning Junebug's pa had dreams of Buck's Creek being a proper town, but it was too high up and got snowed in through the heart of winter. Instead, the town of Bitterroot sprang up four hours down the mountain, just far enough away to be wretchedly inconvenient, in Junebug's book.

Junebug loved the trading post and would have spent all day, every day working there, rather than cooking and laundering and being the general workhorse that she was. Interesting people blew into the trading post—you never knew who you'd meet. Or what they'd bring with them. Once she'd almost taken possession of a stuffed beaver from a man named Garneau; the beaver was marvelous, frozen in a look of perpetual surprise, its mouth open, showing its two jutting teeth. But the best thing of all was that Garneau had dressed the beaver up like a gunslinger. It had a little bandolier around its beaver chest, and a cowboy hat perched on its beaver head. And it even held a gun, carved out of aspen and painted to look just about real. It was the darnedest thing. Junebug would have bought it for sure, if only her brothers hadn't been right there, complaining about how Garneau had ruined a perfectly good beaver skin. Someone, somewhere, now had the pleasure of that beaver, and her brothers had never recognized how nearsighted they'd been. They just didn't know a good thing when they saw it.

As she reached the trading post, Junebug climbed over Thunderhead Bill's snoring body and headed inside, yanking her book off the shelf on her way past. She reached for the inkpot and sent splatters of ink across the page as she scrawled her complaints into the book. She stumbled a little over the word *irascible* and eventually crossed it out and wrote *blockheaded* instead.

Kit didn't take complaints in any form except written. He'd laid down the law on that when she was knee-high, and had even taught her to write so she could follow through. He stocked up on ledgers when he went to town, and made sure she had ink. All that trouble just so he wouldn't have to listen to her moan. Junebug was supposed to put her complaints in the book, and he was supposed to read them after she'd gone to bed. Every day she'd check the book after breakfast, only to find he'd gone through and corrected her spelling. Now and then he bothered to write a response to her complaint. Usually listing all the ways in which she had things upside down and backward, which she didn't appreciate. It was an unsatisfactory arrangement, to say the least. But if it weren't for the book, he'd get away without ever getting a piece of her mind. So at least it was *something*.

As she wrote, Junebug was dimly aware of Roy and Sour Eagle sidling up to the counter. She heard the rustle of newspaper as Sour Eagle folded his old reading paper away and tucked it under his arm. Their companion Thunderhead Bill was still snoring out on the porch. The three old trappers had blown in with the last storm of winter and hadn't seen fit to leave yet. They'd taken a shine to sitting around the porch of the McBrides' trading post all day, gossiping like old women. Not that Junebug knew any old women, but Morgan said they were just like 'em, and Morgan wasn't prone to falsehoods.

"Whatcha writing there?" Roy asked.

Junebug ignored him. She didn't like Roy in the slightest. He was uncouth. Not that Junebug was quite sure what *couth* was, but whatever it was, Roy wasn't it.

"That your complaints book?" Sour Eagle prodded, although he knew perfectly well that it was.

Junebug liked Sour Eagle a sight more than she liked Roy. He was dignified and gentlemanly in his ways. Sweet too. What's more, he told some mean war stories, complete with all the details Morgan said she was too young for. "It is," she agreed, slamming it shut, "and it's just between me and Kit. It ain't for the likes of you. Why, it'd sear your eyes right out of your sockets, the fury in those words."

Sour Eagle respected the power of words. He gave her an understanding look. "You burn the cookhouse down again?"

"It was Morgan's fault." She put the book back where it belonged. No one would dare touch it. Not when there'd be Kit to face if they did. Why, Kit had scared the wits out of Roy just yesterday when Roy had tried to put his hand in the jar of sweet strap candy without paying for it first. Junebug had never seen a grown man cry before. Roy had honked like a goose, his face all red and scrunched up, and Kit hadn't even touched him. Just the idea of Kit's anvil fists had been enough.

"Junebug, are you still in the letter-writing business?" Sour Eagle asked, tactfully changing the subject away from the fire as he watched her rub the wet ink from her palms onto her overalls.

"Well, spit, you know I am."

"Roy here needs a letter writ."

Junebug narrowed her eyes and looked Roy up and down. "He does, does he? Can he pay?" She didn't believe a man like Roy Duncan had a cent to his name. Or that he had anybody to write to. Although she supposed every man had a mother. She'd had a ma, too, once, although her ma was out of mail reach now; Junebug would have given anything to be able to write Ma a letter and tell her how these boys were using her up with chores. Her gaze drifted to the open door and the fenced-off plot by the slow-moving creek. The cross that marked her ma's grave was leaning toward the creek in that wonky old way that it had. What good did a dead ma and three dead sisters do her, she thought, feeling a stab of bleakest misery. Couldn't there be *one* woman to help her?

Junebug had been nine when her mother died. Old enough to remember her, although her memories were bitsy and jagged, like clay smashings after you'd dropped a pot. Just lots of bits of broken clay that couldn't carry water no more. That had been a fearful bad year, the year Ma died. First Maybud had died, and then Ma. And Ma hadn't gone easy. She'd moaned and sweat and scared the wits out of Junebug with all the noises she made in the night. After she died, the boys had buried her next to Maybud and the other girls under the chokecherry tree. Pa must have helped, but Junebug didn't remember it; she didn't remember much of Pa at all. The thick minty smell of his chewing tobacco, the sound of him cracking his knuckles, the way he'd drawl, *Well, now* . . . when you asked him a question he didn't want to answer. That was about it. He'd run off not long after Junebug's ma went under the chokecherry tree. And the less said about that, the better; Pa was a touchy subject around here.

Junebug didn't wish Pa back, but she sure as hell wished Ma and those girls back.

And it wasn't just about the chores. Sometimes she got so lonely—

"I got money," Roy said bullishly, interrupting her thoughts.

Spit. There was no use wishing for what couldn't be.

"I *do*," Roy insisted, his nose all out of joint as he took her silence for disbelief. "Honestly earned."

Junebug fixed him with a calculating look. She reached under the counter and pulled out her sign: "Junebug McBride, Public Letter Writer." "I charge twenty-five cents a page," she told Roy sternly, "and I require payment in advance."

"Is she worth it?" Roy asked Sour Eagle suspiciously. "I cain't be paying for no substandard letter, not in this circumstance."

Junebug took offense at that. "I'll have you know that you cain't find better in these parts. I'm *loquacious*."

Roy blinked. She assumed he had no idea what *loquacious* meant. She wasn't too sure herself, but it was a word Kit used to describe her letters, and it sounded plenty fancy. One of these days she'd get around to looking it up in the dictionary.

"You'd have to be the best," Roy said as he fussed in his pockets, "you're the *only*."

Junebug took in the summer grasses and the shine of the creek through the open door behind the trappers. Beyond the broad meadow the highest peaks of the mountains rose, still snowy tipped, even in the middle of August. There wasn't another homestead for miles, and Bitterroot, the closest town, was a four-hour ride down the mountain. She *was* the only. The only girl on a mountain of men. It was enough to make you want to scream. "You want this letter or not?" Junebug had half a mind to refuse Roy's business if he was going to get lippy with her, and her thoughts had her all out of sorts anyway.

"Sure, I want it." Roy brandished a sweaty handful of coins.

"This a long letter or a short one?" Junebug reached for the paper. She loved writing a good letter.

"Short. I ain't paying for extra words, you hear? I just want to answer the advertisement."

"Advertisement?" Junebug slapped the paper down on the counter and climbed up onto the stool. She peered down at Roy, enjoying the height the tall stool offered. She leaned forward on her elbows. "What advertisement?"

"This one!" Sour Eagle untucked the newspaper from under his arm and unfolded it. He spread it out on the counter.

From where Junebug sat it was all upside down. She turned it around. The *Matrimonial News*. Junebug had never heard of it. She'd seen scraps from various papers as trappers and travelers passed through. Usually the papers were woefully out-of-date, but she sure did like some of the illustrations. She hoped Sour Eagle's paper had some illustrations. Maybe he'd let her have a look once they were done with all the letter writing. Sometimes she got to keep a page or two. Up at the cabin she had pages from papers like the *Chicago Daily Tribune*, which Kit told her was in Illinois (she didn't really know where Illinois was, but she liked the sound of it), and the *Lynchburg Virginian* from Virginia (which was nowhere near here). She also had part of a copy of the *Iron County Register* from Missouri, and even a page from the *Sun*, all the way from New York. Once a trapper had left behind most of a *Wichita Daily Eagle* and, another time, she'd found a few pages of the *Yorkville Enquirer* from South Carolina. And the last time Kit had taken her to town, Junebug had talked him into buying a copy of the *Dillon Tribune*, which was printed all the way over in Beaverhead. That was out-of-date, too, but not by as much as her other papers. Junebug liked thumbing through the ratty pages, reading about places so far off they might as well be on the moon.

The *Yorkville Enquirer* even had a column advertising a circus. It was a double show, with six lady performers and five clowns; the circus had come to Yorkville on April 16, in the year before Junebug was born. There were four little pictures down the side of the column, of people doing tricks while standing on the backs of horses. The horses looked frisky. Junebug would have given anything to see those lady performers and horses. But Buck's Creek was a long way from Yorkville and was unlikely to see a circus in Junebug's lifetime. South Carolina must be quite a place . . . maybe one day she could go see it for herself. Until then, she'd find out more about this Matrimonial place. Maybe they had circuses there too.

Only, as she looked at the newspaper, she found it wasn't like any newspaper she'd seen before. It was nothing but advertisements. And they were all advertisements for *people* . . .

"What is this?" she asked suspiciously.

"The *Matrimonial News*." Roy wrestled the paper off the counter, tugging it out of Junebug's grip. "I'm looking to get a wife."

"A wife!" Junebug was genuinely shocked. *"You?"*

"Why not?" He jutted his chin at her, looking about as obstinate as the cow got when Junebug tried to milk her. "Why shouldn't I have a wife?"

Junebug didn't even know where to begin. His smell? His looks? The fact that he was currently living on a *porch*? And it wasn't even *his* porch.

"I had wives once," Sour Eagle sighed. "Before the buffalo were all killed."

"You can have more than one?" That set Junebug's mind working. There was a staccato snorting from the front porch.

"Looks like Bill's waking up."

"Here." Roy folded the newspaper in half and shoved it at Junebug. His finger tapped a small rectangle of print. "That one."

Young lady of blond type, with no fortune save a warm heart. Any gentleman who might appreciate these meager qualities will find a devoted wife.

"What's *blond type*?" Junebug asked curiously.

"Yeller hair."

"I know what *blond* is." She rolled her eyes. "It's the *type* I want to know about."

"White?" Sour Eagle suggested.

"Where's the coffee?" Thunderhead Bill entered in his usual blustering way, rumpled from his nap. His hat was askew.

"No coffee," Junebug said shortly, her attention still on the paper. "Some of these others have done a better job of it than the blond type. I don't trust her brevity."

"What's *brevity*?"

"She's skimpy on the detail."

"What do you mean, no coffee?" Thunderhead Bill was outraged. He'd become accustomed to a pot being available after his nap.

Junebug ignored him. "This woman won't hear of a man who doesn't have good moral character, and this one wants a man who practices sober living. And *this* one wants business acumen in a husband; age and looks not important. Why doesn't your blond type specify anything like that? I don't trust it."

"Did you burn the cookhouse down again, is that why there's no coffee?"

Junebug glared at Thunderhead Bill over the paper.

"She doesn't specify anything because she's desperate," Roy told Junebug cheerfully. "And that's the girl for me."

Thunderhead Bill pulled his hat from his head in disgust. His wild gray hair sprung up like a grizzled old lion's mane. "I go to sleep for a few minutes and everyone loses their wits. What's happening here that's more important than coffee?"

"You were asleep for more than two hours," Junebug told him. "And we got our wits in hand just fine, thank you. We're finding Roy a wife."

Roy's narrow eyes got narrower. He sure did look like a muskrat. Junebug was none too fond of muskrats since one had eaten her pet frog.

"You ain't finding me anything," Roy sniped. "*I* found her. You're just writing the letter."

"You're being hasty," Junebug assured him. "You don't know anything about her. She could be a poisoner like that lady in Boston."

"What lady in Boston?"

"The one that poisoned her husband and took his farm."

"I ain't got a farm to take."

"There are no farms in Boston," Thunderhead Bill rumbled, gearing up for one of his lectures. "Boston is a civilized place. Who told you such nonsense?"

"You did." That shut him up. Junebug opened the newspaper. "What about this one: *Widow of robust temperament and no debt seeks man of good health*? You're healthy enough. You sure eat like a horse. And I reckon your wife's going to need a bit of robustness to cope with you."

"I like yeller hair," Roy said sullenly.

"Yeller hair ain't good for nothing. What you need is a woman who doesn't mind living on a porch."

Roy sent Thunderhead Bill a searching look. "You explain what yeller hair is good for, will you, Bill? I ain't got the stomach to tell her about the set of a man's needs."

Thunderhead Bill was more than happy to oblige. "Now, Junebug, being of the female persuasion—"

"Persuasion!" she snorted. "Ain't nothing persuasive about it, that I can see. No one listens to females, at least not around here."

Sour Eagle leaned forward sympathetically. "Maybe not when you're a slip of a girl. But one day you'll be grown, and I reckon you'll be right persuasive."

"I ain't a slip of anything, and don't you make the mistake of thinking so. What about this one: *Lady looking to escape the city for a country life*? This is about as country as it gets."

"Being of the female persuasion"—Thunderhead Bill picked up right where he'd left off, like she hadn't even spoken—"you're un- aware of the myriad charms women hold for men."

Myriad. Thunderhead Bill could be a tiresome old windbag, but he sure did know some pretty words. "Myriad . . ." She tried it on her own tongue. It sounded sparkly, like sun on the creek. "How do you spell that?"

But Thunderhead Bill was too busy talking to listen. "And yeller hair is a significant charm. As is a plump cheek—"

"And a plump everything else," Roy crowed.

"You like them fat?" Junebug scoured the advertisements, looking for plumpness.

"Not fat—"

Sour Eagle interrupted. "She's just a kid. None of that."

Junebug looked up, pricked. She didn't like being left out of things. "None of what? What's not fat?"

"Forget the fat, it's not about that. It's about wiles," Roy insisted. "Tell her about feminine wiles, too, Bill," he prodded.

Oh, that sure set him off. Turned out Thunderhead Bill knew a *lot* about feminine wiles, and this time he didn't hold back, slip of a girl or not. Junebug sat, riveted, as he recited all the ways a woman could make a man daft. Sometimes with just a look. Sometimes by *not* looking at him. He told of a woman in Cincinnati who had once struck him dumb just by wearing a frilly dress. *Off the shoulder.* Junebug glanced down at her own shoulder. Who knew? And then Sour Eagle weighed in with a story about a woman's laugh shivering like a cascade of rainfall over rocks.

"When I touched my first wife, it was like I'd captured sparks from the campfire in my bare hand," he said dreamily.

Were they making fun? Junebug's hackles went up. She didn't like being made fun of. "Have you been at the moonshine?" she asked tersely.

"She had a way of looking sideways at me . . ."

He didn't seem to be making fun. He looked like he'd been kicked in the head by a horse; his eyes had gone all far away and unfocused.

"Oh, the looks they give a man . . ." Thunderhead Bill seemed to have been kicked by the same horse. "Sideways, darting, up through the curl of lashes; glancing looks, deep stares, right into a man's soul . . . A woman can cast a spell on a man," Thunderhead Bill sighed, lost in memory.

"A whore once looked straight at me as I was—" Roy yelped as the palm of Sour Eagle's hand came down hard on his head.

"Not in front of the kid."

"You're saying a woman can make you lose your wits just by *looking* at you?" Junebug didn't believe it.

"A *grown* woman," Sour Eagle amended. "They have to be grown or it doesn't work." He slapped Roy again when the muskrat went to speak. "Grown," Sour Eagle repeated. "Ain't that right, Roy?"

"Yeah, that's right," Roy muttered, rubbing his sore head.

"And yeller hair makes you witless?" Junebug considered Roy. "More witless than you already are . . ."

"Yeller hair makes me . . ." Roy searched for a word, inching out of Sour Eagle's reach. "*Wild.*"

Huh. "And you *want* a wife to make you wild? You don't want someone who can bake a perfect peach pie? Because this one here says her peach pie's the best in Georgia." She heard Sour Eagle slap Roy again, even though he hadn't said anything. "Fine. It's your life." She dipped the nib in the ink. "What do you want to say in your letter?"

"*Dear . . .*" She glanced at the number on the advertisement. "*Dear Miss 179 . . .*" Junebug waited patiently for Roy to dictate his letter.

"What do I say?" he asked, sounding a bit panicked.

"Start with a compliment," Thunderhead Bill suggested.

"But I ain't met her!"

"Say something about her good heart."

"Warm heart," Junebug corrected.

"Tell her I like that bit," Roy instructed. "Tell her I'm partial to a warm heart. And to yeller hair. Mention the yeller hair."

"You should probably tell her about you too," Junebug suggested.

"Tell her I'm good-looking."

"I ain't in the business of lying."

"Handsome, then."

"I ain't writing that neither."

Roy scowled at her.

"What word could you use, in good conscience?" Sour Eagle asked, trying to head off an argument.

Junebug considered her options. Roy was a paying customer; he deserved an assiduous response. "I'll get the dictionary." She was off the stool and out the door before they could protest.

When she got to the forge, Kit wasn't pleased to see her. Junebug blamed his perpetual grumpiness on his place of work. It was *hot* in there, especially in August. And this August had been a baking one. Dry as a cow run out of milk. The forge was hotter and nastier than ever. Kit was stripped to the waist, his hair soaked through with sweat, his thick, dark eyebrows drawn together irritably. "What do you want?" He was hammering a new stove, for the new cookhouse. From the violence in his blows, Junebug guessed he wasn't happy about it. The muscles in his arms bulged and flexed, and the clang of hammer on iron just about split Junebug's head in two.

"I need the dictionary." Kit kept all the books in an old trunk in the corner of the forge. Kit had a thing for books. And he had a thing for no one else touching them.

"Why?" He paused to glower as she got her paws on his books.

"I'm letter writing." The dictionary was the only book she was allowed to borrow, and she had to have a good reason for borrowing it. Sometimes he let her sit in the corner and read, but she wasn't much for the indoors. It had to be a pretty miserable day out for her to be happy closed up with a book.

Kit scowled. "You're supposed to ring the bell when travelers come to the trading post. You ain't supposed to serve them by yourself. It's not safe."

"It's not travelers." Junebug yanked the dictionary free from the trunk. "It's just for old Roy."

"He's got someone to write to?" Kit sounded surprised. He paused and watched as she headed for the door. "I don't like you being alone with him."

"I ain't alone. Sour Eagle's there. And Thunderhead Bill." She left before he could make trouble. And she knew he would. Kit was like a rain cloud on a sunny day; he ruined all her fun.

And writing this letter was *a lot* of fun. Without it she'd never have learned about womanly wiles. Or whores. She looked up *whore* in the dictionary. It led her to the words *venal*, *debauched*, and *promiscuous*. It was shaping up to be a *very* interesting day.

When she got back, she found Thunderhead Bill had helped Roy craft a response to the ad without her. "Write it down!" Thunderhead Bill said loftily, tapping the empty page.

"But none of that is true," she said, aghast as she read it back to them. *"Bachelor of means? World traveler?* You're selling some poor girl a false bill of goods!"

"I've got twenty-three dollars to my name, that's *means*," Roy said stubbornly.

"And Roy has spent his whole life traveling this great world of ours," Thunderhead Bill boomed. He seemed inordinately pleased with himself.

"He has?"

"I've been to Billings *and* to Butte."

Junebug rolled her eyes, even though she hadn't been to either. The only place she'd ever been, other than here, was down the hill to Bitterroot. And Bitterroot was only a scratch of a place, even if it was prideful about getting a spur on the rail line.

"What's all this?"

Roy honked in surprise at the growl of Kit's voice from the

doorway. Junebug's rain cloud of an older brother was showing up right on cue, just in time to splash down on all her fun. He hadn't bothered to put his shirt on before he followed her down to the trading post, and he was still all flushed and shiny from the heat of the forge. The sight of all those muscles had Roy shrinking back against the counter.

"Business," Junebug informed him. "I told you, I'm letter writing." She flipped open the dictionary, hunting for words that might do Roy justice, without leading some poor yeller-haired girl astray. She hoped Kit would do his terrorizing quickly and get back to the forge. She had work to do.

"What did I tell you?" Kit scowled at the trappers.

"Pay for the strap candy before you put the hand in the jar," Roy honked.

Junebug's second-oldest brother crossed his arms, as formidable as a mountain. "Junebug's in the trading post. So where are you supposed to be?"

"Not in the trading post." Roy skittered toward the door, looking more like a muskrat by the minute. Kit didn't move out of his way. Roy was left hovering and twitching in his shadow. Kit's inky gaze pinned him to the spot. Junebug could practically hear Roy's knees knocking.

"You three aren't to pass this threshold when she's here alone. And yet here you are . . ."

"I just needed a letter writ . . ."

"You're not to go within ten feet of her."

"Now, Kit," Thunderhead Bill said cheerfully, "you know we'd never harm a hair on her head."

"I don't know any such thing. You're a bunch of miscreants."

Oh, that was a good word. Junebug looked it up.

"I don't think that's quite right," she told her brother, reading out the definition. "I don't reckon they could summon enough energy for villainy. They're more like *varmints*."

Kit had the good grace to take that under consideration. "You're a bunch of varmints," he amended. "And you're not to step foot in this place when my sister's here."

"How are we supposed to trade or purchase under those conditions?" Thunderhead Bill affected a disgruntled countenance. But mostly for the sake of an afternoon's entertainment. Things could get a bit monotonous in Buck's Creek, a town with a population of five, and all of them McBrides. "It seems a strange way to do business, to have a trading post a man cain't trade in."

"You ain't trading, you're yapping."

"I traded that beaver that time."

"And we'll take your next beaver, too, but you're to do your trading when one of us is manning the post, not when Junebug is here alone."

"I just wanted a letter writ," Roy said pleadingly, "and you see her sign, she's in the business."

"This is serious business too," Thunderhead Bill assured Kit. "Roy here is getting himself a wife."

Kit's thick black eyebrows went shooting up his sweaty forehead. "A wife! Now what in hell do you need a wife for?"

Roy took plain offense at that. "And why wouldn't I need a wife? A man's entitled to a wife, isn't he?"

"Is he?" Junebug asked, surprised. "Why?"

"To care for him," Sour Eagle told her. "Every man needs a wife."

Junebug looked up *wife* in the dictionary as Kit herded the trappers out onto the porch. It wasn't a very interesting word. But now Sour Eagle had got her thinking about men needing wives. Wives cooked, didn't they? Most probably without blowing up the flour. And they cleaned, and sewed, and hauled bathwater and the like. Every man needed a wife to care for him . . . and maybe Junebug could use some caring for too.

"You can stand out on the porch and talk to her through the open door. She can hear you from there." Kit was still busily ruining Junebug's afternoon.

"You're an inhospitable man, McBride," Thunderhead Bill told him gravely.

Kit closed the door in his face.

"Why did you have to say that?" Sour Eagle's voice came muffled through the door. "Now he won't bring us coffee and biscuits in the morning."

"And Junebug won't be writing my letter." Roy's voice was less muffled and a lot more spiteful.

"You're bad for business," Junebug told her brother. "This is no way to be writing a letter, with them all the way out there, on the other side of the door." Through the oilcloth over the window, she could see the shadows cast by the three trappers. She stalked over to the window and hauled it open. "How's this?" She read them back the letter she'd written.

They gathered close to the sill.

"What's *torpid* mean?" Roy asked suspiciously.

"It means you like sitting on porches."

He scowled at her. "I'm paying for this?"

"I can change it to *lackadaisical* if you prefer?"

"Will that cost extra? It sounds like an expensive word."

"You should thank me; I was going to say *impecunious*."

"Just write plain, for Pete's sake! I ain't made of money."

"Fine. How about this: *I'm a man who likes yellow hair and watching the sunset from the comfort of a porch. I hope you'd see fit to watch the sunsets with me.*"

"That makes it sound like he's staying," Kit warned from behind her. "He ain't welcome past summer."

"It doesn't say *which* porch."

"What other porch is there?"

"Maybe he'll build her one of her own." Junebug hazarded some optimism. "But if you're going to get ornery, I'll cross out the porch bit."

"How many words is that? Did we fill the page? I can only afford one page; don't go over," Roy said anxiously.

Junebug took a guess at how many words she could fit into the remaining space. "You got about twelve words to spare."

"You should use them, friend," Thunderhead Bill advised. "The page is twenty-five cents whether you use those words or not. No man wants to pay for unused words."

From the corner of her eye, Junebug saw Kit pick up the newspaper from where they'd left it on the counter. She heard him mutter under his breath.

"Twelve words," she mused, wondering how to make a muskrat into a viable marriage prospect. "Why don't we tell her about that bear you said you caught?" Junebug didn't believe he'd ever actually caught a bear, but he did own a fine bearskin, which was piled up out there on the porch. He slept on it, even on hot nights. He said it was softer than a feather mattress. Junebug wouldn't know—she'd never slept on a feather mattress; her mattress was full of dried meadow grass—but she was pretty impressed by that big black pelt.

"*Expert trapper*," Thunderhead Bill intoned, "*seeks frontier wife.*"

"Oh, that's good," Junebug agreed, "and, except for the *expert* bit, it ain't a lie."

"If you get this woman, which you won't, not with drivel like that, what in all that's holy are you going to do with her?" Kit snapped, throwing the newspaper back down. "Where's she going to keep house? You ain't got a house!"

"You should consider getting a bride yourself," Roy sniffed at Kit. "Junebug would sure appreciate the help around here."

"She sure would," Junebug said as she addressed the letter.

"Junebug don't need help," Kit grumped. "She just needs a bit of common sense. Now, give her the money and get along down to Bitterroot to post your nonsense. Junebug has a cookfire to build and dinner to start, and you're all keeping her from her chores."

Junebug watched the three trappers amble off along the creek, disappearing into the tangle of skunkbush sumac by the bend. They wouldn't be back tonight. By the time they got down to Bitterroot, it would be darkening, and they'd hit the saloon because the post office would be closed. They'd come back late tomorrow, all grizzly, with sore heads. Hopefully they'd have remembered to post Roy's letter. And maybe the yeller-haired female would turn up one day and join Roy out here on the porch, and Junebug would finally have the company of another girl. Junebug wondered what girls were like. The few women there were down in Bitterroot wore heavy-looking dresses, even in the hottest hours of the hottest summer days. Except for the girls at the cathouse, who sat on the porch in skimpy cotton, as pretty as flowering fleabane. But Junebug wasn't allowed to talk to them. Which was a blessed shame, as she bet they had a lot to tell.

"That cookfire won't get built by daydreaming," Kit warned. "And Morgan's in a sour enough mood as it is, without pricking him further."

"Oh, he's always sour. I cain't do anything right, so why try, Kit?" Junebug asked, surreptitiously swiping the *Matrimonial News* off the counter and trotting after him as he hiked back to the forge. "How come you ain't interested in a wife?"

Her older brother made a sound like he'd just swallowed a bee. He threw her a dark look. "A wife!"

"Yeah. A wife. A lady. A woman."

"What'd I want a woman for?" He sounded genuinely appalled.

Maybe Kit didn't know about womanly wiles. After all, he'd lived in the mountains his whole life, just as Junebug had. Maybe he didn't know women laughed like falling water and that their shoulders had magic qualities.

"To do chores, for a start," she sighed, not brave enough to bring shoulders into it just yet.

"That's what you're for," he said, disappearing into the forge.

Well, spit. It was just that kind of attitude that boiled her blood. She weren't no *wife*.

Junebug stewed over her situation as she cleared up the spot for a cookfire and hauled wood, and she was still stewing over it as they sat down to eat.

"I caught them trappers bothering Junebug again today," Kit announced over the burned hare that passed for supper. Well, the outside of the hare was burned. The inside was bloody and raw. When they complained, Junebug told them to shut up and be glad it was cooked at all.

The McBrides took their evening meal out in the meadow, around the snapping cookfire, as the long summer night fell lushly, purple and blue and smelling of creek water and grass and night-scented flowering stocks. The katydids were chirping away as a creamy yellow moon rose over the pines. Junebug liked eating out here a sight better than eating in their cabin, which smelled of sweaty brothers.

"I reckon it's time to tell them to move on," Morgan grunted. He was staring disconsolately at his plate of hare. Morgan loved his food, and he was endlessly depressed by Junebug's cooking.

"Move on!" Junebug was outraged. "You cain't move them on *now*, or Roy's yeller-haired girl will never find him."

Morgan, Beau and Jonah were nonplussed. Only Kit had any idea what she was talking about.

"Roy's gone and ordered himself a mail-order bride," he explained.

"Oh, for the love of . . ." Morgan swore under his breath.

Junebug tried to catch the words, but Morgan was good at keeping words from her. Not like the rest of them.

Jonah hooted. "Imagine if he gets one!"

"Imagine the look on the poor gal's face when she turns up to find *him*," Beau laughed. "She'll go running straight back down to catch the first train out from Bitterroot."

"Maybe. Or maybe *we* could keep her," Junebug suggested.

"What on earth would we do that for?" Morgan sounded horrified. "The last thing we need is another mouth to feed."

The problem with her brothers was that they were mountain men. They had no experience with ladies. Not one of them had been spellbound by a pair of shoulders or been struck speechless by a female fixing them with her gaze. They didn't know what they were missing . . .

And they'd never had a peach pie. Junebug was *sure* a peach pie would convince them, even if the wiles didn't.

"We'd do it for the cooking!" Junebug said, her thoughts whizzing about like lightning bugs. How to convince them to get a wife or two . . . or three, or four? "You all know I cain't cook for spit."

"You could if you'd take some care once in a while," Kit told her.

She didn't rise to the bait. She had bigger things on her mind than Kit's petty nagging. "A wife could cook for us. Why, I bet she'd cook hare pie, or something fancy."

They'd all stopped eating and were staring at her. Junebug had put her fork down long ago. She couldn't eat that atrocity. Why couldn't they see that it was unfair to *everyone* to make her cook?

"We don't need a wife for any of that," Morgan told her firmly. "We've got you. And I told you, we don't need another mouth to feed. We'll be lucky to get through the winter ahead as it is. Especially if we don't get another cookhouse built."

Junebug rolled her eyes. They'd have another cookhouse built before the week was out. And if Junebug had her way, she'd have a wife installed in there baking pies before next summer blossomed. Maybe she should gather chokecherries and dry them out, just in case they made good pie . . .

The fire popped and sent sparks dancing into the sky. *When I touched my first wife, it was like I'd captured sparks from the campfire in my bare hand.* She remembered that kicked-in-the-head look Sour Eagle had worn. What Junebug needed was some female to hand her brothers a bunch of sparks until they looked kicked in the head too . . . and then the female could go churn the butter and skim the milk.

Junebug had her heart set on a wife. Because things couldn't go on like this, with exploding cookhouses, and burned-raw hares, and this aching loneliness, which every day grew worse and worse and worse. She fell to sullen silence as her brothers piled up their plates for her to wash. They all took to lazing about as usual, leaving her to the evening chores. Junebug stomped down to the creek to gather water for the washtub.

A bobcat didn't tackle a black bear head-on, she reminded herself. Junebug's brothers might be bigger than her, but she was stealthy. She was also quicker, meaner and craftier, and she had less scruples. They didn't *think* they needed wives, but she knew better. She could place an ad on her own, and find the right woman on her own, and once the wife turned up, what were they going to do? Especially if she found the *right* wife. If she got an extra-wily one . . .

But which brother should she find a wife for first? Morgan was the oldest . . . but he was also the scariest. And stubborn beyond belief. It would take some pretty remarkable shoulders to win him over, and he probably wouldn't even give the poor woman a chance to show a shoulder before he sent her packing. Also . . . Junebug would probably find herself locked in the root cellar with nothing but bread and water for a month if she saddled Morgan with a surprise bride. He'd be a tough nut to crack, even for the wiliest of brides. No, Morgan was too difficult. She'd have to work up to him. Kit was the next oldest, so by rights she should probably find *him* a bride. Although Kit had a temper of his own . . . and a habit of making Junebug work in the forge with him when he wanted to punish her. Junebug hated the forge worse than she hated the cookhouse.

Beau might be better than Kit. Any bride would be thrilled to marry Beau. He was about as pretty as a man could be. But Junebug was still sore at Beau for snapping her best hickory fishing rod. Why should he get a wife to fawn all over him after that? He certainly didn't deserve pie. That left Jonah . . . but he was too young for the kind of woman Junebug was looking for. A wily woman would never be satisfied with a pup like Jonah. No, it would have to be Kit. He was the best of a bad bunch. She'd just have to make sure this wife knew what she was getting into, or the poor woman would turn tail and run the minute she laid eyes on him. He was just so . . . *big.*

Ladies didn't like big, did they? At least not judging by the mustachioed, barbered-looking men in the illustrations in the papers. Look at how Kit had hulked into the trading post today, half-naked and brooding. No lady would want that.

Well. Maybe Junebug needed to take every precaution that the wife was *expecting* a big, grouchy, bossy slab of a man so she didn't run straight back down the mountain when she got here.

Junebug sighed, watching the ripples cross the moonlit creek as she dipped her pail. There was no point in lying. The wife would get up the mountain and see him with her own two eyes. And maybe, just maybe, there was a lovely woman out there who was desperate enough to move to the mountains and live with Junebug's irascible blockheaded brother.

As the moon re-formed on the surface of the water, as whole and shiny as a new coin, Junebug fell to daydreaming of fancy ladies in frilly aprons, baking pies. They'd smell good, like melting sugar and apples, and they'd be kind and soft and give her gentle looks. When her brothers scolded her, the ladies would fix them with their gazes, and her stupid brothers would melt at their feet into useless puddles. And then the ladies would say, *There, there, Junebug, have some pie.*

Consequences and root cellars and working in the forge be damned, Junebug was going to do this. She deserved it.

She just hoped that the woman she found wouldn't mind a man who looked like the base of a mountain and never shaved. Or the fact that he was always sweaty and walking around without his shirt, because the forge was so hot.

But he worked hard; that was something. He could also be pretty funny, especially when he was torturing Beau. And he was the kindest of the lot of them.

Junebug just *knew* she could find herself and Kit a wife. And when it all worked out perfectly and her brothers were eating fresh-baked pies, they would admit what a brilliant idea she'd had, and they would regret how rude they had been. And then Beau would be begging Junebug to find him a bride too. And she'd have to let him down gently (or maybe not so gently) and tell him he'd have to wait his turn, because Morgan was next. But maybe if he got her a new hickory fishing rod, something could be done . . .

As soon as she'd finished her chores, Junebug took a lantern and skittered down to the trading post and took up her pen. She stared at a fresh sheet of paper. How to sell Kit?

There wasn't much point in selling some poor girl a false bill of goods. Not like Roy had tried to do with his yeller-haired gal. No, if she was going to do this, Junebug was going to tell the *truth.*

WANTED

Wife for a blacksmith. Do not expect doting,
nor compliments.
Must be willing to put up with judgment, nagging and
unreasonable expectations. Mustn't mind snoring,
cussing or a filthy morning temper.
Comes with a wealth of land.
Is not too old and not too ugly, has all his own teeth.
Added benefit of knowing myriad big words.
Lady must have charms and know how to use them.
Ability to complain in written form and bake pie essential.

Two

St. Louis, Missouri

Maddy Mooney had been born under an unlucky star. Possibly more than one. Nothing about America had turned out the way she'd expected. For a start, she'd never thought she would end up somewhere like St. Louis, with its belching factories and the heavy smell of slaughterhouses. She'd been promised wide-open spaces, rugged mountain ranges, the bounties of God's green earth. A new life. Opportunity. Instead, she'd chugged in on the Southwestern Limited from New York, on a swampy hot day in May, as rumpled and tired as a used dishcloth, only to find that St. Louis was filthy and smelly and not at all the fresh green Eden she'd been promised. It was a teeming, loud, brash city of breweries and paint factories, flour mills and brick kilns, tobacco processers and ironworks. It was nothing like God's green Eden, and nothing like back home.

Home.

Her mind reeled back to Ireland, like a big fat fish caught on a hook. The feeling of homesickness was so strong it was almost dyspeptic. Maddy hadn't bargained on homesickness like this. It had bitten her before she even got on the ship in Dublin. Venomous, a poison she carried with her all the way across the ocean. Every mile made the homesickness stronger. And it was ridiculous! Because . . . Jesus, Mary and Joseph, what home did she have to be sick for? She hadn't had a real home since she was a wee 'un. Not since the day Father Boylan had come to the house after her mam's funeral, rounding her and all the Mooney children up. He took them all away, like a black-cassocked Pied Piper. Maddy remembered the feel of her baby sister Jean's body in her arms as she carried the poor motherless girl for the last time. Some of the Mooney weans went to distant family, some to workhouses, and Maddy and the older ones were sent into service. Father Boylan had walked Maddy to Ormond House himself and handed her over to Mrs. Egan at the kitchen door. She'd not seen any of her brothers and sister since, and never would again. She didn't even know where poor little Jean had gone.

Maddy had spent all the years since that day in the flat-faced stone manor at the foot of the Slieve Bloom Mountains, scrubbing floors and polishing silver, working her way up from the scullery to a plum role as parlor maid. At night she trudged up the back stairs to the attic room she shared in the eaves with Roisin and Fiona, all of them too tired to talk. They got up before dawn, their narrow window showing nothing but darkness. As she worked, sometimes Maddy saw the mountains out of the vast manor windows, the carpets of bluebells in springtime and the misty flanks of the hillsides in winter. But mostly she looked down at her work.

What was there to be homesick for, when that was your life?

But it turned out you could still be homesick, even if you didn't have a home. You could miss the flat boggy land and that shade of spinach-emerald green that didn't seem to exist anywhere but in Ireland; you could miss the soft rain and the rise of the mountains, and the sound of the church bell on Sundays; you could miss Mrs. Egan's endless pots of tea, and the smell of her ginger biscuits hot from the oven. You could even miss blacking the fireplaces at

Ormond House. All forty-six of them. And Maddy had *hated* black-ing those fireplaces.

Why had she let Mrs. Egan talk her into something as daft as sailing all the way across the steely ocean, away from Ormond House, and toward a place like this?

It's a better life, it is, Mrs. Egan had promised her. The cook had been reading one of Roisin's letters aloud to the maids and foot-men as they sat at the table after a long day, the dishes done and the kitchen scrubbed shiny, a plate of biscuits and a pot of tea fill-ing them up before bed. *And her no better than a third maid before she went,* the cook had sighed, peering over the page at Maddy. *Imagine what a girl like you could do,* she'd prodded.

A girl like her. Orphaned, sent out into service, all alone in the world. A girl so stupid she'd fallen for the oldest trick in the book, and let herself be seduced . . . Oh, the disgrace of it. Every time Maddy thought of it her fists curled tight, fingernails biting blood-red crescents into her palms. She was naught but a filthy sin-ner. Every bit the base bog Irish people thought she was.

She was such an eejit. Every girl in service knew to keep herself tidy. Especially when it came to the men of the manor. But Thomas Ormond had seemed so *sincere.* So lovestruck. And even though she knew, deep down in her bones, that nothing good could come from it, she'd fallen under his spell. And Jesus, Mary and Joseph, it had been . . . *heaven.* For the brief season it had lasted, anyway . . . Afterward had been pure hell.

At least she hadn't found herself with a wean. That was a bless-ing. The kind of blessing that made you cry until your eyes swelled up and you looked like you'd been set on by wasps. All those weeks of fretting. What would she do? Give it away? Keep it? But how? How could she even get through the pregnancy? She'd be sent to the Magdalene Laundries, with all the other fallen girls. Her reputation would be shredded beyond all repair, and she'd never find a decent situation again.

She'd lost her wits, to risk everything. And for what?

For *heaven*. Because when Thomas Ormond had looked at her, she'd felt like anything but a parlor maid. She'd felt like a debutante, or a princess. A goddess. And when he'd kissed her . . . well, the sky had all but rained down on her head.

Eejit.

Because then it was over. And she was just a maid. A *used* maid. One who could count herself lucky not to find herself in the family way. And when Tom Ormond married in the summer, and he and his Right Honorable wife came to Ormond House to stay, Maddy was the one who had to pick his wife's clothes up off the floor and pull their stained sheets from the bed. And he never so much as looked at her. Not once. She wasn't anyone, and most certainly not a goddess. She was just a body in a black dress and a starched apron and cap, following in his wake, cleaning up after him. It took every inch of self-control not to cry. At least not until she was in bed at night . . . then she buried her head under the covers and cried until her face swelled up.

Maddy knew the other girls suspected. Mrs. Egan too. The cook had seen enough in her time to recognize the signs, and she knew the habits of Tom Ormond all too well. Maddy was keenly aware of the silent knowledge in the cook's stare when she suggested America. *A new life.*

Mrs. Egan had pushed Maddy to follow in Roisin's footsteps, hounding her with stories of easy living, opportunity, of a life that held more than long hours of cleaning, six and a half days a week. *Our Roisin married a merchant! She has a place of her own*, Mrs. Egan told her, *and that girl doesn't know a teapot from a chamber pot, bless her. Imagine! Mistress of her own house, with servants of her own!*

Maddy couldn't imagine. Roisin had been an uninspiring milky-looking girl, with watery blue eyes and a wavery voice.

You can have a life, pet. Mrs. Egan had patted Maddy on the cheek. A life.

She didn't really believe it. Lives weren't for the likes of her. The crowded room in the eaves that she shared with Fiona and Mary Frances (now that Roisin had left for the land of milk and honey and gold-paved streets) was for the likes of her. Broken nails and a sore back and dirty linen were for the likes of her. Half a day off to go to church, and sometimes an afternoon to go into town— that was for her. Not America, not a house of her own . . .

But Roisin's letters kept coming. And Thomas and his wife kept coming. And then his wife got fat with a wean, and his gaze started drifting to Maddy again. And Maddy's heart did the old slow turn in her chest, and she knew she was in trouble.

America.

Father Boylan wrote the letters for her and, before the year turned, she had a ticket. The whole thing moved like a storm over the bog, a great gray sliding force that dragged her along with it. The ship out from Dublin was filled with girls just like her: eager, petrified, all of them homesick. Girls from Meath, and Kildare, and Wicklow, freckled and with rough hands, each and every one of them dreaming of water-colored futures, rosy with hope, stiff with wariness. These girls knew a tide could turn, and fast.

In New York they were met by a host of nuns and a walnut-faced priest, who herded them along to the boardinghouse, where they were handed out assignments. Maddy's assignment read *Colonel and Mrs. Hiram Holt Lascalles, St. Louis, Missouri.* Maddy hadn't even known where Missouri was. Sister Ruth had shown her on a map, babbling a bundle of nonsense about "the Gateway to the West" and "God's great Eden." Imagine Maddy's shock when the train pulled into a coal-stained port city, with its brick chimneys spewing filth and its waterways clogged with shipping. What "West" was this? What Eden?

The sight of the place through the grimy train window was enough to make her want to turn around and go home. *You were born under an unlucky star, Madaidh.* Her poor dead mam's voice rang in her head as she took it in. Maddy had heard it so many times in her youth, she'd started to believe it. And if Tom Ormond hadn't been proof enough, St. Louis certainly was. And she *really* believed in unlucky constellations when she met her new employers. Or rather, employ*er*. Because it turned out that Colonel Hiram Holt Lascalles had died of cholera, and not recently. It was his widow Maddy found when she arrived at the house on Lafayette Square. Although calling Willabelle Lascalles a "widow" didn't quite do her justice. *Widow* conjured images of a woman in black, ghostly with grief. Aged.

Not the vibrant, busty, gold-headed parrot of a woman who occupied the yellow house with its brass chandeliers and ostentatious furnishings.

"For land's sake, what took you so long!" Mrs. Lascalles exclaimed, aerating herself vigorously with a feathered ivory fan as she led Maddy in through the front door instead of the servants' entrance. Snapping at Mrs. Lascalles's satin skirts was a small hairy dog with bulbous dark eyes. It had ears like sails, fringed with fur, and it yapped ferociously, its body rigid with suppressed enthusiasm.

"I can't be expected to do for myself, you know!" Maddy's new mistress cried out. She swept up the yapping dog and thrust it at Maddy. "Here, Merle wants attention."

Maddy looked down in horror at the dog. It was baring its teeth, which were small but wickedly sharp. The dog gave Maddy an evil look and growled deep in its throat.

"Don't mind Merle," Mrs. Lascalles cooed. "He's just protective of his mama." She bent to smother the growling animal's nose with kisses.

Maddy's homesickness returned in full force. What she wouldn't give for Mrs. Ormond and her lazy Irish Setters right now.

Unlike Mrs. Ormond's rigid decorousness, Willabelle Lascalles was all plump rosy flesh exploding from a satin gown of eye-watering turquoise. The bustle at her rear was so large it threatened to upend the porcelain curiosities strewn on every surface. She was definitely *not* what Maddy had expected. She didn't bear the slightest resemblance to Mrs. Ormond, who had been as composed as statuary.

The house wasn't quite what Maddy had expected either. She'd imagined a town house, like the brownstones in New York, or a grand estate like Ormond House. Not this lemon-drop confection with three tiers of wedding cake wrought iron balconies, explosions of lace and salmon-colored velvet at the windows, and wallpaper so flocked it was deep enough to gather dust. And gather dust it had, by the look. It was like a neglected house of ill repute.

Maddy also wasn't expecting to be the *only* servant. There had been more, Mrs. Lascalles told her, but they had *absconded*. And the house was in utter disarray. The great ferns in their brass pots were brown and withered, dropping desiccated curlicues on the carpet; there was moldy food in the food safe; the bathroom was an indescribable disgrace; and Mrs. Lascalles's bedroom looked like a whirlwind had gone through it. There were stockings hanging from the iron bed, shucked off like snakeskins. The lady of the house gave Maddy the tour herself, oblivious to the total disorder. Maddy trailed behind, her arms full of the hairy little dog, who perched his paws imperiously on her forearm. He was clearly used to being carried around like a baby emperor.

The tour ended back in the filthy kitchen, where Mrs. Lascalles put in her request for dinner ("Nothing heavy and nothing boiled and, for land's sake, no beans!"), and that was when Maddy realized that she was expected to cook too.

Her! Cook!

She could barely coddle an egg. She was a *parlor maid*. Worst of all, she couldn't read, so she couldn't even make use of the shelf of cookbooks. Maddy protested, but she might as well have been speaking Greek. Mrs. Lascalles didn't seem to hear anything that she didn't want to hear. She left Maddy in the kitchen, surrounded by unwashed dishes and moldering food, with an armful of irritable dog. "The markets are open tomorrow. You can go and restock. I'm sure you can make do with what we have until then," Mrs. Lascalles said cheerfully as she disappeared, leaving a miasma of heavy French scent in her wake.

That was how Maddy Mooney found herself stranded in St. Louis through the spring and summer of '86, solely responsible for the running of a three-story house, at the beck and call of a woman who was prone to ordering up a scented bath in the wee hours of the night and playing nanny to an ill-tempered Papillon. Maddy was scullery maid and cook, parlor maid and housekeeper, lady's maid and butler, dog walker and groomer, even gardener.

And to top it off, she hadn't had a decent cup of tea in months. She also hadn't been paid.

At first, she thought it was an oversight, Mrs. Lascalles being her usual scatterbrained self. But as the weeks drew on, the sick feeling in Maddy's stomach curdled into dread. The purse she was given for market days grew lighter and lighter; the badly cooked fare on the table grew more and more meager. The gas was cut off. And Willabelle Lascalles wouldn't allow conversation about wages.

"That kind of talk is for my financial manager," she'd say with a waggle of her satin-gloved fingers. "Talk to him."

But Maddy didn't know who he was. She'd certainly never *met* the man.

And then she noticed that things were going missing around the house. A porcelain pug dog here, an ivory statuette there. Jasperware, crystal decanters, oriental vases. The piano.

Was it possible that there was no money? That she would *never* be paid . . .

The piano was the final straw. It sent Maddy dashing out at first light to see what she could learn. She wasn't normally one for gossip, but that morning she needed it desperately. Merle followed her, growling, her constant aggressive shadow. The maids of Lafayette Square gathered in the lane after tossing out the night's chamber pots, swapping tales. Maddy wished she knew them better. It seemed crass to dive right in and ask for gossip—but what choice did she have?

Maddy made a beeline for Rosie McCann, the upstairs maid from the biggest house on the block. She was always in the thick of it, whispering and giggling. She seemed a good place to start.

"Good morning," she said brightly, giving Merle a nudge with her boot as he growled.

Rosie lit up at the sight of her. It turned out getting gossip about Willabelle Lascalles wasn't hard—they were all itching to talk about her. And they had a lot to say.

Her employer, Maddy quickly discovered, was "codfish aristocracy." New money. Completely disdained by even the other new-money families. She was crass, vulgar, showy and an utter disgrace. And Maddy got swift confirmation of the widow's financial troubles . . . The gossip came in a flood. Mrs. Lascalles was flat broke.

"Broke?" Maddy didn't bother to keep the dismay from her voice. Her stomach was in knots. "You're sure?"

The maids all nodded. Maddy thought she heard a nervous giggle or two. Absently she scooped Merle up as he started chewing on the hem of her apron. He sounded like a wild animal, but the minute he was in her arms he relaxed, lolling and panting happily. He was a petty tyrant; all he wanted was for her to carry him around. "Tell me everything," Maddy said grimly, steeling herself for what might come.

"The colonel's sons from his first marriage own the house," Dottie from two doors down told Maddy, all but shivering with the delight of sharing such momentous news, "and they're kicking her out. She doesn't have a *cent* to her name."

"Worse," Annie May from the green house next door chipped in, "she's in debt, *huge debt*, and the Lascalleses ain't of a mind to pay it off for her."

Maddy swore. She was owed weeks and weeks of back pay.

Jesus, Mary and Joseph, what was she going to do?

As the pearly dawn became full blue morning, Maddy stalked back to the house, still carrying Merle. What if Willabelle Lascalles *never* paid her? Maddy had nothing. Nothing even worth selling. She'd have to throw herself on the mercy of the church . . . but she hadn't even gone to church since she'd got here. She didn't know a single priest. What if things were different here? What if there was no mercy for a girl like her?

Panic beat in her breast. Panic and fury. That parrot owed her, and Maddy wanted her due.

Inside, she noticed things she'd been willfully avoiding. The dark rectangles on the wallpaper, where paintings had once hung. The empty spaces where furniture had once been, the carpets bearing the phantom imprints of chaises and chairs long gone. The pile of notices building up on the rolltop desk in the parlor (if only she could read them!). The house had a hushed, wary air, as though waiting for disaster to strike.

America had been a colossal mistake. What *had* she been thinking? Damn Thomas Ormond. And damn her for falling for his nonsense in the first place. If it weren't for Tom—and for her own raw stupidity—she wouldn't be in this infuriating situation.

"We need to absquatulate," Willabelle announced as Maddy struggled with dinner. Maddy didn't have the slightest clue what the silly parrot meant. She dipped her head to push a stray lock of hair off her brow with her forearm and tried not to lose her temper. She was frayed with the stress of worrying. And how she'd worried all day, imagining the disasters that might lay ahead. Homelessness.

Hunger. Disrepute. Now she was wretched and fretful and had her hand halfway up a sad-looking chicken to boot; she didn't have time for Willabelle's shenanigans.

"We need to what?"

"Absquatulate! Remove ourselves, absent to elsewhere, *leave!*" Willabelle had a ghoulishly gleeful look, as though she was enjoying the drama. She threw herself into a chair at the kitchen table. Maddy wasn't used to the lady of the house making herself at home in the kitchen. It was disconcerting. But everything about Willabelle was disconcerting. Her purple taffeta bustle bulged out the back of the chair like a tumor as she kicked her fancy heels against the floorboards. Merle took hold of her hem and started up a tug-of-war; Willabelle failed to notice. "We need new diggings. You'd best get packing."

"Let me just finish putting dinner on," Maddy said tiredly. She didn't know what a digging was and frankly didn't care. It was a sticky hot day, and the kitchen was well over ninety degrees. Maddy had sweat through her black dress long ago.

"Dinner? Haven't you heard a word I've said? We're leaving." Willabelle's round face drew in like a cushion that had been sat on.

"Now?" The woman was impossible. She talked like someone from a theater troupe. Willabelle could be as dramatic about her morning toast as she was about an outbreak of typhoid fever. Maddy was sick of it. Why couldn't she behave like a normal lady of the house? Where was the icy demeanor? The adherence to protocols? Why couldn't she treat Maddy like she was invisible? Or at the very least, pay her!

"Now!" Willabelle agreed. "This very minute. Up you go, pack everything in my closet, I'll be needing it all. I'll do the jewels. The rest will have to stay or the boys will have an accounting of me. Their father was never so stingy of heart. Or stingy of anything else." At that point, Willabelle went on one of her dramatically forlorn rambles about her late husband, who, Maddy gathered, had been a shining paragon of knightly virtue. According to Willabelle, the colonel had been a decorated veteran of the Civil War, a *hero*. His Union sword still hung over the mantel, framed for posterity. Maddy did the math and figured that he must have been old enough to be Willabelle's father, since she must have been born *during* the war, or even after it. From the maids in the lane, Maddy had learned that Colonel Lascalles had caused a scandal by throwing over his first wife for Willabelle. The wife had died of grief. Or dyspepsia, depending on whom you listened to. Sometimes in her rambles, Willabelle got his name wrong, reversing the *Hiram* and the *Holt*. Maddy wondered how long they'd been married before he'd shucked off his mortal coil. Long enough to buy Willabelle some fancy jewelry and set her up in this confection of a house, but not quite long enough for her to have a firm grasp of his name.

"Imagine leaving the house to *them*," Willabelle pouted as she sprawled at the kitchen table, unmindful of propriety, "two of the most unseducible men in Missouri." Her nails clicked on the table. "It's a miracle that I've kept the house as long as I have."

Maddy took a deep breath and put the chicken in the oven, which shimmered with scouring heat. She'd never known heat like this. The whole summer had been cloyingly hot, the nights oppressive. It was like being wrapped in wet blankets and dropped in a hot bath. Especially up in the attic, where her cupboard of a room was. She hadn't slept in weeks, even though she was dog-tired. Dog-tired from all the labor she was doing, which she wasn't being *paid for*.

Oh, it was infuriating.

Maddy had worked so hard to whip the house into decent shape, and she hadn't been paid a red cent for all her work. She'd lain awake in her sweatbox upstairs, fretting over money, over her future, over the absolute mess she was in. And after no sleep, she spent the day beating the carpets, which were thick with dirt, scrubbing the stairs and oiling the furniture, and attempting to cook, as the heat weighed her down, sucking the air from her lungs and drenching her unmentionables with perspiration. She felt limp and scrunched and all out of patience. And now this parrot in purple taffeta was telling her to *pack*.

"Mrs. Lascalles," she said, trying to keep her temper. Years of training had kept her in check until now, but today was testing her. "What do you mean *pack*? And . . . *absquatulate*?" Who even used words like that?

"We're in a fix, that's for sure." Willabelle rested her cherubic chin on her hand and fixed Maddy with her round china-blue eyes.

"We?" Maddy didn't know where Willabelle got the *we* from. There was no *we*. Maddy had done all she had a mind to do for this woman. She was going to collect her pay right this minute and head back to New York. Maybe even back to Ireland. All the way back to county Offaly and the bogs. Back to somewhere that made sense.

"I've taken a shine to you, Madeleine." Willabelle had the nerve to flutter her eyelashes, like Maddy was a suitor come calling.

"It's Maddy." She hated the way Willabelle fluffed her name up into something it wasn't. She was plain old Maddy Mooney, and nothing more.

"I've got a hankering to get out of this place. It ain't nothing but a pit of vipers. Uptight ones, at that. Who needs St. Louis? Not us!"

"Us . . ." There she went again. There was no *us*. There was Maddy and the money she was owed, and that was all.

Willabelle blew a raspberry. "That's what I think of those Lascalles boys."

Maddy pressed the heels of her hands against her forehead and tried to draw strength. If only Willabelle could talk straight. "You're being evicted," she said evenly. Dottie and Annie May had told her so gleefully, and now here was confirmation.

"Isn't it an outrage?" The china-blue gaze grew stormy. "I

earned this house. That old flapdoodle *promised* me it would be mine. And then he ups and leaves everything to those sourpusses."

"Mrs. Lascalles, I'm owed wages." Maddy opted for bluntness. This wasn't an ordinary employer, or an ordinary situation. Things were different here in America. There was no housekeeper to speak to, no polite way to approach the matter. There was just Willabelle here at the table, her blowsy golden curls tilting wonkily under the weight of an ostrich feather. "More than three months' wages, to be precise."

Willabelle shook her head and tutted. "Why, those scabby rodents. Imagine, not paying you. You should march right up to Homer and Chester and give them what for."

"I work for *you*, Mrs. Lascalles."

"Willabelle, honey. After all, we're friends now."

Friends? Since when? Maddy looked at the woman like she'd lost her mind. She'd never heard anything so daft in all her life. She was a *maid*. "I've never met any Homer or Chester," she pressed on. "But I need the money that's owed me. I plan to go home."

Willabelle looked startled. "Home? Well. That's going to be tricky."

What was so tricky about it? Maddy felt like kicking something. Just one of the earbobs dangling from Willabelle's ears would pay for her ticket back to New York. "I want what I'm owed," she said firmly. Oh, imagine if anyone from Ormond House could hear her, talking to her employer that way! But she felt truly desperate. Like she was on a cliff edge, and the cliff was crumbling out from beneath her.

"Oh, now *you're* mad at me too." Willabelle's big blue eyes filled with tears. "And me, a widow!" A lace handkerchief appeared, flourished from her creamy cleavage. Willabelle dabbed her eyes and looked skyward. "Darling Holt! You see what's become of me, now that you've abandoned me to this earthly prison."

Maddy didn't know how she did it. It was like a sleight of hand. One moment Maddy was standing her ground, determined to get her money, and the next she was hauling Willabelle's trunks out to a hired carriage. And then she was being whisked away into the sweltering St. Louis evening.

"We'll get ourselves nice and settled tonight and then we'll get this mess sorted out." Willabelle's fan wafted lazily through the torpid air as the carriage jounced toward the river. Merle snapped at the feathers and almost fell off Maddy's lap.

To Maddy's horror, they pulled up in front of a hulking white stone hotel. It looked like a palace. "You can afford this?" Where she found the temerity to ask, she didn't know. The boundaries between servant and mistress were very wobbly tonight.

Willabelle laughed and tickled Maddy's nose with the feathers of her fan. "I can afford to *charge* it."

Maddy sneezed and pushed the feathers away.

"Those Lascalles boys can treat me to my last hurrah in St. Louis."

And what about *me*? Maddy thought as she trotted after Willabelle through a soaring portico. Inside, the walls danced with painted frescoes in the gaslight. Maybe it was the lack of sleep, maybe it was the heat, but the world had gone funny. Shimmery and unreal.

It only got stranger as she followed Willabelle upstairs, to a suite on the top floor. Maddy had never been inside a hotel like this before. It dripped with money. Wood paneling, etched-glass light fittings, thick carpeting, mirrors and shining mahogany. And everywhere she looked everything was kept to the highest standard. There wasn't a speck of dust. The windows were crystal clear. Maybe she could get a job here . . .

"Don't bother unpacking, Madeleine," Willabelle ordered as

soon as they were ensconced in a room that put the bedrooms at Ormond House to shame. She threw her fan on a chair. Out of habit, Maddy picked it up.

"We won't be here long. Draw me a bath, will you? I think better in the bath. I've ordered dinner sent up. We'll be here for the duration, until all our problems are solved."

Maddy did as she was told, her mind racing as she considered offering her services to the hotel. She could earn enough to get back to Ireland in a place like this. It looked clean and well-run. Maddy wondered if they paid their wages promptly.

It sure did niggle letting Willabelle walk away with all those months' wages unpaid though. She'd have to find a way to settle accounts before she changed employers. She'd earned that money.

"Don't skimp on the scent," Willabelle ordered as Maddy drew her bath.

Maddy upended the scent bottle, watching the liquid splash into the steaming water. Pungent clouds of perfume rose in the steam. Maddy sneezed again.

How the woman could bathe on a night this hot was beyond her. Willabelle seemed to spend half her life lolling about in a tub. Maddy opened the windows to alleviate the steam, which had fogged everything and was making the walls sweat. But the night outside was as still and sultry as the washroom. Maddy's hair was already plastered to her head.

"You're a sweetheart," Willabelle sighed, turning her back so Maddy could unbutton her and unlace her stays. Maddy struggled with the buttons and the knot on the laces. She'd never done duties as a lady's maid before her employ with Willabelle.

Dutifully she took the discarded clothes to the armoire and hung them neatly, even though what she really wanted to do was hurl them to the floor. She was tired and hot and hungry. When Maddy returned to the washroom, Willabelle handed her a leather folder stuffed with letters. "Don't let them get wet," she ordered, dropping her robe and lowering herself into the tub. "By the time I get out of this bath, we're going to have found me a husband."

"A husband!" Maddy was shocked. Willabelle said it like she was about to go shopping for a new hat.

"Inspired, don't you think?" Willabelle looked like the cat that got the cream as she sank back into the scented water. Her golden hair formed damp ringlets against her flushed cheeks. "I've been answering advertisements."

"Advertisements!" Maddy was shocked. "What do you mean, advertisements?"

Willabelle closed her eyes and settled back in the steaming tub. "For brides! Do you know how many men there are out west, in desperate need of a woman? And what am I, if not a woman?" She lifted a languid hand. "Think of all those men who've struck gold, or silver—I'm not fussy—or all those ranchers with their thousands of acres. Think of the *money*."

Maddy looked down at the folder in her hands. "You've been answering advertisements . . ."

"So many of them! Because I can't marry just anyone. Not with my tastes."

"How many ads have you answered?" Maddy asked weakly, sinking onto a plush stool by the vanity. She'd never heard of anything so reckless.

"Dozens. A score. Who knows? More than I counted. These are the ones in the final running, and you, honey, are going to help me pick a winner."

"Me?" Oh no. She was just a maid.

"C'mon, Miss Maddy, don't you want your money? Since those Lascalles boys are too cheap to pay you those wages they owe you, I guess I'm going to have to do it. And this is the way I can do it." She grinned. "It'll be so much fun."

Fun? Maddy couldn't think of anything *less* fun. In the morning she'd apply downstairs for a job, she decided. Anything was better than this.

"Off you go, read them out."

"Read them . . ." Maddy flushed. "I can't."

"Sure you can. I give you permission. Land's sake, girl, you've seen me in my altogether, what more privacy do I have left?"

"No, I mean I *can't*."

Willabelle was nonplussed.

"I can't read." Maddy held the folder out.

"But . . . you're *English*."

"Irish." Maddy shook the folder. "I'm Irish."

"Didn't y'all invent reading?"

"I don't think so."

"Well, I never." Willabelle took the folder. "No wonder you wanted to be an American."

But she hadn't. She'd just let herself be blown here, like a leaf on the wind. The truth of it stung. She hadn't wanted to be here at all. She'd spent her whole time in America sullen and resentful. Awake at night, imagining the long hallways of Ormond House, and the feel of Thomas Ormond's mouth . . .

Eejit.

"I'll read them to you, then," Willabelle announced. "And you tell me yes or no."

Look at Willabelle. She was no leaf on the wind. She was the wind itself. A gale of a woman, sweeping through life with destructive force. For a moment, Maddy envied her.

"I wouldn't know what to say yes to," Maddy told her weakly. "What would you be looking for in a husband?"

"Money, silly. And a nice pliable man to let me spend it." Willabelle had bundled the advertisements into groups, each bundle tied with a different-colored ribbon. "I'll read you their correspondence and you give me your opinion."

"My opinion?" Why on earth would Willabelle want *her* opinion? What did she know about marriage and husbands? Or money.

"Think of it like fishing," Willabelle said gaily. "We throw the little ones back!"

By the look of it there were a lot of little ones. Willabelle discarded a bunch before she'd even finished reading them. They fell like confetti around the foot of the tub. And it was up to Maddy to pick them up. In the end, once all the fallen contenders were cleared away, Willabelle had three left.

A miner. A merchant. And a blacksmith.

"What does he mine again?" Maddy asked, refreshing the water in the tub for the third time. Willabelle seemed in no hurry to get out.

Dinner had arrived but was going cold out in the main room.

"I can't leave now. It's my thinking place," she said whenever Maddy suggested leaving the tub in favor of the dining table. Maddy's stomach rumbled loudly.

"What does he mine . . . ?" Willabelle searched the letters. "That's a good question. He doesn't say."

"If he owned a gold mine, surely he'd brag about it." Maddy paused, considering. "But aren't all mines good?"

"*Noooooo*. Not coal. I don't want to get coal dust all over my gowns." Willabelle considered the miner's last letter. "It also gives me pause that he mentions children. Would I have to have anything to do with these children?"

"I imagine you'd be their stepmother," Maddy said mildly.

The letter went floating to the floor, where it absorbed the latest slosh of bathwater, the ink running in spirals on the now-translucent page. "I could end up nursemaid to a pack of kids, covered in coal. No, thank you. Now . . . merchant or blacksmith?"

"Blacksmithing seems like a dirty business too," Maddy ventured.

"True. Let's look at the merchant."

Maddy's stomach was complaining in earnest now. She thought longingly of the roast chicken they'd left behind at Lafayette Square. If they hadn't absquatulated, she'd be sitting down in the quiet kitchen right about now, eating Willabelle's leftovers. Her mouth watered.

Merle kicked up yapping. "He's hungry," Maddy said, snatching him up. "Why don't I feed him?"

"Oh, give him my dinner. I need to lose a few pounds anyway before I meet this bridegroom."

Maddy was in the other room before Willabelle had even finished speaking. She dropped Merle on the bed and pulled the silver lid off the dinner tray. Merle barked. "Hush," she told him. What right did a dog have to a prime steak? He ate better than her every other day; he could sacrifice today, surely? But she cut up a third of the steak and put it on the side plate for him. She added some potatoes, because he loved potatoes, and couple of green beans. Then she sat at the table and stuffed the napkin into the collar of her dress. Oh Lord, she was hungry.

"The merchant lives in Nebraska." Willabelle's voice drifted through the open door. "I don't know that I fancy living in Nebraska."

Maddy didn't know the first thing about the place. She wondered if it was as industrial as St. Louis.

She closed her eyes in sheer pleasure at the first mouthful of the steak. Even cold, it was the best thing she'd eaten in months.

Merle barked. He'd finished his plate. Maddy held out a buttery carrot, and he stood on his back legs to grab it.

"The thing is, I just like the *sound* of the blacksmith." Water sloshed in the bathroom.

"Uh-huh," Maddy said around a mouthful as she mopped up the gravy with a hunk of bread.

"Blacksmithing makes a man terribly well-built," Willabelle sighed dreamily. "Back home in Kansas, I knew a blacksmith who was nothing but muscle . . ."

Tom Ormond had been muscular, Maddy remembered, feeling the old stab right in her belly. An expert horseman, he was lean and ropy. She wondered what he was doing now. His baby would have been born . . .

"And listen to this," Willabelle hooted. *"Lady must have charms and know how to use them. Don't that sound just the thing?"*

Maddy gave the bathroom door a horrified look. "The thing . . . ?" *Charms. Know how to use them* . . . What kind of man *was* this blacksmith?

"You can bet I wrote back and told him that I have charms in abundance."

"You didn't!" Maddy almost choked on her food. The woman was a scandal.

"I most certainly did. I'm an *expert* at making a man lose his wits," Willabelle said smugly. "It's my chief asset."

"Her chief asset . . ." Maddy rolled her eyes at Merle.

"I told him I've had two marriages to practice." There was a playful splashing.

"Two marriages!" That was news to Maddy. "But you're so young!"

Willabelle laughed. "The first one barely counted. It only lasted a few weeks. But Lord, it was fun while it lasted!"

Maddy slipped Merle another carrot. "I hate to think what her idea of fun is," she whispered to the dog.

"Poor Ralphie," Willabelle sighed. "He was such a looker too. It was a shame."

Maddy couldn't resist asking, "What happened to him?"

"Turned out he was already married."

"He *what?"* Suddenly Maddy's own experiences with Tom seemed very tame.

"He had a wife and kids back in Virginia. The rat." But Willabelle didn't sound too sore about it. She laughed again. "I didn't tell the blacksmith that bit."

"How did you find out?" Maddy speared the last of the steak, ignoring Merle's beseeching gaze. "About the other wife, I mean."

"Oh, eventually he sobered up and told me."

"Eventually?"

"He was on a tear when we met," Willabelle giggled. "And that man was a hoot when he was drinking. Lord, he was fun! But a few weeks after the wedding he ran out of cash, and as a result ran out of whiskey. And once he'd sobered up and realized what he'd done, well, he felt real bad." There was a note of regret in Willabelle's voice. "I told him I didn't mind, but he felt too guilty and hopped along home to Virginia."

"You didn't *mind*?" The woman was a perfect heathen! All of Maddy's Catholic upbringing revolted at the thought. Willabelle didn't seem to have the slightest grasp of right and wrong. "You mean you would have knowingly committed bigamy?"

"Oh, listen to you!" Willabelle sounded amused. "Bigamy! Getting all lawyerly on me."

What had the church been thinking, sending her to this woman? She imagined what the nuns and the walnut-faced priest would say if they could see her with Willabelle now . . .

"Is the blacksmith in Nebraska too?" Maddy changed the subject. She didn't want to know how many other skeletons were in Willabelle's closet. She gave Merle the last of the beans and then packed up the plates. She hoped Willabelle had been serious about not being hungry, because there was nothing left.

"No, he's not in Nebraska. He's in Montana!" Willabelle sounded pleased. Maddy had no idea where Montana was.

"I'm ready to get out now, Madeleine! This is the one. I've been reading through our correspondence, and I have a good feeling. He's flirty but blunt. And he has a fine vocabulary. I do love a man who knows some powerful big words."

"I wouldn't think a blacksmith has much call for words and the like," Maddy observed as she gathered up the thick fluffy towel and Willabelle's wrapper.

"Blacksmithing is a profitable business," Willabelle told Maddy as she stepped into the towel Maddy held out. "But it's the *wealth of land* bit I like the best."

Maddy didn't see how a wealth of land was going to pay her outstanding wages.

Willabelle seemed to read her mind. She pulled the towel tight around herself and fixed her big blue eyes on Maddy. "I know you're owed," she said, "and I mean to pay. If you come with me, I'll make sure Mr. McBride settles the debt first thing once we're married. And then, I hope, you'll stay on in my employ."

Jesus, Mary and Joseph, no.

Willabelle's eyes narrowed as she sensed the resistance. Her lips pursed. "You know," she said slowly, "Mr. McBride and I have corresponded about how we'll arrange the household after our marriage. I explained how fearfully badly the Lascalles boys have treated me, only letting me have a single servant. To run *such* a big house. Mr. McBride agreed that it was a powerfully mean thing to do to me."

To *her*? What about to *Maddy*?

"Mr. McBride will provide a much healthier household." Willabelle reached for one of the letters. "See here? He says I may keep house as I wish." Willabelle showed Maddy the letter, which she couldn't read. "I know you've only been a parlor maid to date . . ."

Maddy almost laughed. Only a parlor maid. Since she'd got to St. Louis, she'd been a cook, a footman, a gardener, a dog walker . . .

"But I would love to offer you the role of housekeeper, with the commensurate increase in salary."

For a moment, Maddy was speechless. "An increase? On the *nothing* I get now?"

Willabelle's face crumpled. "You don't trust me!"

No! No, she didn't trust her. And she kept thinking of the value of the earbobs. Just one would more than pay Maddy's outstanding wages. "Mrs. Lascalles," Maddy said, eerily calm in the face of the gathering storm. "I just want what I'm owed. I'm no housekeeper. Or cook. Or anything but a parlor maid. I do an honest job and I just want my honest pay." She gathered her courage to say the thing plainly. "Those earbobs you wore today." Her voice cracked as an image of Mrs. Ormond came into her head. Lord, imagine saying this to *her*. She pushed the idea away. Willabelle Lascalles was no Mrs. Ormond. "Just a single one of those earbobs would more than settle our debt."

"You want my earbobs?" Willabelle seemed thunderstruck.

"No!" Maddy felt like a thief. "No," she stressed. "But you could sell them and use the money to settle my wages."

"Here!" Willabelle dashed from the bathroom and returned with the earbobs. "Take them *both!*" She stood like a child, her hand outstretched. "I didn't think. Of course the earbobs should pay the debt. Take the second one, too, as interest."

Maddy looked at the tourmaline earbobs. She didn't want them. She wanted the money. She couldn't buy a train ticket with these. And she was scared she'd be accused of theft if she tried to pawn them. She didn't look like someone who would own jewelry like this. She tried to explain it to Willabelle, but Willabelle just took everything and twisted it all around.

And by the end of all that twisting, somehow Maddy was going to Montana with her.

"You keep the earbobs, for security," Willabelle said, putting them in Maddy's palm and closing her hand around them. "And when Mr. McBride pays you your money—with interest, I won't forget the interest—you can give them back to me. I do love them so. My dearly departed mother gave them to me."

Maddy's heart gave a squeeze. Her own mam had left nothing to Maddy. She hadn't had anything to leave.

"And then you can decide whether to take up my offer as house-keeper, or whether to catch the train back to St. Louis."

New York. There was no way in hell she was coming back to St. Louis. The place was cursed.

"I don't know where Montana is," Maddy said dumbly, the ear-bobs heavy in her hand. She felt like a leaf on the wind again, all blown away.

"Montana? Oh, it's just a little way out west," Willabelle said cheerily.

But it turned out Montana was more than just a little way out west. It turned out it was a lot out west. On-the-very-edge-of-the-frontier kind of out west. And it also turned out that Maddy's luck was about to get much worse.

Three

Kit McBride slipped away before first light so he didn't have to deal with Junebug. That hellcat was always trying to hitch a ride into town with him, and she ruined the whole journey with her yapping. Kit loved her half to death, but he sure didn't love listening to her yap for the four hours it took to ride down to Bitterroot.

Buck's Creek and Bitterroot were two separate towns, close enough together to be neighborlike, but far enough away to be distinct. Buck's Creek was up a winding track through thick forest. That was their pa's fault. He'd settled in the high mountain meadow thinking it would make a great spot for a town because it was on the Natives' trade trail, but it turned out most settlers didn't want to make the arduous hike uphill and would rather settle on the flanks of the mountain. The winters were marginally kinder in Bitterroot, and it was surrounded by a network of thriving silver mines; it even had a rail spur. On the other hand, up the mountain, Buck's Creek was just a cluster of log buildings. There was no railway, no saloon, no hotel, no mercantile. There was only the McBrides.

Kit thought Buck's Creek was a darned sight prettier than Bitterroot, but it did feel as far away from civilization as the moon. Kit didn't mind being out in the wilds, but Junebug had taken a shine to riding into town as often as she could. She liked to go flitting about like a lightning bug, visiting the post office, which was just a window out the side of the new train station, and the mercantile, gathering up gossip the way a bird gathered twigs for its nest. That girl could talk a blue streak.

Let Morgan have her today. He was due a solid day with her, and it would do Junebug good to have a dose of Morgan's stony silence.

Not that it would stop her from talking.

He could only imagine the state of them both by the time he got home.

Kit felt his mood easing as he headed downhill. It was cold out in the bud of morning, and fall was flushing the leaves with color. As the sun speared over the mountains, the turning leaves glowed like embers: the maples rosy at the tips, the aspens liquid yellow, the larches shimmering into vibrant lime.

Kit loved fall more than any other season. There was something elegiac about it, full of longing. It was like one of those melodies that Jonah played on his fiddle, setting a feeling flickering inside Kit. A mixed-up feeling that made him feel like crying, even though it was sharp with happiness. Fall gave him that same sharpness, that same swell of sadness. This time of year, the cold snapped in overnight, turning his morning breath to cloud, and the sun sparkled on frosty dew. The colors were clearer, fine edged, and the woods bustled with animals gathering and hunting and making ready for winter. Mist rose from the creek into the tender blue sky, and the air smelled of leaves turning, wet earth and currants ripe and heavy on the bush.

He might have been the only human on earth as his horse picked its way down the mountain. Beau and Jonah complained fiercely about the distance between Buck's Creek and Bitterroot, but Kit loved nothing more than the slow ride down the hill, watching the day warm, the wind casting ripples of shadows through the woods, the leaves shivering on the bough. As he rode, his thoughts slipped by like trout in a stream, and he felt like there was nowhere else he'd rather be.

It was always a bit of a disappointment to round the bend and see the town.

Today especially so, as sitting in the crook of a maple was his little sister. Somehow—*how?*—she'd got ahead of him and beat him down the mountain. Kit sighed as he pulled his horse up in front of the maple. Her mountain pony was tethered to the trunk of the tree beneath her, happily pulling up grass.

It was completely unsurprising. She was the fly in every ointment.

Junebug was cradled in the crook, bare feet dangling, her hat hanging off a twig. She'd hacked off all her hair over the summer, sick of wrestling with the tangles, and it was a thick dark shag around her square-jawed face. She was looking triumphantly pleased with herself.

"Junebug," he said tersely, "what have we told you about riding around on your lonesome?"

"I ain't on my lonesome." She sat forward. "I'm with you. Now, anyway. And I would have been with you before, if you weren't so blamed selfish."

"Did you think to tell someone where you were going?" She must have left Buck's Creek well before him, when it was still pitch-dark. There was no way she'd told Morgan where she was going, and Beau and Jonah would still be snoring away like sleeping buffalo. The thought of her riding around in the dark made him feel sweaty with terror. What if her pony had gone down and no one knew where she was? What if she'd broken a bone? What if she'd got lost? The kid was a walking disaster. She could die out there in the woods.

The thought made his blood colder than the creek in January. He could have throttled her for the way she sat there in the crook of the tree, blithely unaware of how she had his heart in her hands. And how she kept scrunching it to hell every time she did something foolhardy.

"You got some nerve, Kit McBride," she complained, totally unabashed by his dismay, "sneaking out at the crack of dawn and not inviting me along with you. You know I wanted to go to town this week." As always, Junebug had a way of ignoring him that pricked him sore. "It's selfishness, pure and simple," she continued, "you hogging a day in town all to yourself and leaving me to Morgan. You know he don't want me underfoot."

"You're not to go riding around on your own," he growled.

"It's settled, then. Since I can't ride home on my own, I'll come into town with you." She dropped out of the tree and pulled her pony away from the grass.

How did she *do* that? She had a way of slithering out of things, silver tongued and slippery skinned. Now he was stuck with her, unless he wanted to give up his day in town and march her back up the hill. And she knew very well he wouldn't, not when he had a package waiting for him down in Bitterroot. The kid was sly that way.

"Besides," she said cheerfully, "I'll be useful. I can go chase down our wagon, the one Thunderhead Bill ain't returned yet."

"Don't even think of it," Kit warned. Thunderhead Bill was camping out at the cathouse. It was no place for a girl like Junebug. "Why not?"

Look at that fake innocence. She knew very well why not; she just wanted to make him say it. Well, he wouldn't. "Because I said so, that's why not."

"And who made you my Lord and Savior?" She swung up into the saddle, as nimble as a squirrel. "Speaking of Lords and Saviors, did you hear Bitterroot is going to build a church? A proper one, with fancy windows and everything."

There she went, off and talking, even as she turned her pony and started down the hill. Her words drifted over her shoulder and clouded Kit's path. So much for a quiet morning alone.

"Now that they've got the train, I reckon they'll be a right metropolis," Junebug said. "Maybe we'll even get the circus."

Kit had no idea what got into that head of hers. "Circus? What in hell do you know about circuses?"

"I know they got lady performers. And Thunderhead Bill says he once saw a man fired out of a cannon at a circus. Imagine that."

"I wouldn't believe even half of what Thunderhead Bill says." And that was being generous.

Junebug paid his sourness no mind. "Half ain't a bad average. Look at Beau. Most of what comes out of his mouth is utter garbage, but then he'll go and tell you how to snare a jackrabbit and you realize he ain't all idiot after all."

Kit suppressed a smile. She sure did have a way of nailing people down.

"I suppose you'll be headed for the post office first?" she said archly, looking back over her shoulder at him.

"I imagine so." He kept his voice even. He didn't like being teased about his packages. They were too important.

"I'll come along too. I want to talk to old Bascom about that ghost train."

Kit groaned. "What ghost train?" What nonsense was Bascom feeding her now?

"That one down in Arizona." She seemed surprised that he hadn't heard of it. "The one that rockets around in the dead of night, with an engine glowing red with overheat, collecting lost souls for its carriages. Bascom said word came from Butte; it's been seen in Utah and Wyoming and they're for certain it's not long for Montana. He's been staying up nights, watching out for it."

"Goddamn, Junebug. You got to stop being so credulous."

"What's *credulous*?"

"Stop believing everything you're told. People have a streak of lying in them, and the sooner you realize it, the better."

"Bascom ain't a liar. He works for the railway. That's some serious respectability, Kit. More respectable than you."

Kit sighed. "He's not lying in a bad way, Junebug. He's just making fun."

She had that mule look again; stubbornness was rooted deep in her. "He wouldn't lie to me. And what do you know, anyway? You've never been off the mountain. Hell, you didn't even see a train till the spur came to Bitterroot. How would you know if there are ghost ones or not?"

"Because there ain't no such thing as ghosts," he told her for the thousandth time.

"Sure there are." She flicked the reins and kicked her pony into a trot. "Ghosts are right there in the dictionary!"

Kit would have to have a word with Bascom. That kid had too fertile an imagination for people to fool around with her. Especially when *he* was the one who had to calm her down when she thought ghosts were crying down the chimney on windy nights.

Kit wasn't surprised when Junebug trailed him to the train station, which was a proper building now and not just a hut. Bascom had even added a white sign that read "Welcome to Bitterroot." He was standing on the porch, all fancy in his railroad uniform, a silver whistle hanging around his neck on a cord. Kit thought he looked like a bantam rooster.

This was pretty much how he spent his days, as the trains were infrequent up here. The biggest excitement of most days was when he checked whether the clock was accurate. And he did that with ritualistic pleasure. Once a week he had the responsibility of winding said clock, and he took that responsibility very seriously. Kit bet Junebug was glad they hadn't missed the event this week; she liked watching old Bascom set his clock.

Bitterroot itself was greeting the morning in its usual sleepy way. The dusty golden sunlight streamed through the firs, glancing off the rill of a creek as it splashed through the middle of town. The place was hardly a fleabite; there was the train station–cum–post office, the hotel, the mercantile, the cathouse, a shack that called itself a saloon, and three or four timber-frame houses. But it was getting bigger. There was silver about, and a bunch of mines springing up, and the flanks of the mountains around Bitterroot were gathering people the way a honeypot gathered flies. By mid-morning the mercantile would have a row of horses hitched to the rail out front and the little dirt street would be bustling. Well, as bustling as a fleabite place could be. There'd be at least a dozen people.

"Good morning, McBrides," Mrs. Langer, the sometimes postmistress, called as she saw them hitch up. Mrs. Langer was German and looked like an old hickory fishing pole. Kit always felt like a bull trout trying to evade her hook; Mrs. Langer fished for information with terrifying persistence. Her son, Fritz, ran the mercantile. His name wasn't really Fritz, but that's all anyone ever called him. He had no wife but a bunch of kids. Junebug was always pestering Kit about how that worked ("How do you get kids without a ma to pop them out?") but he refused to answer. Morgan tore strips off her for asking about missing people. He'd point to the clump of graves under the chokecherry tree. "There ain't good answers to why people are missing, Junebug," he'd say blackly, pointedly not looking at Kit. "Even if they ain't dead, they ain't *here*, and that's no business to be poking your nose into."

Missing people were off-limits, and that was all there was to it. Kit certainly didn't want to be thinking about all the people who were no longer here: Ma, Pa, the girls, Charlie . . .

His mind veered away from thoughts of Charlie. What was done was done, and there was no point in thinking on it. Kit pulled his hat off and prepared for Mrs. Langer's hook to come snagging at him.

"Package came for you, Kit," Mrs. Langer said slyly, in her thick accent.

She was curious as a cat about Kit's packages. She didn't need to be. They were just books. They were more valuable than silver to him, but only books to everyone else. Those books got him through bad times; they eased the ever-present loneliness and filled the nights he couldn't sleep. New books gave him a thrill he couldn't explain. It was like the thrill of hitting hot iron in the perfect spot to shape it, or the thrill of snatching trout from a shimmering creek. His books were so treasured he wouldn't trust anyone with them; if people wanted to know what was in them, he would read them aloud after dinner. He bought books about stars and bugs, about abysses and equality and all sorts of tangled-up ideas. The ones Junebug and his brothers liked the best were the novels: revolutions and wars; love stories on moors and in haunted old houses; jousts and duels; lovers dying and walking about as ghosts afterward. Kit loved the way Junebug leaned into the stories, often literally on the edge of her seat, exclaiming and raging and chattering about the characters like they were real people. They felt like real people to Kit, too, and it was nice to see her feel the same. As much as they enjoyed him reading to them, his brothers didn't really understand it, and his pa had given him hell for it when Kit was a kid. Pa didn't hold with storybooks. But Kit had always felt something loosen inside him when he opened a book. It was the feeling of opening the door to the first spring day after a hard winter; it was a green sap, blue sky, fresh breeze kind of feeling. Like you had lightning bugs flickering on inside you.

Nothing in the world made Kit happier than a delivery of new books.

Every month, Kit sat down and pored over his catalogs. Then

he wrote out his orders, in his careful script, without so much as a splotch of ink astray. He didn't put the name of the catalog on his letters, just the postal address, so Mrs. Langer and the other Bitterroot busybodies wouldn't know what he was up to.

"Another letter to Chicago," Mrs. Langer would say, peering down at the envelope. Or: "Who is it you're writing to in Baltimore?" Or Boston, or New York, or wherever it was he wrote off to. Once it was Canada, and didn't that set Mrs. Langer on edge, trying to work out what was going on.

"No one cares about your dumb books," Junebug had told him a million times, but he kept on with the secretiveness, as squirrely as ever. He'd learned his lesson in childhood. *You're a damn sissy,* Pa would rage, snatching the book out of Kit's hands. Since Pa left, Kit had renewed his love of books, but he didn't need everyone in Bitterroot knowing he had words like lightning bugs in him, ideas and poetry flicking around his head like fireflies in a twilight field. He didn't need them all knowing that he cried when Little Nell died in *The Old Curiosity Shop*, or that every time he finished *Ivanhoe* he was heartbroken that Ivanhoe couldn't be with Rebecca, who was clearly his true love; he didn't want them gossiping about how he mouthed the words to "The Simplon Pass" when he was out stalking in the woods ("Of woods decaying, never to be decayed"), or thinking he was touched in the head for obsessing over Herodotus's accounts of ancient wars already fought and lost.

"Thank you, Mrs. Langer," Kit said evenly, determined to show no trace of excitement. His Thackeray and Hardy would be in that package, big thick meaty books to sit with through the long nights ahead.

Mrs. Langer sat on her stool at the open window, the sill forming a makeshift counter. She had her best black dress on, buttoned up to the chin. She liked to look smart when she was on official business. And even though she was an old battle-ax, she melted a bit when Kit tipped his hat at her.

"This one is heavy," Mrs. Langer observed, holding the package in both hands and considering its weight. The brown paper wrapping was peppered with postmarks.

"Is it now?" Kit took it from her. "Why, so it is." He tucked his books under his arm, his heart giving a leap of excitement at the weight of them, and pulled out his latest letter. "I'll need a stamp, thank you."

Mrs. Langer peered down at the address. "Minnesota? Who is it you write to, Mr. McBride? A lady? Or many ladies . . . ?"

"No ladies," Kit said, as even as ever. "Not even a one. It's just a mail order, Mrs. Langer."

"I don't believe you. A fine young man like yourself . . ."

"I'm going to talk to Bascom," Junebug said abruptly, clearly repulsed by talk of Kit being a fine young man.

"I'll come with you," Kit told her, dropping payment for his stamp in Mrs. Langer's palm. He didn't want to get stuck talking. He wanted to get on with the chores so he could get home and open his books.

"No need." Junebug was already off. She was itchier than a cat today. Kit followed her, sighing.

"Is it time for the clock yet, Bascom?" she was asking as she rounded the corner of the station.

This could take a while. Junebug and Bascom could talk the hind leg off a mule.

Bascom was still there at his post, chest puffed out proudly in his railway uniform. Being stationmaster was the pinnacle of his dreams, even if it was in a fleabite town in the middle of nowhere. "Not yet, Junebug. You know it happens at nine o'clock on the dot."

Junebug looked up at the clock. "What time is it now?"

Kit gave her an exasperated look. "Read the clock."

Junebug hated reading the clock. "No. Just tell me," she said, flat-out refusing.

"Remember the big hand—" Kit prodded.

"Anyone new arrive since I was last in town?" Junebug just talked over the top of him, directing her attention to Bascom.

"Indeed!" Bascom lit up. "The hotel is packed full right now. Rigby don't know what to do with himself. Guess what? A couple of men arrived with the deed to Enoch Teter's claim." Bascom was a feverish gossip, and he dropped his talk of clocks and times immediately in order to fill Junebug and Kit in on the latest train full of arrivals. "Won it off him, they said. Gambling."

"Well, that don't surprise me one bit," Kit sighed. "Enoch Teter didn't have the brains God gave a tadpole."

"And he's gone and proved you right. Got himself liquored up and lost his whole claim. And it was a doozy of a claim."

"So he said," Junebug said scornfully, "but he only ever had a couple of gray rocks to show for it. I don't believe that mine is anything but a big hole full of rocks."

"Those gray rocks got him to St. Louis, didn't they?" Bascom chided.

"Fat lot of good it did him, if he went and lost his claim," Junebug sniffed. She hadn't liked Enoch Teter ever since the day he said her ears were big. Kit remembered her in a white-hot fury about it. Her ears weren't big, it was just that her head was small, she'd insisted. And her hat pushed her ears out and made them look worse than they were. But she'd never forgiven him. Junebug could hold a grudge better than anyone Kit knew.

"What are the new men like?" she asked Bascom.

Bascom shrugged. "Nothing special. One tall, one short. Rough around the edges. Total greenhorns when it comes to mining. Fritz sold them a load of rubbish they'll never use."

Kit bet he had. There were greenhorns aplenty since the silver mining took off, people from the East, the West, and all the countries across the seas. Most of them came in by train, filing off rumpled and dusty, and ripe for the picking, and they moseyed on into Fritz's store and saw the rows and rows of tools (drifting picks and

mattocks, axes and barrows, pails and pitchers), all of them gleaming and new, and they spent up big, believing they'd be the ones
to pull hefty nuggets of silver from the earth.

"Fritz will be needing you to make new cookware, Kit. You'd
best head over today and take his order," Bascom told him.

Kit nodded. Good idea. Cookware was becoming his best
earner. These miners bought his stock almost quicker than he
could make it.

"You'll never guess who else came in," Bascom said, his eyes
sparkling.

"Who?" Junebug was getting itchier by the minute. Kit guessed
she loved the idea of new people to yap at.

"A very fancy lady, in a dress like you've never seen in your life.
Brighter than a sunset. With a bustle bigger than a horse's behind."
Bascom mimed the bustle out the back. "Pretty as a picture, too,
with a head of curls and big blue eyes."

"A lady!" Junebug looked like she'd been stung by a bee.

"We ain't never had any lady so fancy in Bitterroot before,"
Bascom marveled.

Given only eight ladies had ever been in Bitterroot, that was no
wonder. There were the three girls at the cathouse, Mrs. Langer,
the housekeeper and maid at the hotel, and the two women out on
the Bladderpod silver claim. If you added Junebug and the Langer
girls, there were twelve. But they hardly counted as ladies, and
Junebug didn't even own a dress, let alone a fancy one.

"Before you know it Bitterroot will be the biggest toad in the
puddle," Bascom said proudly.

Kit snorted. Bascom had unwarranted highfalutin dreams for
Bitterroot.

"And she stayed, the fancy lady?" Junebug asked, unable to con-
tain her excitement. Kit guessed she was plenty keen to lay eyes on
the woman, balloon of a dress and all.

"When she got off and saw the state of this place?" Junebug

prodded. "She didn't get straight back on the train and head back where she come from?"

"Nope. She's over at the hotel. You need to go and meet her. Just for the dress alone!" Bascom said gleefully.

Kit was sure Junebug had every intention of doing exactly that. But she had one more question. "Do you know her name?"

"Mrs. Willabelle Lascalles." Bascom said it with relish, savoring every syllable.

Junebug made a strangled squealing noise.

"What's wrong?" Kit asked.

"Nothing!" she said hastily. "Nothing at all."

"Wait till you see her." Bascom was smug. "You'll be squealing, too, Kit."

Kit doubted it. He had no plans to meet the woman, no matter how fancy she was.

"Ah hell, Junebug, you've made me late for the clock winding!" Bascom glanced at his clock and swore. He went off for his ladder, flustered and out of sorts. Normally Junebug would have stayed for the theater, but today she had bigger fish to fry.

"I'm going to the hotel," she told Kit, peering at her reflection in the station window; she removed her battered hat and smoothed down her choppy hair. She still looked a fright.

"What are you doing?" Kit asked, amused, even though he knew perfectly well what she was doing. She was preparing to go grill the new arrivals, as she always did. "I ain't going with you," he told her. "I've got to see Fritz at the mercantile."

"Good," she said, licking her palm and running it over her head, trying to get her cowlick to stay down. "Who asked you anyway?"

"What are you so all-fired nervous for?" he asked as she surrendered on her wayward hair and jammed her hat back on.

"I'm not nervous," Junebug snapped. Then she rolled down the sleeves of her shirt and did up her cuffs.

"You look like you're off courting or something," he teased.

She didn't dignify that with a response, but she looked flustered.

"Come on," he laughed. "I'll walk you to the hotel so you can see the fancy lady."

"I can walk myself," she told him, all but tripping over her own feet as she headed for the street. "You go do your chores."

"What if I want to see the fancy lady too?"

She looked horrified. "You said you didn't want to!"

"Well, now you got me wondering if I'm wrong." He was just kidding her, but she was plainly not in the mood for it. The idea of this fancy lady had got her well flustered.

Not for the first time, Kit thought how strange it must be for Junebug to live in a world peopled almost entirely by men. Hell, she was growing up. Soon she'd need a woman in her life. Kit would have to talk to Morgan about that one. Maybe they could organize for Junebug to spend more time in town. Somehow . . .

She sure did love zipping around like a gadfly, gossiping and sticking her nose in other people's business, visiting with Mrs. Champion and Ellen at the hotel and gathering up news.

Kit caught up and fell in beside her. "Don't worry," he laughed when she scowled. "I won't get in your way. I just thought I'd walk you there and get a glimpse of this wondrous sight. I never did see a lady with a behind like a horse."

The hotel was nestled between the firs. Not much of Bitterroot had actually been cleared. The place was really just a forest with some houses in it, and a dirt road scratched through the trees. Rigby's Bellevue Hotel sat in its sea of firs, a rawboned, two-story wood frame, with a fat lip of a front porch jutting out. Rigby had tried to fancy it up a bit, with some white lacework edging, but it was like putting a dress on a pig. Recently, he'd painted the whole thing a sagebrush green and put some cane chairs and rockers on the porch, as though hoping he'd actually get some decent guests, instead of the miners who tended to rent beds one night at a time, licing up his sheets. Rigby could often be seen lingering on his porch, waiting for business.

Today it looked like his chairs were being used for a change. Bascom was right; Rigby finally had some customers. Kit almost cannoned into Junebug when she stopped dead. She looked peaky.

"What's wrong?"

"Nothing." The crazy kid went and hid behind a fir.

Kit glanced back at the porch. It wasn't like Junebug to be nervous. But it was a regular old party over there. And these miners looked more civilized than the norm; most of them were in suits, like they were off to church. They were circled around a big old cane chair, which had a high curved back. It hid the woman in it from view, but there was a billow of a shining yellow skirt.

"You can go now," Junebug ordered him.

"She ain't going to bite, Bug," Kit said kindly, assuming she was daunted by the prospect of meeting a proper lady. "In fact, she'll probably be as mannered as all get-out."

"I never thought she'd bite." Junebug had her stubborn look on. "I just don't want you coming and scaring her."

"Scaring her?" Kit was startled.

"She'll need to be prepared for the likes of you," his sister told him firmly.

"I ain't scary." Kit didn't know what went on in the damn fool kid's mind.

She rolled her eyes. "Old Roy just about wets himself when you so much as look at him."

"Old Roy ain't normal. Besides, you ain't scared of me," he pointed out.

"Yeah, well, I ain't scared of anyone."

"Except this fancy lady, apparently."

"I ain't scared!" And with that she yanked the brim of her hat down and stalked off toward the hotel. She got halfway to the porch and then veered suddenly, headed back toward the mercantile instead. Kit laughed. Looked like she was going to give herself time to gather her courage before she introduced herself to the woman on the porch of the hotel.

Kit only hoped that, when they eventually met, the fancy lady lived up to her expectations.

As he went to follow her, he caught sight of the McBrides' wagon, parked crooked outside the cathouse. It was the wagon Thunderhead Bill had borrowed. Thunderhead Bill's mule hadn't even been unhooked, poor creature. It honked and hawed when it saw Kit. He sighed. He guessed Bill had got himself good and liquored up again and passed out inside the cathouse.

"No need to fuss," he soothed the mule, crossing the street and rubbing its nose. "We'll get you sorted out." Calmly he set to work unharnessing the mule. It just about bolted, it was so happy to be free. "How long have you been here, boy?" he asked, giving it a good scratch behind the ears. He glanced up at the shuttered cathouse. Everyone was sleeping off a long night, by the looks. "Let's take you round to Rigby's stable and get you some feed. You've eaten your way through the clover, but nothing beats a good sack of oats, eh?"

Kit led the mule across the road and around behind the hotel. He sighed. He'd have to spend some money he'd rather not spend lodging the mule. Rigby wasn't one to be neighborly; he'd want to be paid for the stabling. Kit would add the cost of it to Thunderhead Bill's tab at the trading post, a tab that the old coot was unlikely to ever pay. Still, Kit felt sorry for Bill. He hadn't had an easy life. Half–Bitterroot Salish, half-white, raised by a brutal old trapper in the mountains, Thunderhead Bill nursed a pain so deep it was a fissure through him.

"We have a saying, we Crow," Sour Eagle had said once as they watched Bill, drunk, thrashing in the creek after falling in trying to wash his face. "You are without relatives." Sour Eagle's voice was full of compassion. "It's an insult. But I no longer know who it's supposed to be insulting."

Kit thought on that a lot over the summer. The weight of relatives. The weight of their absence. He was thinking on it now as he rounded the corner of the yard, with the mule in tow, and ran smack bang into a woman. She was bent double over the water pump, crying her heart out. He didn't have time to register her presence before he walked into her, and his bulk sent her head over heels, flipping into the mud beside the pump. She had something to cry about before, but she had even more to cry about now.

Splatters of muck hit Kit and the mule, and the mule bucked, honking and hawing like a shot goose. Kit fought to control him, worried his hooves would hit the woman in the head.

"Hellfire, are you all right?" He kept tight hold of the mule, struggling. The poor old thing was out of temper after a night in harness. "Lady?"

There was no response. She just lay there in the mud, like a dropped rag doll. Lord, had he hurt her bad?

Kit hurried to tether the mule to a juniper bush and rushed to the poor woman's aid. "I'm sorry," he said, squatting in the mud at her side. "I should've taken a wider berth around the corner."

She spluttered. It was a relief to see her move.

She was only a little bit of a thing, trussed up in an ugly black dress and a now-muddy white apron. Kit helped her sit up, gingerly taking her by the muddy arm.

"I'm so sorry." He couldn't seem to stop apologizing. It felt powerful bad to knock a lady over that way. He felt like an oaf.

"That's one way to get the sense knocked into you," she said, spitting mud. She sounded dazed but lively enough. She had a strong and mighty pretty accent. The melody of it made Kit shivery. It was like a cascade of falling water; arioso. Now there was a word he didn't get to use much.

She was staring at him now, vaguely alarmed. He was used to

that. He was a big man; it made people wary. And he *had* just sent her flying, so she had reason for some alarm. Maybe Junebug had been right to call him scary. She met his gaze and her eyes widened. If she was surprised, Kit was lost for words. Her eyes were the deepest shade of blue that Kit had ever seen on a person. They were the color he imagined sapphires to be when he read about them. They had the same sense of depth he imagined sapphires had too. The same hidden sparkle. But they also put him in mind of forget-me-nots and harebells and deep fall skies.

God, look at him. He knew so few young women, just the sight of one sent him stupid.

But she sure was pretty. Her oval face was pointed at the chin, and she had a pert nose covered in a dusting of freckles. Even with her sitting there covered in filth, it was clear as day that she was a fine-looking woman.

"Did you hit your head?" Kit asked gently. She looked dazed.

"Erm . . . I don't think so." Circumspectly, she pulled her arm away from his grasp and reached up to feel her head. She glanced around and moaned. "Not more blessed laundry!"

He'd clearly caught her in the middle of her chores. There was a half-filled pail, and a wicker basket, now tipped on its side in the mud. Its contents were a slop of muddy cloth.

"I'm powerful sorry." Kit sat back on his heels. She was a bedraggled sight, sitting there in the puddle by the pump, in the middle of her now mucky clothes.

Thunderhead Bill's mule hee-hawed.

"I reckon he's wanting to apologize too," Kit said, trying to coax a smile out of her. He bet she was even prettier when she smiled. He moved to help her as she went to stand.

"It's my own fault for blocking the thoroughfare," she sighed. She had a way of looking at him sideways, her sooty lashes trembling against her mud-speckled skin, that made him feel rather thickheaded.

"Hardly," he disagreed. "A body has every right to be using a pump." Although she hadn't been using the pump, had she? She'd been bent over it, like all the bones had melted out of her, weeping up a storm. Kit wondered what had made her cry like that. And whose fault it was.

She sighed and started gathering up the mucky clothes. "No rest for the wicked."

God, that voice. It made him daft. It was too pretty for words.

"Is there anything I can do to help?" Kit asked, bending to pull a skirt from the mud.

"Take me back to Ireland?" She slopped mud off her apron with her bare hands. "I'd best be getting these clean again. I'm sorry I got in your way." She had a formal way of talking. Deferential like.

Kit laughed. "*You're* sorry?" Hell, she was serious. "Honey, you didn't do anything. It was all me and the mule."

The mule hee-hawed again.

"See? He agrees with me."

Not so much as a smile. She merely apologized again and slopped away, her wet skirts heavy against her legs. She did glance back at him as she slipped through the washhouse door, and that glance made his stomach go weak. But there wasn't so much as a flicker of a smile.

Who *was* she?

She must have come in on the last train, Kit thought as he collected the mule. He looked back at the washhouse. The poor thing looked worn-out. He felt terrible for adding to her troubles.

He wondered if there was anything he could do to make it up to her . . .

Maybe flowers? Girls liked flowers, didn't they? They did in the books he read, anyway. His little sister was more partial to a new fishing rod than flowers, but this one didn't seem the fishing rod type. There weren't many flowers around in November, most of the wildflowers bloomed themselves out by the end of summer, but after he'd sorted Thunderhead Bill's mule, Kit wandered the woods behind the stable, trying to find enough to put in a bunch. He managed to make a fistful of late-blooming wild roses, with a couple of wallflowers and some flowering buckwheat mixed in. He gathered his nerve and headed for the washhouse.

But as he neared, he heard splashing. And not the kind a washboard made.

She was cleaning the mud off herself, he realized, flushing. She'd been well and truly soaked in it . . .

Unbidden, images flooded his mind. Images of that black dress peeled away, of a washcloth swiping mud, of dewy clean skin revealed . . .

Hell. Those were thoughts to make a man half-daft. And he might be a backwoodsman, but he wasn't backward enough to barge in on a lady at her toilette.

Feeling vaguely ridiculous and more than a little transparent, he took his offering to the kitchen door instead, knocking as he stuck his head in. "Good morning," he greeted Alice Champion.

"Kit." She was surprised to see him. "Junebug's not here."

"I know." He felt absurdly bashful. "I've just . . ." He cleared his throat. "I've got flowers." He held out his modest pink-and-white bunch. The wallflowers nodded on their long necks.

Alice blinked. "I see that." She seemed totally nonplussed.

"For . . ." Hell. He didn't even know the girl's name. "She has blue eyes," he said helplessly. Only that didn't quite do her justice, did it? "Harebell blue, like a June field."

"For the love of . . ." Alice leaned forward on her fists and took a steadying breath. "Not another one."

Another one? Kit frowned.

"Do you have a message you want to give her too?" Alice asked, sounding bewilderingly irritable about it.

"Just that I'm sorry."

"You're sorry?" Alice sighed, and came to collect the flowers.

"I'll pass it on. I'd let you pass it on yourself, but Miss Blue Eyes is busy right now."

Kit blushed. It was his fault she was busy bathing. He'd gone and flung her headfirst into the mud. He felt terrible. Imagine how hard she had to scrub to get that thick pump-puddle mud off.

No. Don't imagine. Imagining did disturbing things to him.

"I really am sorry," he said. "Please tell her that."

"You're sorry. I'll tell her." Alice was businesslike. "Anything else? Or just you're sorry? Twice over."

"Just that." Kit felt himself grinning as he left the hotel. He gave the washhouse a last look and patted the water pump on his way past. He hoped the flowers would go a way toward making her less sad.

As he headed to Fritz's, he realized he hadn't asked Alice Champion what the blue-eyed girl's name was. He could have kicked himself. But then again, it gave him a good excuse to come back, didn't it? And he might wear his nicer shirt when he came. Maybe shave first. It had been a long time since he'd shaved.

As he wandered up the street to the mercantile, he was lost in thoughts of blue eyes and that arioso voice.

Four

"I haven't a baldy notion why you didn't tell her to wash her own unmentionables in the first place," Maddy muttered to herself as she scrubbed the linen on the washboard with ragged fury. She couldn't believe she was washing Willabelle's clothes for the second time in a day!

How was her luck, being knocked into the mud when she was carrying *clean* clothes! If only the big brute had knocked her over *before* she'd washed them. Maddy had been at the end of her tether even before the rough-looking frontiersman had collided with her. The journey to Bitterroot had been long and arduous. It had involved multiple trains, through Missouri, Minnesota, Wisconsin, North Dakota and finally Montana, in carriages crammed with prospective miners swapping tips about dynamite and glory holes and steam engines. Maddy didn't think she would ever scrub herself free of the dust and soot or get the smell of sweaty men out of her nose.

Willabelle could only afford for them to travel third class, so they sat upright the entire way, elbows jarring each other, Merle squirming on their laps. Willabelle made Maddy sit by the window, as she didn't like the billowing steam and the stench of oil, and through that window Maddy had seen more of America than she ever knew existed. The distances were unfathomable; she thought Ireland could have fit into the Great Plains alone more than a dozen times over. As the train headed westward, she'd seen the regal roll of the Mississippi, with steamboats gliding like swans on its shining length; eaten catfish and frizzled ham in half-dime lunchrooms; navigated the beehive of a station at St. Paul, where more than one hundred trains departed every day; and she'd seen the vast plains themselves, where the clouds chased shadows over seas of grass, waves of grain rippling in the wind, tossing their heavy heads. The far-flung stretches of land boggled the mind, as did the variations—mountains and rivers and hills and plains. It was nothing like the predictable spinach-green undulations of home.

Not unexpectedly, Willabelle was a nightmare to travel with. She complained like an angry toddler, and then she took a shine to a sleazy miner named Garrett who talked of nothing but the silver on his claim. Maddy could practically see the nuggets sparkling in Willabelle's eyes. Mr. McBride might have some stiff competition; Maddy hoped for his sake (and hers, since she needed him to pay her way home) that all those blacksmithing muscles would turn Willabelle's head from Garrett's promise of silver.

As the days slid by, Maddy had the disconcerting sense of being dragged farther and farther into the wilderness. She wished she'd kept hold of Willabelle's earbobs, instead of letting her lock them back up in her safe again. It had felt too risky to carry them on her person, but without them she was hostage to Willabelle's whims. And those whims had thrown her to the four winds of fate. She felt like she was falling off the known map, into a world that would swallow her up and never spit her back out again.

And then they got to Bitterroot.

Maddy's heart sank when they stepped off the train. She thought there must have been a mistake. This wasn't a town; it was a train stop in the middle of a forest. The land wasn't even cleared. The main road was just dirt—and there was a creek running through the middle of it! Nothing was clean. Even the sunlight was dusty.

There was only one hotel in town, and it still smelled of the pine it was built from. Willabelle had booked herself a big double room (on credit—the poor hotelier had no idea she was flat broke) and relegated Maddy to a cramped servant's room in the eaves. And then she'd dumped her trunk of filthy laundry on Maddy and sent her out to the washhouse.

Maddy had been so tired. And as she'd worked her way through Willabelle's clothes, slogging back and forth to the pump for fresh water, she'd given in momentarily to her despair. Look at the place! It was barbaric! And look at her, working her fingers to the bone for a flibbertigibbet who didn't even have two pennies to rub together!

Her mind spiraled through all the wickedly bad choices she'd made to lead her to this point. This was her punishment for being naught but a hussy. She worked herself into a lather thinking on it, and collapsed over the pump and cried like she hadn't cried since Thomas Ormond had thrown her over.

And then, her stars being what they were, she got knocked face-first into the mud by one of the brutes of Bitterroot. She'd been so shocked, her tears had dried up.

The mud was a thick mineral tang in her mouth and nose. She felt it squidging between her fingers. Couldn't a girl even have a *cry* in this place without the world turning upside down? She'd felt like flinging mud at the lout.

The cursed man had knelt by her side, and he was the biggest man Maddy had ever seen, with arms the size of Christmas hams and thighs like tree trunks. His chest was as wide as a draft horse's. And he had a thick dark beard and strong eyebrows. She wouldn't like to run into him at night. Or when crying over a water pump . . .

He was definitely *not* the kind of man she should be flinging mud at, she'd thought with a shiver.

But he turned out to be a gentle brute. His eyes were liquid darkness, full of concern, and his voice was husky and soft. It seemed incongruous coming out of a man so rough. The gentleness contrasted starkly with his looks. When he called her *honey*, Maddy felt a bit giddy. No one had been this concerned for her in months. Not since Mrs. Egan back home. It made Maddy realize that no one had even held her gaze, person-to-person, since she'd reached America. And why would they? She was just a servant.

This man didn't just meet her gaze; he stared. Like he could see right through to the center of her. And his soft brown eyes were so *warm*. Kind.

Everything had just been so *bad*. She was lost, she was alone; everything was so wild and remote, and she had no idea where to turn for help. She was exhausted by this place and by these people, and by America as a whole. She missed the smallness of Ireland, the speck of Crinkle, the stiff order of Ormond House, where a girl knew what was what. Even facing Thomas Ormond and his Right Honorable wife didn't seem so bad anymore. At least it was predictable. Not like here, with woods so endless everything seemed like something out of a frightening fairy tale.

The man's kind stare made her want to spill her hurt out. To ask for help. Which was absurd, because he was a total stranger. A rough Bitterroot frontiersman who couldn't be trusted. Shouldn't be trusted.

When the enormous man helped her up out of the mud, he was so strong that she felt weightless. He set her on her feet and steadied her. And he kept apologizing, more sorrowful and earnest with every repetition.

Maddy had pulled away and brushed herself down, flustered by the attention and the courtesy. Her hands came away from her uniform covered in muck. More blessed laundry, she realized, spying the clean clothes sprawled in the mud. She didn't know if she could face that washhouse again. And look at the state of her!

He set to apologizing again.

"It's my own fault," she'd assured him, as she'd been trained all her life to do. It was her job to stay out of the way. To be invisible, just part of the furniture. If someone tripped on a stool, they didn't apologize to the stool.

He laughed and his laugh was a revelation. It was deep, honest. Free. She risked another look at those eyes. Jesus, Mary and Joseph, they were beautiful eyes, with thick curling lashes framing them, pretty as any girl's. How did such a man have such pretty eyes? Maddy got a bit lost in them.

"No rest for the wicked," she'd said awkwardly, pulling away to gather the laundry up.

"Is there anything I can do to help?" he asked, and she almost threw herself at him then and there.

"Take me back to Ireland?" she blurted.

Lord, he was big. Big and some lash. Shoulders like you wouldn't believe.

Imagine the sight of him out of that shirt . . .

What on earth was she thinking? He could be a murderer for all she knew. He looked rough enough.

Not with those eyes, a little inner voice sighed.

No. Definitely not with those eyes.

"Eejit," she muttered, coming back to herself, bent over the washtub, scrubbing everything for the second time. What was she doing fantasizing about some backwoodsman? Did she *want* to get herself stranded out here, at the very edge of the world? "You're nothing but a brainless eejit. Look at you. Scrubbing her nasties and thinking about your man, instead of telling that parrot to get stuffed and climbing on the first train out of here." She huffed as she worked the washboard. "Ah yes, but with what money? It's all well and good to—"

"Good morning," a perky voice said from the doorway of the washhouse.

Maddy startled, slipping on the washboard and banging her chin on the top of it. She swore.

"That's a good word," the voice observed. "What does it mean?"

Maddy touched her chin gingerly as she glared at the intruder. Did she look like she wanted company?

The company in question was a lanky girl in a set of denim overalls too big for her; they looked in desperate need of a clean, as did she. She was holding a battered old hat in her grimy hand, and her choppy dark hair was mussed in every which way. She wasn't wearing shoes, and her feet were brown with dirt.

Maddy didn't think it was a good morning at all and wasn't in any mood to make chat with strangers. Especially a child as raggedy as this one. "Good morning," she said shortly, returning to her chores.

"Them clothes sure got you sore bothered, don't they?" the girl said cheerfully, leaning against the doorjamb. Maddy wished she wouldn't. The washhouse was rickety and was liable to fall right over with her leaning on it like that.

"Well, if you're going to moan, you might as well put your back into it, that's what I always say," the girl laughed. "And I must say, it was good to hear it. Quite snapped me out of my nerves."

"I thought I was alone," Maddy grunted, returning to the washboard. She fell into a rhythm, the percussion fractious and vexed.

"A fair enough assumption in Bitterroot. Although I heard the hotel was full, so there must be folks about."

Maddy felt the girl's frank stare. She had the manners of a guttersnipe. This town was nothing but miners, brutes and gutter-snipes. Oh no, now she was thinking about your man again, him of the incredible shoulders . . .

"You're new," the girl continued. "Did you come on the train?"

Maddy grunted an assent.

"What brings you to Bitterroot?"

"Matrimony," Maddy said dryly, before she could think better of it.

"Matrimony!" The kid sounded gleeful. Then there was a long pause.

Maddy glanced up. The girl was giving her a troubled look.

"*You're* getting married?" she sounded doubtful.

"No."

There was another pause. "You're parsimonious with your words, ain't ya?" the girl observed. "I cain't say it's a quality I admire. My brothers can be tightfisted with words, too, and it irks me to no end. *You're here for matrimony but you ain't getting married . . .* it's like a riddle."

Maddy sat back and rubbed her sweaty forehead on her arm. She wished this child would just go away. The laundry was going to take her forever as it was.

"You're a servant!" the girl announced triumphantly as she worked it out.

"My, you're a bold one!" Maddy scolded. "Did no one ever tell you not to talk to strangers? Let alone ask questions that you've no right to be asking."

"There ain't no strangers around here."

Lord, the child was exasperating. "*I'm* a stranger."

"Not now that I've met you, you ain't."

Maddy might have been startled into a laugh if she hadn't been so exhausted. "Honestly. You don't even know my name."

"But I will, as soon as you tell it to me." The irritating child pulled up a low stool and sat on the other side of the copper, directly opposite Maddy. Her gaze had the quality of a watchful cat.

"You must work for someone pretty fancy. We don't get servants much in these parts. Except for Ellen and Mrs. Champion at the hotel, and neither of them are much good at it." The girl cocked her head. "You're a maid, right?"

"Right," Maddy said sourly.

"And you do laundry." The kid sounded inordinately pleased.

Maddy felt like slopping Willabelle's wet drawers in her lap. There was nothing to be pleased about when it came to laundry. "Did *no one* tell you the story of Little Red Riding Hood?" Maddy demanded. She had palpitations at the thought of what might befall a girl around here, especially a girl as forward as this one was. Those miners at the hotel might be dusting off their manners for Willabelle, but they were no gentlemen. "Talking to strangers isn't safe, especially for a young girl! Now get on with you."

"I ain't as young as I look." The girl grinned, and Maddy blinked. Her smile lit up her face, like the sun coming out from behind the clouds. "And you ain't no wolf," the girl said gently, as though trying not to hurt Maddy's feelings.

"I might be," Maddy snapped. "You don't know yet."

The kid's grin only got wider. "Well, if you are, I reckon I'd be keen to know a lady wolf."

"Not if I ate you up."

"So, the lady you work for is here to get married?"

The girl was incorrigible.

"Who's she here to marry?" she continued, ignoring Maddy's irritation. "I'd know him—I know everyone. Did she answer an advertisement? Is she nice?"

The barrage of questions was discombobulating. Maddy had had enough. "Who do you belong to?" she asked tersely. Whoever was responsible for this kid needed a talking-to. She peered over the girl's shoulder, out at the yard.

"Who do I belong to?" The girl seemed astonished by the question. "What a queer thing to ask. I belong to myself."

"I mean, where are your parents? You oughtn't be left to wander around, bothering people."

"I don't reckon talking is bothering. People usually like me talking to them. You will, too, as soon as we're better acquainted. I reckon you're just out of sorts because you don't like laundry."

Well, that was true enough. "Who does?" Maddy rolled her eyes as she stood up. She was going to find out who this child belonged to. She didn't have time for this.

"Laundresses might like laundry?" the girl hazarded.

"No, they hate it too." Maddy dried her hands on her apron. "Every laundry maid I've ever known would rather be doing anything else. It's hot, it's sweaty and it's endless."

The girl's smile grew even brighter, if such a thing were possible. "That's heartening! I thought it was just me. I'll have to tell Morgan it's everyone. It'd be good for him to know it's the laundry's fault, not mine." She reached into the wicker basket next to the copper and pulled out one of Willabelle's skirts. It was stiff with mud. Maddy felt herself shudder at the sight of it. She'd been putting that one off. How was she ever going to get all that mud out?

"What did she do, roll around in the creek?" the girl asked with her perpetual cheeriness.

"Something like that." Maddy moved to the doorway and examined the yard for sight of the girl's parents. There was no one out there.

The girl stood up. "I can help you, if you want. I'm an expert in these things. You should have seen the state of my brothers' long underwear after last winter." The kid gathered up the filthy skirt and opened the door to the stove, which was burning merrily, heating another copper of water.

Before Maddy had quite realized what was happening, the mad girl had thrown Willabelle's skirt into the stove and swiftly closed the door.

"There you go," she said, pleased with herself. "Problem solved."

"What are you *doing*?!" Maddy felt like she'd been kicked by a horse.

"You were never getting that skirt properly clean again. That mud stains. It's better off burned." The kid actually seemed to expect gratitude.

She'd *burned* Willabelle's skirt! Maddy exploded. "*I'm* the one who'll be blamed for this!" She didn't have it in her to listen to Willabelle throw another tantrum. Oh, she could have pitched the girl in the stove too! "She'll be furious!"

Not just furious—she'd dock Maddy's pay. The pay she wasn't even paying!

"Will she now?" The girl cocked her head and pursed her lips. "She's got a temper, has she, this woman you work for?"

"I want your name." Maddy folded her arms and gave the girl her sternest look. She was done being everyone's doormat. "And I want to know where your parents are."

"My name's Junebug." The girl thrust her hand out, as though expecting Maddy to shake it. "And I don't rightly know what my parents have got to do with anything. But if you have to know, Ma's dead and Pa's run off."

Maddy didn't shake her hand. "Junebug isn't a proper name, and if you don't have parents, you belong to someone, and I want to know who."

"Junebug mightn't be a proper name where you come from—where is that, by the way, because you talk funny—but it is here."

"I don't talk funny at all."

"You do. If someone played the fiddle, you'd sound like you were singing. Are you southern?"

"Irish," Maddy snapped. Her head ached. This girl had a knack for getting her all turned around. "And I still want to know who you belong to!"

"Irish, huh . . . Ireland's a long way off! I'd be keen to hear about it." The mad girl seemed thrilled. "My brother read me a book about an Irish girl once, *Molly Bawn*. She was a hoot. Have you read it?"

Maddy wasn't getting swept up in talk about a book she hadn't read and couldn't read. "Your brother!" She leapt on the scrap of information. "Is he the one responsible for you?"

"You sure have got a bee in your bonnet about me belonging to someone."

"I want recompense for that skirt! I'm not paying for it."

"Oh, that." Junebug flicked her hand dismissively. "It was already ruined. I'm happy to tell her I did it. Just tell me her name and point me in her direction."

Maddy was going to do more than that! She was going to march the girl in to Willabelle herself. The last thing she needed was Willabelle deducting the skirt from the pay she was owed. "Her name is Willabelle Lascalles, and she's out on the porch. I'll escort you." Maddy gestured to the door.

"Willabelle Lascalles!" The kid grinned ear to ear.

Maddy didn't see what she had to be so pleased about.

"Well, I'm right looking forward to meeting her." Junebug swept through the door and headed for the hotel. "Don't fret, I'll tell her that her skirt was beyond saving."

"And that you burned it," Maddy insisted.

"I'd think you'd be happy you don't have to wash it," Junebug said blithely. "Seems like you got the good end of the stick . . . Hey. I just realized I don't know your name. I reckon you need pulling up on your manners, not introducing yourself. I may have been raised in the wilds, but even I know it's polite to shake hands and give your name. Don't think I haven't noticed you didn't shake my hand. Don't they shake hands in Ireland?"

Lord, the girl could talk. Maddy had intended to drag her to account, but instead she was jogging in her wake, trying to keep up.

"If you don't tell me your name, I'll have to make one up for you," Junebug announced. "I need to address you as something."

"You can't go making up names for people!" Maddy scolded as they reached the back door of the hotel.

"Sure I can. All names are made up anyway."

"Well, you won't be making one up for me."

"Shame. I can think of some names that will suit you."

Maddy almost asked what they were but then mentally shook herself. "My name is Maddy, you bold wean."

"Pleased to make your acquaintance, Maddy." Junebug was sunny as she pushed open the door to the hotel kitchen. "Good morning, Mrs. Champion!"

The smell of yeast and rising dough hit Maddy full in the face as she followed Junebug into the kitchen. The room was flooded with sunshine and dusty with flour. Mrs. Champion, the hotel's housekeeper, was a short woman with an excess of energy and a soft heart. But her softheartedness wasn't on display today; she was pummeling a lump of dough as though she wanted to commit violence as they came in.

Junebug sneezed as she walked into a cloud of flour. "Remind me to tell you about the explosive properties of flour," she told Mrs. Champion. "You've got a disaster in the making here."

"Oh, good morning, Junebug, pet. There's no bread yet, I'm afraid, if that's what you've come for. I'm well behind today." Mrs. Champion was flustered and sour.

Junebug turned and pulled a face at Maddy. "That's not what I'm here for."

No. Maddy was sure it wasn't. Mrs. Champion's bread was dire. It didn't matter how much butter or jam you smeared on it, it tasted like wood pulp.

"I've come to meet one of your guests," Junebug said brightly.

Mrs. Champion's gaze flicked to Maddy, who felt like she'd lost control of the whole situation.

"Is she still out on the porch?" Maddy asked, trying to regain a semblance of authority. There was no need elaborating on who the *she* was. Mrs. Champion and Maddy were of a similar mind about Willabelle. Maddy could see the cloud cross the housekeeper's face.

"And where else would she be?" Mrs. Champion gave the dough a violent pounding. "She's insisted on high tea. High tea! We don't do high tea. Do you know," Mrs. Champion told Junebug and Maddy, "that fool Rigby wanted me to bake a cake! A cake! When there's still all the breakfast dishes need doing, and the bread to get on with. When I said no, do you know what he did?"

"No . . ." Junebug was transfixed.

Oh no. Maddy saw where this was going. Once Mrs. Champion got started, she talked as much as Junebug did. And Maddy had no time or inclination for it.

"He got Bonnie to bake one!" Mrs. Champion railed.

"Bonnie!" Junebug exclaimed.

"Never mind about the cake," Maddy interrupted, impatient. "We need to talk to Willabelle."

"Never mind about the cake!" Mrs. Champion exclaimed. She and Junebug were both astonished. They turned on her.

"You're only saying that because you don't know who Bonnie is!" Junebug told her.

"No, I'm saying it because it's irrelevant, no matter who Bonnie is." Maddy pushed open the kitchen door. "Come on with you now."

"I'm only coming because I want a slice of cake," Junebug told her.

"Rigby will want you to pay if you want cake," Mrs. Champion warned as Junebug followed Maddy. "He's putting on airs for Her Majesty."

"It's okay. I've got money from my letter writing." Junebug paused. "What did you just call her?"

"Her Majesty. Her Grand Highness. Her Royal Pain in the Derriere," Mrs. Champion muttered into her dough.

"I don't like the sound of that," Junebug said in dark tones.

"Come on." Maddy took Junebug by the arm and led her through the empty dining room. She didn't want the girl to back out now. Talking to Willabelle was a trial at the best of times; add this chatterbox of a child and she might not get back to finish the laundry until well after suppertime.

"*Is* she a royal pain in the derriere?" Junebug asked.

"One doesn't speak ill of one's employer," Maddy told her, without enthusiasm.

"But if one did . . . ?"

Maddy didn't answer. If one did, one would let loose the floodgates . . .

Five

Willabelle was holding court in one of Rigby's high-backed cane chairs. She was decked out in canary-yellow satin, with an enormous fluffy yellow feather curling from her pile of blond hair. She was glowing, the sun around which everything orbited. The porch was crammed with miners. Every seat was full, and the porch rail was hidden, as men lined it, elbow to elbow. All of them had their gazes trained on Willabelle.

"Well, if that don't beat all," Junebug breathed as she and Maddy reached the front door. They paused to take in the crush on the porch. "She's got some serious wiles, don't she?"

Maddy didn't reply. She was too irked. Here she was, sweaty from labor, while this bright canary of a woman sat in the cool shade of the porch, with men fluttering about, handing her cake.

"Junebug!" Rigby, the threadbare hotelier, noticed them hovering at the front door. Alarmed, he darted over. "Not today!" He shooed the girl.

"I'm with her," Junebug said stubbornly, stepping closer to Maddy. "And I want cake. I ain't had cake in an age. My brother Kit made me chocolate cake for my birthday last year," she confided to Maddy, "but I ain't likely to get it ever again, since the recipe burned down with the cookhouse."

"I just need her to talk to Mrs. Lascalles," Maddy told him, ignoring Junebug's chatter about cake.

"Now?" Rigby seemed flustered. "We're in the middle of high tea!"

"You got tea?" Junebug lit up. "I ain't never had tea!"

"We got coffee." Rigby was sour.

"You've always got coffee. How is this different than usual?"

"I don't want you making a scene and scaring off all my customers," Rigby hissed at them. "You can wait here till high tea is over and then you can talk to her!"

Maddy gathered her patience. "Please, Mr. Rigby, I have chores to do. It will be quick."

"And I don't got all day neither," Junebug chimed in. "I'm a busy person, I'll have you know."

But Rigby wasn't amenable. And Maddy was loath to make a scene—it went against all her training.

"Why don't you give us some of that cake and we'll wait inside until your high tea is done?" Junebug suggested. She seemed fixated on the cake, which was sitting proudly on a table in the middle of the porch. It was a layered yellow sponge cake, bursting with cream and strawberry jam.

"That cake is not for the likes of you," Rigby snapped.

Maddy was unsurprised. Junebug was delusional to think she could join in with teatime, looking the way she did. She clearly had no idea of the way of things. "Come on, Junebug, you can help me with the laundry until this is over and then we'll talk to her." She wasn't letting the girl out of her sight until Willabelle heard about the skirt.

"Fat chance," Junebug said, undaunted. "I want that cake." She fished in the pockets of her overalls. "Here," she told Rigby, flourishing coins. "I can pay."

Maddy saw the emotions warring on the hotelier's face. He

didn't want Junebug ruining his fancy high tea, which he'd pulled together to impress Willabelle (the man had even repurposed one of his lace curtains to make a tablecloth), but he was also clearly a sucker for a shiny coin.

"I won't sit on the porch," Junebug promised. "I'll go sit in the dining room, away from your fancy guests."

Rigby took her money.

"I want a slice for Maddy the Maid too!" Junebug called as he plowed toward the cake table.

"Oh no . . ." Maddy protested, out of habit. But she stopped herself. The cake did look good.

"In the dining room," Rigby told them sternly as he handed over the plates.

"You've been stingy," Junebug complained, looking at the slivers of cake. "I paid good money! You go right back and put more on those plates or I'll park myself out there in the middle of your darned high tea." She scowled at him.

To Maddy's astonishment, the hotelier did it. He didn't look pleased about it, but he did it.

"You got to watch him," Junebug sniffed. "He's tight as a gnat's chuff."

"Junebug!" Maddy said, shocked. Honestly, the girl was completely undomesticated. "That's no language for a lady!"

Junebug shot her a cheeky grin. "Sorry," she apologized. "I'm used to the company of boys." Then she straightened, looking pleased. "You think I'm a lady?"

"Dining room!" Rigby interrupted, thrusting plates holding fat hunks of cake into their hands.

"I don't have time for this," Maddy complained as Junebug headed happily back to the dining room.

"Sure you do. That laundry ain't going anywhere."

Well, that was God's honest truth. Maddy followed her into the dining room, where Junebug had pulled up a chair at the table by the window. As Maddy joined her, she realized they had a clear view of the circus out on the porch.

"She always this popular with men?" Junebug asked. The girl was transfixed as Willabelle giggled and simpered and cast sideways glances at all and sundry.

Maddy grunted. She turned her back on the display. She'd seen enough of it on the train. Her mouth watered as she considered the cake. It was highly improper for her to be sitting here in the guests' dining room, eating cake in the middle of the workday . . . but look at this place. Everything about Bitterroot was highly improper.

Maddy speared the cake with her fork. It was the only payment she'd get today for all her labors, so she might as well enjoy it. And, oh Lord, it was good. Chewy and airy and vanilla sweet. The cream was a cloud of pleasure in her mouth.

"You ever notice that her eyes don't smile?" Junebug observed. For someone who had been fixated on cake a minute ago, she sure was slow to eat hers.

Maddy looked over her shoulder at her employer, following Junebug's gaze.

"They don't match the rest of her," Junebug said, disgruntled. "She looks like a goshawk hunting squirrels."

That was as apt a description as any Maddy could think of for Willabelle.

"Are all fancy ladies like her?"

Maddy thought about it. "Not all. But I guess they have to hunt husbands . . . so a lot are." She remembered Tom Ormond's wife. She was prone to a lot of trilling laughter, too, and her eyes were often watchful and cool.

"She's here to get married, huh . . ." Junebug prodded. She turned away from the window and gave Maddy her full attention.

Maddy wasn't one for gossip. She simply nodded, hoping Junebug would get lost in the pleasure of the cake and drop it.

But Junebug had other ideas. "And she's already got a man picked out from an advertisement."

"Yes." Maddy frowned. "How did you know about the advertisement?"

Junebug rolled her eyes. "You think we get women out here any other way? You seen any other fancy ladies in these parts? If there were ladies here, the rest of us wouldn't know so much about laundry," she muttered. "And we might get cake more often." She finally turned her attention to her plate. "So tell me something, Maddy the Maid: if she's here to get married, why is she out there hunting husbands?"

Maddy shrugged, staying tight-lipped. Every bit of her training screamed at her to stay quiet. One didn't gossip. Even if one's employer was a scheming, self-involved defaulter of payments.

"She always dress this fancy?" Junebug asked, changing tack.

Maddy shrugged again.

"Humph." Junebug wasn't pleased by her reticence. She picked the cake up in her hand, the cream smooshing between her fingers, and bit a hunk out of it.

"Use a fork!" Maddy scolded, waving her own. "For Pete's sake, your hands are filthy!" Oh, this child needed serious parenting!

"It's good," Junebug said through a mouthful of cake. "You know who made it, don't you?" Her eyes shone as she jerked her head in the direction of the cathouse across the street. "Bonnie's one of the girls at the cathouse. My brothers think I don't know what goes on over there, but I do."

Maddy choked on her mouthful.

"I looked up *whore* in the dictionary," the girl said smugly as she licked cream off her fingers.

"Jesus, Mary and Joseph!" Maddy was shocked to her core to hear the word come out of a child's mouth. It wasn't a word she was used to hearing coming out of *anyone's* mouth.

Junebug blinked at the strength of her reaction. "What?"

"That's not a word for a lady," Maddy said tightly.

"I ain't a lady."

"You most certainly are not. But you should be!" Maddy was horrified. "You keep talking about your brothers—don't you have any sisters?"

"Sure." Junebug's pink tongue licked a blob of cream off her thumb. "Dead ones."

Maddy's heart squeezed. Poor wayward wean. "So, it's just you . . . and a bunch of men?" Maddy could only imagine what kind of men, given the state of her.

Willabelle's chiming laugh sounded, and Junebug's attention returned to the porch. "What does she do?" the girl asked.

"Do?" Maddy was still thinking about the girl's plight. Look at her. She was filthy. She hadn't even washed her hands before she ate out of them.

"Yeah, do. If you do all her laundry and the like . . . what does *she* do?" Junebug demanded. "Does she cook?"

"No!" Maddy actually laughed at the thought.

"Clean?"

"No."

"Garden? She good with growing vegetables?"

Maddy shook her head.

"Can she milk a cow?"

Maddy tried to imagine it and giggled.

"So what in hell does she do? Other than beguile men?"

"I think that's about it," Maddy said honestly. "Although she likes to shop too."

"Shop! For what?"

"Clothes," Maddy sighed. "That I have to wash."

Junebug was frozen, cake in hand, staring at Maddy. She cleared her throat. "Are you staying with her, when she marries this man from the advertisement?"

"Not ever!" Maddy couldn't stop herself. The thought was too appalling. "As soon as she pays me the wages I'm owed, I'm on the first train out of Bitterroot!" The thought was almost as sweet as the cake. Once Willabelle was Mrs. McBride, and had access to funds, Maddy would be free.

Junebug's cake squished as she clenched her fist. "But who'll clean her clothes when you go?"

"I haven't a notion and I don't care," Maddy said firmly. "But I doubt it'll be her."

"C'mon." Junebug shoved the remains of the cake into her mouth, cramming it in until her cheeks bulged. She stood up and wiped her hands on the tablecloth. "Let's get this over with," she said through the mouthful of mashed-up cake, striding off to the porch.

"But Rigby . . ."

All that came back was a string of muffled curses. Maddy went bright red. She'd never heard such words in her life.

"I got a confession to make," the girl said as she planted herself in front of Willabelle Lascalles.

By the time Maddy reached the porch, the ragamuffin had already found Willabelle and started in on her speech. Willabelle was out of sorts, Maddy noted, because the miners were taking their leave and heading en masse down to the mercantile to buy supplies for their new lives on their claims. Rigby had taken the dirty dishes to the kitchen, and Willabelle was now devoid of male attention. Maddy knew how irritable that made her. Willabelle glanced up at the raggedy girl and immediately dismissed her as not worth talking to.

"Where's my shawl?" she demanded of Maddy instead. "It's getting cool. You know I catch a chill easily, why didn't you bring my shawl?"

"It's on the arm of your chair," Maddy told her, trying not to roll her eyes. She stood behind Junebug, half blocking her exit, half feeling the urge to offer moral support.

"It's a confession that concerns you," Junebug announced, stepping sideways so she returned to Willabelle's field of vision.

"Shouldn't you be mucking out a stable, or chopping wood, or making yourself useful?" Willabelle sighed, fixing Junebug with her cool blue gaze. "Rigby won't be impressed to find you here harassing the guests."

Maddy saw Junebug's shoulders go rigid. Lord, the woman could be rude.

She might have met her match with this urchin though.

"I ain't harassing anyone," Junebug protested. "I'm only *talking* to you."

Willabelle pulled her shawl around her shoulders and examined Junebug from head to toe. Her gaze lingered on Junebug's filthy bare feet. "Who do you belong to?"

"Why do people keep asking that?" Junebug shot Maddy a dark look. "I belong to *me*." She crossed her arms. "I hear you've come for the purpose of matrimony," she announced bluntly.

Oh no. She wasn't letting this get hijacked. Maddy stepped in. "No. She wants to talk to you about your skirt," she blurted.

Willabelle's eyebrows shot up. "My skirt?"

"Not yet." Junebug had come over stubborn. Willabelle would do that to people. "Your maid says you're here for matrimony." She crossed her arms.

Maddy flinched as Willabelle shot her a scathing look. "Gossiping, Madeleine?"

"Maddy," Maddy corrected automatically.

"She weren't gossiping," Junebug snapped. "In fact, she's the least gossipingest person I've ever met. It's downright infuriating. I had to work like the devil to get what little information I got."

"I should dock your pay for such indiscretion," Willabelle told Maddy primly.

Maddy flushed, feeling a lick of anger. Dock her pay? *What* pay?

A bellow from the street was the only thing that stilled her tongue. She was so frayed she might have given Willabelle a piece of her mind, but a wild yell echoed through the town.

Across the street, an old man stood on the steps of the cathouse, staring in horror at the hitching post. He was a fright, his iron-gray hair sticking up like a lion's mane. He looked like he'd never bathed in his life. And he was drunk.

He followed up his enraged bellow with a string of curses that rivaled Junebug's. "Someone's stolen my mule!" he yelled. "Where is he, you crooked bastards!" He kicked at the hitching post.

"Oh my." Maddy took a step back toward the door.

"The mule's bad enough," the old man railed. "But if you think you can steal a wagon from the McBrides, you got another think coming! Ain't no one survives a McBride who's been wronged!"

"Ain't that the truth," Junebug said fervently.

"McBride!" Willabelle was on her feet like she'd been stung by a bee. She met Maddy's gaze, and her blue eyes were full of raw panic. "Did he say *McBride*?"

"He surely did," Junebug said. The girl looked like she was enjoying the show immensely.

McBride! Maddy's stomach fell to her feet. Oh no. Please no. That old man couldn't be . . . *Look* at him. There was no way he had enough money to pay Maddy's back pay, not the way he was carrying on about not being able to replace the mule, let alone the wagon.

"He ain't wrong neither. There'll be hell to pay if someone's gone and stolen the McBrides' wagon. When I got here it was parked right there in front of the cathouse." Junebug sat down in the cane chair Willabelle had just vacated, and put her feet up on the railing.

"The *cathouse*." Willabelle was very pale as she clawed at Maddy's arm. "Madeleine. He was in the cathouse."

"Of course he was," Junebug told them. "Why else would he come to town?"

Maddy felt like Willabelle might cut off her circulation, she was squeezing so hard; she unhooked Willabelle's talons from her arm. Her own heart was racing. What were they going to do? If *that* was Mr. McBride, Willabelle certainly couldn't marry him. Even if she did marry him, there wouldn't be any money. They were trapped!

"Why else would he come to town . . ." Willabelle echoed. "You mean he doesn't live in town?"

"Him?" Junebug jerked her thumb in the old drunk's direction. He was stumbling back inside the cathouse. "No, he doesn't live in town."

"Where does he live?" Willabelle didn't sound like she really wanted to know the answer.

"Mostly on the porch of the trading post." Junebug grinned at her. "It's up the mountain, on the Natives' trail."

"Up the mountain. *That* mountain?" Willabelle's gaze turned to the end of the "street," where the mountain rose sharply.

"Yeah, that's the one." Junebug grinned.

"What else do you know about him?" Willabelle was all business now. She fixed her cool gaze on Junebug, who was reveling in the attention.

"What do I know about him . . ." She grinned up at Willabelle. "I know he's got all his own teeth."

Willabelle blanched.

Oh dear Lord, it *was* the McBride Willabelle was here to marry! Maddy remembered the advertisement: *Is not too old and not too ugly, has all his own teeth.*

Not *too* old. And not *too* ugly.

"Do you need to sit down?" Maddy asked weakly as Willabelle gave a soft moan.

"You'd best sit down in a chair while you can," Junebug suggested, "as he don't own any. Should you be thinking you could sit in one of his." She glanced at the street. "Looks like he don't even own a mule anymore." Then she swore and jumped out of her chair. "Hell, that's my brother come down the hill for me."

Maddy followed her gaze. A man on a horse appeared at the tree line at the end of the street. A *big* man. Almost as big as the brute who had knocked her into the mud puddle . . .

"I'd best head him off. It's better to get him before he's too mad," Junebug sighed. "Although he's had a few good hours to build up a head of steam. You'll probably hear him yelling from here . . ." She jammed her hat on her head and scooped up a hunk of cake off a discarded plate with her bare hand. "It was nice to meet you, Maddy the Maid. And good luck with your nuptials, Miss Lascalles." Junebug winked. And then she was off like a jackrabbit.

It was only when she was halfway down the street that Maddy remembered the skirt. "Hey!" she called, but Junebug was too far away to hear her.

"We need a new plan," Willabelle said slowly. She was still staring at the stairs to the cathouse, where the old drunk had stood moments before.

"The advertisement said he had a wealth of land . . ." Maddy reminded her. "Maybe he's not as bad as he seems . . ." But she didn't believe it and couldn't really even pretend that she did.

Willabelle snorted and shot her a scornful look.

Comes with a wealth of land. The advertisement hadn't said he *owned* the land, though, had it . . . Maddy took in the vast forest all around them. And what was all this, if it wasn't a wealth of land . . .

"I'm leaving," she blurted. The decision came swiftly, like a change in the weather. Her fingers fumbled at the apron ties. "I'm selling your earbobs and buying a ticket on the next train out of here." Willabelle could dig those earbobs out of her safe and make good on her promise. Maddy didn't even care where the next train was going, so long as it was to a town that had connections to a major city. The man who valued the silver from the mines could value the earbobs for her, and hopefully give her what they were worth. She didn't even mind if she got less than their worth, so long as it could get her train tickets. She'd go back to the walnut-faced priest and ask to be sent home to Ireland.

"No!" Willabelle panicked. "You can't! Those were my mother's!"

"Fine, give me something else to sell. I want what I'm owed!" Maddy took the apron off, folded it and dropped it on the empty cane chair. "I'll be upstairs packing my things," Maddy told her firmly. "You can bring me the jewelry and settle our accounts."

A gale of righteousness blew Maddy off the porch and into the hotel. She didn't care what the silly parrot did next, so long as she paid Maddy what she was owed.

"Oh, Maddy, I forgot!" Mrs. Champion was sweaty from her endeavors with the bread when Maddy stalked through the kitchen. "More flowers came for Her Queenship while you were in the washhouse earlier. Take them up, would you?" She gestured at a bunch of wildflowers sitting on the bench in a jug.

Maddy snatched up the flowers from the jug. "Who are these ones from?" she asked dryly as she headed for the back stairs. She had no intention of giving them to Willabelle. The woman had a roomful of flowers as it was; every spare surface of her room was covered with jars of the things, messy little bouquets, as filled with weedy-looking bits as they were with flat-faced wild roses. Maddy didn't understand why all these men couldn't see what an ugly warty-souled toad Willabelle really was. How could men be so stupid?

"Kit McBride," Mrs. Champion called after her.

Maddy stumbled over the bottom step. She could have screamed. They'd come all this way, on this harebrained mission to marry the man, and look where they were now! Who married a total stranger?! This was what came from such lunacy. You ended up with an angry old drunk man who lived on a *porch*.

He did pick a nicer bunch of flowers than most, Maddy noted.

"He said to tell her he was sorry," Mrs. Champion added. "Be sure to pass that on, won't you, dear? He said it twice, so it's important. And I'd hate to let him down."

He was *sorry*! For selling a false bill of goods? Oh, what use was his pitiful bunch of flowers. Could flowers buy a train ticket?

Maddy took the stairs two at a time and dropped the flowers in the chamber pot in her attic room. She was getting out of here.

Six

She was a total eejit. A bog-stupid, clod-headed, scramble-witted complete and utter *eejit*.

Willabelle was gone.

Maddy had waited for Willabelle to come with the jewelry, but of course she hadn't come. Maddy wasn't really surprised. She had been expecting a fight. After a couple of hours, Maddy put on her hat and coat, gathered her bag and headed down to confront her ex-employer. She rapped on the door.

There was no answer.

What a coward, Maddy thought. Still blown on righteous winds, she let herself in.

Willabelle's room was in complete disarray. That wasn't unusual. What *was* unusual was that her trunks were gone. In fact, *everything* was gone, except for the dog and a pile of dirty laundry. Discarded in the corner were soiled underthings, a pair of muddy shoes and two of Willabelle's gowns, which had almost irredeemably filthy hems. She'd also left a note, which Maddy couldn't read. Merle was curled up right in the middle of the bed, blissfully dozing, looking for all the world like he didn't mind being abandoned.

For mercy's sake, who abandoned their *dog*?

Willabelle Lascalles, that's who. Frantic, Maddy took the note downstairs to the kitchen. Between them, Mrs. Champion and Ellen managed to read it to her. And it was horrifyingly absurd.

Dearest Madeleine,

I have decided to settle my account with you by gifting you the blacksmith. Please. Don't thank me. It turns out he isn't without means, after all. I know it's more than I owe you, but you deserve a happy life with a wealthy man. If my heart hadn't been lost to another, I would snap him up myself. But love has claimed me, and who am I to argue with Cupid?

This is the least I can do to reward your loyal service. I am also leaving you some of my best gowns. Do be kind to the turquoise satin—you know I love it so.

That *witch*. Maddy had never been so furious in all her born life. *Gifting you the blacksmith!* She was insane. And Maddy didn't believe in the least that McBride had means. The man looked like he lived at the bottom of a bog! And *best gowns*! Dirty gowns, more like. Left for Maddy to wash.

What fool of a man could she have run off with? Who would have had the coin to tempt her?

Garrett. It could only be Garrett and his damn fool silver mine! Oh, imagine that parrot of a woman flapping about in a mining camp! Maddy hoped she fell down a shaft.

"What blacksmith?" Ellen asked, confused.

"Kit!" Mrs. Champion clamped her hand over her mouth. "Oh my, Kit McBride! *That's* why he brought her flowers!"

"Kit? Kit *McBride*?" Ellen was shocked. "But he doesn't even notice girls! Now, if it were Beau . . ." Ellen gave a moony sigh.

"That's what all those letters were about!" Mrs. Champion was hopping about with excitement now. "The letters, Ellen! The letters Mrs. Langer told us about! *Him*, off writing to people all over the country. He was looking for a *wife*."

"And he picked *her*?" Ellen's nose wrinkled.

"She is very pretty, you have to admit. And men go silly for a pretty woman."

"But he couldn't very well tell she was pretty from a letter."

Maddy stared at the scratchy lines on the page. They made no sense to her at all, and not just because she couldn't read. What was the madwoman thinking? *I have decided to settle my account with you by gifting you the blacksmith!* The *blacksmith*!

She didn't want the damn blacksmith. She wanted her twenty-eight dollars!

Maddy didn't know whether to laugh, cry or throw things.

"I can't believe it. Kit McBride," Mrs. Champion clucked. "He's such a lovely man. She would have been a lucky woman."

"Lucky! Imagine *her*, up there on the mountain!" Ellen didn't agree. "She wouldn't last a minute. There ain't no cane chairs and high teas on the McBride porch!"

"I wouldn't mind being in her place," Mrs. Champion cackled. "Up there with not just Kit, but that Morgan too! Oh, I wouldn't know where to start!"

"Mrs. Champion!" Ellen was scandalized, but the housekeeper just kept cackling.

"I can't wait to tell Mrs. Langer about this! A mail-order bride for Kit McBride." She shook her head. "And him so secretive about it." Mrs. Champion seemed to remember Maddy standing there. "Oh, pet, you should take her up on it. You won't regret it. Kit is a prize!"

Maddy frowned. Something was fishy here. The man Willabelle had pointed out to her hadn't been any kind of prize. He'd looked like a raggedy old raccoon.

"If I were ten years younger, I would have married him myself!

Lord, what a man." Mrs. Champion wasn't joking. She was coy as a schoolgirl, flushed and flustered at the thought of Kit McBride. She was *serious* about fancying the raccoon.

Only . . . what if the raccoon wasn't the right McBride . . .

"That man over at the cathouse," Maddy blurted. "The one who was yelling about his stolen mule . . . with the wild gray hair . . ."

Mrs. Champion was hard to distract from her fantasies about the blacksmith, but eventually Maddy broke through. "You mean Thunderhead Bill?" the housekeeper said, confused.

"Thunderhead Bill . . . McBride?"

Mrs. Champion and Ellen hooted with laughter. "Oh, my goodness, no, although you'd be forgiven for thinking so, given as how he's lived on their porch for the best part of a year."

Their porch. "He's not a McBride?" Maddy was struck with the blunt force of it. Junebug! That little hellion had lied to them!

"No." Mrs. Champion gave her a puzzled look. "What gave you that idea, pet?"

A little raggedy girl with the mouth of a sailor, that's what gave her that idea.

"Can you tell me . . ." Maddy didn't know where to begin. "I . . ." She threw up her hands. "Oh, Mrs. Champion!" She collapsed in a kitchen chair and tried to gather herself. And then it all poured out of her. Arriving in St. Louis, working without pay, the train ride, the shock of finding out that Willabelle wasn't going to marry Mr. McBride after they came all this way, Willabelle's disappearance . . . her eternal gullible idiocy.

"Oh my." Mrs. Champion hung on every word. "You poor love," she clucked. She whipped up a pot of coffee and served a plate of her burned biscuits. "No need for them at breakfast tomorrow, now that Her Majesty has run off. Eat. You need some sweetness."

The biscuits were about as edible as shoe leather, but it was a kind thought.

"It's like something out of a story," Ellen said, her eyes wide. "Now you should go throw yourself at the mercy of the Mc-Brides . . . If this was a story, you'd run up there, and they'd rescue you, and then you and Beau would fall madly in love."

"It's *Kit* looking for a wife," Mrs. Champion reminded Ellen. "Not Beau."

"But Beau's the handsome one."

"How many are there?" Maddy asked, dispiritedly picking at the blackened crust of a biscuit.

"There are four of the boys, and then the little one," Mrs. Champion said, happy to settle in for a gossip. "Not that she's little anymore. She's a handful, too, that one. Morgan took on the raising of her and the others when their father ran off. Poor Morgan."

Four boys and the little one . . .

Junebug.

"And they're up the mountain?" Maddy tried to control her voice. The hard biscuit cut into her as her fist clenched around it. She remembered the way Junebug was quizzing her in the dining room. *Does she cook?*

But who'll clean her clothes when you go?

Junebug had clearly decided she didn't want to be doing laundry for Willabelle Lascalles . . .

"They've got their own little township up there," Mrs. Champion said cheerily. She clearly liked these McBrides. She got all rosy with happiness when she talked about them. "Buck's Creek. It's in the prettiest broad meadow, with the creek running right along through it. Only it's more of a stream than a creek; I don't know why they call it a creek. It's wide and deep enough to be packed with trout."

"A township?" Not just a trading post on a Native trail . . .

"The start of one, anyway. There's the trading post and the forge. Kit's a powerful good smith and his forge is neat as a pin. He's busy as all get-out now that we've so many miners. He should move down to Bitterroot, instead of hauling his wares down that mountain, but they do a roaring trade up there in the trading post, with the trappers, and see no call to leave. Morgan brokered a deal with the American Fur Trading Company. People back east pay a lot of money for those furs. Fancy ladies like your Mrs. Lascalles like their hats and mufflers and such. But what good is money really, up there? The poor things have a hard time in the winter; they get snowed in for months." The information came out of her in an avalanche. "I keep telling them to get a winter house down here in town, at least for the sake of the girl. But they don't listen. I think they like it there, all by their lonesomes. I wouldn't, myself."

Clearly not. She loved to talk. Maddy wondered how Junebug coped—she loved to talk too.

"And Thunderhead Bill lives with them?" Maddy asked gingerly.

"Oh no, pet. He and Sour Eagle and Roy just camp up there. Morgan's been trying to move them on since spring."

Maddy could understand why, given the state of Thunderhead Bill. "Morgan's one of the brothers?"

"The eldest. He looks a fright but he's really a gentle soul."

"Gentle!" Ellen scoffed. "He's as gentle as a mountain lion."

"Even lions are gentle with their own," Mrs. Champion said fondly.

"Kit really told Mrs. Lascalles that he'd pay your outstanding wages?" Ellen asked Maddy.

"So she said, but I was an eejit to believe it." Maddy uncurled her fist and dropped the biscuit onto her plate. It made a *thunking* noise.

"But it might be true! And he's not short of money."

"I don't believe she ever even mentioned me to him." Maddy had no faith in Willabelle anymore. Not a scrap of it. Oh, she could scream. She was stuck here.

Maybe the hotel needed another maid . . . maybe she could work for enough money to get her ticket out of here.

"But you said he sent train fare for you?" Ellen insisted, fired up with the romance of it all. "She must have told him about you."

It was only romantic when it wasn't happening to you, Maddy thought sourly. She didn't find it romantic at all that some backwoodsman had gone advertising for a bride.

"They're good boys, those McBrides," Mrs. Champion assured Maddy. "Kit McBride is an honorable man; if he said he'd pay your wages and send you home, then he will. He wouldn't leave you stranded, not when he has some responsibility in you being left like this. I'm sure he'd at least give you fare for the train."

"For certain he would," Ellen agreed.

"I couldn't ask him." The very thought appalled Maddy. She'd never even *met* the man; she couldn't ask him for money. And it wasn't his fault that Willabelle had absquatulated. Imagine how he was going to take *that* news. He thought he was getting a bride!

"Nonsense. Of course you could ask him. It ain't your fault that you're stuck here." Mrs. Champion was firm.

"It's not *his* fault either," Maddy insisted. "The poor man is expecting a wife! Not a housemaid begging for handouts."

Mrs. Champion patted her hand. "You leave it to me, pet." She bustled out of the kitchen, and when she came back, she was carrying a portable writing desk, with fresh ink and paper balanced on top. "Now, I think it would be best if you went to Buck's Creek yourself to sort this out. Kit's not likely to be back in Bitterroot for the next week, and you don't want to waste time hanging around, not when you could get yourself out of these parts on the Friday train to Butte."

The Friday train! Maddy's heart squeezed at the very sound of it. The impossible hope that she could get out of here . . .

"I really don't feel comfortable taking money from a strange man," she said, but her protest was weaker this time.

"None of that. No nice girl deserves to be abandoned, and no decent man like Kit would stomach it, believe you me." Mrs. Champion dipped her nib in the ink. "I'll do my best to write him a letter—you can give it to him when you get up there. I'll put the whole story here and vouch for your character. Those boys know and trust me; they'll come to your aid. And maybe next time Kit will be more careful about the type of woman he chooses to take to wife."

"But—"

"No buts! I'll ask Bill and Sour Eagle to escort you up the mountain."

"Bill!" Maddy squawked. The raccoon? "As in *Thunderhead* Bill?"

"I know he looks a mess, but he's a sweet man, really. And his mule wasn't stolen, it was just stabled."

"I can't be alone with him! Them, I mean. Not out in the middle of nowhere. It's not seemly!" She could be raped and murdered and dumped in a ravine!

Mrs. Champion tapped her pen against her lip. "No. Fair enough. You're right, it's not seemly. Although, you'd be perfectly safe. Those two have all the threat of a pair of Canada geese."

"I got bit once by a Canada goose," Ellen said darkly. "It rushed right at me, flapping and snapping."

Mrs. Champion rolled her eyes. "And did it hurt?"

"No, but it sure knocked the wind out of me. I'm just saying, sometimes a goose isn't just a goose." She pursed her lips. "I'd best go with her."

"Oh no, you don't. I know what you're up to. You've got chores to do; I ain't losing you for a day just so you can go mooning after Beau McBride. I'll go. But only so far as the edge of the woods, pet. I can watch you cross the meadow from there, just to make sure you get there safe, and still get back in time for supper."

This was moving too fast. Maddy really didn't like the idea of barreling up the mountain and into the poor man's home. He didn't owe her anything. "I really don't think—"

"Now, now, no need to thank me."

"But—"

"It wouldn't be Christian to do less." And then Mrs. Champion was off to hunt down Thunderhead Bill and his friend, muttering about borrowing horses.

Maddy felt shocked, like she'd just been trampled flat on a busy street.

"She's a force, isn't she?" Ellen commiserated. "But it's a good plan. You wait and see. Those McBrides will have you on the Friday train and you'll be happy as anything. Unless you fall in love while you're up there . . . that Beau McBride could tempt a saint!"

"You can't wear that." Ellen was appalled when Maddy came downstairs, carrying Merle under one arm and her carpetbag under the other.

Maddy looked down at herself. It was her cleanest dress. It wasn't her fault she hadn't had time to scrub the mud off the other one. This one was clean but faded under the armpits and threadbare at the neckline. Usually her apron helped disguise its state. "It's all I have," she said defensively. Mrs. Champion was in an all-fired rush to get going before the day was wasted, and she didn't have time to do anything about her dress.

"Go put on one of those fancy ones Her Queenship left behind." Ellen turned her around and marched her back upstairs.

"I can't wear her clothes!"

"Of course you can. She said in the letter she left those dresses for you!"

"They're not appropriate!"

"And yours is? You look like an old crow," Ellen giggled as she propelled Maddy into Willabelle's abandoned bedroom. Maddy had straightened up as best she could. The place was still scattered with bunches of wildflowers, but she'd hung the undergarments over the end of the bed, piled the discarded letters and papers on the desk and stripped the bedding. She'd left the gowns folded on the end of the bare mattress. Ellen snapped up the turquoise satin.

"Not that one," Maddy protested. "It's ridiculous."

"Fine. But you're taking it with you. Maybe you can sell the fabric when you get where you're going. It looks valuable."

That was a good point. And Willabelle *had* left it to her. Maddy let Ellen cram it into her carpetbag.

"This one it is, then." Ellen held up the gaudy plaid taffeta. It was bright cobalt blue and scarlet, shiny as a newly minted bell, except for the stained hem. "Lucky she left some of her rear-end padding behind," Ellen giggled.

"Really, if this one isn't good enough, I should just wear my black." Even if it was still muddy from her fall in the pump puddle.

"You'll look like a beggar! Don't you want to look respectable?"

Maddy did feel like a poor relation in her faded servant's dress. She would look the complete beggar, turning up on Mr. McBride's doorstep. It was too humiliating for words. She'd never been a charity case in her life. She'd been a hardworking girl, earning her keep . . .

For the sake of her pride, she let Ellen coerce her into the plaid. She'd promise to pay Mr. McBride back, she resolved. Once she had a job, she'd save every penny and send it to Bitterroot for him to collect. She wouldn't ask for charity, but a loan . . .

She wasn't as buxom as Willabelle, so the dress wasn't as fitted as it should be, she thought ruefully as Ellen buttoned her up. It hung in loosely rustling taffeta folds.

"It's still better than your old rag." Ellen tossed the faded dress in the corner.

"Hey! I'll need that." Maddy fetched it back.

"What on earth for?"

"For next time I have to do laundry, or clean out a fireplace, or scrub the floor. I'm hardly wearing *this* to work, am I?"

"You'd best take his letters too," Ellen said, sifting through the pile on the desk. "To prove you are who you say you are."

That was a good point.

"Lord, he was blunt about himself, wasn't he?" Ellen giggled, struggling to read through one of the pages.

"Don't read that—it's someone's personal mail."

"Don't expect grooming. I reckon I've shaved about twice in all my born life. And I cut my hair with a hunting knife, but only when it gets past my collar," Ellen quoted.

"Is that true?" Maddy didn't like the sound of that at all.

"Yes." Ellen rolled her eyes. "Why do you think Mrs. Champion melts at the sight of him?"

She melted at the sight of an ill-groomed man? That made no sense.

"Here." Ellen folded them up and handed them to Maddy. "Put them in your pocket. I'd be giving him them letters, so he knows you're speaking plain."

Maddy's stomach was in knots. None of this felt right. But nothing had felt right for a very long time.

"Oh my," Mrs. Champion exclaimed when Maddy came downstairs in Willabelle's dress. "Don't you look a picture."

"It's not very practical for traveling," Maddy admitted, aware of the pooling of the stained hem on the kitchen floor. She was a little too short for it.

She cleared her throat. There was something that worried her more than the state of the plaid. "I should probably tell you now that I can't ride a horse. I mean, I never have . . ." And horses scared her. They were so *big*. How people bounced along on their backs the way they did, without falling off . . .

Out of the blue, she remembered the hunts at Ormond House.

The horses gathered in the courtyard, their breath frosty plumes in the autumn air. Tom Ormond in his fancy red coat and black velvet cap, full of grace on his dappled gray, charging after the dogs like he was flying. The smell of sweat on him after, as he found her and pushed her against the wood-paneled wall of the corridor, kissing her until her head felt like she'd been drinking the Christmas brandy.

"Oh, don't you worry about riding," Mrs. Champion assured her, breaking into her memories like a splash of cold rain. "I borrowed Fritz's wagon. I would have borrowed Rigby's but the man's such a nag. I'd never hear the end of it if something happened to it. Come along, then, let's get away or I'll never be back before midnight."

Ellen followed them out into the yard, where a rough plank wagon sat tethered to a couple of stolid-looking ponies. "Say hi to Beau for me," Ellen said shyly.

"We'll do no such thing, you brazen girl." Mrs. Champion gave her a scolding look. But there was a twinkle in it.

Maddy dropped Merle onto the buckboard and then struggled to climb up to join him. Willabelle's ridiculous plaid skirts kept tripping her up. Eventually she hauled herself in, skirt and all. The caging of the bustle bent under her weight as she sat down, but the skirt ballooned up on either side of her and she had to push it down. There was barely any room for Mrs. Champion next to her.

"Well, this is cozy, isn't it?" the housekeeper said cheerfully as she took the reins. "I do love an outing. I don't get much call for them these days, so this will be a rare treat."

Maddy's stomach was churning. Jesus, Mary and Joseph, she was about to climb a mountain to beg a complete stranger for money. How utterly absurd. Imagine if Mrs. Egan could see her now!

"Maddy, my pet, this is Thunderhead Bill and Sour Eagle." Mrs. Champion called out the introductions as they passed through the gate onto the dirt road. Thunderhead Bill and his friend were flanking the gate. Sour Eagle was dressed in a buckskin vest and leggings, with a white collared shirt and a wide-brimmed brown hat. He had a long face, framed by shining jet-black hair, and a straight, serious mouth. He and Thunderhead Bill were both armed with rifles. Maddy nodded a nervy hello. Thunderhead Bill was red-eyed and none too steady in his saddle; it didn't take a genius to realize that he was dead drunk. And in the morning too. Sour Eagle, on the other hand, was sober in every sense of the word.

Sour Eagle tipped his hat at Maddy. "Good day, miss." He fell in beside her. He had a fatherly air.

"Fine weather for a drive, don't you think, Bill?" Mrs. Champion chattered away to Thunderhead Bill, who took the road on her side of the wagon.

"It ain't fine at all. The weather's turning," he disagreed, his voice thick with the drink.

"Oh no, I doubt it." Mrs. Champion looked up at the bright fall sky; Maddy copied her. "It's a beauty of a day."

"Going to snow." Thunderhead Bill dug in, uncaring of the cloudless sky and buttery sunshine.

"Listen to him," Mrs. Champion clucked. "Snow! It's only November, Bill!"

"Big snow."

"He's often right," Sour Eagle told them mildly. "Bill's got a nose for snow."

"Got nothing to do with noses," Bill slurred. "The beavers have been overly busy. And there ain't a goose to be seen; they've all flown."

Maddy held Merle close as they trundled up Main Street. She could feel his little heart racing against her palm as she listened to Mrs. Champion and Thunderhead Bill disagree about the likelihood of snow on this sparkling day. The Langer children were out on the porch of the mercantile as the wagon passed; they waved energetically, and Sour Eagle and Mrs. Champion waved back.

Taking it as an invitation, the children chased the wagon as it rat-tled its stately slow way out of town. Merle twisted in Maddy's arms and yapped. She held on to him tight. Jesus, Mary and Jo-seph, she didn't want to lose him in the woods—how would she ever find him again? She fished in her carpetbag for his lead and tied it to his collar. She wrapped it around her wrist.

"We're in this together," she whispered, giving his big furry bat ears a scratch. "Don't you even think about leaving me." It was comforting to have familiar company, even if it was only Merle.

They turned the bend as they left town, and the Langer chil-dren fell behind. Almost immediately, Maddy felt the thick hush of the woods press in on them. Towering firs were interspersed with shivery-leaved trees in autumn colors. The road became a track and rose into a sharp incline, wending its way through a for-est so deep Maddy was sure they were bound to get lost.

"Where's Roy?" Mrs. Champion asked Thunderhead Bill, set-tling in for a gossip as she drove. Maddy listened with half an ear as she watched the woodland rock by. Squirrels darted from tree to tree, gathering nuts; birds flickered in between the boughs, swooping and bouncing on frail twiglets; and once she thought she saw a goat.

It was cool in the shadows of the forest. The sunlight freckled through the canopy, but it was barely a kiss of warmth on Maddy's skin. The higher they went, the crisper the air felt, tinged with the cold of a frosty night. It smelled of leaf mold and mushrooms, of soil and groundwater.

"Are you here to marry?"

Maddy jumped when Sour Eagle spoke. He'd been silent for most of the journey. "I beg your pardon?"

"Are you here to marry?" He was examining her in a way that made her frightfully uncomfortable.

"You *know* about the marrying?" Mrs. Champion interjected, sounding gleeful. "Isn't it something! Who knew our Kit was looking for a wife? You did, plainly! But no one else would have guessed. Mrs. Langer and I have been tearing our hair out, guessing at the contents of them letters."

"Roy asked for yeller hair," Thunderhead Bill rumbled. "He'll be sore disappointed with this dark-haired one."

Maddy flushed, feeling strangely insulted, even though she most certainly was not here to marry this Roy fellow.

"This one's not for Roy," Sour Eagle said implacably. "This is Kit's wife."

"No, no," Maddy said hurriedly. "There's been a mistake . . ."

"Damn straight. Roy clearly specified yeller hair." Bill wobbled and almost fell out of his saddle.

"Sour Eagle, you'd best take care of him," Mrs. Champion sighed, "or he'll break his neck."

Maddy was relieved when Bill and Sour Eagle dropped back, with Sour Eagle taking Bill's mule by the reins. "How many brides are they expecting?" she asked Mrs. Champion anxiously, remembering all of Willabelle's letters falling to the floor around her tub. Maybe Willabelle wasn't the only person writing to more than one spouse at once . . .

"Just you, pet."

"Not me," Maddy reminded her. "I'm not a bride." Thank God, because who would want to live out here, with only the goats and squirrels for company.

"Look." Mrs. Champion pointed to the patch of blue above. "There's a goose, Bill! You're wrong about the snow!"

"That's not a goose," he said firmly. "It's a falcon."

"Never."

"Geese don't fly alone. They pair up."

Maddy couldn't care less about geese and falcons and pairing up. She just wanted to get her train ticket out of here.

Seven

"Morgan! Yoo-hoo!"

Maddy clung to the sides of the rickety wagon while also trying to keep hold of Merle. They'd emerged from thick woods into a high mountain plain. It was a wide bowl of a place, grassy green, with a fast-moving stream running through it. The track had become indistinct in the meadow, and the wagon jolted and bucked over rocks and tussocks. It reminded Maddy of the ship out from Ireland, when it would hit heavy swells and send her rolling.

"Morgan!" Waving her arm madly, Mrs. Champion rose to her feet as the wagon rattled to a halt next to the stream.

The day was passing, and the shadows of the mountains fell across the far meadow, but the stream was still in sun, spangled and silvery. The ruddy glow of the afternoon light caught a building Maddy assumed was the McBrides' trading post. It crouched on the banks, its roof steeply pitched and its porch a wide brim. There was no glass in the windows, only oilcloth, and the porch rails still resembled the tree branches they'd once been. Stepping from the shadow of the porch was a great big bear of a man. Even from this distance Maddy could tell he was bewildered to see them.

"That's Morgan," Mrs. Champion told Maddy proudly, as though she'd made him. Maddy wondered if she expected to be congratulated. Her face had gone all pink. She flicked the reins and the horses started forward again. Merle yipped as he and Maddy almost jerked right out of their seats.

"I can't stay!" Mrs. Champion chattered freely as she clattered the wagon closer to the bear standing on the steps of the trading post.

Up close he was fearsome looking. He wasn't quite as big as the backwoodsman who had knocked her into the mud down in Bitterroot, but he was close. He had a thick black beard, a mess of tangled black hair and eyebrows that drew together over a piercing glare. His red-and-black flannel shirt stretched over arms that looked like they could squeeze the life out of a person. Lord. If this was Junebug's older brother, no wonder the girl had no manners! He looked like he might have been raised by bears!

Maddy held Merle tighter. This had been a bad idea. She'd just get Mrs. Champion to turn right around and take her back down the mountain.

"No, really, I can't stay," Mrs. Champion insisted, even though no one had said anything to the contrary. She sounded like she'd been asked in for tea, which she most certainly had not been. "It's powerful late in the day; if I don't get off now, I'll never make it back before it's pitch black. Down you hop, dear." She gave Maddy a gentle shove, never turning her blushing face from Morgan McBride, who was without a doubt the scariest man Maddy had ever seen. Maddy didn't move.

"Down." Mrs. Champion shoved her harder. Then she reached into the back of the wagon and picked up Maddy's carpetbag. "Here you go, Morgan, love." She dropped it to the pillowy grass. "You take it for her, won't you? Go on, dear. Down." She put her hand between Maddy's shoulder blades and shoved. "I'll leave you safe here in Morgan's capable hands."

Maddy tumbled from the wagon, barely keeping her feet. Merle yapped.

The bear of a man blinked. He clearly didn't know what was happening but knew he didn't like it.

"I meant to have Thunderhead Bill and Sour Eagle bring her this far—I wasn't going to come across the meadow—but Bill fell off his mule, stone-cold drunk, so *I* had to bring her the whole way. Now I'm at risk of being stuck out after dark, so I can't stay." Mrs. Champion sounded regretful as she turned the wagon around. Maddy almost ran after her.

"Wait!" Too late, the bear seemed to realize what was happening.

Maddy jumped. His voice was as scary as he was.

"Alice!" he bellowed. "What the hell!"

But Mrs. Champion had whipped her horses into a trot and was jouncing away across the meadow already.

"Alice!" He lunged off the step of the trading post and Maddy flinched. The bear frowned, looking back and forth between her and the departing wagon.

Maddy took a step backward and gulped. This had been worse than a bad idea, she thought, feeling her stomach turn shivery with terror.

"Who the hell are you?" he growled.

Maddy panicked. She was all alone, in the middle of nowhere, with the most terrifying man she'd ever seen. Jesus, Mary and Joseph, what was Mrs. Champion thinking, leaving her alone in the wilds with a man like this?

She just panicked. There was no other explanation for it. "Kit McBride," she blurted. Words seemed to have deserted her.

"Kit McBride?" He looked astounded. And even scarier than before, if such a thing were possible. "You're telling me *you're* Kit McBride?"

She shook her head, the panic growing by the minute. Oh my

God. "His bride," she blurted, meaning to go on to tell the story of Willabelle and the whole disaster, but he cut her off.

"His bride!"

The bellow was too much for her. Increasingly terrified, Maddy backed away. Not looking where she was going, she stepped straight into a rabbit hole, and she stumbled. And then there was nothing but pain.

She screamed fit to break the world. She'd never felt pain like it—and it was only made worse by her fear. She'd fallen down at his feet! She was helpless and at his mercy!

Vaguely, Maddy heard Merle explode into a frenzy of barking.

"Stop that!" The bear came at her, and she couldn't help it, she screamed even more.

She tried to crawl away from him, but her foot was well and truly stuck in the hole. And holy of holies, it hurt so bad.

"Stop screaming," the bear ordered.

"Get away from me!" Oh my God, she was trapped, and he was looming over her. And she hurt so *bad*.

Merle hurled himself at the bear, growling and snapping, doing his best to protect her.

"Morgan! Junebug! What the hell is going on!"

Heaven help her, there was another one! She was trapped and there was a whole *den* of them!

Oh, the pain. It crashed in a series of sickening waves. She was cold with it. Her stomach wobbled. Oh, she was going to be sick.

"Calm down," the bear hollered over his shoulder. "It ain't Junebug!"

"Well, what the hell!"

Maddy started to cry. Her teeth chattered and her head swam. Merle's manic yapping filled the air. She felt the press of him as he backed into her, standing guard, snarling at the bears.

"I think she's broken her leg," the bear growled.

"Who?" The other one was getting closer, and he was a growler too.

"Your *bride*."

"My what?"

Their voices were sucked away from her, as though she were on a train rocketing down a track. She was going to faint, she realized in shock. She'd never fainted in her life, and this was the worst possible time to start, but—

"I tell you, she said she was your bride!" Morgan was seething.

Kit ignored him. Now wasn't the time. Not when the poor girl was sprawled unconscious in the dirt. "What in hell happened?" He eyed the snarling little squirrel of a dog. It was guarding her as though its little life depended on it.

"Rabbit hole, I reckon," Morgan said. "Just wait until I get my hands on Junebug."

Kit didn't have a clue why Morgan was blaming Junebug for a rabbit hole. "C'mon, boy," he soothed the dog, inching forward. "You've got to let me have a look at her. I can't help her if you won't let me look at her." He squatted in front of the fierce little thing and held his hand out for the dog to sniff. It growled. "I won't hurt her, I promise."

"For the love of God, Kit. Just pick the thing up." Morgan reached over and grabbed the dog by the scruff of the neck. It writhed helplessly, snarling like it wanted to bite his hand off.

"Didn't anyone ever tell you that you can catch more flies with honey than with vinegar?" Kit sighed.

"Yeah, you. But my way's faster."

Kit inched toward the woman. "Lady?" She was collapsed on her side, her face pressed into the meadow grass. Her fancy dress had ballooned up around her. Gently, he pushed it down. Her leg was well and truly stuck. "I hope it ain't broke," he said ruefully. He put a hand gingerly on her shoulder. The taffeta rustled under his grip. "Lady?" She was out cold. Kit was worried she couldn't breathe, with her face pressed to the ground. Carefully he took her head in his hand and turned her away from the grass.

"Hey!" He knew her! It was the woman from the mud puddle next to the water pump. She was white as a ghost, but it was definitely her. The same oval face with the pointed chin, the same smattering of freckles, the same thick black eyelashes.

"You know her?" Morgan sounded suspicious. He tucked the dog under his arm. It got busy savaging the sleeve of his shirt, but Morgan barely noticed.

"Yeah. I mean, kind of." Kit brushed the girl's hair off her face. She was clammy. "We're going to have to get that leg out of the hole."

"She'll scream something awful." Morgan dropped the dog and rolled up his sleeves to help. "How do you know her? Is it true? She your bride?" He sounded shocked and hurt. The furious little dog latched on to his ankle and growled triumphantly. Morgan ignored it. "Why didn't you tell me about her?"

"Bride? What? *No.* Don't be absurd. I just ran into her in town."

"Absurd? You know what's absurd? This fancy lady showing up out of the blue, announcing that she's your bride and then snapping her leg right in two and ruining my quiet coffee."

"Your quiet coffee? That's what you're worried about? And hopefully her leg ain't snapped at all, let alone in two." Kit ran his hand down the woman's leg. It didn't seem broken.

Morgan swore. "I'll go get a shovel. We'll dig her out."

Kit bent over the girl. "Hang in there, honey. We'll get you out and fixed up." Her eyelashes fluttered against her translucent skin. Hell. She looked like she was coming round, but it might be better if she stayed out. She was going to wake up to a world of pain. "You got a knack for ending up in the mud, don't you?" he told her, stroking her hair to keep her calm. She stilled again. Kit was worried. It was hard to tell how serious it was, with her leg hidden down the rabbit hole like that.

"We got a lot to talk about once she's sorted out," Morgan complained, putting his back into shoveling. As usual, Morgan calmed himself by taking action. He was better when he was tiring himself out doing something. The dog was still firmly attached to his ankle.

"Watch out," Kit ordered, wary as the shovel head bit into the earth. "Don't cause her pain." He guarded her leg while Morgan dug her out, making sure the shovel didn't come too close to her and that the burrow didn't collapse in on her.

"Like, how you know her, for a start," Morgan huffed. "How in hell do you know a lady this fancy?"

"I told you, I ran into her in town." Quite literally. Ran into her and knocked her elbow over head into the mud. "Only she wasn't this fancy then." He wondered if she'd got his flowers. Was that why she was here? To thank him?

He shook his head at his own whimsy.

"Please tell me you didn't propose to the first pretty woman you ever met?" Morgan grumped.

Kit silently urged him to go faster. He was terrible worried. "Have you been out in the sun too long? Why do you keep carping on about marriage?"

"She said she was your *bride*," Morgan reminded him breathlessly.

His bride? Kit didn't know what to make of that.

"I was all set to blame Junebug until you said you knew her."

"What in hell would you blame Junebug for?"

The woman groaned and the sound made Kit's heart pinch. But it was good that she had the energy to groan.

"You're all right," he told her softly as she stirred, pressing a hand to her forehead. "We've got you. You're all right."

She cried out when they eased her leg from the decimated rabbit burrow.

It wasn't broken, Kit thought with relief as he ran a hand down her leg. But she sure was going to be sprained and bruised and sore. He had to rip her skirt to get her free of it; the tangle of it was causing her pain. Underneath the skirt was some ridiculous contraption. It looked like some kind of animal trap.

"How in hell do you get her out of that?" Morgan asked.

"Carefully." Kit managed to find the buckle around her waist to release the soft cage of an underskirt, and between the two of them they managed to get it off. Once she was down to her bloomers, they had the chance to get a good look at the leg.

"That ain't nothing," Morgan observed unhelpfully. "It's nowhere near as bad as Junebug's arm was. What's all the fainting about?"

"Hush up," he told his brother, jerking his head at the girl.

"She's out cold."

"She still might be able to hear you." Kit tied a thick pad of the ripped plaid taffeta skirt to her leg in a makeshift bandage to keep her leg still and considered how he was going to lift her. They had to get her out of the dirt and grass, to somewhere they could clean and tend her.

"What . . . ?"

Hellfire, she was waking up. She opened her eyes blearily, her face a rictus of pain.

"Hush," Kit soothed. "You've hurt your leg, but you'll be just fine."

"My leg?" She struggled to focus. She frowned, confused. And then she seemed to recognize him. "You!"

"Me," he agreed, trying to soothe her with a smile. "But this time it wasn't my fault."

She was turning an alarming shade of green. "I'm going to be sick." He held her head and tried to calm her as she panicked, turned and vomited into the grass.

Morgan grunted, unimpressed by the theatrics, but Kit felt for her. The pain was clearly bad. He held her and waited for the vomiting to end.

"I need to move you, honey," he said gently, once she'd wrung herself dry. "I'm awful sorry, because it's going to hurt."

She whimpered. The poor thing was weeping now.

"I'll do my best not to hurt you. Can you hold on for me? It's about twenty steps to the trading post. You just need to hang in and then I'll lower you down on the porch."

"No . . ."

"There's no other way."

She was losing all her color again. Even the green was gone. It might be a blessing if she'd faint.

"You want me to help?" Morgan asked.

The woman flinched at the sound of his voice.

"No, I reckon it'll be easier on my own," Kit said mildly. Morgan plainly scared her. "You ready?" he asked her.

"No," she whimpered.

"I promise I'll make it quick."

She pressed her white lips together and nodded.

Kit lifted her. Her fingers clawed into him, and her harebell-blue eyes went wide with shock. She made a strangled noise.

"You're all right, honey," he soothed. "I've got you."

"I'll get water." Morgan peeled off to get fresh water from the creek to clean her up, the dog harrying him, while Kit carried the woman onto the porch of the trading post. Her teeth were chattering, and she was shivering like an aspen leaf in a gale.

"Now, I'm going to put you down, honey," he said, moving as slowly as he could and trying not to jar her. But even with all his best intentions, she screamed fit to wake the dead.

Eight

"It's ghosts," Junebug insisted. "There was a woman murdered right by the creek by that old French trapper Gendron. I bet that's her, still screaming."

The screams had shattered through the woods when she was out hunting with Beau and Jonah, scaring the wits out of all three of them. The boys had taken her out to cheer her up after Morgan had laid into her about sneaking off into town on her own.

"Damn it, Junebug, there ain't no such thing as ghosts," Beau told her impatiently. He kept his rifle ready and started for home. "And even if there were, they wouldn't be going around screaming in broad daylight." He sounded more nervous than Junebug liked.

"It ain't broad daylight in the forest, is it? It's all dim in here."

"You said she was down by the creek. It ain't dim there."

"I said she was *murdered* down by the creek; there ain't nothing to stop a ghost walking about. In fact, ain't that what they do? Go walking about, scaring people?" She followed her brothers back down to Buck's Creek, both scared and exhilarated by the ghostly screaming. It was her life's ambition to see a ghost in the flesh: Or not in the flesh, as the case may be.

"And old Gendron never murdered anyone. He couldn't even trap a squirrel," Beau said tersely.

"That's 'cause he was cursed," Junebug said with satisfaction. "That murdered woman cursed him and scared all the squirrels away. He never caught another thing again."

The screams shrieked up the hill again, bloodcurdling in their intensity.

"Ghost or not, we ain't catching anything, either, with that racket," Jonah sighed. "I had my heart set on something fresh for dinner too. I'm sick of salt beef." He had all the sensitivity of a plank of wood, talking salt beef when there were ghosts about.

"Who do you reckon it is?" Beau asked, equal parts curious and disturbed. "There ain't no women up here. And hush up, Junebug. Don't you say nothing about no ghost."

"Whoever she is, she's having a time of it," Jonah said. "It sounds like *she's* being murdered."

They fell into silence, each of them holding their weapon a little tighter. Junebug only had her splintered old slingshot, because the boys wouldn't let her handle a gun, even though she was a crack shot. Or she would be, if they'd let her shoot.

"Who'd be doing the murdering?" Junebug asked. "There ain't no one up here but us and old Roy." Her skin was goose pimpled at the sounds of those screams.

"Well, it ain't us," Jonah said, "so it must be Roy."

"Roy's dumber than a mud brick but he ain't a murderer."

"Maybe that's Morgan screaming," Beau suggested, trying to ease the tension. "Maybe he tried to eat one of your biscuits."

"There ain't nothing wrong with my biscuits!"

"If you like lead shot for breakfast. Those things would break your teeth."

Junebug would like to break Beau's teeth. He was always such a critic. Junebug would like to see *him* try to make biscuits. It wasn't as easy as it looked.

"She's stopped screaming," Jonah observed. Now he was sounding a little nervy too.

The unnatural hush of the woods slowly crackled away as the animals started moving again. It wasn't until the birds started up that Junebug registered how quiet it had been.

It was definitely a ghost. Animals didn't like ghosts.

"You think she's dead?" Jonah whispered to Beau, turning his back to Junebug, as though they meant she wouldn't be able to hear him. Junebug hated it when they did that—tried to keep things from her. It was as infuriating as all get-out. They treated her like she was a child, when she clearly wasn't.

"Junebug, you wait here with Jonah." Beau had his bossy voice on. "I'll go ahead and make sure it's safe at home before you come down."

"How will we know if it's safe?"

"I'll whistle."

"What if you don't whistle? What if you get murdered?"

"Then my ghost'll come back and warn you off," he said dryly.

Junebug didn't like that thought at all. Beau was annoying enough as a live person; imagine how impossible he'd be as a *ghost*. All of that aside, she really didn't like the idea of him going off alone. Those screams had her wound tight. Her palms kept going hot and cold, and her heart kept forgetting to beat.

"You think that lady really was getting murdered, Jonah?" she asked, inching close to him as Beau slunk off.

"I don't know, Bug." He moved to stand in front of her and shouldered his rifle. "Hush now though. Keep your ear out for murderers and the like. Just in case."

Just in case.

"What does a murderer look like?" she asked. What if she didn't recognize one when she saw him?

"Ill favored," Jonah said grimly.

Junebug prepared some shots for her sling. She'd like to see an ill-favored murderer try to take her and Jonah. Although she'd be a sight more useful if they'd let her have a gun.

It seemed like they were waiting up the hill forever. The minutes drew out, filled with the thick noises of the woods. Every nerve strung tight, Junebug strained to hear more than just the squirrels. She almost died when a pine cone tumbled from a branch above their heads. She leapt about a foot in the air and grabbed at Jonah.

This haunting business was a trial, that was for certain.

Eventually they heard Beau whistle, a sharp sound in the cool afternoon air.

Junebug let out her breath. She hadn't been aware she was holding it. "There you go, he's fine."

Jonah exhaled too. Then he adjusted his barely-out-of-adolescence manliness and puffed out his chest. "Come on, Bug. I'll take you down now."

"You'll take me down!" she mocked. "Don't go acting like you're some kind of hero. You didn't do anything."

"I protected you, didn't I?" He got his scowling face on.

"Sure." She rolled her eyes. "About as much as I protected you. And who says I need protecting? I ain't one to mess with. If anyone's taking anyone, I'll take *you* down to Buck's Creek." Junebug was giddy with relief after all that tension and darted past him and down the hill. "Come on, I want to see the ghost!"

Junebug tore through the wheatgrass, dodging pine trees as she ran. She held on to her hat, her arms flapping.

"Junebug!" Jonah chased her, sounding alarmed. "You'll hurt yourself!"

Spit. She wasn't going to hurt herself. She ran in these woods every day. She burst through the tree line and into the wide mountain meadow of Buck's Creek. There was nothing out of the ordinary that she could see. Their cabin, on a gentle rise upstream from the trading post, was the same as ever, while, downstream, the trading post stared out across the creek in its usual implacable way. The meadow had fallen into shadow as the sun sank behind the mountains, and everything had that sweet grass smell as the earth breathed out in preparation for nightfall. There wasn't a trace of a murdered woman, corporeal or ghostly.

She jogged through the grasses, hearing nothing but the rush of the creek and the soughing of the wind in the pines. It was only when she saw Morgan that the hair rose on the back of her neck. He hulked on the porch of the trading post, gripping the rail with both hands. Even from here she could see that he was mad. She knew the look of Morgan mad. He had a way of lowering his head and becoming all shoulders, like a charging bull elk.

He watched her jog toward him with an intensity that frightened her. He didn't yell. He didn't come down from the porch and stalk toward her. There was no fire and brimstone. There was just this seething, pulsing lying in wait.

Junebug's jog slowed to a shuffle and then to a stop. Uh-oh. What had she done now? He couldn't still be stewing about her creeping off down to Bitterroot this morning, could he? He'd already yelled at her for that, for Pete's sake!

No, this was something else, something worse. He looked mad enough to swallow a horned toad backward.

She racked her brains, trying to think what she'd done.

Nothing, except . . .

Hell.

Surely not. Surely, surely not.

But then Morgan held something up. In the aqueous twilight, the sheaf of paper had a pale glow.

Ah, spit! Her luck was the worst! Junebug's mind raced through the possibilities. Had he found Junebug's hidden mail? Had Mrs. Langer twigged to what she was doing and had the nerve to open one of her letters and show it to Morgan? Which was completely unlawful. Or (*surely not!*) had Willabelle Lascalles arrived . . . ?

Had that flashy goshawk come barging up here to spoil every-thing?

Junebug had taken an immediate and muscular dislike to the woman. She scowled as she remembered Willabelle out on Rigby's porch, all superior and snotty. All Junebug's hopes had gone up in smoke. It was galling, to say the least. And now that she no longer wanted the woman for a wife, on no account did Junebug want her up the mountain, beguiling Junebug's brothers. Junebug had enough to do as it was, without adding Willabelle Lascalles's laundry to her pile of chores!

Honestly. Her bride order had gone wrong in ways she never could have imagined.

The mail-order bride was the only thing she could think of that would make Morgan this furious. Junebug hadn't burned any-thing down, or smashed anything, or lost anything. Not that she could remember, anyway.

But maybe she was riling herself up for nothing. Maybe it was the ghost that made Morgan look so bull elk–ish. Maybe the ghost was causing this fury. Maybe the ghost had written all the letters clenched in that hand of his . . .

But if the ghost was the cause of Morgan's latest conniption, his glaring at Junebug didn't make sense. The ghost wasn't Junebug's fault.

Willabelle Lascalles, on the other hand, was.

Junebug considered running back to the woods. It wasn't win-ter yet; she'd get through a night or two without freezing to death. And there were plenty of huckleberries about to eat.

But what was the point? She'd have to come back and deal with Morgan eventually. And he wasn't the type to cool off with time; he was the type to get himself more het up. She'd only make things worse if she made him wait before he could yell at her. He'd have thought up plenty more to say. If she got it over with now, he'd run out of words. Morgan wasn't quick with words; he tended to have a limited supply, unless you gave him time to work on it.

"Hell, Junebug." Jonah came staggering and huffing to a halt next to her. "You've got to stay close! What if you'd run straight bang into a murderer?"

Maybe she *had* run straight bang into a murderer. She considered Morgan's unnatural stillness. Maybe the screaming had been Willabelle Lascalles . . . maybe Morgan had gone and scared her straight to death. And maybe he was fixing to do the same to Junebug.

Only he'd have something coming, because she didn't scare easy.

Why didn't he *do* anything?

"What's going on?" Jonah demanded. "Why's he got his face on? What have you done now?"

"I haven't done anything. Maybe he's glowering at *you*." Junebug was sore pricked. Why did they always treat her like she'd been up to no good?

Jonah sighed. "If you've burned the cookhouse down again . . ." He started trudging toward the trading post, looking glum at the thought of listening to Morgan and Junebug fight again.

Clearly not. The new cookhouse was still visible near their cabin, plainly safe and well. Junebug kicked at a clump of meadow grass. There better be a ghost in that trading post, to make this worth her while, or today was going to be a complete bust.

She set her shoulders and stalked toward her smoldering eldest brother. She noted the way he didn't even glance at Jonah as he slunk past him. Morgan was so fixated on Junebug that it was like Jonah didn't even exist.

Morgan was such a bullish blockhead, Junebug seethed as she stomped through the meadow toward him. All horns and a thick head. She was so sick of his bossiness, and his temper, and his refusal to accept that she was a person with a smart head on her shoulders. Hell. She was more capable than the lot of them put together! They wouldn't *cope* without her. So why did he persist on treating her like she was a silly little girl?

"Who'd you go and kill?" Junebug asked belligerently as she reached the ramshackle trading post. She stood stolidly at the base of the steps, out of arm's reach. "We heard screaming."

"I ain't killed no one," Morgan growled. "Yet."

As always, Junebug's heart raced like a rabbit in the face of Morgan's anger. She never showed it though. She wouldn't give him the satisfaction.

"Explain yourself." He handed the sheaf of paper down to her.

He was such a horse's ass. Why didn't he just yell at her and get it over with?

Junebug kept control of her face as she took the papers and looked through them. There was still just enough light to see that they were her letters to Willabelle. Stupid goshawk woman. If only she hadn't been such a ridiculously impractical person, this could have ended very differently. And Junebug couldn't help but think of all that wasted work, all those hours, writing all these letters. Look at this one. It was a work of art. She'd captured Kit perfectly, every ~~irascible~~ blockheaded inch of him.

"Well?" Morgan barked.

"I don't know what these are." She'd try brazening her way out first.

If possible, Morgan's glower grew blacker. "I can't believe your nerve. Lying to my face."

She really thought he should be used to it by now. Besides, it was *his* fault she lied. If he were easier to talk to, she wouldn't *have* to lie.

"I know you wrote those letters." He leaned forward, more bull elk than ever.

Junebug feigned shock. "Me? These are clearly signed *Kit* Mc-Bride."

"In *your* hand."

He really was looking murderous now. Lying may not have been the best tactic. Oh well, she was in it now. And she'd never been one to lose her nerve.

"Looks like Kit thought my idea of finding a wife was a good one," she said, putting her hands on her hips, "if he's gone and ordered himself a bride. Guess he thinks you should have taken me more seriously."

Morgan's knuckles were turning white as he gripped the porch rail.

She might be pushing this too far, she thought nervously.

"You've got no right impersonating him," Morgan spat. "It ain't lawful! And to have the gall to place an *advertisement* in his name! And to write to some poor stranger, misleading her like that. You're out of control."

Hardly. She was perfectly *in* control. Unlike him. He looked fit to snap that porch rail in two. She refused to be bullied like this. Her idea was a *good* one. If he had half a brain, then he'd recognize that, instead of being a total jackass about it. She'd written in good faith; she hadn't misled anyone. And Willabelle had willingly come to get hitched. It wasn't like Junebug had *abducted* her.

"You're being overemotional," she told him, knowing that would boil his blood. She was irked, and she got sharp-tongued when she was irked. "If you'd calm down, you'd see I haven't *done* anything. Except to hear someone screaming and come down here to rescue you." That last bit was just to needle him, which was reckless, but it sure felt good.

"You want to know who was screaming?" Morgan asked through gritted teeth. He didn't wait for her to answer. "*Her*, that's who!" He jabbed his finger at the pages in Junebug's hand.

Ah hell. So Willabelle *was* here. Damn it. Now she'd have to placate Morgan *and* get rid of Willabelle. Because she certainly didn't want to *keep* her; the woman was a complete trial. Today was just the most objectionable day.

Maybe the screaming was because Willabelle had got a good look at Buck's Creek and realized what she'd got herself into, Junebug thought hopefully. Or maybe she'd got a good look at Kit . . . He'd been looking a fright today. And while she'd endeavored to prepare the woman in her letters, it was hard to do Kit justice.

And all aside from Kit, Morgan himself had probably scared the life out of her.

Maybe getting rid of her wouldn't be too hard . . . Maybe Junebug just needed to step out of the way and let her brothers be themselves . . .

"*Her?*" Junebug echoed Morgan, still opting for feigned innocence. He didn't believe her lies, but it sure did irk him, so it was worth continuing. "Her, who? Honestly, Morgan, you're making no sense! Have you been drinking the moonshine in broad daylight? Ma would be rolling over in her grave."

"Get up here," he snapped.

Get up there? On the porch? With him? No. That didn't seem like a good idea.

"Don't you want to meet the woman you deceived?" he growled.

Junebug couldn't help snorting at that. She'd already met the stupid goshawk. And if anyone had been deceived, it was *her*. Junebug had told nothing but the unvarnished truth about Kit; it was Willabelle who had spun falsehoods. Molasses cake and all. Junebug didn't think that canary-clad nightmare had ever baked a cake in her life, despite what she'd said in her letters.

"She's come all the way from Missouri, according to them letters. Expecting to be a wife." Morgan was righteous in his rage.

Junebug scowled. Morgan was worried about *Willabelle?* Had that goshawk worked her wiles already? Because if so, the woman worked *quick*.

"Get inside and see what you've done to her," Morgan demanded. His steely gray eyes were as flat as a winter sky.

What *who* had done to *who*? Junebug didn't like what he was suggesting. She hadn't done anything to Willabelle except promise her a husband, flaws and all. There was no law against that, was there?

The goshawk was obviously in there bewitching Junebug's hulking fool brothers. Morgan here was clearly stupid from all those wiles.

Junebug wondered if it was possible to get a woman who was a little bit wily, but not too much. And how she could fish for one like that in the *Matrimonial News* without getting the wrong sort of catch. This first attempt had been nothing short of a disaster.

"Get inside. This minute." That vein in his forehead was twitching again. It was always a sign that she should walk careful.

Fine. She'd go inside, but not because he told her to. She'd go in there because she wanted to gauge the situation and to see how hard it would be to unbewitch her brothers. *Not* because Morgan was growling at her.

"After you," she invited as she took a slow walk up the stairs.

He didn't take her up on the invitation, and she had the displeasure of squeezing past him to get to the door. Honestly. He was such a *lump*.

She got inside to find the place was hotter than a July day. They had the stove going, and the trading post was stuffy and warm. She could barely breathe with it. And it just made everything stink from the pile of tanned hides stored in the loft.

Beau and Jonah were clumped around the stove, blocking her view of Willabelle. They were definitely beguiled, she thought grimly, taking in the way they were hovering. They'd both removed their hats and were holding them nervously. Since when did they have the manners to take their hats off indoors?

The goshawk was on a makeshift mattress on the floor; Junebug could see her white feet sticking out. They'd piled up a bunch of furs for her to rest on. That told Junebug all she needed to know. Those furs were worth a lot of money; Morgan never let Junebug so much as touch them, and now here was the goshawk lying on a whole passel of 'em.

Kit was squatting at her side, ministering to her. God, look at him. He looked worried as all get-out.

Maybe she'd fainted. Ladies were always fainting in Kit's books. They'd get a shock and faint dead away. Sometimes just the *thought* of a shock sent them swooning. Junebug imagined that the goshawk's bustle had probably cushioned her fall. That thing had been enormous.

She felt Morgan looming behind her.

"Look at her," he ordered.

What did it *look* like she was doing? Dancing a jig? She was plainly looking at the woman. Not just the woman but her dog. Junebug hadn't known that she had a dog. It was a bedraggled muddy-looking thing, its long fur all matted and stuck through with leaves and twigs. It was sitting right by the goshawk's white feet, keeping guard. Now and then it would look up at Beau and Jonah and growl, its teeth like a row of needles.

Jonah and Beau were also growling, but not at the dog. "You ordered a *woman?*" Jonah radiated disbelief.

No. She'd ordered a *wife.*

"You need a good whipping," Beau snapped.

If they laid one hand on her, they'd regret it. Junebug was glad she still had her slingshot. She'd use it too.

"Get out of the way and let her see what she's done to the poor woman," Morgan ordered.

Jonah and Beau stepped aside, and Junebug swore. She couldn't help it. The words just burst out. Because there on the floor was . . . not the woman she was expecting.

It wasn't the goshawk at all.

It was the goshawk's maid. The dowdy one who'd been all in black, who'd been out of sorts in the Bellevue's washhouse. The poor woman was in a serious swoon.

"What in hell happened?" Junebug asked, shocked. She turned to glare at Morgan. "What did you *do*?"

"Me?" He flushed a deep brick red. She could see it even though he was mostly beard. "Since when do I go around hurting women?"

"She hurt her leg," Kit said calmly, not looking up. "It went down a rabbit burrow."

"And it weren't nothing to do with me," Morgan said, still all angered up. "Much."

Junebug was all discombobulated. Where was the goshawk? The maid wouldn't be here all on her lonesome. Junebug took stock of the trading post, but there was no sign of Willabelle Lascalles that she could see.

Where *was* she?

"This is what your scheming comes to!" Morgan snarled. He was still all red and bothered. And getting up a head of steam to orate on all of Junebug's failings. "Your damn fool schemes have consequences, Junebug! Look at Miss Lascalles there! Look at the state of her!"

Kit sat back on his heels. He looked up and met Junebug's gaze. The disappointment in his dark eyes cut Junebug to the quick more sharply than all of Morgan's words. "He's right, Junebug. Miss Lascalles is hurt bad. And all because of you and your hare-brained plan to trick her here."

Harebrained? There was nothing hare about it! And she hadn't tricked her—she'd told the *truth*.

Wait. Why did they keep calling her Miss Lascalles? She was the *maid*.

"I didn't trick anybody," Junebug said, her mind all at work. They didn't think *this* was Willabelle Lascalles, did they?

"I read those letters," Morgan said darkly. "So you can drop the act. We know everything."

Everything, her sweet behind. They knew next to nothing. Her mind was tumbling over itself as she tried to think things through. Had they assumed the maid was Willabelle, just because she'd arrived with the letters . . . or was something else going on here?

"You keep calling her Miss Lascalles?" Junebug fished, creeping closer. It was definitely the maid, even though she wasn't wearing the ugly black uniform she'd been wearing in Bitterroot. This dress was a fancy shiny bright thing, with puffy sleeves, more like something the goshawk would wear.

Kit was out of temper too. "Drop it, Junebug. You know who she is and so do we. Stop pretending."

They really did think it was Willabelle. How curious.

This was almost as interesting as a ghost would have been.

"She said that was her name? Miss Lascalles?" Junebug prodded.

"What she *said*"—Morgan sounded about ready to throttle her—"was that she was Kit's *bride*."

Curious as hell. The *maid*. What was she up to, coming up here, pretending to be Willabelle Lascalles? That took some brass, didn't it?

"What in hell were you thinking!" Morgan had well and truly lost his patience with her. He was so loud he made the oil lamp rattle on the bench top.

"Enough!" Kit snapped. He rose to his feet. Ugh. The two of them towered over her, making her feel like she was trapped at the bottom of a well. "You'll wake her up, and when that happens she'll be in a world of pain. Morgan, you can yell at Junebug while she gets supper ready. Jonah, I want you to get over to the forge and damp down the furnace. And then you and Beau can head over to the Ella-Jean Mine and see if they still got that doctor there."

"But it's getting on nightfall." Jonah didn't sound pleased.

"You can get as far as Bitterroot, and head out from there at first light," Kit snapped. "Tell the doc it ain't broke but we'd like him to check on her anyway. Just in case."

"What if the doc ain't there?" Beau asked.

"Then get on into Butte."

"No doctor's coming all the way up here," Jonah complained.

"I don't care if you have to kidnap him, you get him here," Kit said tersely. "And what are you standing there gawping for, Junebug? Go get supper. She's going to need to eat to keep her strength up. Make a broth or something. We'll deal with you later tonight." He sank back down to minister to the unconscious woman. None of them moved. "Get!" he growled.

They got.

"You better hope she doesn't get an infection," Morgan warned Junebug, "or you'll be in more trouble than you've been in before, in all your born life."

"Thought I already was," Junebug muttered.

"Take your fighting outside," Kit growled. "If either of you disturbs her, there'll be hell to pay."

Junebug noted the way he put a damp cloth to the maid's forehead, the softening of his gaze, the worried furrow of his brow.

Wait. Was Kit . . . *beguiled*? By the *maid*?

It had never occurred to Junebug that Maddy the *Maid* could be the wily type . . .

She barely listened to Morgan's epic scolding as she headed to the new cookhouse. He lit the lantern so she could see her work, and didn't let up the vociferation, not once. She was too caught up in her thoughts to take it in, but she didn't need to listen to his blustering, she'd heard it all a thousand times. Nothing she did was right. Blah blah blah.

As she scrubbed the filthy potatoes, she thought of Maddy working the washboard as she cleaned Willabelle Lascalles's fancy underwear. Maddy was strong, wiry. A worker. And wasn't that just what Junebug needed?

Indeed it was.

Was it possible that Providence had smiled on her today? What better wife could she hope for than one trained to serve?

"I don't know what you've got to smile about," Morgan snapped.

No, he surely didn't. But he'd find out soon enough.

Nine

Kit, Morgan and Junebug spent the night in the trading post, watching over the poor maid, who was feverish and pained. She never did rouse enough to eat the broth Junebug had made. Which was probably for the best, Kit mused, as it was terrible. Junebug had really just thrown some vegetables in a pot with some water and an old scrap of salt beef. None of them could stomach it, except the muddy little dog.

As the night wore on, the poor woman worsened. Every time she moved, she cried out with the pain of it. Her face grew hectic with color, two bright circles burning like rosy coins on her cheeks. And she sweat something fierce. Her dark hair was plastered against her head, and droplets rolled down her face. Kit murmured soft reassurances and wiped her forehead with a cool wet cloth. He was powerful worried about her.

"You'll burn her alive if you keep stoking that fire," Junebug told Kit when he put another log in the burner. "It's stifling in here; we don't need it any hotter."

He ignored her and kept stoking away. She'd ordered him a *wife*, he thought numbly as he tended to the blaze. A wife! He was too shocked to be angry. It was extreme, even for Junebug. Where had they gone wrong? She seemed to have no idea of right or wrong, appropriate or inappropriate, acceptable or unacceptable. And this was flat-out wrong, completely inappropriate and totally unacceptable. What in hell were they going to do with her?

What did four men know of raising a girl? Nothing! This stunt proved it.

"Everyone knows you feed a fever, Junebug," Morgan snapped at her when she went to complain again. "Leave him be, he knows what he's doing." Morgan was antsy, pacing about and fiddling with the stock on the shelves. Kit knew he was feeling everything Morgan was feeling, and more. Morgan took more than his share of responsibility for Junebug, and he took each of her failings as his own.

A wife!

Junebug had picked *this* woman out for him. Kit looked down at the woman stretched out on the furs. He felt a mess of feelings at the thought of it. Too many tangled-up feelings to know what was what.

"Feed a fever?" Junebug snorted. "You mean by burning someone half-alive? That's just wrongheaded. She looks powerful hot and uncomfortable, and I don't reckon you burning her up has helped one bit. If anything, it seems to have made her worse." Junebug bustled about, flinging open the doors and rolling up the oilcloth at the windows. "The least we can do is try and cool her off." The night breeze skimmed in off the creek, fresh as new frost.

"Damn it, Junebug. Ain't you done enough?" Kit snapped. "Close them back up. You'll be the death of her."

"Just try it." Junebug was bullish. "For a few minutes, at least. If I was sick, I'd rather breathe fresh air than tanned hides; and if I was burning up, I'd rather get cool than keep hotting up."

"*Hotting up* ain't a word." Kit turned back to the woman. She took a deep shuddery breath. Her face was flushed and dewy with sweat. He frowned. The cool swirls of air seemed to ease her fret-fulness, but he was anxious it would make her worse . . .

"I know it ain't a word," Junebug said sourly. "It's two words."

They lapsed into tense silence, each of them watching Willa-belle Lascalles. The fresh breeze skittered through the trading post, blowing out the oily smell of Junebug's broth and the stink of hides and wood ash. Gradually, Willabelle Lascalles soothed, slipping into calm sleep.

Kit sighed, feeling a swell of relief. "Hopefully she'll sleep all night," he said, pulling the furs up gently, trying not to disturb her.

"You're welcome," Junebug told him tartly.

Kit ignored her. He didn't know what to say to her. A damn wife!

"Hell. When her leg went down that hole, I near about lost my nerve," Morgan said, leaning both hands on the bench and lower-ing his head. He sounded shaky. "The sound of her screaming . . ."

Kit knew what he meant. He shuddered at the memory of it. He'd felt her screams go right through him. "I need a coffee after that." He reached for the pot.

"Coffee?" Morgan was appalled. "After this goddamn afflicted day? You need something stronger than coffee." Morgan went to the safe, where they kept the good liquor, and brought out the whiskey. He poured long splashes of amber liquid into the tin mugs and handed one to Kit. "You did a good job with her," he told Kit, still sounding unsteady. "I got no touch with women. Looks like you do."

"Not all of them." Kit took a gulp of whiskey and turned his gaze to Junebug. "Show me this wretched ad you placed," he said, after the whiskey had fortified him. He stared at her like she was a mule deer come stumbling into the trading post and he was try-ing to decide whether to shoot her or just let her go gamboling free back to the woods.

He didn't know what went on in that head of hers.

Morgan gave a caustic laugh and sat down on the sacks of flour. "An ad! For a wife. For *you*. Imagine."

"I don't have to imagine," Kit said tightly, gesturing to the sleeping woman by the stove. "She's right here."

"Oh God." Morgan rubbed his hand over his face. "What are we going to do with you, Bug?"

"Thank me?" she suggested. She was looking mutinous, as always.

How did she not know how all-fired *wrong* this was?

"Seriously, show me the ad." Kit tapped his mug on the bench.

"I don't have it," she said, her chin going up in the air. "We don't get the *Matrimonial News* in these parts." At least she'd dropped all her lies and the pretense that she didn't know what they were talking about. "We don't get any newspapers at all. It's a sore shame, too, as we got no idea what's going on in the world without a newspaper."

"Stop changing the subject," Kit warned. "I don't want to hear about newspapers or the world; I want to know what the ad said."

"I have a draft of it." Junebug paused. Then she grinned. "I'm only telling you because I'm so darned proud of it. It took ages to get it right. Wait here." She climbed up into the loft and headed for her secret hiding place. The one they knew about. Kit was sure there were others they didn't know about. The kid was too wily for them.

He met Morgan's gaze. His older brother looked as grim as he felt. She was actually proud of unlawfully impersonating someone. Of lying to some poor woman and dragging her out here into the wilderness, with promises of a matrimonial match that could never happen. Because Kit sure wasn't getting hitched. And certainly not to some woman ordered in the mail, like one of his catalog books!

Junebug dropped the advertisement down to Kit. It fluttered and landed near his feet.

Gingerly, he picked it up, as though it might burn him. Above him, he was aware of Junebug sitting on the edge of the loft, watching him read it.

Wanted: Wife for a blacksmith. Do not expect doting, nor compliments . . .

Gobsmacked, he read the entirety of the ridiculous thing. He shook his head in disbelief and handed it to Morgan. "Where'd you leave the bottle?" Kit wandered off to find the whiskey.

"Must be willing to put up with judgment, nagging and unreasonable expectations!" Morgan made a choking noise as he read it. "You didn't put that!" He glanced up at Junebug. She didn't deny it.

Kit poured himself a double measure.

"Mustn't mind snoring, cussing or a filthy morning temper?"

Junebug nodded. "Well, it's true, ain't it?"

"Has all his own teeth?"

Kit downed the mug in one fiery swallow.

"As far as I know he does. I wasn't too sure, but I hazarded a guess that he at least had enough that she wouldn't notice any missing."

Kit glared at her.

"What?" she demanded.

"And you got replies to this?" Morgan said, bewildered.

Kit's gaze slid to the woman asleep on the furs in front of the stove. What kind of woman responded to *that* advertisement?

"Sure. People appreciated the honesty, I reckon."

Kit returned to glaring at her. "Honesty? I don't snore."

"You do. Like a hog."

Morgan laughed.

"What are you laughing at? You're supposed to be disciplining her for this!" The shock was wearing off—Kit was definitely feeling some rage now.

"She's right. You do snore like a hog. Grunty like."

"What about the other bits. The nagging and judging? That

don't describe me at all; that's you." Kit scowled at him. Why wasn't Morgan tearing strips off her? Not only had she advertised for a wife, but she'd slandered Kit in the process!

Morgan didn't seem in the least offended. In fact, he seemed to agree. It was irksome.

"It's both of you," Junebug told them. She was safe out of arm's reach, all the way up in the loft.

"And *unreasonable expectations*?" Kit threw his hands up in disbelief.

"I stand by that."

"You stand by that." He was disgusted. Enraged. And lots of other feelings besides. He poured himself another generous slug of whiskey and then handed the bottle to Morgan.

"You want me to cook and clean," Junebug said mutinously, "and wash and mend, and tend the vegetables, and look after the animals, and all the rest of it, like I'm your *wife*. Well, I ain't your wife. So, I thought, since you were so all-fired fixed on getting me to act the wife, that you must want one. So I got you one. You're *welcome*."

"Lazy as a house cat," Kit muttered. "And you threw in the bit about the pie because . . . ?"

"I like pie." She was getting testy. "I ain't going to apologize for *that*."

"Does *she* bake pie?" Morgan asked dryly, nodding his head in the direction of the woman in front of the stove.

"The letters said molasses cake," Junebug muttered.

Kit swore and turned his back on her. He leaned against the bench and stared down at the woman. Molasses cake.

What in hell did a woman that pretty want with a snoring, cussing, not-too-ugly mountain man? A woman like her could get any man she wanted. Come to think of it, why was she answering ads in the first place, let alone an ad for a man this undesirable?

Hell, she was as pretty as a speckled pup. She must have men lining up.

"Ability to complain in written form." Morgan snorted as he returned to reading Junebug's advertisement. "She nailed you true there."

Kit didn't respond.

Morgan looked up at Junebug. "You know this was wrong, I hope. Because if you don't, I despair."

"Wrong!" Junebug was outraged. "If you don't see why this is *right*, then *I* despair. You pair of blockheads!"

Kit took back the bottle of whiskey and headed out to the porch. He couldn't trust himself not to speak his mind. And he loved his sister too much to speak it now, when he was this angry.

"I'm just at my wit's end with her, Kit." Morgan had sunk into a gloom. He and Kit had both moved out onto the porch, where they sat, passing the bottle back and forth and listening to the wind in the pines.

The moon was waxing, a big old silvery bell, its reflection wobbling in the water. The breeze carried the smell of fall leaves and loamy earth. Kit loved the way the meadow grass rippled, the blades chased stony white by moonlight, and the way the mountains stood like family around their meadow. He could hear the lap of the creek as it rolled between its banks and the shivering sigh of leaves waving in the forest. The air was icy fresh. There'd be a rime of frost on the creek come morning, he reckoned. The first lace of winter ice.

Usually, the meadow and mountains soothed him. But not tonight.

The cry of a snowy owl out hunting echoed through the violaceous evening.

He and Morgan had a clear view of their unexpected guest through the open door, and Kit kept a careful eye on her, worried that her fever might return. Junebug had fallen asleep upstairs in the loft. Morgan had gone to check on her not long ago. He said even in her sleep she looked out of sorts. It did unpleasant things to Kit to know she was unhappy. He didn't like it. Even if she *had* gone and impersonated him and ordered up a wife.

"I mean, what do I know about raising a girl, Kit?" Morgan moaned, stretching his legs out in front of him and morosely watching the creek slide by.

"Nothing," Kit sighed.

"That's right. Nothing." He rubbed his face. "God, I hate this place."

Morgan had never wanted to stay. If he hadn't come home for a visit when Ma had died, his whole life would have been different. And he never forgot it.

"I mean, I can't wrestle it out of her the way I could with the boys," Morgan said, exasperated, snatching the bottle off Kit. "With Beau and Jonah, I could get them down in the meadow and take them on, head-to-head, simple like."

"I think we've got different definitions of *simple*," Kit said wryly. He turned his chair so that he was facing the door. "I'm getting a crick in my neck checking on her all the time."

"She's fine."

"The fever might come back."

Morgan sighed. "And look at this, now we've got *another* girl. Hell. We can't handle the one we've got."

"I used to think you were doing fine, Morgan. Even if you couldn't wrestle her." But now . . . Now Kit felt a measure of despair about his little sister. The thing was . . . she ran rings around them.

"I think she'd probably win a wrestling match, anyway," Morgan said morosely. "She's smarter than me, you know."

"She's smarter than all of us," Kit sighed. "And dumber, all at the same time."

"Can you believe she wrote that advertisement?"

"Yeah. I can. It's Junebug."

They fell into thinking, one looking in at the trading post, the other looking out into the night.

"You reckon she's lonely, huh?" Morgan didn't like that idea. "I guess it ain't easy being the only girl."

"I guess not."

"I mean, she don't even own a dress . . ."

"A dress? What's a dress got to do with it? And do you reckon she'd even want one?" Kit was surprised. "She's always seemed happy enough in Jonah's old overalls."

"How do we know? Dresses are girl things, and we don't know nothing about girl things."

"What else do you think she wants?" Kit mused. He couldn't quite imagine Junebug in a dress. "A mother?" Kit guessed. His gaze drifted to the silhouette of the chokecherry tree.

"Not a mother. A *wife*. You heard her. She reckons we've been making her act like our wife . . ."

"It's reasonable to get her to do chores, Morgan."

"But *all* the chores . . . ?"

"She don't do *all* the chores."

"Maybe she's right, though, Kit. Maybe we do need a woman around here." Morgan gave Miss Lascalles a thoughtful look. "Someone who can teach Junebug about growing up. About the kinds of responsibilities that a girl needs to take on."

"You're not suggesting that I actually marry this woman, I hope?" Kit was appalled.

"No, of course not."

"Well, *you're* not marrying her!" He was even more het up by that idea.

"No, I damn well ain't!" Morgan was horrified.

"What the hell are you talking about, then?"

"She's sore injured, isn't she? She ain't going to be able to travel for a while. I reckon we get our little sister to take care of her for the duration. Keep them together. Let this Miss Lascalles teach our Bug a thing or two about being a lady." The more Morgan thought about it, the better the idea sounded. He couldn't teach Junebug squat about womanhood. He didn't know the first thing about being a lady, and nor did he want to. "Miss Lascalles looked a thorough lady getting down from that carriage, fancy dress and all. Gentle mannered . . . You ever think that sometimes God works in mysterious ways, Kit?"

Kit was silent.

"How long do you think it'll be until Miss Lascalles heals up?" Morgan mused.

"I don't know," Kit mumbled. For some reason, the idea of her healed up and leaving put him even further out of sorts.

"And that's provided she don't get an infection. It could be longer. And if the snows come early, she might get stuck here. Maybe for the whole winter . . . You reckon winter is long enough for Bug to learn how to be a lady?" he grunted. "Probably not. But it would be a start . . ."

"What if Miss Lascalles don't want to stay up here with us?" Kit asked, his heart jumping beats in his chest. "This is a damn fool idea, if you ask me. We ought to get her back down to Bitterroot before the snows come."

"Of course she wants to stay! She came up here to marry you, didn't she? And you read those letters; Junebug was plenty honest about what she should expect, so she must know what she's in for," he laughed. *Do not expect doting, nor compliments!*"

Kit groaned. "That kid will be the death of us."

"Got all your own teeth at least." Morgan seemed much more cheerful now that he had a plan.

"It's no thanks to you I have my own teeth. You almost knocked them all out a thousand times over trying to wrestle me." Kit knew he was sounding sour.

"Did I win?"

"Nope. It was only ever a draw. You ain't never beaten me."

"That's 'cause you're so solid from all that blacksmithing. If you were built normal, you wouldn't stand a chance." He passed Kit the whiskey. "Here, we should celebrate the fact that you found a woman willing to marry you."

"Very funny."

"Considering you snore like a hog, it sure is."

Ten

Pain chased Maddy through her dreams. She ran through the back corridors and servants' stairs of Ormond House, through light as dim and thick as a watery grave, trying to outrun the hurt, but she was too slow. And she hurt so bad. In and out of delirium, she saw a stove, and her dreams warped until she was blacking fireplaces again, on her hands and knees, weeping because Tom Ormond was getting married, weeping because she was so grateful that she wasn't pregnant, weeping because she was so deeply and completely alone.

"Hush." A hand pressed against her head, like her mam's had when she had nightmares as a wean. It was large and cool. Maddy wept. She missed her mam so much.

Vividly, Mam swam into her dreams, not sick the way she'd been in the end, but hale and laughing, holding Jean's hand as they walked to the little church in Crinkle. The bogland stretched flat behind her, the clouds scudding in the broad sky. Mam's hair was dark and shiny, her eyes bright blue and full of impishness. She was like Job in the Bible stories, she said as she walked, trusting in the Redeemer, even though life was full of grief and trials.

KIT McBRIDE GETS A WIFE   153

Jesus, Mary and Joseph, Maddy missed her. The sight of her in dreams made Maddy's heart hurt, like someone had sliced into it with a paring knife.

Ah, Madaidh . . . my love. She felt the press of Mam's hand on her head. The warmth of her love. *Rest now. Sleep.* The hand stroked her hair, and a cool breeze brushed over her like a sigh. Maddy drew a shuddering breath. *He wounds, He binds up, He shatters, His hands heal.* Mam had said that on her narrow bed, as she lay dying. *His hands heal.* It was from the Book of Job. She'd mumbled it through her fever, that and her favorite, which was a mishmash of what the priest said at weddings: *Without love, I am a clanging cymbal.* The words broke through her dry lips, rustling on her withered breath.

Shane . . .

Shane, Maddy's father. Mam had called for him a thousand times as she lay in bed. She'd been panicked at the end, unable to breathe, buried in her own body. Calling out for Maddy's father, who'd died of typhoid fever, leaving her alone and impoverished with all the weans.

He wounds and shatters.

Without love.

Was Maddy dying? She felt the same overpowering sense of desperation that she'd seen in her mam. The coldness of being alone. And without love.

"You're all right." The voice came through the watery gloom of Maddy's half-waking dreams, strong and certain, a deep rumble. "You're all right. Sleep now." The hand was slow and kind as it stroked her head. The feel of it steadied her. *You're all right, honey. Sleep.*

She did. And when she woke, it was morning. A cold blue morning, filled with the sound of birds and the smell of icy water and grass and a sooty stove. The pain dragged her up from sleep, but she surfaced with a clear head. Jesus, Mary and Joseph, she was in agony. Her leg was swollen and raging.

The bear! She sat upright, her heart pounding, her gaze skipping around the small oblong room, looking for the threat.

She shook her head. No, it hadn't been a bear. It had been a man. A McBride.

It all came back, the horrid moment of being left by Mrs. Champion, alone with the towering black bear of a man, with his wild hair and terrifying scowl.

Who the hell are you?

And then her leg had gone out from under her, and she'd been in agony. She remembered struggling as someone moved her leg around, causing pain like she'd never felt in the whole of her life. The bear had held her down, she remembered with a shudder, while the other one sent shattering pain through her.

The other one . . .

Jesus, Mary and Joseph, it had been the man from Bitterroot! The one who'd knocked her flat into the mud. The brute with the incongruously beautiful dark eyes.

Was *he* a McBride too?

She was trapped here, injured, at the mercy of two enormous and brutish men. Her leg throbbed inside the makeshift bandages. How was she going to get out of here?

Where even was she?

Maddy took in the log building, which was dim and shadowy in the breaking dawn light. The windows showed a plum-colored sky, but nothing more. The walls were dotted with pegs, from which hung all manner of goods: bridles and tack, ropes, hats and coats, sailcloth. There were shelves full of dry goods, and stacks of sacks and barrels.

This was the trading post.

Maddy herself was on the floor, resting on a pile of furs in front of a potbellied stove. She didn't think she could get up. Her leg throbbed without mercy.

"You're up!"

Maddy flinched. She felt so helpless.

"Spit, you look all right!"

It was the barefoot girl. The one from Bitterroot, the one who'd thrown Willabelle's skirt in the fire and never told Willabelle about it, even though she'd promised Maddy she would. That had been a bad day, through and through.

Wait . . . was that yesterday? Today? Days ago? Maddy was unsettled to find she'd lost track of time.

The girl came in from outside, her breath pluming in the dawn light. There was a yap and then Merle trotted in, too, his tail managing to wag even though it was thick with mud. He was a sight. Like a clod of earth, fresh turned.

"You don't look fevered no more!" the girl exclaimed.

Junebug. That was her name. Maddy's sluggish thoughts started to gather speed.

She was in the same filthy overalls that she'd been wearing in Bitterroot. She came in carrying two dented pails full of water, still barefoot, still bold. "I reckon you're milking it so you don't have to haul no water."

"What happened to me?" Maddy took in her position on the floor. Someone had built a comfortable pallet for her there, nested with soft furs. She was near the stove, warm even though she was laid on the drafty ground. Someone had been very considerate of her.

"You went down a rabbit hole. Here." The girl dropped her pails and dipped a mug into one of them. She squatted next to Maddy and offered her water.

Gratefully, Maddy drank. The water was icy and sweet. She felt the cold run through her, settling her head.

The girl sat and crossed her legs. Merle climbed into her lap and made himself comfortable. He was panting, his tongue flopping, his black eyes shining with pleasure.

"He's been chasing muskrats," the girl said, giving him a scratch.

Merle barked.

Maddy was still struggling to absorb the girl's presence; she couldn't think about Merle and muskrats. "Junebug . . . You're Junebug. We met in the washhouse . . ."

"Oh, good, your brain ain't damaged, then. Sometimes when people get fevers, they forget who they are. It happened in one of Kit's books. The lady hadn't a notion who she was and then there were hijinks. But I don't think I've got enough energy for hijinks today; I didn't get much sleep last night, with all Kit's snoring. I'm surprised you managed to sleep through it. It got me thinking that maybe the fever had hurt your brain. I reckoned only a brain injury could induce a body to sleep through all that racket. Morgan went and slept out on the porch, Kit's snoring bothered him so."

"Kit?" Maddy blurted. "As in, Kit McBride . . . ?" Was the *bear* Kit McBride? No, wait. That was Morgan, she remembered. *Morgan! Yoo-hoo!* Mrs. Champion's ghostly voice rang in her ears.

"That's the one." Junebug glanced at the door, as though to make sure they were still alone. "I reckon since we got a minute alone, we'd best clear the air, don't you? Because I know you ain't Willabelle Lascalles, and you know you ain't Willabelle Lascalles."

Willabelle? What? Maddy frowned. "No, I'm Maddy Mooney."

"I remember. Maddy the Maid."

"I worked for Willabelle," she reminded Junebug.

"I ain't one to judge," the girl said, looking solemn. "So don't be afeared of a scolding from me."

What was the silly girl talking about? Oh, Maddy's head hurt.

The girl saw her wince and took the mug off her and refilled it. "Here, drink some more. You sweat buckets last night; you're probably dry as a bone."

"I don't know why you'd scold me," Maddy said as she drank.

"That's what I'm trying to say, I won't."

None of this was making sense. Maybe she did have a brain injury . . .

"It's no skin off my nose if you want to pretend to be Willabelle Lascalles."

Maddy choked on the water, spraying it all over herself. "I *what*?"

"The woman was a hardship, that's for certain. I ain't never met a more trying person in my life. Except for Morgan. And maybe Beau. Jonah sometimes. But they weren't in the same basket as that Willabelle."

"Wait. Slow down. You think I'm pretending to be Willabelle?"

"I know she got scared off. And I consider that a triumph. The last thing I want is that goshawk up here, making my life a misery. And I can see as how you might see this as an opportunity. I didn't at first, but I've been thinking on it all night, and I reckon being a wife is a darned sight better than being a maid."

"A *what*?" Maddy's stomach was churning. What was this ridiculous child blathering about? Maddy's wits felt about as swollen and useless as her leg. She couldn't quite work out what Junebug was trying to tell her.

"I got no call for a nincompoop in a pretty dress," Junebug was saying now, "but you're another kettle of fish. *You* I'd consider keeping."

Keeping? *What*?

"Oh, thank heavens, you're awake."

Dear God, it was the bear! He loomed in the doorway, looking twice as terrifying as she remembered, a solid mountain of a man with a mane of tangled black hair and a formidable beard. Maddy heard herself make a small whimpering sound and hated herself for it.

"Junebug, stop harassing the poor woman."

"We'll talk later," Junebug whispered to Maddy.

Maddy hoped not. She hadn't enjoyed that conversation at all. "There's been a mistake," she blurted. "Please . . ." Her voice trembled and she found she was on the edge of tears.

"Calm down." The bear's black eyebrows drew together.

Jesus, Mary and Joseph, he was dismaying. The kind of man you had nightmares about.

"I don't reckon growling at her to calm down is helpful," Junebug told him as she slipped past him and disappeared outside. "Try being nice to her." Merle bounced out after her, leaving Maddy alone with the bear.

"I am being nice," the bear bellowed at her back. Then he stepped into the room, and Maddy moaned. What was he going to do to her?

Was she supposed to ask for help from these brutes? Because this Morgan McBride didn't look like the helpful type. He looked like the type you needed help to get away from.

"You're in pain?" He stopped, frowning fiercer than ever.

Maddy nodded jerkily. She was. But worse than the pain was the fear. This man made her weak with it. Barely able to speak. She remembered the sensation of her leg going out from under her, the wicked pain, him towering over her. *Who the hell are you?*

"You hurt your leg," he said gruffly.

Her leg. Was it broken? Jesus, Mary and Joseph. What if it was broken? Would she heal? What if she couldn't walk properly? How would she manage if she was lame?

"Bad," the bear added. "You screamed a lot."

Maddy felt like she'd been hit by an icy gale. Every part of her went cold. No. She couldn't be lame. How would she earn her keep?

Maddy started crying.

The bear made a strangled noise and looked at her in horror. "Christ," he swore. "I'm sorry. I ain't no good with women." He fled.

Maddy collapsed back on the furs and covered her face with her arm, dissolving into tears. *He wounds, He shatters*, she thought, sobbing. Oh, she rued the day she was ever born.

"You'd best come," Morgan urged Kit. "She's crying."

Kit glanced up from the eggs in the pan. "She's awake? That's good." He'd set to fixing a solid breakfast, hoping to encourage her to get something down. She needed to eat if she was going to recover. When he'd left the trading post, she'd still been fast asleep, still peaceful and unfevered, thank God.

"Yeah, but she's crying. Come quick."

"The pain?"

"I guess so." Morgan looked at a complete loss. He'd never been good with tears. It was lucky for all of them that Junebug wasn't a crier. Wrestling was more his style, and Miss Lascalles didn't look the wrestling type.

"You cooked!" Junebug's head popped up as he carried the breakfast past the woodpile, where she was gathering an armful to replenish the cord he'd used the night before. She looked like a beaver popping up out of its dam. Miss Lascalles's little dog popped up, too, sniffing the air.

"What are we having?" Junebug asked.

"It ain't for you," he said shortly. "You're capable of cooking your own."

"Hardly." She scowled.

"Don't be lazy. Eggs ain't hard, Junebug."

"They are when I cook them." She followed him with her haul of wood. He could practically feel her glare boring into his back.

Kit could hear the soft sound of weeping as he reached the trading post. He picked up speed, worried. He hoped Miss Lascalles wasn't suffering too much. His heart pinched when he saw her, her face turned to the stove. She didn't storm when she cried; it was just a steady and heartbreaking downpour.

Feeling awkward, like he was invading her privacy, Kit knocked on the open door as he came in.

She made a noise and looked over to him, fear etched over every inch of her.

Hell, he'd have to keep Morgan away from her. He forgot how scary his older brother could be, especially to people who didn't know him. Morgan was all bluster, but people never knew that. And why would they? He looked rougher than a bear just out of hibernation.

Maybe Kit should ask him to shave. He was less intimidating without the beard.

"Good morning," Kit said gently, keeping his movements slow and careful so as not to startle her. He figured soothing a woman wasn't too different from soothing a skittish horse; something he was good at, since he'd shoed more than a few in his time. No sudden movements, no loud noises. "I made you some eggs. You need vittles after the shock of yesterday."

Her blue eyes were distrustful as he approached. She pulled the blanket up all the way to her chin.

"My brothers have gone for the closest doctor, but he's all the way down at the Ella-Jean Mine," Kit told her calmly, "so he might not get here for a couple of days. If you eat up, I'll check your leg."

She looked genuinely terrified at that.

"I brought fresh coffee too. It'll fortify you." He lowered the plate and mug within her reach.

She stared at them like he was offering her poison.

"They're good eggs," he promised.

"They are," Junebug seconded, coming in behind him with her wood, the dog dancing at her heels. "If you ain't hungry, I'll have them."

Kit ignored her. She was eating Miss Lascalles's breakfast over his dead body. He put the plate on the floor next to her and collared the dog as he darted forward to steal the eggs. "They're not for you . . ." He paused. "What's his name?"

"Merle," Maddy said.

"Beast," Junebug spoke at the same time.

"Merle?" Junebug sounded plain appalled. "You called your dog Merle?"

"He's not my . . ." Miss Lascalles bit her lip, which was still wobbly from crying. Kit was just glad she was talking. That was a definite improvement on mute terror.

The dog in question yapped. Kit wasn't sure whose side he was on. Merle was a right peculiar name for a dog. "Junebug, you can't go renaming people's dogs," Kit sighed.

"I can if they're named something as dumb as Merle."

"Junebug," he snapped, then immediately wished he hadn't, because it made Miss Lascalles flinch. And flinching obviously caused her pain.

"What? It *is* a dumb name. I reckon Miss Lascalles here even agrees with me. Beast is a much better name."

"I'm sorry about Junebug," Kit apologized to the poor woman. "She was raised by wolves." Keeping hold of the dog, he put the coffee mug on the floor next to the plate of eggs.

He moved away and sat on the flour sacks, keeping the wriggling dog in his lap. He rubbed the back of Merle/Beast's neck, aware of the way the solid little body was poised to leap at the eggs the minute he relaxed.

Miss Lascalles sat there for a few minutes, like she was run to ground by a mountain lion and trying to decide what to do. At least she wasn't crying anymore. Eventually she took up the plate and tried the eggs. Kit had known she must be hungry.

"They're good, thank you," she mumbled, keeping her gaze on the plate.

Junebug scowled at him and dropped her wood on the pile with a clatter.

"Go get your own," he told her. "Miss Lascalles wants to eat in quiet."

"No!" Miss Lascalles was horrified.

Kit felt absurdly hurt.

"It's not seemly," she said quickly. "To be alone with you. With any man . . . Junebug needs to chaperone us . . ." She seemed highly anxious.

Kit blinked. Oh. He flushed, feeling every inch the backwoodsman. Of course. Just like in his books.

"But *I'm* alone with him all the time," Junebug said.

"You're my sister," Kit said. He still felt like an oaf. "You don't need a chaperone with your own brother."

She was thoughtful. "Wait. Does this mean that even if you marry him, you can't be alone with him? That I have to follow you about everywhere, doing all this chaperoning, on top of my other chores?"

"Junebug!" Kit could have kicked her. She had all the tact of a wild bull. He wasn't planning on marrying Miss Lascalles, or anyone. But poor Miss Lascalles didn't know that yet. He didn't want to lead her on, but he also didn't want to add to her current distress. They could talk about the whole sorry marriage situation later, when she was feeling better.

"Marry you?" Miss Lascalles spluttered into her coffee. "*You're* Kit McBride?"

Kit found himself blushing again. She sounded so shocked. "I am," he admitted. All of the things Junebug had written about him in the ad came swimming to the front of his mind. The snoring, the ill manners, the bossiness, the temper . . . *not too old and not too ugly* . . . Hell.

Why had she ever answered the ad, given that description? Even now, with her face swollen from crying, her clothes filthy and her leg in a state, she was a good-looking woman. Better than good-looking. Beautiful. Her eyes alone were stunningly blue, a spring shade so vital it rivaled the bluest sky.

"I didn't know which one was Kit . . ." she said weakly. She'd started blushing now too.

"That's him." Junebug had finished restacking the firewood, badly, and was staring openly back and forth between Kit and Miss Lascalles. Kit could practically read her mind. His scheming little sister plainly still had matrimony on her mind.

Well, she could get it off her mind. Because he had no intention of marrying, even if the option was this blue-eyed, music-voiced beauty.

"Junebug, go get yourself some breakfast."

"If I go, you go. She cain't be alone with you, remember?" Junebug grinned at him. She was enjoying herself, the little hellion.

Kit could have sworn. The last thing he needed was Junebug underfoot while he ministered to Miss Lascalles.

"I'm done," Miss Lascalles said quickly, putting the plate down. She wasn't anywhere near done but was obviously keen to get rid of them. "It was delicious, thank you."

"He's a decent cook," Junebug said. "He's just stubborn and don't cook much 'cause he thinks I should do it."

"She should do it." Kit couldn't help himself. Junebug's laziness always irked him.

"She *does* do it," Junebug said sourly. "And have a look at the size of him! Guess how much he can eat? Can you cook?"

"Junebug," Kit said warningly.

"What? Since when is asking someone if they can cook not allowed?"

"I really am sorry," Kit apologized, feeling like he'd done nothing but apologize since he'd met Miss Lascalles. "I'm not joking, she really was raised by wolves. Rude ones." He put the dog down and rolled up his sleeves to get to work on her leg. Merle the Beast immediately ran for the leftover eggs and licked the plate clean.

"Wolves," Junebug muttered. "Don't flatter yourself. And how come the dumb dog can eat the eggs, but I cain't?"

He ignored that. "Junebug, can you get some more water? Keep the door open so you can see us; that should count as chaperoning."

"Please . . ." Junebug prodded.

He rolled his eyes. "Please." As soon as she was gone, he knelt beside Miss Lascalles. She seemed nervy. That he could well understand, after the pain yesterday. He got a bit nervy himself just remembering it. "I'm going to unwrap the leg," he told her calmly, even though he wasn't feeling terribly calm. His heart couldn't seem to decide on a rhythm.

Junebug returned with fresh water and peered over his shoulder as he unwrapped the wounded leg. Miss Lascalles sat forward to watch, too, rigid as a tentpole, her jaw clenched so tight that he fancied he could hear her teeth cracking.

Relief swept him as he saw the leg was swollen but straight. And not as bruised as he'd thought it might be.

Miss Lascalles wasn't so relieved.

"Well, that don't look like anything," Junebug said, disgusted, leaning so close that Kit could feel her breath against his ear. "I've had hangnails worse than that."

He didn't deign to reply.

"Is it broken?" Miss Lascalles reached out and touched his biceps nervously. He felt it all through him, like a shot of moonshine.

Startled, he met her gaze. Such a shade of blue. He felt more than a bit drunk. "No," he said huskily. "It's just sprained."

"Did I carry on this bad when I broke my arm?" Junebug asked. She sounded genuinely curious.

"No," Kit sighed, still lost in Miss Lascalles's harebell eyes. He realized he was staring and flushed. He cleared his throat. "You swore a lot and kicked, and it took both Morgan and Beau to hold you down while I set it."

"I gave Morgan a black eye," Junebug said in satisfaction. It was an old family story, one they told often.

Kit checked that Miss Lascalles was still breathing. She was so pale.

"Kit?"

"What?" He was irritated by Junebug's constant blathering.

"She'll be all right?"

He looked up, surprised. The kid was giving him an impatient look.

"That's all she wants to know. If she'll be all right or not. Look at her."

He had been looking at her. It made him soft in the head.

"You'll be fine," he said. Best not to look at her square on, he decided, turning back to her leg.

"Oh, thank God." She went limp, sagging into him. "I didn't know how I'd ever work again if I went lame . . ."

"You won't be lame," Kit assured her. "Not so long as you rest up now and allow the swelling to go down."

"Maybe we should put honey on it," Junebug said thoughtfully.

"What?" Kit peered up at his sister, who was considering the shelves around them. He could practically read her mind. "No," he said shortly. "No honey. She just needs to elevate it and rest until the doctor comes."

Miss Lascalles seemed heartened by talk of the doctor.

"I'm serious," Kit's fool sister continued, heading off to hunt among the shelves. "Sour Eagle swears by it. He says he got gored by a bull elk once and slapped some honey on it and it was good as new in no time."

"I'm sorry about her," Kit sighed, taking a cloth and using the fresh pail of water to clean Miss Lascalles's swollen leg.

She squeaked, and he looked up to find she'd gone bright red. She shuffled and tried to pull her skirt down.

Kit felt a hot wave of shame. He'd been washing her naked leg. That certainly wasn't proper, was it . . . "Junebug," he said hoarsely. "You come do this. It ain't right for me to be doing it."

Junebug swore. "I ain't a workhorse, you know." But she took the cloth off him and was gentle as a lamb as she cleaned Miss

Lascalles up. Kit kept his gaze averted. The silence was deeply awkward. He felt big and oafish and completely uncivilized.

"You reckon I should go find some honey next?" Junebug said helpfully.

"Only if you're going to eat it," Miss Lascalles said sharply.

Kit risked a glance at her. She and Junebug were staring each other down. Junebug was the first to look away. There was a measure of fire in her, then, Kit thought, and the notion made him warm in the most disconcerting way.

Eleven

"We need to talk." Maddy snagged Junebug as she delivered lunch. It was her second day on the bed of furs in front of the stove on the floor of the trading post. She was still in pain, stiff from the floor, embarrassed about using the chamber pot with Junebug's assistance and in despair about the way the two bearish McBrides kept calling her Miss Lascalles.

She had to correct it. She also had to talk to Kit McBride about the whole issue of her train ticket. She didn't think she had the nerve to ask for her twenty-eight dollars' back pay, but she was desperate enough to broach the train ticket. Only how was she ever getting out of here with her leg in such a state!

At least Kit McBride was the kinder, gentler bear. The one with the melting dark eyes . . .

By the time Junebug arrived with Maddy's lunch, which was a near-inedible plate of fried ham and a slab of gluey bread, Maddy had gathered herself enough to tackle things head-on.

"I'm not Willabelle Lascalles," she told Junebug firmly.

"Lucky for all of us, on that count," Junebug said as she dug out the coffee tin and readied the pot. She'd brought her own lunch along and gnawed on chunks of fried ham as she worked. "We already talked about this, Maddy the Maid. You sure you didn't damage your brain?"

"You know who I am, so why are your brothers calling me Miss Lascalles?" Maddy demanded, putting her plate in front of Merle and letting him at the horrid ham.

Junebug gave her an odd look. "Because you told them you were Kit's bride."

Maddy blinked. "I most certainly did not!"

"Morgan said you told him you were Kit's bride, and then you fell down a rabbit hole. I know it was his fault, somehow, because he's got his guilty face on. I reckon he scared you after you told him you were here to marry Kit, and you hurt yourself running away."

"I said no such thing!" Maddy racked her brain to remember what she *had* said. Not much at all, from memory. She'd been too panicked by Morgan's size and ferocity to be able to say much of anything. *Kit McBride.* She'd said that. And then . . . oh no . . . *his bride.*

She groaned. "I was trying to tell him about Willabelle. *She* was supposed to be Kit's bride."

Junebug pulled a face. "Thank God that never happened. What a nightmare. I didn't last one conversation with her. How on earth did you put up with her?"

"I didn't have a choice," Maddy sighed.

"Is that why you came up here, to run away from her?"

"Not exactly."

"Well, what exactly?" Junebug put the coffeepot on to boil and fixed Maddy with her full attention. "Go on. Tell me. I'm a good listener. Even Morgan says so. Although he says I'm a better talker. He also says even if I do listen, it doesn't mean I'll do what I'm told." She sounded bizarrely proud of that fact.

"It's complicated," Maddy told her.

"I'm good at complicated!"

"No one is good at *this* complicated." Maddy tried to work out how much to tell her. "She abandoned me."

Merle yapped.

"And him," Maddy added. "She ran off with a miner. I'm owed months of wages and I've got no way to get back east. She said your brother would give me train fare back." Well, she'd actually said she was gifting Maddy the blacksmith . . . but Maddy wasn't telling anyone *that*.

Junebug's eyes were as wide as saucers. "That *bitch*."

Once again, Maddy couldn't believe the mouth on the girl. She hadn't been raised by wolves, she'd been raised by *sailors*.

"How dare she lead me on like that?" Junebug raged. "Even if I didn't want her, she had no right. And to tell you that we'd pay your way, after throwing us over like that? And she just *left* you?"

Merle yapped.

"And left you too," Junebug amended, reaching down to scratch his ears. "Poor little Beast." She poured Maddy a mug of the thick tarry coffee.

"You wouldn't have any tea, would you?" Maddy peered distastefully at the sludgy coffee. What was with Americans and coffee? Did no one drink tea out here? "I haven't had a decent cup of tea since I left Ireland," she sighed. They'd made tea for her in New York, but the nuns were stingy with the leaves and it was like drinking colored water.

"Tea?" Junebug squinted at the shelves. "You know, we do. I saw some when I was hunting for honey—I didn't even know we had tea." She went off rummaging. "Here we go." She opened the tin and took a sniff. "How do you make it?"

Lord, the child was wild. "Boil water," Maddy advised. "Then pour over the leaves and steep it."

"That's it?"

"Add cream and sugar if you want to."

"Well, that makes sense. Anything would taste good with cream and sugar." Junebug found a pot and got some water on to boil.

"How much did the goshawk owe you?" Junebug asked.

Maddy told her.

"Well, spit. Surely her yellow dress was worth that? It looked costly enough. Couldn't she have sold her dress?"

Maddy pulled a face. Dress or earbobs . . . yes, she could have found a way.

"Who did she run off with?" Junebug demanded.

"Garrett."

"He the one that took old Enoch Teter's claim?"

"I don't know who he got it from; he won it gambling."

"That's the one." Junebug dumped tea leaves into the pot. Maddy winced. She had doubts that this would be a decent cup of tea.

"The nerve of her." Junebug was outraged.

"You need to strain the leaves out," Maddy said hurriedly. She was likely to end up with a mouthful of tea leaves if she left this to Junebug.

"You came up here to get help?" Junebug prodded. She was stirring the pot of leaves like it was soup.

"Yes," Maddy sighed. "I can't afford a train ticket, and Mrs. Champion convinced me that your brother would do the honorable thing and help . . ."

Junebug didn't respond to that. She was busy pouring out the tea. "I got sugar but no cream. I reckon you need sugar right now." She fetched the sugar bag and poured a heft into the mug. She sniffed it. "Smells all right." She handed Maddy the mug.

It wasn't the best tea she'd ever had, but Maddy didn't care. It smelled of the kitchens at Ormond House. She could practically hear the clink of cutlery being polished and the homely sound of Mrs. Egan humming to herself. It fortified Maddy enough for the conversation at hand.

"I need your help," she told Junebug bluntly. "You need to tell your brothers that I'm not who they think I am . . ." She pulled a face. "I don't imagine your brother Kit is going to take kindly to hearing about how Willabelle has absquatulated, and I don't fancy being the one to tell him."

"Absquatulated!" Junebug lit up. "Now *that's* a word. What's it mean?"

"Run off," Maddy sighed, remembering Willabelle declaring her decision to absquatulate back in St. Louis. "Removed herself, absented, left."

Junebug gave Maddy an admiring look.

"It's not my word," Maddy told her, pricking her bubble. "It's hers."

"It's your word now, I reckon. You used it with aplomb. That means with assurance. Self-confidence. Poise. That one's the dictionary's word, not mine." Junebug poured herself a cup of tea as well and sweetened it with a long pour of sugar. "Look, Maddy the Maid, we need to talk frank."

Maddy blinked. Wasn't that what they were already doing? How much franker could they be?

Junebug sat on the floor next to Maddy and took a long slurp of her tea. "It tastes like larkspur smells." She took another slurp. "I could get used to it."

"Let *me* make it sometime and it will taste better," Maddy suggested.

Junebug grinned. "That sounds like a good deal." She cocked her head. "Can you make cake?"

"I've never tried," Maddy admitted.

"Pie?"

Maddy shook her head. "I'm not really a cook."

Junebug couldn't hide her disappointment. She put her tea down. "Maddy the Maid, I'm in a bind. If we could talk frank, that would be appreciated. If you could keep what I say just between us, that would be even more appreciated."

Maddy had a sinking feeling that she wasn't about to like what Junebug had to say. She also noted that Junebug abruptly seemed much older. She wondered how old the girl was. It was difficult to tell, given the overalls and the hacked-off short hair.

"The thing is . . . it weren't Kit who advertised for a wife," Junebug told her. "It was me."

That was not what Maddy was expecting her to say.

Junebug ran a hand through her shaggy hair, pushing it back from her face. Her gray eyes were solemn. "I was the one who wanted a wife." She looked grim, but only for a moment. Resolutely, she looked Maddy in the eye. "He didn't know I advertised, or that I wrote the letters, or that I proposed to Willabelle on his behalf."

Maddy had thought she was beyond shock, given the past months, but it turned out that she could still be shocked. *Very* shocked. "You . . . ordered him a wife without him knowing?"

Jesus, Mary and Joseph, that explained the bear's ferocity when Maddy had arrived. Imagine what the two of them must be thinking, a woman fetching up out of the blue, claiming to be a bride! Maddy felt sick to her stomach. But also relieved. They wouldn't mind at all, then, when she told them she wasn't actually Willabelle Lascalles, and that she had no intention of matrimony . . .

Oh. But if Kit McBride hadn't known about her, then . . . he'd never promised to cover her back pay . . . and it wasn't at all appropriate for Maddy to ask him to pay for her train ticket out of here . . .

Oh God. What a mess. What was she to do? She couldn't stay here. But looking at the state of her leg, she also couldn't leave. Here she was, imposing on these poor men, who didn't want her in the first place.

"Do you have any idea how much work it is looking after four men?" Junebug sighed.

Maddy was sure it was a lot of work, especially given the size of the two brothers she had met—and there were two more on top of them. But that didn't warrant lying to people on such a grand scale!

"I needed help," Junebug admitted. "I *need* help. And I thought a wife would be a good idea. I *still* think it's a good idea," she sighed. "But my brothers don't see the sense in it."

"They're hardly likely to change their minds if you shove a strange woman in front of them," Maddy snapped. Honestly, the silly girl was out of her mind! Maddy wouldn't be in this position if Junebug hadn't been such a schemer; Willabelle would have chosen someone else, someone who lived in a proper town, not out in the middle of the wilderness. Someone who didn't have rabbit holes for a girl to break her leg down! Someone who could have paid her wages . . .

"Ah," Junebug said, "there's where you're wrong. Putting a woman in front of them is *exactly* what I need to do. The thing is, they've been stuck up here their whole lives. Morgan's the only one who's traveled, and he only ever traveled with a bunch of cows. The lot of them have no idea about women. They don't know what they're missing! But I do."

"Oh, do you now?" Maddy was getting irked. This girl had up-ended their lives: hers, Willabelle's, the bear's, Kit's . . .

"I do!" Junebug nodded vigorously. "They're missing *sparks*. They should be walking around looking like they've been kicked in the head. They should be distracted by shoulders and gazes and smiles. They should be daffy with it. And I shouldn't be washing their long underwear or cooking their dinner."

The girl made next to no sense.

"You know what I *should* be doing?" Junebug demanded. "Fishing! And book learning. Making friends. Not playing the wife to a bunch of ungrateful blockheads! If they want a wife, Maddy the Maid, then they should go and marry one!"

Maddy groaned. "They don't want a wife, though, do they!" she told Junebug. "And even if they did, I'm not her."

"I'll win them over," Junebug said bullishly. "But you're right, you're not her." She finished her tea in one long swallow. "The thing is, if we tell them, things will just get more complicated than they already are. I mean, why make things worse?"

Maddy didn't like the glint in Junebug's eye. "Why not just tell them the truth?" Maddy said sternly.

Junebug made a disgusted noise. "Tell them I picked the worst wife ever? Then they'll *never* let me pick another one."

"I doubt they'll let you anyway." Maddy was getting sore sitting up. She lowered herself back down into the soft furs. She hated being incapacitated like this. She felt too vulnerable, too helpless.

"Look. I have money," Junebug told her. "I've been saving up my letter-writing money for this bride business. Roy's been spending big on his hunt for yeller-haired girls, so I'm sure I've got enough to get you a train ticket."

Maddy's breath caught. She certainly hadn't been expecting that.

"We both know it's my fault you're here. Not Kit's. So, it seems fitting I should pay for your ticket out. On one condition . . ."

Oh, here it came. Maddy deflated. There was always a condition. What did she have to do?

"You keep pretending to be Willabelle."

What? Oh no. No, no, no.

"Hear me out." Junebug didn't let her speak. "Kit don't want you, right? He don't want any woman. Or so he says. So you're in no danger of finding yourself hitched." She paused. "You don't want to be hitched, right?"

"No!" Maddy was appalled by Junebug's vaguely hopeful look.

Junebug shrugged. "Thought I might as well ask."

"This is crazy. Why can't you just tell them I'm Willabelle's maid?"

Junebug groaned. "Because they already think I'm witless. I don't need them to know that all my plans went upside down on me. Let them think I did a good job of this, and found a good woman, and that the only reason it's not working is because they're too stubborn to admit I'm right. Please . . ." She fixed Maddy with a beseeching gaze. "Here." She fumbled in the bib pocket of her overalls. "Look. I have the money." She held out a wad of bills. "See? This will more than buy you a train ticket home."

It surely would. Junebug held a healthy bundle of cash in her chapped hand.

Lord, she *could* get out of here. Maddy felt wobbly with relief.

"You don't have to lie, not really. Just answer to the name, that's all. And who will it hurt? Nobody at all," Junebug begged. "One woman's the same as another to Kit; he don't want any of them. And if you're leaving these parts, what does it matter who people think you are?"

Maddy couldn't really argue with any of that.

"As soon as your leg's healed up, off you go, with no one the wiser."

Her leg. Maddy stared at the throbbing swollen thing that used to be her leg. How was she going to get down the hill and onto a train? "How long do you think it will take to heal?" She was scared of the answer.

"Kit says not long." Junebug pulled a face as she looked at the leg. "I'd be betting on a couple of weeks."

A couple of weeks! "I can't pretend to be Willabelle for a couple of weeks!"

"Sure you can. And you don't have to pretend to *be* her. Who the hell wants her around, even if it's only someone *pretending* to be her? She's the last person I want around here, pretend or not. This isn't about pretending to *be* her; this is just about answering to her name."

Maddy blinked, not sure any of that actually made sense.

"Here, I'll get you another cup of tea and you can think about it." Junebug flashed the money as she stood up. "I reckon you'll see that it's a good deal."

Good deal? As far as Maddy could see, it was the *only* deal.

Twelve

Maddy was relieved when Kit offered to carry her outside. She was heartily sick of being supine on the floor of the stuffy trading post, next to the sooty stove. Kit noted her restlessness; he seemed to notice everything.

"Would you like to sit on the porch for a bit?" he asked shyly. "You'd have to keep your leg propped up, but at least you can look at something other than our dusty rafters."

Maddy was more than happy to accept his offer, even though every time she moved, her leg blazed with pain. But she was willing to put up with any amount of pain for the change of scenery. She'd stiffened up something terrible from lying on the floor, and she was sick to death of the rafters, and the floorboards, and the landscape of dust that had collected under the shelving.

Kit McBride apologized when she hissed with pain as he gathered her up. He apologized a lot; he even apologized for apologizing. And he apologized more than ever when she tried to snag a blanket to cover her state of undress.

"Hell, I'm sorry, you ain't clothed. I forgot." He helped her cover herself.

"I have another dress in my carpetbag," Maddy said, feeling naked in her undergarments. She held the rug over the tattered bodice of Willabelle's plaid dress. "It's not clean but at least it's not in streamers."

"I'll have Junebug clean it for you first," he promised. "I should have thought of it, I'm sorry. We'll get you bathed and in fresh clothes before tonight." He flushed. "I mean, Junebug can help you. I didn't mean *we* . . ." He was turning the color of a ripe tomato. "I was just wary of moving you . . ."

"I wasn't criticizing," Maddy hurried to assure him. She wished she could simply put another dress on right now. She'd rather be dirty and clothed than sitting out in her undergarments and a blanket. But she was too embarrassed to push it.

He went off apologizing again, his cheeks shining red above his thick beard. "I'll get it sorted."

He was such a contradiction. Burly, big and about as masculine as a man could be, but also gentle, shy and courteous. Maddy had never met a man like him. Look at the way he carried her, as though she were as light and fragile as a brittle autumn leaf, careful of her leg as he eased them through the doorway and into a day so bright that it made Maddy squint. His arm was like a beam under her, solid and sure.

He smelled of woodsmoke and sunshine and alpine air. It was a fresh smell. Good. She could see the pulse beating fast in the hollow of his throat as he lowered her into the wooden rocking chair on the porch.

Maddy gritted her teeth against the pain as he pulled a stool over and lifted her foot onto it. She kept tight hold of the blanket, painfully aware that she was only in her bloomers from the waist down.

"I'm sorry," he apologized for thousandth time. "But you need to keep the leg elevated or it'll swell right up."

They both looked at her leg. Her foot was like a swollen water bladder.

"More than it already is," he said helplessly. "I'll get you some extra blankets. It gets cold in the shade." He disappeared inside.

It was the strangest thing. Maddy had never before in her life had anyone wait on her. She didn't remember ever being idle or laid up. No one had worried over her before, the way this big bearish blacksmith did, or fetched her blankets or had concern for her comfort. Even Tom Ormond had been rough more often than not. He'd certainly had none of the tenderness of this mountain man. And Kit McBride was the last man Maddy would have expected tenderness from. No, actually, his brother was probably the last man. Kit was second to last.

You just didn't expect giants to be this gentlemanly. But here he was, gingerly spreading another woolen blanket over her. "I saw Junebug tried to make you tea," he observed. "She left the pot on the stove." He cleared his throat. "Would you like another cup?"

Maddy blinked. She was more used to people asking *her* to make the tea. "I'd love one," she admitted. My, it felt good to be on the other end of this.

"Milk and sugar? I'd offer cream, but we don't have any." He seemed bashful about it.

"Both, please." Oh, she could get used to this, she thought, nestling under the blankets as he strode off toward the creek, where the milk pail was sitting in the shallows, keeping cool.

The trading post had a magnificent view. From here Maddy could see the whole of the creek as it ran through the meadow. Now *this* was what she'd imagined when Sister Ruth had talked about the West. *This* looked like the wild frontier. Buck's Creek was tucked against the hip of the creek, which really was more of a stream than a creek. The shining waterway snaked through a wide expanse of high mountain meadow. The woods hemmed the broad meadow on all sides, sprawling up the mountainsides in a brilliant patchwork of autumn color. The forest blazed red and orange, yellow and lime green. The mountains themselves were mighty, dwarfing her memory of the gentle Slieve Bloom Mountains back home. In fact, they made the Slieve Blooms look like hillocks.

The perfume of the place was heady: the mineral tang of the water flowing by, the drying grasses, the fragrance of brittle leaves. There was the pungent aroma of hay and oniony greens, and other scents foreign but fine. A frisky cool breeze was skittering through the meadow. It blew the cobwebs from Maddy's head.

Upstream, she could see a log cabin, nestled in a curve of pines. It wasn't big but it sure was sweet. It had a modest front porch large enough for a single chair, a pane-glass window next to the front door and a loft above, with a window staring straight down the stream to the trading post. Between the cabin and the trading post was a small hut, down closer to the water; blue smoke curled from a stovepipe poking through the roof. And then there was a large barn, surrounded by fenced paddocks, and a squat timber building with wide-open double doors and a fat black iron chimney. Maddy guessed that must be the smithy.

Everything was splashed with golden sunshine the color of cider. Faintly, Maddy heard the sound of Merle barking happily as he chased muskrats or rabbits through the tall grass. She watched Kit McBride pull the metal milk pail from the frosty creek and lower the dipper into the milk.

"You have a beautiful home," she told him as he returned with a cup brimful of milk.

He smiled.

Oh, what a smile could do. His whole countenance changed, like a lamp had been turned on. His dark eyes shone, and his teeth were white as starched sheets in his black beard.

"It's glorious at this time of year, ain't it?" he said, pausing to glance back at the sun on the wooded mountains. "Wait until sunset. You won't have seen anything so pretty in all your born days."

Maddy's heart was pounding as he disappeared inside to make her tea.

What was *that*? The man smiled and her heart drummed fit to accompany a brass band? By the time he emerged with her tea, she'd managed to calm herself. She kept her gaze fixed on the mug as she took it, not wanting to risk a heart attack by witnessing another smile.

"I'll send Junebug up to collect your washing," Kit promised. "And here." He held out a small handbell. "If you need anything, just ring." He put it down on the porch next to her chair.

Oh my. Now she really did feel like the lady of the manor.

She watched him go. For all his size, he moved with grace, easy in his body. His shirt was stretched tight across his broad back. Maddy remembered the soft well-washed feel of his shirt against her cheek, and the smell of the sunshine and creek water embedded in its weft. His wild black hair ruffled in the breeze.

Maddy felt oddly light-headed as she watched him go. He was a fine man.

But then . . . *oh* . . . she drank the tea.

And it was *good*.

Suddenly "fine" didn't seem to do him justice.

"I don't want to shave." Morgan glowered at Kit like he'd just suggested that Morgan dance naked through Bitterroot.

Kit had found him down in the root cellar, where he was taking stock and getting things in order for winter. It was frigid down there; it made Kit realize that winter might be closer than they'd hoped. The creek had been crocheted with frost at the edges this morning, and the grass had glittered with crystals instead of wet dew in the rising sun, and now, down here in the cellar, the earth felt frozen through already. Hell. It would be a long winter, if it started this early.

Morgan was always well prepared for the cold, ever since that first year he'd come back to find them half-starved after a brutal season of snow and ice. He stocked far more than they'd ever need, forcing them all to pickle and salt and jar everything they didn't eat. This year he'd slaughtered an extra hog and salted it down. Kit doubted they'd get through it all, but when a blizzard hit, he was always glad for Morgan's hoarding.

"I wish Junebug had saved the rest of the cucumbers from the damn rabbits this year," Morgan complained as Kit came down the steps into the dugout cellar. "We could have used a few more jars."

He was in one of his states, stressed about things that would probably never come to pass. That was Morgan's way. He was a worrier.

He was also stubborn as hell, and not amenable to Kit's suggestion that they shave their beards off.

"We scare her, looking like this," Kit said placidly, pitching in to help Morgan rearrange the cellar, making sure that everything would be easily accessible during a storm. "I reckon shaving would help with that."

Morgan gave Kit a sour look. "Maybe our faces would just scare her more."

"You're just worried that she'll take a shine to you if she sees your pretty face." Kit ignored the absurd spurt of jealousy he felt at the idea.

Morgan grunted. It wasn't exactly untrue. The last time he'd shaved his beard off, the women in town had all about swooned at his feet. He hadn't enjoyed it. "She'll cope with me and my beard just the way I am."

"She just about faints away at the sound of your voice."

"Shaving my beard off ain't going to help none with the sound of my voice, now, is it?"

Kit sighed. Not for the first time, he wished Morgan were of an easier temperament. "Would you consider trimming it at least?"

"Jesus, Kit, what's got into you?" Morgan paused over a barrel of beer. "Since when do you care what my whiskers look like?"

"Since I started playing doctor to a lady who is plumb terrified of us, that's when," Kit snapped back. "It'd make my life easier, Morgan, if she didn't shrink away every time that I came near her. And if she didn't set to weeping every time you so much as looked at her."

"That ain't happened since yesterday," Morgan muttered. "Ah hell. Fine. I'll shave. But I'm letting it grow right back, you hear? I ain't freezing my face off all winter just to make some fancy lady feel better. She can get a look at me and see that I ain't nothing to be afeared of, and then the whiskers come back."

Kit was happy enough with that. Without his beard, Morgan had dimples. It was hard to look scary when you had dimples winking away at people. "I'll help you finish in here, then we'll get shaving."

Morgan groaned. "You cain't let it wait until morning?"

"Nope." Kit rolled a barrel his way.

"I hate to think what you'd be like if you actually wanted to marry the woman."

"This is just a practical solution to a problem, Morgan," Kit told him. "Nothing more."

"Sure it is. You planning to wear your good shirt to supper to-night too?"

Damn it. He had been. But not because he was planning to court or marry the woman, for Pete's sake. Just 'cause . . . well, just 'cause.

He sure as hell didn't like the way Morgan was smirking.

"Do *you* want to look after her and her leg?" he snapped, knowing Morgan didn't have the stomach for it.

"Hell no!"

"Then shut up and make my life easier, would you?"

"What bug crawled up your nose?" Morgan sounded on the verge of laughter, which wasn't at all like him.

Kit felt all antsy and out of sorts. The thing was, that Lascalles woman did odd things to him. Hell, the way she felt in his arms, when he lifted her . . . the swell of her breast pressing against his chest, the look of her hand on his arm, the plump curve of her lower lip. Everything about her drove him to distraction. It had him washing his good shirt this morning and hanging it in the sun to dry; it had him planning to shave; it even had him thinking about trimming his hair. It was daft.

Maybe the shaving was a bad idea. But it was too late now. Morgan had worked out that he'd got under Kit's skin and was now hell-bent on shaving.

"You reckon I should lop the lot or keep a mustache?" he mused, adopting a tone that was so irksome that Kit wanted to thump him.

"I could try for some of them muttonchops, like Fritz wears?"

Kit blocked him out. He was just too irritating. The two of them hauled water from the creek and heated it on the cookhouse stove. Morgan had decided that if they were going to shave, they might as well go the whole hog and wash too. Kit was beginning to regret the whole thing.

"She's a pretty little woman," Morgan said as he took the scissors to his brushy beard. Clumps of black hair fell to the floor.

Kit made a noncommittal grunting noise. He dunked his head in the warmed water and scrubbed his face and hair with the sludgy soap Junebug was so bad at making. She'd tried to improve the lye and tallow scent with handfuls of sweet clover, which made the whole thing smell weirdly like hay. Still, it was better than the year she'd put nodding onion in, and they'd all reeked of sharp green onions for months.

"What are you doing?"

"Think of the devil, and she appears," Kit sighed.

Junebug stuck her head in the door and sniffed. "Why are you using the good soap?"

The good soap. She was flattering herself there. The stuff was a vile goo. He'd have to show her how to make proper lye again. Kit reckoned she'd been using softwood ashes instead of hardwood. Again. No matter how many times he told her that you needed hardwood ash, she got lazy and used whatever was on hand. No amount of sweet clover could turn a poor soap into a good one.

"Are you shaving?" Junebug sounded shocked. "Oh my God, Kit. Morgan's shaving!"

"I sure am." Now that he was doing it, Morgan had thrown himself into it with gusto. Mostly because it was annoying Kit. The scissors had cleared the thicket down to a solid black stubble.

"I don't really remember what you look like under there," Junebug said. She came in and pulled herself up to sit on the workbench so she could watch.

"Don't you have chores to do?" Kit growled. He scrubbed his face dry.

"I've done 'em. I washed all them dresses like you told me to. The two black ones took forever; they were filthy. One of them was so threadbare it just about fell apart on me. I reckon it's done for."

"Hell." Kit felt a stab of guilt. "We ruined her best dress when we were fixing up the leg."

"What's this *we*?" Morgan asked, lathering up with the hay-smelling goopy soap. "I didn't ruin no dress."

"It's your fault she went down the hole in the first place," Kit muttered.

"Don't fret, she's got another fancy one." Junebug had narrowed her eyes and was evaluating them. "It's bright blue and shiny. Not blue-blue," she corrected. "Kind of pale silver-blue, but bright. A bit like the belly feathers on a bluebird."

"You're a poet, Bug," Morgan said. "No wonder you managed to snag yourself a wife."

"What's with him?" Junebug asked Kit suspiciously. "Why's he acting all like that?"

"All like what?"

"Happy." Her lips thinned. "He ain't never happy. I don't trust it."

Neither did Kit. Morgan was entirely too chipper.

There were only two reasons for it that Kit could see, and he didn't like either of them. One: Morgan had got it into his thick head that Kit was trying to pay court to Miss Lascalles and was now out to torture him. Kit didn't like that idea at all. Not least of all because he wasn't courting anyone, so it was a wrongheaded notion. Two: Morgan had taken a shine to Miss Lascalles himself. *She's a pretty little woman.* Kit liked that even less. Hell, Morgan scared the wits out of the poor woman. She'd probably faint dead away if he pressed a suit.

Only . . . now Kit had got him to shave, and his dimples were out.

Damn it. Maybe this had been the dumbest idea Kit had ever had.

"When I'm done, Bug, do you want to give me a haircut?" Morgan asked as the razor rasped over his square jaw.

A haircut! Kit scowled.

"What in hell do you want a haircut for?" Junebug asked, astonished.

"Ain't you heard? We got a lady here for supper. I might wear my good shirt too." He winked at Kit.

Damn it.

Thirteen

"Aren't any of my clothes dry?" Maddy asked Junebug, a touch desperately. An old trapper had turned up over the course of the afternoon and had a habit of staring that made Maddy feel more naked than ever.

He hadn't introduced himself. He seemed entirely struck speechless by her presence. He'd ambled up, carrying the carcass of a deer over his shoulder, and, when he saw her, he'd stopped dead, his mouth falling open. Maddy had been on the verge of ringing the bell for help when Junebug came jogging toward the trading post.

"Go on, Roy, get," Junebug said when she arrived, kicking the trapper off the porch. "She ain't one of your yeller-haired girls, so stay away from her, you hear?"

Roy the trapper got, but only as far as the creek, where he made camp on the bank and kept right on staring.

"You going to skin and dress that deer or just let it go to waste?" Junebug called.

Only then did he seem to remember that he'd come in with a deer.

"I need something to wear," Maddy pleaded, pulling the blanket even tighter around herself. "He keeps staring at me."

"Roy, you look this way one more time and I'll slap you upside the head," Junebug called furiously down to the trapper. "You're making her skittish."

"Even aside from him," Maddy hastened, worried that Junebug thought the warning would be enough, "there are your brothers to worry about. It's not decent, me sitting here without a stitch on."

"You're wearing your bloomers, ain't you?"

Maddy glared at her. "Of course I'm wearing my bloomers, but bloomers aren't *clothes*."

"The only scrap of clothing you got that ain't wet and on the line is that shiny blue one," Junebug sighed. "That bluebird dress is one of hers, ain't it? It don't look like something a maid would wear. I was too scared to wash it 'cause I never washed something that shiny before. I thought I might ruin it."

Maddy didn't care if Willabelle's turquoise dress was completely inappropriate, she had to wear *something*.

"I got no idea how we're going to bathe you either," Junebug admitted. "Kit told me to get you washed up, but how in hell we're going to do that, I don't know." She considered Maddy, still sitting in the rocking chair on the porch. "I'm going to have to get someone to bring you inside."

"I can hop," Maddy suggested. She was still disconcerted by her reaction to Kit earlier and wasn't ready for a repeat of being cradled in his arms. Just the thought conjured that scent of pine trees and sunshine and woodsmoke, and the memory of the scent caused an unnerving squeezing sensation in her belly. Also, an absurdly vain part of her didn't want him to see her again until she was washed and dressed.

One of Junebug's dark eyebrows rose dubiously. "You can hop?"

"I can hold on to you and hop one-legged." Maddy was firm. She was strong, she could do it, so long as Junebug helped her balance.

She didn't need carrying. Getting out of the dim trading post and into the shining bright autumn day had fortified her. The peace of the meadow and the swirling creek had soothed her shredded nerves, and being up off the floor and sitting in a proper chair had unkinked her muscles. The fresh alpine air cleared her head, and the sunshine gave her warmth. And if her leg spiked with pain whenever she moved, well, at least the pain was less than it had been lying on the furs this morning.

"You'll faint again," Junebug warned. "And if you faint and hurt your leg, Kit will skin me alive."

"I won't faint." Maddy gripped the arms of the chair and grimly pulled herself up onto her good leg. "I'm not a fainter."

"You've fainted three times since you got here."

"I have not!"

"Once, then. But it was a good long one."

"And with good reason!" Maddy gestured for Junebug to come closer. "Don't give me a reason and I won't faint." She struggled to get an arm around Junebug's shoulders as the girl took her by the waist and bore her weight. "Thank you." Nervously Maddy took a hop away from the chair, careful to keep her hurt leg up off the floor. It was hard work. She broke out into a sweat; the thought of banging her leg and experiencing that indescribable pain again made her shivery with dread.

She lost her grip on the blanket as she hopped; it sagged and almost tripped her.

"Goddamn it!" Junebug caught her and tried to wrench the blanket out of the way.

Maddy squealed. "No! The trapper! He'll see me!"

"Roy, you close your eyes right this minute!" Junebug hollered. "If you look, I'll never write another letter to another yeller-haired girl so long as I live!"

"He's looking, isn't he?" Maddy felt sick at the thought.

"Nope. But let's make sure." Junebug hollered down to the trapper again, sounding fiercer than ever, "Turn your back too! The lady don't want your greasy eyes all on her!"

Maddy strained her neck trying to see what he was doing. Astonishingly, he'd obediently turned to face the mountains, granting Maddy her privacy.

"He ain't as bad as all that," Junebug sighed. "Not that I like him, mind. But he's not as bad as I first thought. You should see the things he wants me to write to those yeller-haired girls. On the inside he's really just a big bag of mush."

Hop by agonizing hop, Maddy managed to get herself inside the trading post.

"I don't want to go back down on those furs," she protested, when Junebug steered her in that direction. "I'm done with lying on the floor!"

"Fair enough." Junebug led her to the stool by the counter instead. By the time Maddy pulled herself onto the stool, they were both sweating and huffing.

"You don't look like much, but you sure weigh a ton," Junebug observed.

"Thanks," Maddy said sourly.

"I'll go get some water for you to wash with." Junebug headed back out into the bright afternoon.

Maddy steadied herself, both hands on the counter, and caught her breath. Her heart was racing. She'd got so weak in such a short time. It was sobering and made her feel even more vulnerable.

Junebug went to and fro, bringing water and toweling, soap and on the final trip, the armful of turquoise satin that was Willabelle's fancy dress. The hoopskirt and bustle had been ruined, Maddy realized, which meant the skirt would hang in big clumps of material. Oh well, it wasn't like she'd be walking around in it. And it would be easier to sit in without the cage.

Junebug made short work of heating water on the stove. She closed the door and pulled the oilcloth blinds down over the windows and lit a lamp for Maddy to see by.

"You don't need me to wash you, or anything, do you?" Junebug asked awkwardly. She didn't look thrilled by the idea.

"No." Maddy's cheeks burned. "I'm perfectly capable of washing myself." Although she wasn't sure she was . . .

"Here." Junebug pulled a chair from next to the stove and put it in front of Maddy. She helped Maddy hop over to it and then put the pails of water and the soap and toweling in easy reach. "I'll sit over here in front of the door, so no one can walk in. I'll keep my back turned, but you yell out if you need help, you hear? Don't be all shy if you're hurt." Junebug snagged a ledger off the shelf and collected the pen and ink off the counter on her way. "I got things to write anyway. Kit needs to know it ain't acceptable to growl at me all the time."

"You said you write people letters? For that trapper and others?" Maddy asked as she struggled out of the plaid bodice. Lord, she could smell herself. She stank of stale sweat and pain and fear, and there was the mineral iron and clay smell of mud mixed in too. Imagine what Kit McBride must have thought of her noxiousness when he carried her outside. It was amazing she hadn't knocked the man out cold with the stink. No wonder he'd suggested Junebug bring her soap and water.

"Indeed I do." Junebug took the hint and kept up the conversation while Maddy bathed. It felt too awkward for both of them to sit and listen to the splashing. "I've even got a sign. I'm the town's public letter writer. I work for the folks of Bitterroot, too, although most of them can write on their own, so they don't have much call for me."

Maddy grunted with pain as her bad foot brushed the floorboards. She scrunched her eyes closed and gritted her teeth until the wave of agony receded.

"I wish there were more folks to write letters for." Junebug kept talking, although she paused in sympathy whenever Maddy groaned. "I like hearing what people write to each other. Once a trapper came all the way from Canada to hunt for beaver, and he got me to write a letter to France. I always wondered if it got there, and if the French person on the other end could even read English."

Maddy tried to control her breathing as she contorted herself on the chair, scrubbing at herself with the soapy cloth. The soap was soft and stank of lye and rendered fat. Someone had squelched some vegetable matter into it, but it didn't improve the smell much. Maddy remembered Willabelle's fancy English and French bar soaps with longing. The heady scents of mimosa, sandalwood, rose, lemon and violet used to rise from those long baths she took, flooding the whole house with perfume. Maddy would kill for a scrap of one of those bar soaps now. Mrs. Egan had a good recipe for lemon-and-rosemary-scented soft soap, she remembered. She'd settle for a good soft soap like that one.

"Would you write a letter for me?" Maddy asked Junebug, thinking that she should write for that soft soap recipe. She could give it to Junebug as a parting gift.

Only she'd be long gone by the time Mrs. Egan's letter arrived. She imagined the post from Ireland to the backwoods of Montana would take a fearfully long time.

"I would!" Junebug sounded sprightly with pleasure. "Who would you write to? Your ma?"

"No, my mother isn't with us anymore," Maddy told her. "She died a long time ago. I was thinking of writing to Mrs. Egan, the cook at the big house where I used to work, back in Ireland."

"Ireland! I forgot that's why you talk funny."

"*I* talk funny? Have you heard yourself?" Maddy put her elbow into scrubbing the mud off her good leg.

"My ma's dead too," Junebug said pragmatically. "She died when I was a kid."

Like she wasn't a kid now.

"How old were you when *your* ma died?" Junebug paused and then said all in a rush, "Sorry, I'm not supposed to ask about missing people. Don't tell Morgan or Kit that I asked. And don't answer if I've tore your heart out or nothing. But I don't get why no one talks about this stuff. I'd be happy to tell you about my ma, if you cared to know."

It took Maddy a moment to take in the rush of words. "Oh." She collected her thoughts. "I don't mind. It was a long time ago. I was thirteen, old enough to go into service."

"What's that? Maiding and the like?"

That was one way to put it. "Yes, maiding and the like. I started at Ormond House as a scullery maid and worked my way up from there."

"What's a scullery maid?"

Maddy explained, remembering the days spent under sour old Polly, the kitchen maid, toiling dawn to dusk, scouring the flagstone floors, scrubbing out the stove, washing every pot and pan a thousand times over. Oh, it had been backbreaking work.

"That's me!" Junebug said, bright with recognition. "I'm a scullery maid. Only not paid."

Maddy laughed. "Scullery maid and laundry maid and cook, I bet."

"Yes." Junebug's voice had wonderment in it. "You're the first person to see it."

"I didn't see it. You told me, that day in the washhouse."

"You're the first person to hear it, then." Junebug sounded happy as a lark. "Tell me about this Ormond House. How many maids were there? More than just one Junebug, I'm guessing?"

Maddy laughed again, imagining Junebug McBride let loose in Ormond House, burning laundry instead of washing it. "So many more. There was a whole staff for a house that size. The housekeeper, the butler, Mrs. Egan in the kitchen, the valets and ladies' maids and then all the junior staff: footmen and pages and boot boys; between maids, chamber maids, house maids, kitchen maids, laundry maids, scullery maids. But that was only when the family was in residence. Some of them traveled with the Ormonds. I didn't. I was always at the house."

"Hellfire, that's an army!"

"A family," Maddy sighed, remembering mealtimes in the servants' hall, the jokes and the teasing, the spats and feuds, the romances and heartbreaks.

"Were they family? Did you have brothers and sisters there?"

"Not at Ormond House." Maddy finished scrubbing off the dirt and patted herself dry. "I had lots of brothers and sisters though." Maddy's stomach churned, as it always did when she thought of her lost siblings, of the phantom press of little Jean in her arms.

"Had?" There was a tense pause. "Sorry, I'm doing it again. Morgan says there's no good answers when it comes to missing people and that I'm sticking my finger into open wounds."

That was a vivid image, Maddy thought with distaste. "Don't worry, it's not an open wound. It closed over long ago." She could tell Junebug was burning with curiosity. "I had nine brothers and sisters."

"Nine! Hell. Oh wait . . ."

Maddy heard Junebug counting softly to herself.

"Hey. I have nine too. If you count all the dead girls."

Maddy started in horror. "All the what?"

"Out there under the chokecherry tree with Ma. Eliza Jane, Carrie Ann, Maybud and the baby that never got a name. The girls all died off. But not the boys. Morgan, Kit, Beau and Jonah. And then there's Charlie, Kit's twin, who we don't talk about. That's nine. Then me, makes ten. And you're ten too."

Charlie, Kit's twin, who we don't talk about. Maddy filed that information away for later.

"I'm the youngest now," Junebug continued. "But before some of the girls died, I was third to youngest. Are you the youngest?"

"No," Maddy said absently. "I was one of the oldest. The second oldest."

"Like Kit."

"I don't suppose there were spare undergarments dry?" Maddy asked, looking at her muddy bloomers with distaste.

"Nope. But you can wear a pair of my shorts if you want."

"You're smaller than me."

"Yeah, but my shorts are all stretched out and baggy—you'll be fine. They were Jonah's before they were mine."

"Wait," Maddy said sharply, when Junebug made to leave. "Don't you dare leave me here like this alone. Anyone could walk in."

"I could put a sign up: 'Don't walk in'?" Junebug suggested.

Lord, the girl was naive. "Sometimes people walk in even when you tell them not to," Maddy told her. She needed some schooling in the ways of men. Men who weren't brothers.

"Huh." Junebug was clearly pondering that. "I could give you a gun?"

Jesus, Mary and Joseph, she kept forgetting how rough these people were. "Never mind. We'll worry about bloomers later, after I have the dress on. Could you help me wash my hair?" Maddy wrapped the toweling around herself and waited for Junebug to help. She untangled her hair from the squashed bun, trying to unknot it with her fingers as Junebug prepared to douse her. Her hair stank too. Lord, she must have sweat herself through several times over. It was a sour smell. Horrid.

"This is going to be messy," Junebug warned, dragging a large tin tub over from the wall. "Here, lean your head over this."

Anxiously, Maddy swiveled sideways on the chair, trying to keep her leg well away from the tub. And away from Junebug, who bounced around like a puppy. Maddy leaned over the tin tub and held her breath as Junebug tipped a pail of water over her head.

The girl was surprisingly gentle as she soaped Maddy's hair.

"I ain't never washed anyone's hair before," she said, her fingers snagging in Maddy's knots.

"You're good at it," Maddy sighed, enjoying the ministrations.

For a while there was just the sudsy sound of hair washing.

"You need a better soap recipe," Maddy told her as the pungent lye got up her nose.

"I know, it's awful, ain't it? One time I got a bar of soap for my birthday. The boys went and ordered it. Soap and a cookbook and a new fountain pen, which was about the best thing anyone has ever given me, hands down. I asked for a rifle, but if I couldn't have a rifle, the pen was a pretty good present. That bar soap was sure fancy though. It smelled like roses. And so did I afterward. If I washed my hair with it, I smelled like roses for days; one time I washed my clothes with it, too, and, spit, I smelled so fine the bees started following me around."

Maddy laughed.

"I tried to make rose soap afterward, but it didn't smell anywhere near the same."

Maddy bet it didn't.

"Over you go, bend and I'll rinse this out. You should be glad I took the time to stick some flowering clover in it, or it would smell even worse."

Maddy didn't think that was possible. She held her breath as Junebug poured water over her head, but even so the stink of tallow and lye got up her nose. She could taste it.

"I reckon old Fritz has got some soap in the mercantile," Junebug said guiltily. "Mrs. Langer puts comfrey in it to sweeten the smell. And sometimes they stock some fancy soaps that the girls in the cathouse buy. Maybe we should get some while you're staying with us."

Lord, Maddy wasn't sure she liked the idea of smelling like a girl from the cathouse. But maybe anything was better than Junebug's soap, even smelling like a whore.

———

"I can see that would be a right pretty dress," Junebug said slowly, once they'd fought to get the turquoise silk over Maddy's head. "With the right underthings."

"And the right body," Maddy added, pushing at the billowy loose fabric where her breasts should have been.

"It's not that you don't have a good figure," Junebug assured her. "It's just that Willabelle Lascalles has enough figure for two women . . ."

Maddy pulled a face. She felt like she was in a silk sack. Oh well, clothes were clothes, weren't they?

"Want me to go fetch you some undershorts?"

Maddy didn't really want to wear Junebug's stretched-out old bloomers, but her own were damp now, and muddy to boot.

"Sure," she sighed.

"I'll wash yours and they'll be good as new tomorrow." She went bounding off.

Junebug had left her ledger and fountain pen on the counter. Not for the first time, Maddy wished she could read. She looked up at the row of ledgers on the shelf, full of words she'd never understand. It was funny to think scruffy little Junebug could do it and she couldn't. She'd love to be able to pick up that pen and write to Mrs. Egan and all the others around the table in the servants' hall, to tell them about her adventures.

And they *had* been adventures, she thought with a start.

Such adventures that she never could have imagined on that day when she set out from Ormond House for Dublin, to catch the ship to America. Adventures in New York and St. Louis, on trains from Missouri to North Dakota, and now up here at the top of the world, in a meadow populated by giants, a staring trapper and a sweet scruffy girl.

Life was strange. And maybe her mother had been wrong

about her unlucky stars. Maybe they weren't unlucky, so much as adventurous . . .

"Here!" Junebug came bursting back in, out of breath from running, bearing a pair of colorless baggy shorts in one hand and a hairbrush in the other. The shorts had a drawstring waist but were otherwise completely shapeless. Junebug snorted with laughter as she considered the shorts and then Maddy in the turquoise dress. "These have got to be the least fitting things to wear under *that* dress."

Maddy wholeheartedly agreed. But at least they were easier to get on than bloomers would have been. Her own bloomers were torture to get off over her swollen leg. She swore at the pain.

"Thatta girl," Junebug said approvingly. "I never did see the point of crying when you can pitch a fit instead. Swearing feels a hell of a lot more powerful than weeping does."

By the end Maddy was doing both. Whose stupid idea had it been to bother with underwear? Oh my God, the pain . . .

"Ah hell." Junebug didn't seem to know what to do. She patted Maddy awkwardly on the shoulder. "There, there . . ."

Maddy took a shuddering breath. The awkward patting was weirdly comforting, as was the fact that Junebug just stood there, waiting it out. There was something soothing about the girl. She had an implacability that was reassuring.

With Junebug by her side, she managed to pull the horrid shorts on over her leg. When she was done, she was exhausted.

"Come on, Maddy the Maid, let's get you out into the fresh air again. I'll brush your hair dry, if you want?"

Maddy nodded, dashing the tears away with the back of her hand.

With the aid of Junebug's strong arm, Maddy managed to get to her foot, holding her throbbing leg up off the floor.

"What in hell are we going to do with all this skirt?" Junebug mused. "You hop in this and you're liable to break your neck."

Without the support of cage and bustle, the turquoise skirt was pooled on the floorboards at Maddy's feet like a shiny bright puddle. Maddy reached down and grabbed a fistful and hiked it up. It pulled on her leg and she hissed.

"Here." Junebug grabbed a fistful, too, and pulled the skirt up, more gently. Maddy's bare leg and foot were on full display. "Roy," Junebug yelled as she escorted her hopping companion out to the porch. "Turn your back and close your damn eyes!"

When they got out onto the porch, Maddy saw Roy was doing exactly as he'd been told. He had his back resolutely to them. He'd also made an incredible disgusting mess of the deer all over the creek bank.

"Junebug," Maddy huffed, "can I look at something other than that mess?"

"Only if you can hop down the steps."

Maddy clenched her jaw. "I can do it."

Junebug laughed. "Over my dead body. Sit your ass down in that chair. I'll get Kit or Morgan to come carry you down to the meadow. I'll cook out tonight and you can keep me company as I work. I like having you around. But there's no way you're hopping off this porch. You'll break your other leg." She stopped dead next to the rocking chair. "In you get."

Despite her desire to get away from Roy and his massacred deer, Maddy collapsed into the chair, trembling. She would have hopped down those stairs, she thought stubbornly. But it was a relief not to have to. Even if her heart was kicking up again at the thought of Kit McBride carrying her.

"Let's brush your hair first," Junebug said. "You tell me more about this Ormond House while I brush it. Do those ladies' maids brush the ladies' hair like this?"

"Yes," Maddy sighed, leaning back, exhausted from the simple act of washing and dressing. And hopping. She thought of Tom Ormond's wife and her lavish coiffures. Tom's wife had shining auburn hair, which glowed like polished brass against her decorative hairpins. Sometimes Maddy had to clean the fallen strands of her hair off the rug.

"Do those ladies have fancy bedrooms?" Junebug asked. She was surprisingly gentle as she brushed Maddy's hair dry, working the knots patiently and calmly. She coaxed every detail she could out of Maddy about Ormond House, about the furniture, gleaming with beeswax polish; and the quilts on the beds, fat with duck feathers; about the mirrors, gilt-edged; the wallpapers and wainscotings; the chandeliers, crystal in the public rooms, brass in the private rooms; about the thick Aubusson carpets; and the silver-backed hairbrushes come all the way from Paris. Junebug was fascinated by the idea of gaslight and plumbing and all the luxuries of a great house.

"Hell, Roy, you don't still have your back to us!" Junebug cried in exasperation when Maddy's hair was finally dry and she looked up from her task.

Roy the trapper was still dutifully standing with his back to them on the bank of the creek. A giggle escaped Maddy at the sight of him. She had a feeling he probably still had his eyes scrunched closed too.

"Goddamn it, Roy, you don't have the good sense God gave a goose," Junebug railed at him, waving the hairbrush. Which he couldn't see, because he had his back turned to them.

Maddy's giggles bubbled over.

"Turn around, you dolt, and get back to your deer!"

Roy did as he was told. Sort of. He got halfway turned around and caught sight of Maddy on the porch and started staring again.

Now Junebug was giggling too. "Hell, Roy, ain't you never seen a woman before?"

"Poor Roy." Maddy tried to squash her laughter. It wasn't right to laugh at the man.

"There ain't nothing poor about him." Junebug stuck the hairbrush in her back pocket. "I'll go round up one of the boys to carry you to the campfire." She leaned on the porch rail. "Hey, Roy! Get that deer chopped up into steaks and I'll cook 'em for supper. You can join us."

The old trapper broke free of his freeze at that. "Cain't Kit cook 'em? You'll just ruin 'em."

"Ain't you got no manners, you old muskrat? I just asked you to supper and you go complaining about my cooking. Do you want me to withdraw my invitation?"

Maddy pressed her lips together to stop the giggles. She must be overwrought. It wasn't that funny. Only the sight of Junebug and the mangy trapper trading insults made her buoyant with laughter.

They were so cheerful about their animosity. And clearly enjoying themselves as they spat at each other over the deer.

"What the hell are you two yelling about?" Kit's deep rumble broke through the argument, making Roy the trapper jump a mile. He almost left his boots.

Maddy turned, her heart skipping a beat before she even laid eyes on him. But then she *did* lay eyes on him . . .

Oh.

Oh *my*.

Ohhhhh *my*.

Maddy felt like she'd been dropped from a great height.

Standing there, in the meadow grass, the late sun striking him sideways and haloing him with dusty light, was the single most beautiful person Maddy had seen in her entire life.

His jaw was blunt and square, the line of it so strong it seemed outlined in ink; his cheekbones were high and hollow; and his lips were . . . Oh Lord, there weren't words for those lips, with their pointed corners and plump curves. His eyebrows were black slashes above eyes the midnight darkness of a night river.

"You shaved," Maddy blurted.

Her heart was stumbling like a horse fallen mid-gallop. Her head felt light and floaty. Jesus, Mary and Joseph, was she going to faint again?

His gaze moved from Junebug and Roy to her, and she was falling again. An endless, slow, drifting fall, sending her stomach skyward and her heart rolling over. His midnight-water eyes swept her from head to toe. She felt weak. Not even Tom Ormond had done this to her, she thought dumbly. Especially not without even touching her.

"I shaved," Kit McBride agreed, and the rumble of his voice sent a cascade of sparks through Maddy.

She was falling and on fire all at once.

And all because he'd shaved.

Fourteen

He was in trouble. He'd suspected it before now. But the sight of her in that blue dress did him in. He felt like a stunned rabbit, knocked out by a slug from a slingshot.

Kit hadn't known it was even possible for a woman to look this good. He'd read about it but never really believed it. He'd also read about these aerial swoopings of the heart, but he hadn't believed them either. They were things that happened in books, not in real life . . .

But now here he was, with a flying heart, struggling to breathe, unable to think straight. Because of a blue dress. No, screw the dress. It wasn't the dress. It was *her*.

Miss Lascalles was sitting in the rocking chair on the porch, leg extended, face turned to catch the breeze. Her black hair was straight and shining. The wind sent strands rising like threads of silk. The blue of the gown made her eyes luminescent in the fringing of her black eyelashes. Her skin was the color of skimmed milk, and her lips were rosy pink, thin on the edges and rising to a plump strawberry in the center.

"Kit, she's coming with me to the campfire while I cook. We're eating out tonight. Roy's got deer steaks." Junebug was talking, but Kit was having trouble registering the words. His heart felt mighty strange. Everything felt strange. Like he'd stepped through into another world, one that had been here all along but he just hadn't been able to see.

"Pick her up, would you?" Junebug snapped her fingers in front of his face, and he blushed. Goddamn it, he was staring like a fool. And now that he didn't have his beard, everyone could *see* him blushing.

"What?" He frowned at his little sister, who was buzzing like a mosquito fresh hatched off the creek.

"Pick. Her. Up. She wants to come with me to the meadow now that Roy's gone and fouled up her view."

"I got you dinner, didn't I?" Roy snapped. "How'd you expect to get steaks without a little mess?"

"You coulda done it somewhere else. Who up and butchers a deer right in front of the porch?" Junebug griped.

Kit's gaze drifted back to Miss Lascalles, who had turned a blooming shade of pink. Hellfire, it was becoming. It made her blue eyes even bluer. "You want to go to the meadow?" he asked, his voice none too steady.

She pressed her strawberry lips together and nodded shyly.

As he climbed the porch steps, the air got a charge, like there was lightning coming, only there wasn't any lightning. He met her gaze, and everything slowed down. He could hear the slow thunder of his own heart, the creak of the boards under his heel, her breath catching.

This was what the poets were on about. *This.*

And all that's best of dark and bright / Meet in her aspect and her eyes . . .

Hell, the way she tilted her head to look up at him when he reached her. The white arch of her neck, with the flutter of her pulse in the hollow . . . it made him daft. Even the scent of

Junebug's sweet clover soap, which wafted from her shining hair, addled him to the point where he could barely speak in full sentences.

"Come," he grunted, as graceless as Roy out there with his deer. He bent to scoop her up. She lifted her arms and looped them around his neck. He heard her hold her breath as he slid his arm under her sore leg.

"All right?" he asked. Then he made the mistake of looking into her eyes. "Harebells in spring, blue as blue." Hell, he'd said it aloud. He felt his ears burning, red as beets. He couldn't believe he'd spoken. He looked like the worst kind of backwoods hick. Worse even than old Roy.

Her harebell eyes went wide, and then she looked away. She'd gone beet red, too, now. He was an idiot.

As though from a great distance, he heard Roy and Junebug bickering.

"What's going on?" Roy demanded.

"What do you mean, what's going on? He's taking her to the campfire."

"But why are they looking at each other like that? Like they been hit on the head or something."

"You going to get those deer steaks or not? Stop yapping and start butchering or I'm uninviting you."

"You cain't uninvite people once you've invited them. It ain't civil."

"Well, neither is gossiping about people being hit over the head."

"Who's gossiping! I only asked what was going on!"

"None of your business, that's what's going on."

"I'm sorry about those two," Kit mumbled as he straightened and started toward the meadow. He took the stairs gently so as not to jar her leg.

"I know," Miss Lascalles said softly. "They were raised by wolves."

He felt a frisson of intimacy. "Sometimes I think they *are* the wolves."

Hell. She smiled at that, and he just about dropped her. Goddamn, she was pretty. One of her incisors was very slightly crooked, and it caught on her lip in the most adorable way.

Her body fit neatly against his as he carried her. She was warm, and she made Junebug's nasty soap smell so good.

"I almost didn't recognize you without the beard," she said huskily.

All kinds of him tightened at the sound of that musical accent, in that husky voice. "I hope it wasn't too much of a shock," he managed to say. "I thought we might be scaring you, all roughed up like mountain men. I got Morgan to shave too." Which had been a colossally awful idea. He didn't want her to see Morgan's dimples and have her head turned.

"You still look like a mountain man," she said, and, hell, that *smile.* "Just one who shaved his beard off."

How could you feel a smile in your toes? He didn't know, but somehow you could. He should have worn his nice shirt, he thought witlessly. He'd decided against it because of Morgan's teasing, but now he wished he'd ignored Morgan and dressed up. Look at her in her pretty dress, and here he was in his threadbare old shirt. Morgan would probably wear *his* good shirt, and then Kit would be competing with dimples *and* good clothes. Goddamn Morgan.

It was only as Kit reached the burned-out remnant of their old kitchen campfire that he realized that he didn't know where he was going to put her. He couldn't perch her on one of the logs— she wouldn't be able to put her leg down. And he didn't want to put her on the ground and ruin her dress. Damn it. He looked around for a solution.

When he saw one, he didn't like it.

It was Morgan, coming down from the cabin, carrying a chair.

He'd put on his good white shirt, which shone like ice in the westering sunlight, and he'd actually had the nerve to slick his newly shorn hair back.

As if all that weren't bad enough, he also had the gall to smile, his teeth white and even, and his damn dimples flashing.

"Who's that?" Miss Lascalles asked, confused.

"My brother," Kit growled, unimpressed as Morgan came swashbuckling through the meadow grass, settling the chair next to one of the logs. He arranged it so Miss Lascalles could prop her injured leg up on a log, conciliatory as a lovestruck suitor. Unbelievable.

Morgan was completely unperturbed by Kit's glower.

"Your brother. Which one?" Miss Lascalles whispered to Kit. "I was in so much pain; I don't remember meeting this one."

Getting Morgan to shave was definitely the dumbest thing that Kit had ever done. Not only was Miss Lascalles no longer scared of him, she didn't even know who he was. Her gaze followed him as he set up the chair.

"Which one?" Kit echoed, unable to keep the sourness out of his voice. "That's Morgan."

"No!" She was genuinely shocked. She glanced up to see if he was making fun.

He most definitely wasn't; he'd never been less amused in his life.

"*That's* Morgan?" She sounded like she didn't believe him.

"Ugly, ain't he?"

"Here you are, Miss Lascalles," Morgan called over. "A throne fit for queen, especially one with a beat-up leg."

"Thank you." Damn it, she was blushing again. But this time because of Morgan, not because of him. It was a disagreeable state of affairs.

"Oh good, you got her a chair." Junebug came scampering up, the dog gamboling after her. Miss Lascalles's dog was getting filth-ici by the hour. He was also carrying a dead shrew and looked about as far from a lady's lapdog as it was possible to get.

"I did get a chair," Morgan agreed, with uncharacteristic cheeriness. "Only Kit don't seem of a mind to put her down."

Junebug didn't look pleased. "Put her down," she ordered. "She and I got talking to do while I cook. You don't get to hog her."

"Hog her? You had her all afternoon." Now he was sounding like a petulant child. Hell, his family drove him up the wall.

"Come on, it'll be getting dark soon," Junebug groaned. "And I got lots to do before we can eat. If y'all want to fawn over the lady, why don't you make yourself useful and go get her some blankets. She'll get cold just sitting there. It is November, you know."

Fawn! Kit wasn't fawning. If anyone was fawning, it was Morgan.

Irked at his sister, Kit lowered Miss Lascalles into the chair. Morgan barged in, helping her get her leg onto the log. Kit felt a hot lick of jealousy to see him touching her. Stupid, because what right did he have to be jealous? None.

"You heard her, Kit, best fetch the lady some blankets." Morgan grinned at him. Kit could have thumped him.

The only consolation was that as Kit headed back to the trading post for blankets, he could hear Junebug bossing Morgan around. If Morgan did as he was told, he would be off fetching firewood and not hovering over Miss Lascalles. That was something.

When Kit got to the trading post, he saw the tin of tea leaves and had an idea. Blankets would keep her warm, but a nice hot mug of tea would keep her even warmer. He whistled as he put the water on and fixed her tea. Milk and sugar, he remembered. Let's see Morgan beat a hot cup of tea.

It got dark early this time of year, and as Kit returned to the meadow, laden with blankets and trying not to spill the tea, their high mountain pasture fell into evening shadow. Pale moths appeared from the grasses, luminous in the lavender evening.

Morgan had got a fire roaring in their outdoor kitchen camp, and the moths were flickering toward it in soft puffs. Overhead, coral-colored clouds streaked the sunset sky. The katydids were chirring, and the last birds of the day were winging home.

"Tea!" Miss Lascalles lit up when she saw his offering. She cradled the tin mug between both hands and gave him one of those heart-stopping smiles. He unfurled the thick wool blankets, wrapping one around her shoulders and draping one carefully over her good leg. "Oh, you make a magnificent cup of tea, Mr. McBride." She inhaled the fragrant steam and closed her eyes in bliss. "I never thanked you this morning, but that was the best cup of tea I've had since leaving Ireland."

"It's Kit," he corrected her.

"Kit."

The sound of his name from those lips got his sap stirred up.

"I thought I was getting time with her," Junebug complained. "Why do you have to ruin everything? Go away. I want to hear more about that house she lived in."

"You're here, aren't you?" Morgan said, taking a seat on the log next to Miss Lascalles. "And so is she."

"But you're here too." Junebug crossed her arms. She was put out. "And so's Kit. Go tend the animals or do whatever it is you normally do while I cook. She was telling me stories."

"We don't mind if you keep telling stories," Morgan assured Miss Lascalles, his white teeth glowing in the lavender twilight.

Miss Lascalles shot Junebug a worried look.

"These stories aren't for you," Junebug told her brothers firmly. "They're for girls only."

Kit felt invisible. He didn't like it.

But then he saw the way Miss Lascalles darted sideways looks at him as she sipped her tea, and he felt warm from head to toe.

"Junebug tells me she had a talk with you, Miss Lascalles," Morgan rumbled. "Or I guess it should be Mrs.?" The bastard was leaning forward, creating a sense of intimacy. "It's *Mrs.* Lascalles, right?"

What? What was this about? Kit glanced at Junebug. She'd stiffened and was watching Morgan with a wary expression. Miss Lascalles had also stiffened, her hands clenching around the mug.

Mrs.? She was *married?*

Kit's bones turned to lead at the thought. But then his head cleared. She couldn't be married; she was here to marry *him.* Maybe she was widowed . . .

"I read the letters," Morgan continued, "I hope you don't mind."

Now Miss Lascalles was looking genuinely panicked. Kit felt a deep sense of unease. How come she looked so upset? He hoped she wasn't going to be too devastated when he broke the news that he couldn't marry her . . .

"Junebug says she told you Kit didn't write them," Morgan said bluntly. He might have shaved and be smiling more, but he still had all the tact of a bull elk.

"You told her?" Kit was surprised. He'd been expecting to have to break the news himself. And how come Morgan knew about this, but Kit didn't?

"It seemed the right thing to do." Junebug adopted a righteous expression. It didn't suit her.

"Hush up, Bug. Nothing you've done so far in all this has been the right thing to do," Morgan said.

"But you just said—"

"Hush. I'm speaking to our guest." Morgan had no patience with her. He put his smile back on and turned back to Miss—Mrs.?—Lascalles. "I went and dug out the letter you wrote back. All the letters you wrote, when you thought you were writing to Kit."

"You what!" Junebug was outraged. "You went through my private things!"

"Your nefarious, crooked, unlawful things," Morgan corrected. He was unyielding, still leaning forward, staring at their guest in her shining gown. "I know you thought you were writing to Kit here, but, trust me, he would have written a nicer letter than the ones you received."

"Hey!" Junebug protested. "I write *good* letters."

"You wrote a shameless load of nonsense."

"I told the *truth*."

Kit didn't know what was happening. Miss—Mrs.?—Lascalles stole a helpless glance at him. He shuffled a little closer. "You're married?" he asked softly.

"Erm . . ." Miss—Mrs.?—Lascalles stared wide-eyed at Junebug. She seemed frozen.

Junebug herself was close to pitching a fit now. "You got no right poking in my things, Morgan!"

"The thing is, Mrs. Lascalles, I'm at a loss as to why a lovely lady like yourself would be interested in the 'man' that wrote those letters." Morgan had grown sly. Kit didn't like it.

Miss—Mrs.?—Lascalles made a helpless noise.

"I'd thank you not to go putting her on the spot like this, Morgan," Junebug railed. "Honestly. She's a guest, not a prisoner to be inquisitioned."

"*Inquisitioned* ain't a word," Kit said, mostly out of habit.

"Of course it is," Junebug snapped. "When I get a minute, I'll look it up in the dictionary and prove it to you."

"I ain't inquisitioning anyone," Morgan disagreed. He was strangely calm.

"*Inquisitioning,* on the other hand, most definitively ain't a word," Junebug complained to Kit, "so why don't you correct *him?*"

"Because he respects his elders." Morgan dismissed her and turned back to Miss—Mrs.?—Lascalles, who was blinking and looking significantly uneasy.

"And also because it *is* a word." Kit scowled. He didn't like how close Morgan was leaning in. Morgan and Miss—Mrs.?—Lascalles were in their own little brassy cocoon of firelight.

"How is *that* a word and *inquisitioned* ain't? Spit, you're unfair." Junebug was gathering steam.

Kit couldn't care less about words right now. In fact, he wished everyone would stop hurling them about and would just shut the hell up. She was *married*? He wanted to know more about that. And he also wanted to hear her answer to Morgan's question. Why *had* she written all those letters? Hell, why had she answered an advertisement for a mail-order bride in the first place?

"Junebug told you what she did? That she's the one who placed the ad?" Morgan asked Miss—Mrs.?—Lascalles. He was staring her in the eye, direct as could be. Kit wished he wouldn't do that. He was apt to get spellbound. Or *she* was. Someone was, and Kit didn't want it happening, unless he was involved.

"Erm . . ." The poor woman was looking plainly uncomfortable, darting glances at Junebug.

"Junebug"—Morgan's voice took on a warning tone—"you said you explained things to her."

"I *did*." Junebug was sounding out of patience. The two of them were liable to butt heads any minute. For once, Kit didn't mind. If Miss—Mrs.?—Lascalles saw Morgan in full head-butting fight, she wouldn't be so beguiled by his dimples.

"She knows I wrote them well-written, truthful letters," Junebug declared. "She *liked* those letters, if you remember, or she wouldn't be here."

"What did you like about those letters?" Morgan asked, resting his chin on his hand. The absolute bastard. He was fixing her with those gray eyes of his, his dimples gentle dents in his hollow cheeks, radiating charm. Why couldn't he have the grace to be his usual bull elk self? "She didn't make Kit sound too appealing," Morgan noted.

"Erm . . ." Miss—Mrs.?—Lascalles was white-knuckling the mug of tea. "What did I like about them . . . I . . . erm . . . thought blacksmithing was a good honest trade . . ."

"The morning temper didn't put you off?" Morgan prodded. She blinked.

"Or the judgment? The nagging? The cussing?"

Kit flushed as she shot him a horrified look. Junebug really hadn't painted him in a fair light.

"Clearly it didn't put her off," Junebug sniffed. "She's here, ain't she?"

"Patently." Morgan smiled. "And it's *Mrs*.?" He'd returned to where he'd begun, still smiling, but immovable. That was Morgan for you. "That's right, ain't it? *Mrs*., not *Miss*?"

Kit held his breath as he waited for the response.

"Erm . . . yes . . . *Mrs*." Miss—Mrs.!—Lascalles took a careful sip of her tea, staring at the fire. A knot popped, sending sparks swirling into the darkening sky.

"Widowed?" Morgan was like a dog with a bone.

"Yes," Mrs. Lascalles sighed. She was looking peaky.

"That's enough," Junebug interrupted. "You're the one always telling me not to go asking after missing people, and now here you are doing it."

Morgan took that one on the chin.

Kit stared at Mrs. Lascalles with new eyes. Widowed. She was young to be widowed, but wasn't that the way of the world . . . Her downcast gaze hid her thoughts. Was she remembering her husband? Had she loved him terribly?

"It must have been a blow to get here and to find out that Junebug had lied to you," Kit said softly. He couldn't even begin to imagine what she must have been going through. Even without the leg.

"Jesus, Kit!" Junebug erupted. "I didn't *lie*. I did the goddamn opposite of lying. I told her everything about your cussedness. I even told her about the damn snoring."

"I don't snore," Kit said tightly. His stomach was sour and churning. He felt weirdly exposed, embarrassed.

"You do snore, like a big old hog," Junebug snapped. "And it's best your poor wife knows it before she gets stuck next to it every night of her life."

Kit groaned. Mrs. Lascalles was right there next to him, radiant as an angel, listening to his wretched family list all his flaws. Could this night get worse?

Of course it could.

"She's right," Morgan told Mrs. Lascalles kindly. "He does snore just like a hog. But she was also right about the myriad big words. And he does have all his own teeth."

Kit was definitely taking this up in a wrestle later. And if Morgan had never won before now, he certainly wouldn't win this time.

"It must have been a shock to learn that Kit didn't write all those letters. Or even the ad." Morgan cocked his head. "Although maybe not. After all, what kind of idiot would write so baldly about himself? Look at Kit here, denying the fact that he snores. That kind of pigheaded refusal to mark the truth is normal in a man."

"I don't snore," Kit told Mrs. Lascalles, more than a little desperately. "No more than anyone does."

"He does," Morgan disagreed amiably. "He sounds like a wild hog with a chest cold."

"An *aged* wild hog with a chest cold," Junebug added.

Kit was startled to hear a giggle. Mrs. Lascalles had her strawberry lips tightly pressed together and her gaze fixed on the fire. But the giggle had clearly come from her.

"I don't think it's fair to sell someone a false bill of goods," Junebug declared. "It was important that his wife know what she was getting into."

"You don't mind a man who stinks of sweat and smoke, I hope?" Morgan asked Mrs. Lascalles. "Junebug didn't put that bit in, but that forge of his smokes him surer than a slab of bacon."

She gave Kit a sweet sideways glance. "I'm sure it's not as bad as all that."

"Oh, it is," Junebug disagreed heartily. "The only thing I got wrong was the looks bit. I ain't seen him without a beard in a while, and I didn't realize he'd grown into his face."

Now there was a definite giggle.

Kit scowled at his sister. "When are you cooking these steaks?"

"As soon as Roy brings them up."

"Ain't you got nothing to prepare to go with them?"

Junebug pulled a face.

"Mrs. Lascalles said she was a good cook in her letters," Morgan said smoothly. "Maybe she has a good idea what you could make to go with the steaks?"

Kit noted the panic again. She was either very shy or Morgan made her very nervous. It was probably the latter, and hopefully it was nervous in a bad way, not in a good way.

"Erm . . . back home . . ." She cleared her throat. "Colcannon mash," she said abruptly, sounding firmer. "I think a good colcannon mash would go fine with steaks."

"I'm sure it would go fine," Junebug said, "only we don't grow no colcannons around here."

The giggle flowered into a full-blown husky laugh this time. It made Kit feel like he'd taken a straight shot of moonshine.

"Colcannon isn't a thing you grow," she laughed. "It's just the name of the recipe."

She was more relaxed with Junebug than she was with Kit and Morgan. And no wonder, with Morgan inquisitioning her, and with Kit being painted as an aged warthog.

Junebug eyed her appreciatively. "Is it good, this colcannon thing?"

"It's amazing." Mrs. Lascalles glowed like one of the sparks from the fire. "Do you have potatoes?"

"Sacks of them." Junebug rolled her eyes. "You should see our root cellar. Morgan stocks it like we'd need to feed every single body in Montana over the winter."

"Winters are nothing to underestimate up here," Morgan said firmly.

"Do you have cabbage?" Mrs. Lascalles asked him.

"Of course." Morgan seemed offended that she should even have to ask.

"I hate cabbage," Junebug groaned.

"You won't hate it in this," Mrs. Lascalles promised. "You'll need potatoes, cabbage, butter, green onions and milk."

"Are you sure about this?" Junebug was evaluating Mrs. Lascalles. "You definitely know how to cook this?"

"She said in her letters she was an excellent cook, didn't she?" Morgan said cheerfully.

"This I can do," Mrs. Lascalles told Junebug firmly. "Trust me."

"You're not doing anything," Kit reminded her. "You're laid up with the leg. I'll help you." He volunteered before Morgan could. "You can guide me," he said, then he blushed, thinking about all the ways he wouldn't mind being guided by Mrs. Lascalles. "Go get the ingredients, Junebug."

"Roy!" Junebug hollered as she stalked off out of the firelight and into the night. "You're cooking the steaks; Kit and the lady are making colcannons." She seemed cheerful enough as she headed for the root cellar.

Mrs. Lascalles had gone all rigid and panicked looking again. Kit realized it must be because there was no one to act the chaperone now that Junebug had gone.

"She won't be long," he assured her, "and we'll be perfect gentlemen."

"Well, we would, if we knew how gentlemen were supposed to be," Morgan said.

Kit glared at him.

"To get back to the topic at hand . . ." Morgan was back to leaning his elbows on his knees and getting all intimate again. Mrs. Lascalles pulled away and was all but hiding behind her tin mug.

"I reckon it must have been a shock to find out that you ain't going to marry Kit after all."

She darted a look at Kit, definitely looking panicked now.

"I mean, you came all this way, thinking one thing was going to happen, and then finding something completely different. And then hurting your leg to boot." Morgan scratched at his bare jaw. "It's a terrible responsibility raising a girl as wild and imprudent as our Junebug. Ain't it, Kit?"

Kit made a noncommittal noise, not sure where Morgan was going with this.

"But this is definitely the worst thing she's done to date. The kid needs a woman around. She's got no mother, no sisters, no aunts . . . no female to show her the what's what of being a woman."

"The what's what . . ." Mrs. Lascalles echoed.

"I mean, did she even tell you she existed in those letters?" Morgan asked. "Because she sure as hell didn't in the ones I read."

"Well, no," Mrs. Lascalles said.

"So, for a start, finding out when you get here that there's a kid to raise, that must be a startlement."

He was talking like the woman had come to marry *him*, Kit thought acidly.

"Yes, I suppose you could say she was a startlement . . ."

"Did you know about the rest of us?"

"Well, no," Mrs. Lascalles admitted again.

"Being stuck in the woods with four backwoodsmen—" Morgan stopped as Roy lurched into the circle of the firelight, carrying a trayful of steaks.

"Four backwoodsmen and a bunch of mangy old trappers," he amended. "Being stuck in the woods with all of us is a damn sight different from marrying a single blacksmith."

"Yes," Mrs. Lascalles said fervently. "Yes, I suppose it is."

"Let's get to the nub of things," Morgan said.

They weren't at the nub yet? It had sure felt pretty nubby. Kit was tense as hell, wondering what Morgan was going to say next. He knew Morgan wanted the woman to stay for a while so Junebug would have a woman around, but, so far, he wasn't enjoying Morgan's methods.

Mrs. Lascalles looked about as tense as Kit felt.

"For all Junebug swearing black and blue that she ain't, she's gone and sold you a false bill of goods," Morgan said solemnly. "Ain't that right, Kit?"

Mrs. Lascalles's gaze flickered to Kit.

"Yeah," he admitted grudgingly. Particularly the bit about the snoring.

"Kit ain't in the market for a wife, are you, Kit?"

"No." That didn't come out as easy as Kit would have liked. Damn it. He *wasn't* in the market for a wife. He *wasn't*.

"Junebug's lawless impersonation, her forgery, has led us to this very sorry state," Morgan sighed. "And I cain't do nothing but apologize to you." There went the damn charm again. "Apologize and offer to pay your way back to where you came from, as soon as you're fit to travel."

Kit saw the flash of joy on Mrs. Lascalles's pointed face, and he felt absurdly hurt.

Morgan saw it too. Kit noticed his black brows draw together and he had a moment of looking like his usual bearish self, even without the beard. "You ain't upset?" he rumbled. "I was afeared you'd be upset, coming all this way for a husband and going back again empty-handed."

"Oh," Mrs. Lascalles said breathlessly. "I mean . . . of course . . . of course I *was* upset. But then . . . with the . . . Junebug . . . I mean . . ." She turned to Kit. "You don't want me," she blurted.

"Oh God, it ain't that." Now he was blurting too. "You're a fine woman. A *fine* woman. The finest. But I didn't know you were coming; I mean, I never ordered any wife. It was all Junebug. But if I was going to order a wife—which I didn't—you'd be . . ." Perfect. That's what he almost said. She'd be perfect.

Although how he could know that when he'd barely had a conversation with the woman was beyond him. But, somehow, he did know it, deep down in his gut, beyond words and rational thought.

"But he didn't order a wife," Morgan rumbled.

"No," Kit sighed, "I didn't." He met her gaze. He couldn't read the expression in it, but there was no anger. There was something else, something more complicated.

"I understand," she said, in that stomach-tumbling, spine-tingling musical voice. She turned back to Morgan. "It's very generous, you offering to pay my way."

"It's the least we can do." Morgan sat back, seemingly satisfied with the way things were going. Kit knew there'd be some kind of catch to the offer; he waited to find out what it was.

"But I can't take it." Mrs. Lascalles didn't even give Morgan a chance to show the catch. She refused him outright.

Kit's heart leapt. She couldn't take the money? Why?

"Junebug has already offered to pay my fare back," Mrs. Lascalles told them firmly. "And it seems far more fitting that she foot the bill, since she's behind this tangle."

"She did?" Morgan and Kit were equally astonished. They exchanged a glance.

"Junebug offered to pay?" Morgan didn't sound like he believed her.

"Just this morning. She feels terrible about the whole thing."

You could have knocked Kit over with a feather. Junebug felt terrible about something she'd done?

"Hellfire, you're having a good effect on her already," Morgan laughed. "I knew you would. That's what I wanted to talk to you about. I was hoping to make a deal with you."

"A deal?" Mrs. Lascalles sounded wary again.

"Yeah. A train ticket for some lady lessons."

"Lady lessons?" Mrs. Lascalles sounded absolutely gobsmacked.

"It doesn't have to be anything formal," Morgan hurried to add. "Really just spend time with her while you're here. She's not been around ladies much, and it would do her good. We don't want her growing up to be a cussed old trapper or backwoodsman, now, do we?"

Kit thought Junebug might have a word or two to say about that.

"I'll tell you what," Morgan said. "If Junebug buys you a train ticket, I'll replace that gown we ruined when you hurt your leg. New bustle thing and everything. In exchange, you teach her some manners. Like I said, nothing formal like. The kid is contrary as a cat. If she thinks you're trying to teach her anything, she'll do the opposite. But she's caught by you, Mrs. Lascalles, I can tell. She'll be watching you like a hawk, and she'll learn a world of things just by watching you."

"But—" Mrs. Lascalles bit her lip. "I just don't think I'm the right person. I'm not . . . well, grand enough for this kind of thing."

"You look pretty fancy to us. Doesn't she, Kit?"

"Yes," he said, his voice embarrassingly sincere.

"And look at us." Morgan spread his arms and held himself up for inspection. "Do we look like we could teach any girl how to be a lady?"

"Well . . . no." Mrs. Lascalles couldn't suppress a smile. "But you don't need to buy me a gown. It's my own . . . pleasure . . . to spend time with her."

"You say that now," Morgan sighed, "but give it a few days." He held out a hand. "We owe you a dress anyway. Deal?"

"Deal."

Kit was blighted with jealousy as he watched them shake hands.

"What in hell are you doing?" Kit demanded, following Morgan to the root cellar, once Junebug was back at the campfire, chattering away to Mrs. Lascalles about the unstomachable qualities of cabbage. She hadn't brought the cabbage. And wouldn't bring it, no matter how much Mrs. Lascalles told her it was necessary to the dish. In the end, Morgan went for it, Kit in tow.

"What does it look like I'm doing?" Morgan sighed. "I'm getting the cabbage. I'm also getting beer while I'm up here. There are steaks and fancy potatoes, a lovely woman, and I'm wearing my good shirt. We might as well make a party of it." Morgan was full of pep as he strode through the night meadow to the root cellar, startling the nocturnal wildlife as he went. Rabbits bounded off through the grass, and Kit could hear Mrs. Lascalles's filthy little dog tearing around after them in the darkness. That dog better hope he didn't catch one, as the rabbits around here were bigger than he was.

"I don't care about the cabbage or the beer," Kit snapped. "I mean, what's with the inquisition, and the deal? You didn't talk to me about any of this."

"No, I didn't, did I?" Morgan shrugged. "Did I need to? You were there when it happened."

"But . . ." Kit didn't even know what he was really mad about. Was he mad because she was here to marry him? Or mad because now she wasn't?

He was all mixed-up and inside out.

Morgan paused on the lip of the root cellar. "Come on, little brother, cheer up. How often do we have a pretty lady stay for supper?"

Never, that was how often. And once she was gone, Kit doubted it would ever happen again.

"Enjoy it, Kit," Morgan told him, clapping him on the arm.

"You don't have to marry her anymore, so you can relax and enjoy her company."

"I never *was* going to marry her," Kit reminded him.

Morgan laughed. "This time our Junebug has bitten off more than she can chew," he said as he tossed Kit a couple of cabbages and then turned to wriggle a keg of beer out from the row in the cellar. "By the time Mrs. Lascalles leaves, Junebug's going to have a whole new perspective on womanhood."

Kit didn't appreciate Morgan's newfound levity.

"It's a shame we sent Jonah for the doctor and he ain't here with his fiddle," Morgan said as he hefted the keg. "Music wouldn't go astray on a night this fine." He eyed Kit. "Why don't you go put your good shirt on. I saw it on the line. Everyone else is looking their best."

"Junebug and Roy ain't."

Morgan started back to the cookfire. "No skin off my nose if you want to look a poor second to your big brother."

Fifteen

Oh, *my*. Maddy was transfixed as Kit McBride rolled up his sleeves to help her make the colcannon. She'd never in her life seen forearms like his. It wasn't just the size of them, it was the definition; his muscles were long and thick and firm under his sun-bronzed skin. Swirls of dark hair only served to accentuate the granite musculature.

Imagine what the *rest* of him was like!

No, don't. Now wasn't the time. Maddy could feel herself losing grip on her composure. It was hard enough as it was to act sensibly around him, without picturing him shirtless.

You'd think a man so big would be thick fingered, she marveled, but he was deft. The slices of cabbage were finer than any she'd seen, and the knife was an efficient blur in his hands.

"Do you cook often?" she asked him. Her voice came out a bit unsteady. She could blame his arm muscles for that.

"More than I should," he said ruefully. "It's supposed to be Junebug's job, but sometimes a man actually needs something edible after a hard day's work."

She didn't doubt it. Maddy had experience of Junebug's cooking, and her tea.

"What now?" he asked once he'd finished slicing the cabbage.

"How are the potatoes?" Maddy couldn't seem to stop staring at him. Look at him! As he bent over the pot, his soft green-and-blue flannel shirt stretched tight over his shoulders—his ridiculously huge shoulders, which tapered down to a waist that seemed narrow in comparison, although all of him was big. Look at his thighs. They were like tree trunks. Thick, muscular, strong . . .

Best not to look, Maddy thought with a hard swallow. Looking did alarming things to her. Her insides were like the tide, swirling and surging.

"They look ready to me."

Ah, not looking wasn't helping. When she didn't look at him, she got the full impact of his voice, which was deep and as warm as hot tea. She gave up and watched as he drained the potatoes. After a minute, she realized he was watching her back, waiting for the next instruction. She was glad it was dark enough to hide her blush.

"Now we fry the greens." We. The word hung between them. Maddy felt it. She thought he did too. He met her gaze, and she had the most delicious sensation, like falling but slower, dreamier. Like being submerged. In the firelight, his gaze was liquid darkness.

"Don't overcook them! Go on, get away. I'll do it," Roy's voice crashed through the spellbound moment.

"I never wanted to do them in the first place," Junebug griped back at him.

If it hadn't been for Junebug and Roy interrupting, Maddy might have drowned in Kit's eyes all night long.

"We fry the greens," Kit repeated huskily, and Maddy didn't think it was her imagination that the we was stressed.

"Make sure you melt them in butter," she said, trying to regain her composure. What on earth was wrong with her! She pretended to shift on the log, making herself more comfortable so she could avert her gaze. He was a mountain man, rough, unmannered. There was no reason to be so daft.

Are you mad? Have you seen him? Her inner voice was breathless. *Look at him!*

He *was* nice to look at . . . for a mountain man.

For any man. He might be the finest man that ever lived.

Yes. Maddy doubted there could be one finer . . . Her gaze clung to those forearms again as he scraped greens into the spitting butter.

"Don't use so much butter!" Junebug squawked. She was watching him too. "I'm the one that has to churn it all, and it takes a lifetime!"

"The recipe calls for it," Kit said, winking at Maddy.

Oh Lord. Maddy felt that wink through every last inch of her.

"Mrs. Egan always said, 'When in doubt, add butter,'" she told Junebug, glad of the distraction.

"Who's Mrs. Egan?" Kit asked curiously as he stirred the greens.

"The cook . . ." Maddy bit her lip, remembering she was supposed to be Willabelle. She cleared her throat. "My cook."

"And this is her recipe?"

Maddy nodded, wondering what Mrs. Egan would think if she could see her now, in this fancy dress, sitting here ordering a beautiful man around . . . *You were right, Mrs. Egan, this is a better life . . .* It just wasn't *her* life. It was Willabelle's.

"That's too much butter!" Junebug protested again once the colcannon was cooked and Maddy told Kit to hollow out a valley in the middle of the mash and add a whole chunk of butter. The butter melted like a golden lake into the pot of cabbage-and-green-onion-streaked mash.

"Have a bit," Maddy told her, "and then tell me it's too much butter."

"If it means I have to churn more of the stuff, it's always too much butter," Junebug complained, but she rammed her finger into the mash, scooping it through the melted butter in the center.

"Junebug!" Kit swatted her lightly with the wooden spoon. "Where are your manners?"

"I suppose it's too much to hope that you washed your hands before you started cooking," Maddy said dryly.

"Well, spit," Junebug moaned, her eyelashes fluttering with pleasure. "That might be the best thing I've ever eaten in my whole life."

"Better than the chocolate cake, eh?" Kit said. "Guess that gets me out of making it again."

"It's about even with the cake," Junebug said, sticking her finger back in the pot. "And you ain't ever made it again anyway."

Kit took her by the wrist and yanked her finger out of the mash. "Stop being such an animal. Get a spoon."

Junebug stole the wooden spoon off him and scooped an enormous wedge of colcannon from the pot.

"Leave some for everyone else, you hog," Morgan told her.

Once the steaks were ready, they settled down to eat, the fire snapping and crackling merrily.

Maddy liked these McBrides. She understood why Mrs. Champion had lit up at the thought of them. They were good craic. They never stopped talking. Their conversations and arguments looped one over the other, like interlocking circles, each one spinning at a different tempo. Sometimes even they lost track of which conversation they were in and fell into disagreements, even though they were talking about completely different things, so there was no point at all in disagreeing.

They teased each other mercilessly, their humor dry and quick and close to the bone. And for all their roughness, they were a thoughtful bunch. She'd been pampered like a queen. She was warm and cozy in her blankets, the fire was bright, flames licking at a sky so full of stars there was barely any darkness between them.

Roy's steaks were cooked to perfection. It might have been the best meal Maddy had ever had.

"You're an amazing cook," Kit said appreciatively as he consumed a mountain of colcannon.

"You cooked it!" Maddy laughed. "I just told you the recipe." But she blushed just the same at the praise.

"You'll have to do it again," Junebug sighed.

It was about the only recipe Maddy knew, aside from porridge and coddled eggs, so if they wanted her to cook, they'd be getting it again, like it or not.

"More beer?" Kit offered to refill her mug.

Maddy let him. She didn't normally drink, but the beer did a marvelous job of dulling the pain in her leg. Fancy, she thought, she'd come all the way up here to *beg* for a train ticket and they'd offered to buy her one twice over. She hadn't even had to broach the subject! And all she had to do was answer to the name Willabelle Lascalles and spend time with Junebug.

It was hard to believe that she'd ever been scared of Kit and Morgan. Well, Morgan. Kit had never scared her much. He'd been too gentle, too kind. Too . . . everything.

"Thank you." She took the beer gratefully when he returned. "It's very good."

"Abner makes it, down in Bitterroot," Kit told her, taking a seat beside her.

Lord, he was fine. His shirt was unbuttoned at the collar, showing his solid neck, the clear line of his collarbones and a curl of dark hair. The tin mug looked like a toy cup in his big hands.

"Our brother Beau makes beer, too, but it ain't as good."

"It ain't good *at all*," Morgan chipped in. He'd stretched out on the grass, his back against one of the logs. He looked mighty pleased with himself. "Beau's beer tastes like sour sweat."

Maddy laughed. "I think I'll stick to this one."

"His sour mash stinks up the whole root cellar," Morgan sighed. "I wish he'd give it away and just let us drink Abner's in peace."

"Who wants seconds?" Roy asked. "There's plenty."

Maddy did. She'd never had venison before, let alone fresh venison steak, cooked right on an open fire. The smell was mouthwatering and the flavor incredible.

"I'll get it for you," Kit offered. He put his plate down and took hers to collect another steak. They heard a happy growl, and Maddy gasped as she saw Merle bearing down on Kit's steak. The little wretch seized it and dragged it off the plate and onto the grass, growling low in his throat the whole time.

"Merle!" Maddy couldn't believe how wild he'd become. "I'm so sorry."

Kit groaned. "It's my own fault. I should have remembered that he was around."

"He's so badly trained," Maddy commiserated, forgetting for the moment that Merle was supposed to be her dog.

"Hey, look at that," Junebug called, pointing with her knife. "He likes Maddy's mash better than he likes your steak, Roy."

Sure enough, Merle had left the steak lying on the grass and was snout deep in the colcannon, lapping away happily, his muddy tail whacking through the air enthusiastically.

"I'll share mine with you," Maddy offered Kit. "The serve is too big for me anyway."

"You need it to keep your strength up," he told her. "Don't worry, there's more on the grill. I'll get another one."

They sure didn't make men like him back home, Maddy thought giddily as she took the plate from him. The smile alone . . . The white, even teeth. The pointed corners of his lips . . . And then his constant, unwavering kindness. What a lethal combination.

There were no plates left, so Kit tossed a steak into the pot with the leftover colcannon and brought the whole pot back to the log next to Maddy. He scooped the mash out first. "It's so good," he told her, sighing with happiness. He reminded Maddy of Merle, and she giggled. The dog had that same look as he lapped up the mash.

"Is this your Mrs. Egan's invention or a family recipe?" he asked.

"It's an every-family recipe back home," Maddy told him. Her family hadn't had too many recipes. They lived a scratched-out life, always struggling. There was a lot of fried bread and pandy. Pandy was the poor person's colcannon, without all the greens. Especially the way Mam made it, without even the cream and butter. It was just squashed-up potatoes, with the potato water used in place of the dairy. Sometimes there was porridge, made with groats. Mam stretched that out for all eleven of them, until it was more of a watery gruel than a porridge.

But she couldn't tell Kit any of that. He thought she was Willabelle Lascalles. A fancy lady, in a fancy satin dress.

"What about you?" she asked. "Do you have any good family recipes?"

He thought about it. That was the thing about him. He wasn't rash. He considered things carefully. It was a very attractive quality in a man. "Ma used to make bread," he said slowly. "All kinds of bread. Soda bread and sourdough, rye and barley, buttermilk bread, molasses rolls . . ."

"Molasses rolls . . ." Morgan marveled. "God, I haven't thought of those in years. I loved those rolls. They were fat little dark things, thick and squelchy, but they tasted like heaven."

"Ma made molasses rolls?" Junebug's ears pricked up.

"You used to eat them by the trayful," Kit laughed. "Junebug only had to smell a whiff of them, and she'd come tearing in . . ."

"Why don't I remember that?"

"You must remember it. You went and picked a wife who promised you molasses cake," Morgan teased. "I read those letters; the molasses cake featured pretty heavily."

"Do you remember how to make them?"

"I never made them," Morgan sighed. "Ma did all the cooking. It's probably what wore her out."

"It was all the babies what wore her out," Junebug said pragmatically. "I'm never having babies. I got no plan to end up under a chokecherry tree."

"She used to feed her yeast every morning," Kit told Maddy, bringing the subject safely back to bread. He was good at that. He often steered his brother and sister away from difficulties. "She'd scoop out half the yeast for the day's bread, and then feed it more flour and water. She kept it in a clay pot, with a cork lid."

"I remember that." Junebug sounded surprised. "It smelled all sour. But also kind of like green flowers." She paused. "Ma's hands smelled like that too."

"My mam's hands smelled like potato starch," Maddy said. "Potato starch and milk."

A melancholy silence fell for a minute, as they all sank into memory. The fire popped and crackled, and the katydids sang.

"My mother smelled like gin," Roy said gruffly, breaking through the silence.

"Gin!" Junebug exclaimed, sounding an equal measure of shocked and thrilled.

"She sweat it right out through her pores." He stared into the fire. "I used to go looking for her when she went missing, and I'd find her in one gin sink or another. Back in Angel Meadow that was, in Manchester."

"Manchester? Is that back east?" Junebug was riveted.

"Nah, in England."

"I never knew you were from England, Roy."

"I never told you. Thought you might have guessed from the accent."

"I guessed Canadian."

"Well, you guessed wrong." Roy had a sorrowful look. "You don't get much gin in these parts, but every time I smell it, I miss her."

"Jeez, Roy." Junebug looked poleaxed. She gave him a pat on the shoulder.

"Venison!"

Maddy screamed as a voice boomed right behind her, from out of the darkness. She spilled beer and cubes of steak down her blanket.

"You wretches are eating venison, while Sour Eagle and I starve!" Thunderhead Bill reared out of the darkness and into the firelight. His gray hair was wilder and more matted than the last time Maddy had seen him, when he was passed out by the side of the trail.

"Hellfire, Bill, you scared the life out of Mrs. Lascalles!" Kit snapped. "Don't you know not to go sneaking up on folks?" He helped her brush the steak cubes off herself. "You're liable to get yourself shot."

Maddy was trembling. It was silly being so afraid. But she wasn't used to the wilderness, and, even surrounded by protective McBrides, all the wild darkness made her nervous.

"He didn't sneak," Junebug said. "I saw him coming across the meadow. Him and Sour Eagle both."

"I saw the mess by the creek," Sour Eagle said placidly, shuffling into view. "You left all the best bits still in the carcass. The night creatures are at them now."

"You'd best have left something for us." Bill's hungry gaze swept the circle.

"There ain't no colcannon left, but there's still some deer," Junebug told him, cramming in her last forkful of mash before Thunderhead Bill could ask for any.

It was the strangest collection of dinner companions Maddy had ever had. She sipped her beer, her stomach full of good buttery mash and well-cooked venison, and watched Thunderhead Bill and Sour Eagle steal empty plates to eat from. Merle was on his belly, cradling Kit's dusty steak between his front paws, gnawing on it happily. He wasn't really eating it, so much as having a chew. His belly was all round and fat from the colcannon. She hoped it wouldn't make him sick.

The firelight created a cone of light and warmth in the darkness. Beyond it, the grasses sighed in the breeze, and the woods were filled with night noises: the cry of owls out hunting, the rustling of small creatures, the breath of the wind in the firs.

Maddy sighed. She felt far from home, but for the first time since she'd left Ireland, maybe even for the first time since she'd left Crinkle when she was thirteen, that felt all right. The thick scatter of stars overhead was comforting, even though they made her feel small. She was just another moth flitting through this starry night, just another katydid scratching out its song. Just another person around the McBrides' campfire, full of food and good cheer. Listening to them talk was a solace. How could anyone feel lonely at this campfire?

"Snow's coming," Thunderhead Bill announced, tearing through his steak.

Maddy doubted it. It was crisp but not cold enough for snow. The sky was a clear canvas, inky blue and sparkling with lights.

"No beavers out," he said sagely. "They've stocked themselves up with extra this year, dams the size of canoes. Going to be a bad one."

"It's only November," Morgan sighed, resting his head on the log behind. "Don't go wishing fall away, Bill."

"I ain't wishing anything. It's just what is. You seen any bears about?"

"Bears? No, can't say as I have."

"That's 'cause they're all tucked up already. Mark my words."

"We never see bears about," Junebug complained. "It's one of my chief disappointments in life, that I don't see more bears."

Maddy shivered. She didn't fancy seeing a bear.

"Cold?" Kit asked, noting the shiver. He stoked the fire up, throwing another log on.

"No, just thinking about bears."

"We've only got black bears in these parts. They ain't so big," Kit told her. "We see them sometimes come to the creek to fish."

"That's a flat-out lie," Junebug pouted. "I ain't never seen a bear fishing in our creek. Kit's been telling me that one for years. But I look and look, and no bears."

"It's 'cause she scares 'em off with all her racket," Kit murmured to Maddy as he sat back down.

She suppressed a smile. She bet Junebug did. The girl was a born talker. Maddy thought silence would probably cause her physical pain.

She watched across the campfire as Junebug orated about bears to the trappers, her striking face animated. Her mop of hair flopped as she gestured vigorously. Sour Eagle listened patiently, but Thunderhead Bill and Roy took issue with just about everything she said, which gave Junebug a chance to get herself good and bothered, which she liked to do.

Lady lessons.

How absurd that Morgan and Kit wanted *her* to teach Junebug how to be a lady. She was a *maid*, for heaven's sake.

But they were right about their sister; she was turning out like the trappers and mountain men all around her. She cussed like a sailor, spat, ran around barefoot and acted the complete wilding. That was all well and good now, but what about when she was grown?

And she was so naive, Maddy thought. It was fearful. Look at her now with those trappers. A girl could come to real harm, particularly when she was grown . . .

"How old is Junebug?" Maddy asked Kit. She'd been trying to guess, but with the baggy overalls and the shaggy short hair and the general lack of manners, it was impossible to tell.

"Fourteen."

Maddy almost spat her beer. *"Fourteen!"*

She never would have thought fourteen! Twelve maybe. But *fourteen.* Forget all that being "well and good" *now*, the girl was full-grown already! Or nearabout.

She didn't have her brothers' height, that was for sure, and she was skinny. There was no sign of womanliness in those overalls. But . . . *fourteen.*

Maddy had gone into service a full year younger than that. And she'd known girls to have their own weans at that age.

Junebug seemed so frightfully young! Not at all fourteen.

"She's lived a sheltered life up here," Kit said, reading her mind. Maddy guessed her shock was written all over her face.

"I can see why Morgan's so set on these lady lessons," Maddy said. Oh my. Look at the girl, sitting there with those trappers . . . "You shouldn't leave her alone with them," Maddy said tightly.

"We don't."

"She shouldn't . . ." Maddy paused, watching as Junebug exploded into laughter. She shouldn't what? Enjoy the comfort of her own campfire? But not all men could be trusted; she needed to learn that. And it wasn't always the violent ones. It wasn't always an attack. Sometimes it was a soft seduction, a charming. Sometimes they got you to do your own surrendering, so they never needed to attack.

As Maddy stared at Junebug, something tumbled into place in Maddy's head. A way of seeing her past, of understanding what had happened with Tom Ormond.

He shouldn't have tarried with her. He shouldn't have charmed her into his bed . . . Jesus, Mary and Joseph, there hadn't even been a bed. There had been corridors, and corners. Hasty meetings, which she'd thought of as passionate but in retrospect seemed cheap . . .

He'd used her. And she'd had so much to risk, while he'd risked so little. He'd risked nothing.

Someone needed to tell Junebug about those risks. Without taking the shine from her eyes or the laughter from her lips.

Lady lessons.

She did have lady lessons to teach, she realized, but they didn't have much to do with fancy clothes or how to dance or sew. There were other kinds of lady lessons, the kind of lessons their mothers had learned the hard way.

I got no plan to end up under a chokecherry tree.

The kinds of lessons that maybe Junebug already had an instinct for.

With all three trappers in Buck's Creek, Maddy and Junebug were escorted to the cabin to sleep.

"Men in the trading post, ladies in the cabin," Kit said firmly.

"I ain't no lady," Junebug complained.

"That's for damn certain," Morgan muttered.

"I'm sleeping out by the cookfire," Roy said stolidly, already bunking down.

"No, you ain't." Thunderhead Bill kicked him. "You'll freeze to death in your sleep when the snows come."

"It ain't going to snow, you old coot. It's clear as glass out tonight."

"There's a change coming." Thunderhead Bill was stubborn. He hounded Roy until he got up, complaining, and shuffled down to the trading post.

Maddy had been dying of curiosity about the cabin, up there on the rise up the creek. She clung to Kit as he carried her up the slope. Morgan followed with the chair and blankets, and Junebug led the way with a lantern. Merle was darting around her feet, tripping her up.

The cabin porch was a fourth the size of the trading post's. Morgan put the chair back in its place next to the front door, under a window that gazed out onto the creek.

"This is where you live?" Maddy breathed as Junebug flung the door open, and the lamp illuminated the room.

It was like something out of an enchanted story. Maddy had no idea how all these giant men fit inside. Kit had to duck his head to get under the doorframe.

The cabin was made of enormous rough-hewn logs. The ceiling was surprisingly high, an A-frame, leaping with shadows as Junebug moved the lantern. The room held a proper fat brick fireplace, flanked by rocking chairs, a bench, and two bunks hewn right into the wall. There were two windows on opposite sides of the room, double casements, hung with simple calico curtains.

"That's where Beau and Jonah sleep," Junebug said cheerfully, pointing to the bunks in the main room. "Morgan and Kit are in here." She slid a door open at the back of the room. It was a solid wood partition on sliders. It rolled across the bunks in the wall, screening them off.

"How clever," Maddy breathed.

"That was our pa's idea," Junebug said proudly.

"The only decent one he ever had," Morgan muttered.

Kit carried Maddy to the open doorway so she could see inside. Two wooden single beds sat on either side of a window. Pegs on the walls hung hats and overalls, long underwear, belts, coats.

"And I'm up in the loft!" Junebug announced, showing Maddy the ladder up to a nook in the A-frame. "I've got a window too. It's got the best view in all of Buck's Creek."

"I'll have to come up and see it when my leg's better," Maddy said, craning her neck to look at the loft space.

"Until then, you'll stay here," Kit said gruffly, lowering her to the bed in his room.

Maddy blushed, painfully aware of the innuendo.

They were alone. Morgan had gone to fetch Maddy's carpetbag from the trading post, and Junebug was poking around up in her loft.

Before he released her, Maddy reached up and stroked Kit's face. She didn't know where she found the courage. Maybe from the beer. But she'd wanted to do it all night, ever since he'd arrived back at the fire in his clean shirt. And now that they were alone, she found the daring to do it. His skin was warm and stubbled.

"You're very beautiful," she breathed.

He didn't speak. He merely stared down at her with those mesmerizing dark eyes.

She felt trapped in honey. Sweet, slow time.

She knew desire when she saw it. He wanted her. *Her.* Maddy the Maid.

His gaze dropped to her mouth, and she knew he was going to kiss her. And Jesus, Mary and Joseph, she wanted it more than she'd wanted anything in her entire life.

He bent, and she shivered with the magic of it. The moonlight flooding through the window, the filigree of lantern light around the door, catching his cheek; the smell of the campfire on him; the heat of his breath and body . . .

"Damn Bill won't stop carping about snow." Morgan's voice shattered the magic. Kit flinched back, all but dropping her to the mattress. Morgan's presence was a violence; he moved through the cabin loudly, his boots stomping on the floorboards. Maddy's carpetbag thumped on the bench. "Junebug, get that damn lamp down here. It don't help anyone up there in your loft!"

"It helps me."

"I'm sorry," Kit breathed, rubbing a hand over his face. "I don't know what I was thinking."

Was he apologizing? For trying to *kiss* her? Lord, the man could apologize for anything! Maddy watched in astonishment as he fled.

Her heart was pounding. Not being kissed by Kit McBride was a thousand times more exciting than being kissed by Thomas Ormond, she thought, feeling dazed. And being kissed by Thomas Ormond had seemed pretty good. Until now . . .

Maddy collapsed back against the mattress, staring at the ridgepole. She listened to the McBrides bickering in the outer room, and she knew the exact moment Kit left. It was like a cord stretched tight, pulling part of her out into the night.

"I'll leave you with Junebug, Mrs. Lascalles," Morgan called. "Make sure she takes care of you properly. Get down from that loft, Junebug. You got to sleep in there with her till she's healed, damn it, we talked about this."

"I'm coming, I'm coming, keep your hat on."

Maddy heard the door slam as Morgan left.

Eventually Junebug appeared in the doorway, holding up the lantern and grinning from ear to ear. "Come on," she demanded, "which one is it?"

Merle yapped and trotted in. He stood next to Maddy's bed, looking up at her expectantly. It was too high for him to jump up. Fortunately, as he was too filthy to be allowed on the bed.

"What?" Maddy propped herself on her elbows, ignoring the dog.

"My brothers. Which one? They scrub up fine, don't they? You got to be in love with one of them. So, which one?" She was so earnest it hurt.

Maddy laughed. "Love doesn't work that way."

"Sure it does! Like getting kicked in the head by a horse," Junebug said. She hung the lamp on a hook and threw herself on the bed opposite, still grinning. "It just hits you."

Merle yapped. Junebug didn't seem to care about getting her brother's bed dirty. She reached down and scooped him up. He happily settled himself next to her, collapsing in a ball.

"Love takes time," Maddy told her firmly. But her heart was skipping and jumping. And she kept seeing Kit bending over her, his dark eyes full of unspoken promises.

"Balderdash," Junebug said, just as firmly. "I've read the books. Love ain't no slow-growing rose. It's a horse kick to the head. At least the kind of love you want is." She propped her chin on her hand. "You'll tell me eventually which one kicked you. I know it was one of them."

"Oh really? And how do you know that?"

"You look kicked."

"I look kicked?"

"You surely do!" Junebug laughed. "And I'm betting on not needing to buy you that train ticket when your leg's healed."

"Well, that's a bet you'd lose," Maddy told her. Dear Lord. Imagine being stuck here in Buck's Creek for the rest of her days . . .

Sixteen

The storm came out of nowhere. When Maddy and Junebug went to sleep, the sky outside the window was starry bright. It was cold but not arctic. But when they woke in the depths of night, the wind was shrieking at the eaves and rattling the windows in their frames, and Merle was barking frantically. He'd tumbled off the bed and was standing in the middle of the room, ferociously growling at the window. He'd worked himself into a complete state.

Sleet and ice pinged at the panes of glass. It sounded like someone was throwing handfuls of gravel at the window.

"Spit!" Junebug said. "We'd better get the storm shutters closed!" Then she remembered that only Maddy was with her in the cabin. "Hell. I guess that means I better do it."

"You can't go out in this!" Maddy was appalled. "You'll get blown away."

The wind shrieked down the chimney in the outer room. Like a banshee, Maddy thought with a shiver.

"And now the ghosts are starting up," Junebug groaned. She turned up the lantern and threw herself out of bed. "I can do it from in here, don't worry. This ain't going to be pleasant though. You might want to pull your quilt up."

As soon as Junebug unlatched the casement window, the wind blew it open with force. The two halves flung back into the room, slamming against the walls, and a wicked glacial tempest threw pellets of ice. Maddy felt flayed. Clothing scudded off the hooks and the lantern leapt, sending fearful shadows yawing up the walls. Merle whined and squirmed under the bed.

The wind was a high scream. Maddy couldn't shake the thought of banshees. All her life she'd been scared of banshees, ever since she'd heard the shriek across the bog the night before her mam died.

Junebug swore black and blue as she leaned through the window to pull the storm shutters closed. The moment she yanked at them, the wind gave a shove and they slammed closed, almost hitting Junebug full in the face. She didn't get them latched before the gusty wind sucked them back out again.

"Watch your fingers!" Maddy warned. She'd wriggled into a sitting position and was preparing to slide down onto her good leg. She could hear the windows in the outer room shuddering in their frames, and upstairs the window in the loft was complaining loudly in its joists. It wasn't a good sound. "Once you've done that one, you do the loft," Maddy said, pulling herself upright. "I'll start shuttering the others." Merle whined from under the bed, and ice clattered on the roof above.

Maddy held on to the low bed, bent double as she hopped to the door. She wobbled, every muscle tensed, prepared for the pain of knocking her leg.

There was an abrupt cessation of the wind in the bedroom and a muffled quiet as Junebug got the shutters latched tight. She closed the windows over and then dashed past Maddy, headed for the loft. Maddy hopped along the wall, keeping her hand on the sliding partition to steady herself. They'd left the lantern in the bedroom, and it was dark in the outer room. Maddy almost tripped on a rag rug and swore as she brushed her sore leg against it.

"That's a good word," Junebug called down from above. "What does it mean?"

Maddy wasn't about to tell her. She finally reached the casement window on the far wall. The other window wasn't complaining as loudly, as it was sheltered by the small front porch, but this one was taking the brunt of the wind and was creaking and groaning something fierce, the glass chattering in the frame. Maddy had nothing to lean on; she tried to balance on one foot as she opened the window. Just as with the bedroom window, this one exploded inward the moment it was unlatched. Maddy was glad she was prepared for it, or she would have gone flying. Leaning into the wind and resting her hips against the sill to steady herself, Maddy strained to reach the shutters. She had to keep her head turned because of the viciousness of the wind and ice. Her fingers were numb and burning sore. Blindly, she felt for the edge of the shutter, leaning out into the whipping cold. She felt the hook holding the shutter to the outer wall and managed to ease it up. But, of course, the wind caught the lip of the shutter and hurled it at her. The wooden shutter rapped her hand and shoved her back into the room. Maddy screeched and almost went down. But she gripped the sill for dear life and managed to stay upright. Just.

"Maddy?" Junebug called down. "Are you all right?"

"Just wrestling with the shutter," Maddy yelled back, pushing her damp hair from her forehead. "Not to worry. You?" Her voice could barely be heard over the roaring of the wind. Ice shards speared at her from the darkness. They felt like tiny razor blades.

"I can't get the shutters up here unhooked," Junebug yelled back.

Well, Maddy was hardly able to climb up to help, was she? "You can do it," she urged. "Keep trying." She heard Junebug let loose a string of epithets that would make a pirate blush.

Gathering her strength, Maddy tackled her own shutters again. The one she'd managed to unhook was banging violently in the gale, slamming back and forth against the house. She was liable to get hit in the head trying to unhook the other one. But what choice did she have? As she gingerly leaned out through the open side, trying to unhook the second shutter, she heard an almighty cracking sound from the darkness.

It sounded catastrophic. Like the earth was splitting itself open. What in heaven's name was *that*?

Terrified, Maddy got her frozen fingers to fumble the hook and free the second shutter. In one mad scramble, she got them closed and locked. The shutters shimmied and bucked against the lock as the wind pummeled them. Maddy closed the glass windows in front of the shutters, and things were quieter, except for the howling of the wind down the chimney and the sound of Junebug swearing up in the loft. Maddy struggled to regain control of her breathing. She felt like she'd run ten miles in a windstorm. She was soaked through too. Willabelle's silk was bound to be ruined. She should never have slept in it; it was just that the thought of getting it off over her sore leg had been too much.

One more window to go. Grimly, Maddy hopped to the window next to the front door. Thank goodness for the protection of the porch; this one wasn't nearly so hard. Once she'd shuttered it, the front room fell to total blackness. The lamp spilled golden light from the bedroom. Maddy hopped to fetch it. The darkness only made the roar and moan of the storm outside seem more frightening. She was tired now, and as she hopped, she kept bumping the toes of her bad leg, which caused her no end of pain.

Gritting her teeth through the pain, she hopped the lantern back to the main room, hanging it from the hook on the ceiling beam. It swayed in the wind eddying down from the open window upstairs.

Up in the loft, Junebug was still swearing and wrestling with the shutters. By the sound of it, she'd got them unhooked at least. They were slamming and banging something awful. Maddy wished she could help. She paused at the ladder, holding the rungs and gazing upward. "Are you all right?" she called.

All that came down were curses.

And then abruptly Junebug won the battle and the shutters locked closed.

"Did you hear the tree come down?" Junebug said excitedly as she scooted down the ladder. Her hair was soaked through, and her face was slick with icy water. Her skin was bright red from the cold.

"Was that what the cracking was?" Maddy felt a wave of relief. "It sounded fearful."

"It must have been a big one." Junebug took in Maddy's be-draggled state. "You look a fright."

"Thanks." Maddy lowered herself down onto the bench. "I thought for sure it was a banshee."

"A what-she?"

"Banshee. A fairy woman, wailing. She only wails right before one of your family dies. It's a fearful thing to hear."

Junebug's eyes were enormous. "You've heard it before?"

Maddy nodded, shivering at the memory.

"And someone died?"

"My mam."

They heard a whine and both flinched. Then Merle's little face appeared around the doorway of the bedroom, his popeyes anxious. Maddy laughed nervously. "You don't look like a banshee, you big eejit."

"You're a coward, aren't you?" Junebug told him, even though a moment before she'd been just as scared. "What kind of Beast are you?"

He lowered his chin to his paws and shivered.

Junebug went over and gave him a scratch. "Come on, let's light a fire and cheer this place up."

Whining, he slunk at her side as she went to the oversized chimney. The thing looked like it belonged in a much bigger house; it dominated the room.

Maddy reached for her carpetbag, which Morgan had left on the end of the bench. "I'm going to change out of this sodden thing."

"Good idea." Junebug set to building a fire.

It was a good idea, only there was no sign of her clothes in the carpetbag. "Junebug, do you know where my dresses are?"

"Oh hell!" Junebug jerked up, banging her head on the lintel. "Oh *hell!*" She rubbed her head and fixed Maddy with a panicked stare. "Oh hell, Maddy the Maid, I'm so sorry!"

Maddy's stomach sank. "Sorry for what?"

"I left them on the line!"

Maddy groaned. Great. Her dresses were probably blown all the way down to Bitterroot in this gale. Not just her dresses, but all her underwear too! She looked down at the sodden turquoise silk with the mud-stained hem. What on earth was she going to wear?

She might have to take Morgan up on that offer of a new dress, after all.

"Don't fret," Junebug told her, although she was clearly fretting. "I'll find you something to wear." She gazed around the room frantically. "I know." She pulled open the chest in the corner and rummaged around. "Here!" She held out an armful of clothing.

"What is that?" Maddy took a well-worn sleeve and pulled the garment from Junebug's grip.

"Long underwear!" Junebug said brightly. "They'll keep you warm."

The sand-colored long underwear was soft with age and wear, bobbled and well used.

"They're better when they're worn in," Junebug promised, reading her dubious expression correctly. "More comfy!"

Maddy sighed.

"And then you can wear these." Junebug held out a pair of overalls, similar to the ones she was wearing. "And this!" The last was an enormous knit cardigan the color of port wine. "It's Beau's but he hates it. I made it for him last winter."

Maddy noted the cardigan had an inordinate number of wonky holes.

"I dropped a lot of stitches," Junebug admitted. "And I never remembered when I was supposed to be knitting and when I was supposed to be purling, so the pattern's a bit odd. But it's warm."

"I don't think I can wear the overalls," Maddy told her. "I'll never get them over my swollen leg."

Junebug's face fell.

Maddy tried to summon some gratitude. "But that cardigan is so big, I'm sure if I button it up it will look like a dress . . ."

"It doesn't have buttons." Junebug was shamefaced. "I never got around to them."

Oh. She couldn't wear it open over long underwear. Not when Kit and his brothers were around!

"Give me a minute," Junebug begged. "I'll see what else I can find!"

She went off into the bedroom, and Maddy heard muttered curses. "Aha!" she heard finally.

Junebug came out, bearing a thick blue-and-green flannel shirt. "Here we are. This is one of Kit's. It's so huge it'll be just like a dress. Then you can throw the cardigan over it too. How about that?"

She was going to look ridiculous.

"Come on, I'll get that fire going and you can get out of those wet things. Do you need help?"

No, she didn't need help. The silly dress was so loose on her, she could just slop it off. She wriggled it over her head as Junebug fussed with the fire. She should be glad the long underwear was so stretched out and worn, as they slid easily over her leg.

Her leg wasn't looking great, Maddy thought. All the movement and banging it around had left it even more swollen, and her toes were cold and blue. She rolled the long underwear up over her knee so she could keep an eye on it. She'd best keep it elevated.

She buttoned herself into Kit's shirt, dipping her head to sniff the fabric. It smelled like him. Smoke and sunshine. Once she had the cardigan on, she pulled herself to her foot.

"What do you think?" She held her hands out, wobbling a little on her single foot.

Junebug looked up and laughed. "You look like a kid who got into her dad's clothes."

The shirt came down to her knees. She could have fit a whole other person in there with her. And while the cardigan was speckled with wonky holes and ribbed in odd places, it was thick and warm and cozy, like wearing a soft blanket. The long underwear was soft as velvet against her skin. As Junebug had promised, she was comfy. She just looked ludicrous.

Oh well, it wasn't like she was going anywhere. By the time she had to get down to Bitterroot, the turquoise would be dry, if water stained.

"You got all the shutters closed?" Kit came barreling in just as Maddy settled in a rocking chair by the fire, her foot propped up on a rough-hewn stool. Junebug had hung the turquoise dress on a hook to dry, and Merle was sprawled on the hearthstone, his furry ears twitching nervously at the sound of the wind.

Kit was dusted in white, and eddies of snow came swirling in with him. He was bundled in a thick oilcloth coat and a misshapen woolen hat.

"It's snowing!" Maddy was surprised. "It was all ice a moment ago."

"Yeah, it's settling in," Kit said gruffly, closing the door against the powerful push of the wind. "Going to be a bad one." His eyebrows were furred white, and his cheeks were chapped from the cold. Maddy bet he missed the protection of his beard. "I ain't seen snow like this in November in years. It's bitter cold out."

"Did you hear the tree go down?" Junebug asked, excited. She came tumbling down the ladder from the loft. She'd also changed into long underwear and a huge knit sweater. Her sweater was covered in pulled threads and bobbles. It looked older than she was.

"You sure those loft shutters are locked tight?" Kit said, looking worried. "You remember what happened that time they blew open and the window cracked. Took us an age to get new glass up from Butte."

"Yes, they're locked tight." Junebug rolled her eyes. "And so are the ones in the bedroom. Maddy did the ones out here, but they look sound enough to me."

Kit glanced at Maddy, surprised. "You did that, even with your leg?" His gaze swept her. "Is that my shirt?" he blurted.

Maddy blushed. "Yes," she said, aware of her state of undress, her legs bare except for the long underwear and the bandage. "The dress got wet when I was doing the shutters, and my others . . ." She glanced at Junebug. "Fell victim to the storm."

"You left them on the line," Kit groaned. "Damn it, Bug."

"How was I to know it was going to blow a gale? It was fine when we went to bed."

Maddy thought about Thunderhead Bill, who'd been predicting snow since the day she'd met him . . .

Kit was distracted. "I'm going to help Morgan with the animals. We'll need to get the barn battened down, and then I'll sort out the forge. We'll get everything else winter-proofed, and then I'll be back. Do you need anything?"

Maddy didn't feel it was the right time to mention her swelling leg. But she didn't need to. He'd already noticed it.

"I'll sort that out when I get back," he told her. "Don't move.

Junebug, she's not to move so much as an inch, you hear? That leg needs to stay still and elevated."

"Aye, aye, Captain." Junebug flopped into one of the chairs by the fire. "You don't want me to help, then?" She sounded very happy about it.

"You're helping by looking after Mrs. Lascalles." He prepared to go back out. "You can start by making her some coffee and toast."

"It's the middle of the night!"

"You planning on sleeping?" He radiated disbelief. The shutters were rattling, and the ghostly shrieking scraped down the chimney. The flames spat as the snow melted as it gusted down the flue.

"No, guess not."

"Be careful," Maddy blurted as he went to open the door.

He gave her a quick smile and then he was gone.

Jesus, Mary and Joseph, Junebug was right. He smiled at her, and she felt like she'd been kicked in the head.

The storm intensified after he left, and Maddy couldn't help but worry. The wind seemed like it was about to blow the cabin to bits—how on earth could he survive out there?

"He'll be fine," Junebug said every time Maddy fussed. She'd stuck a hunk of thick-cut bread in the toasting cage and was holding it over the fire. They finally had some decent coals glowing.

Drafts blew through every last chink in the walls, nipping at Maddy's bare feet. She asked Junebug to fetch her a quilt off the bed. Junebug came back with one for herself and Merle, too, and they made themselves a nest right in front of the fire.

"Don't you think he's taking a long time?" Maddy asked.

"Nope. There's a lot to do." Junebug tried to hand her the toast. Maddy shook her head. She was too anxious to eat.

"Make toast, he says," Junebug muttered, "but no one wants the toast." She fed it to Merle, who was perpetually hungry, even when anxious.

Maddy jumped every time the wind pummeled the door, thinking it was Kit back.

"It really does sound bad, doesn't it?" Eventually even Junebug started to get nervous. The fire was leaping erratically, pushed down by the gusts blasting down the chimney, and the wind was loud as a train rocketing past. But a train with endless carriages that kept coming and coming and coming.

"What are they *doing*?" Maddy asked testily. "Shouldn't he be back by now?"

"They'll be shuttering up all the outbuildings," Junebug told her. She shuffled closer, until she was sitting right next to Maddy. "And then they'll probably string rope lines from building to building, so we've got guide ropes during the blizzard. Normally they set those up before the first blow of winter—this caught us all off guard."

"It didn't catch Thunderhead Bill off guard," Maddy said. She lowered a hand to rest it on Junebug's head. The girl leaned into her.

"No, it sure didn't. He's a wily one, ain't he? Remind me to listen to him more."

They lapsed into silence, but the sound of the wind was too unnerving.

"Tell me more about that house," Junebug said.

"There isn't much more to tell."

"Tell me about the food."

"The food?" Maddy sighed, thinking back to Mrs. Egan bustling around the kitchens. "What kind of food?"

"What about winter food. What would they eat on a day like this? Did it snow there?"

"Not much. The mountains would get snow but mostly not thick like, just a dusting. Mostly we got rain and fog. It was a moody place." Maddy tried to remember what Mrs. Egan would make on a sodden winter day. "Mrs. Egan used to bake a lot in winter. There were always biscuits to go with pots of tea. Cookies, I mean. Mrs. Ormond was always calling for fresh pots of tea to keep the chill out. Mrs. Egan had these little jam tarts she'd make, that she'd serve hot. You could burn your mouth on the jam if you weren't careful."

"I wish we had jam tarts instead of bread," Junebug sighed.

"And the kitchen always smelled of custard and spices." Maddy remembered the perfume of nutmeg settling in for the season. Cinnamon and cloves, ginger and allspice.

"Did you ever have pies?" Junebug asked dreamily.

"Oh my, did we ever. Mrs. Egan used to make a beef and dark ale pie that would haunt your dreams, it was so good."

Junebug looked up at her, startled. "Beef and *ale*?"

"And she made a shepherd's pie with a buttery potato crust that crackled when you bit into it." Maddy was making herself hungry.

"And you really can't cook?" Junebug was forlorn.

"I only started cooking when I got to St. Louis to work for Willabelle. And I wasn't very good." Maddy pulled a face, remembering the awful soups she'd made. And the half-raw roast chickens, followed by the dried-out and deflated ones. She'd never got roasting right.

"Your hair is all tangled," Maddy said. "Want me to brush it?"

Junebug groaned. "I hate brushing my hair."

"That's probably why it's in such a state," Maddy told her primly. "If you get the brush, I'll tell you about all the Christmas desserts. Trifle and pudding and Italian ices."

Maddy hadn't even got past the brandy custard, or battled half the knots on Junebug's head, before the door whammed open and Kit and Morgan shuffled in, looking like frozen bears. A wall of snow came in with them. They were carrying burlap sacks, which they dropped to the floor with a clatter.

"Tarnation, you look blue!" Junebug exclaimed, jumping to her feet. "I'll get the water."

Water? Maddy was left holding the hairbrush, feeling helpless.

Kit and Morgan made low grunting noises as they closed the door and stomped their feet. Kit's jaw was clenched, Maddy noticed, almost like his teeth had frozen together. A muscle jumped in his cheek.

"Get your shoes off, quick," Morgan growled, his voice shaky.

Junebug dragged a tin tub in front of the fire. There was a make-shift work area in the corner, with a small table and cook pots. There were two pails of water, which Junebug lugged to the fire.

"Don't heat them too much," Kit said gruffly. "It ain't supposed to be hot."

"I know," Junebug snapped. "This ain't my first rodeo."

"Can I do anything?" Maddy asked.

"Stay put," Kit told her, "and look after that leg."

She wished she could do *something*.

They shucked off their coats and hats and peeled down to their shirts. Both of them hurried to unlace their wet boots.

"Goddamn that hurts," Morgan moaned.

Junebug splashed the just-warm water into the tub. "Get your feet in quick."

"It's my hands that hurt bad," Kit said as he dragged a stool over next to the tub. He sat down and thrust his blue feet into the water. He yelped in pain. That muscle in his cheek was leaping away. He bent and submerged his hands too.

"It stops the frostnip from setting in," Junebug told Maddy.

"Get some coffee on, Bug," Morgan ordered as he yanked a rocking chair close to the tub and shoved his feet and hands in with Kit's.

The two of them made pained noises as they wriggled their fingers and toes.

"There's the tin of tea in one of those sacks," Kit told Junebug. "Heat some water for that too."

Maddy felt a glow as she realized he was organizing tea on her behalf.

"You've used up all the water on your feet," Junebug reminded him.

"So, get some snow," Kit snapped. "God knows we got plenty of that."

"It's bad out there?" Maddy asked them as Junebug climbed into Morgan's oilcloth slicker and pulled on her boots.

"Worst I've seen," Morgan admitted. "Don't leave the porch, Bug."

"I wasn't planning on it," Junebug said sourly, buttoning the enormous coat to the chin. It was so big on her that it dragged on the ground. She pulled on a woolen hat and grabbed the pails.

"Mittens!" Kit snapped. "Put your mittens on."

"But it's just the porch."

"You want to end up in here with us?"

Junebug considered the sight of them both contorted over the tub and went to fetch her mittens.

As soon as Junebug stepped outside, Morgan was in a state, worrying about Beau and Jonah, who'd been gone for a couple of days. "What if they're stuck out in it?"

"They'll be fine," Kit reassured him. "They're probably at the Ella-Jean Mine, or back in Bitterroot already with the doctor." But he was worried too.

"They could also be stuck halfway between the two," Morgan snapped. "And they don't got a shred of winter wear on them. Hell. Why didn't I think to tell them to take winter gear?"

"Because the weather's been mild," Kit reminded him. "Who knew this monster was coming?"

Maddy found she was clutching the hairbrush in a death grip as she listened to them. Look at the state of them after an hour or two out in the storm; how could anyone survive longer?

They hushed as soon as Junebug returned with her pails packed with snow. She was rigid with cold, her teeth chattering. "That's colder than a witch's tit!" she howled.

"Junebug! We got a lady here!" Kit snapped at her. And then he apologized to Maddy.

"Ah, don't apologize to her, she knows way worse words." Junebug kicked the door closed.

Maddy blushed. One of the first lady lessons would have to be on the value of knowing when to keep quiet about things. Things like the curse words a lady said in private.

"Get those hot drinks on, Bug," Morgan grunted, clearly in pain as his hands and feet thawed. "My insides feel like they're frozen solid."

"Please let me do something!" Maddy begged. She felt like a shag on a rock.

"When they get their hands and feet out, we have to rub the life back into 'em," Junebug told her as she swung the cast-iron pot hanger over the fire. She put the water on to boil and then put a rack over the flames and put the coffeepot on it. "I'll do Morgan, 'cause he has the foulest feet."

"Hey," Morgan protested.

"It's true," Junebug told him, fetching toweling. "They're genuinely disgusting." She dropped the toweling in Kit's lap. "Dry off your hands and give them to her while you keep soaking your feet." She held out a small round tin to Maddy. "Here, use the lanolin; it makes the rubbing easier."

She'd clearly done this more than a few times in her life.

Maddy's nose wrinkled as the pungent smell of lanolin wafted up from the tin. It was a woolly smell.

She felt shy as she watched Kit dry his hands on the towel. He was looking skittish, not meeting her eye, but focusing with intense concentration on wiping each and every droplet off his skin.

"Now," Junebug said brusquely, grabbing Kit's left hand and yanking it toward Maddy. "What you do is this." She swiped a blot of lanolin and showed Maddy how to rub the warmth back to Kit's frozen hands.

"Here, your turn." She dropped his hand heavily into Maddy's care.

"You're still so cold!" Maddy was shocked. "Does it hurt?"

"It's just pins and needles, that's all," he said gruffly.

"Red-hot pins and needles," Morgan corrected. "Goddamn, Junebug, be gentle, would you?"

Maddy used her thumbs to massage his cold hand, taking it slow, afraid of hurting him. She kept her eyes on the job, aware of the thickening intimacy between them. She ran her thumb up the lifeline of his palm, feeling the muscularity of his hand. Finger by finger, she stroked circular motions. Dimly, she was aware of Junebug chattering away to Morgan, and of the crackle of the fire and the moan of the blizzard. Her focus narrowed to the one large hand, to the whorls of dark hair at his wrist and on the backs of his fingers.

"Hurry up and do the next one, or I cain't give him his coffee."

It was only when Junebug snapped her fingers at Maddy that Maddy realized she was the one Junebug was talking to. She looked up and found that Kit was staring at her, mesmerized. His shining dark eyes held hers. She swallowed. Jesus, Mary and Joseph, she was in trouble. The way he looked at her had her imagining all kinds of sin.

He held out his other hand and she took it. She slid her fingers into the tin of lanolin and turned her attention to the cold hand, trying to banish thoughts of sin. But, oh, it was hard to do. She wondered if his chest had the same dark whorls of hair, if his skin was this smooth all over, how this muscular hand would feel running down her body . . .

"Hellfire, you're spoiling him." Junebug crashed in again, thrusting a mugful of coffee at Kit. "Look at him, he looks like a cat. A big fat old happy house cat, full of cream and sitting in the sun."

Kit snatched his hand back and took the coffee. He cleared his throat. "Thanks," he said gruffly.

"Now's the less fun bit," Junebug sighed to Maddy. "Their nasty feet . . ."

Maddy didn't think Kit's feet were nasty at all. They were large and pale, the tendons clearly defined, the toes long and well shaped. Dark hair swirled at his ankles. Maddy ran her thumbs up the sole of his foot, and he let out an involuntary moan.

"Dear God, that's good."

The sound of that groan made Maddy feel loose and liquid. She risked glancing up. He was still staring at her, hungry. She wondered what might happen if they were alone . . . what she might *let* happen. Oh, sod that. What she might *start*.

She ran her fingers between his toes, and his lips parted. His stare grew more intense, heated. Maddy smoothed her palms over the back of his foot and around his ankle. He looked like he could pull her into his lap at any moment. She explored every last inch of his foot and then moved to the next one. He was spellbound.

The way he looked at her . . . no one had ever looked at her like that before, not even Tom. Kit McBride stared at Maddy like she was water in the desert, oxygen after being submerged in the ocean. He looked at her like he *needed* her.

"Warm now?" she asked huskily.

"Warm," he agreed, his gaze dropping to her lips. And then wandering to the open buttons at the neck of her shirt. *His* shirt.

"Tea." A mug appeared in front of Maddy's face.

Junebug had the worst sense of timing.

Maddy took it, her lanolin-coated hand slippery on the handle, trying to hide her irritation.

Junebug leaned close and whispered in her ear, "Kicked. In. The. Head."

Seventeen

The storm raged for days. It wasn't so much a single blizzard as a series of them, all piled one on top of the other. The snow heaped up past the porch, burying them in the cabin. Kit and Morgan tunneled up to the surface and religiously kept the tunnel dug out so they didn't suffocate. The also hiked up and made sure the chimney was clear.

Once a day the two men took an expedition to the barn to feed the animals and then to the trading post to make sure the old trappers were still alive. Alive and not eating them out of strap candy, Morgan said sourly.

"We'll be gone awhile," he murmured to Maddy the first day, giving Junebug a surreptitious look. "Maybe you could distract her with lady lessons while we're gone each day?"

Maddy had followed his gaze to where Junebug was morosely scrubbing the breakfast frypan. She chafed at being shut up in the cabin. "Of course," Maddy said, clearing her throat, wondering where on earth she'd start. The girl didn't have the basics down, let alone the finer points . . .

Tea! She could teach Junebug about tea. The girl had a dire way with it, and teatime was an integral part of being a lady, wasn't it? Maddy remembered Mrs. Ormond's famous afternoon teas: the fine bone china tea set laid out on the starched lace tablecloth; the hothouse roses spilling from the vases; the cake trays artfully arranged with cucumber sandwiches and cakes; and the ladies, as pale and pretty as flowers in their gowns, holding the delicate china handles daintily, their little fingers aloft. Maddy remembered the smoky perfume of the exotic teas Mrs. Ormond would buy for the occasion, with poetic names like Assam Bold and Lapsang souchong, and the sound of tiny silver spoons tinkling on saucers. Maddy never served at table, but sometimes she had to go in and clean up a spill, or fetch and carry, and the sight of those ladies gave her a thrill. Clothed in rustling silk and taffeta, ribboned and jeweled and powdered, they were soft handed and softer voiced.

A string of increasingly filthy words exploded from Junebug, startling Maddy from her memories, and there was a clatter as the girl threw the frypan aside. "I hate this blasted thing! It don't never get clean no matter how I scrub it."

Imagine Junebug at Ormond House, having tea with those ladies! The image was so incongruous that Maddy giggled.

"I don't know what you're laughing about." Junebug wasn't amused. "You ain't the one who has to wash up. I should shove my leg down a rabbit hole too."

Maddy considered how to go about this. Maybe it was best to tackle it head-on. Junebug wasn't the type to play games with. "Your brothers asked me to give you some lessons in how to be a lady," she said bluntly.

"They what?" Junebug perked up, looking interested.

"They thought I could teach you some of the basics." She hurried to set Junebug's expectations low. From what she'd seen of the girl so far, she was prone to flights of fancy. The wind rattled the shutters, and she remembered Junebug's chatter about ghosts. "It will help pass the time," she said optimistically. "For both of us."

"What kinds of things are you thinking?" Junebug cocked her head. "Dancing? In Kit's books ladies are always off dancing."

"Not dancing." Maddy shook her head. She didn't have a clue how to dance.

"Beguiling?"

"What?" Maddy blinked. As usual, Junebug caught her off guard.

"Do I have to get my shoulders out? 'Cause it's mighty cold. Probably too cold. What do ladies do when it's too cold for shoulders? Is that where the dancing comes in?"

Maddy decided to just ignore her talk of shoulders and dancing. Who knew where Junebug got her odd ideas? "I thought we'd start with tea."

"Tea!" Junebug was startled. "What's tea got to do with beguilement?"

Maddy's head was starting to hurt again. "Forget the beguilement. Today's lesson is on tea."

Junebug didn't seem enthused.

"Let's start with making it," Maddy suggested.

"Start with? Does that mean you want me to drink it too?"

"After you learn how to pour it."

"I know how to pour it. What do you think I am, an imbecile?"

It didn't get easier from there. But Maddy managed to win her over by telling her stories about teatime at Ormond House; Junebug would go along, so long as she was entertained. And she was full of questions.

"Why'd they cut the crusts of the sandwiches like that?"

"How in hell do you stir it without clanking? That ain't stirring a spoon so much as dipping it."

"What do you mean, sugar comes in lumps? How do they lump it?"

"What idiot thought of dumping a lemon in their tea?"

"How many cakes can you have before they tell you to stop?"

Most of the time Maddy didn't know whether to laugh or cry.

But by the time Kit and Morgan came back in from the cold, Junebug had managed to brew, pour and drink a pot of tea in an almost ladylike way. Ladylike for Buck's Creek, anyhow. And it was a pretty big *almost*.

"How did it go with the lady lessons?" Kit asked Maddy quietly. He and Morgan were frozen through again and had the ordeal of soaking and rubbing to suffer.

It was the part of the day Maddy liked the most.

As Maddy rubbed the life back into his frozen hands and feet, she found all of Kit's secret spots, the ones that made his eyelashes tremble and his breath catch. He was more desirable than a man had a right to be . . .

"It went well, I think," Maddy said, a trifle breathlessly. "Not that I'd want to take her to tea with the queen just yet."

He laughed. "The queen wouldn't know what hit her."

The sound of his laughter made her stomach turn shivery, and the feel of his skin under her hands was like touching sparks from the fire. Maddy could have sat there rubbing his feet all day long.

As the storm intensified and the temperatures plummeted, Kit and Morgan hauled the single beds out from the bedroom and set them up by the fire, as it was too cold out of the main room, away from the flames. Morgan closed off the partition and kept the fire stoked until the single room was cozy warm. The wicked blasts of cold air through the knotholes were a sharp reminder of the dangerous freeze outside. Maddy was ensconced in the bed, piled with quilts and treated more like a queen than ever. Morgan and Kit slept in Beau's and Jonah's bunks, while Junebug and Maddy had the single beds, and Maddy got firsthand experience of Kit's snoring.

The first night she woke in shock, her heart pounding, fearing a wild animal had found its way into the cabin. A bear or a wild boar . . .

But then she realized what it was. And as she heard Junebug groan and Morgan mutter, she got the giggles.

"You'd best be glad you're not marrying him after all," Morgan whispered to her. "Or you'd have to live with that for all your lifetime to come." He let out an imitation of Kit's snore.

"It's worse than *that*," Junebug said, barely keeping it to a whisper. "It's more like this . . ." She let out a noise like a congested warthog.

Maddy's giggles escalated. Then Kit emitted a snortingly loud snore and she lost her composure and had to bury her face in the pillow.

Morgan started laughing, and then Junebug caught the giggles, and before long the three of them were crying, they were laughing so hard.

The next day they only had to look at each other to set off again, and poor Kit had no idea what was happening. At least he didn't until Junebug mimicked his snort. At that point he scowled at them. "I don't snore!"

Maddy thought she'd burst something internal, she laughed so hard.

"I don't!"

"I should have put *inveterate liar* in that ad too," Junebug giggled.

"You should teach her manners today," Kit said sourly as he jammed his woolen hat on and headed out with Morgan.

Manners? Maddy would have to work up to that. She wasn't capable of miracles.

"What are we doing today? It better not be more cooking," Junebug warned her. "I get enough of that in my regular life." Junebug was lounging on a stool by the fire, elbows resting on her spread legs.

"Making tea isn't cooking," Maddy scolded her.

"Sure it is. You put a pot over the fire, that's cooking, in my book."

She looked like a scruffy boy sitting there, Maddy thought rue-fully, legs akimbo. It gave Maddy an idea. "Today we're going to practice walking and sitting."

Junebug looked disgusted. "You're not serious."

"I'm very serious," Maddy told her. "A lady doesn't sit with spread legs."

"She would if she wore pants," Junebug said, disgruntled.

"No, she wouldn't."

"Well, this one would." Junebug crossed her arms. "I know how to walk and sit just fine. I want to learn proper lady things."

Maddy didn't want to hear more about shoulders and beguile-ment. "These *are* proper lady things. You have to walk before you can dance."

Junebug scowled.

"We'll need a book." Maddy remembered the way Tom's younger sister used to walk up and down the stairs with a book on her head, practicing her posture. The maids had all giggled about it in the kitchen, but if it was good enough for Lucy Ormond, it was good enough for Junebug McBride.

"Good luck with finding a book," Junebug snorted. "Kit's tight with them. He don't let anyone use them, at least not out of his sight."

"Something like a book, then. It needs to be flat and heavy-ish."

Junebug burst into a tirade about books having nothing to do with walking, but she went up to the loft and fetched a hard-backed ledger as she did it. "Here," she sighed. "You can use my complaints book. This is a new one; my regular one is down in the trading post."

"Your what?"

"My complaints book. Kit makes me write down all my com-plaints."

Maddy didn't know what to make of that.

"He says if he had to listen to me, he'd never get any work

done, so he makes me write it all down." She opened her book and flicked through the pages. "You can bet I'm putting this stupid lesson in here."

"It's not stupid."

"It is. I'll have to get the dictionary out to find enough words for how dumb it is." Junebug snapped the ledger closed. "So, what do I do with this, other than write down how stupid the lesson is?"

"You put it on your head."

If looks could kill, Maddy would have dropped dead on the spot.

"You're making fun," Junebug snapped.

"I'm not. You put it on your head."

"Why in hell would I do that?"

"Ladies don't curse," Maddy chided.

"This one sure as shoot does."

"Just put it on your head, please." Oh, she was a trial.

Junebug put the ledger on her head. It slid straight off. She made no move to pick it up again.

Maddy sighed. "The aim," she said, striving for calm, "is to keep a straight back, and to balance the book on your head as you walk."

"Are you telling me," Junebug demanded, "that ladies walk around with *books* on their heads?"

Lord, grant me patience, Maddy thought, casting a glance skyward.

"Is that why they wear those big old hats all the time? To hide the books?"

"The aim is to glide," Maddy instructed her.

"Glide?" Junebug wrinkled her nose. "Do boys do this too?"

Maddy was nonplussed. "Erm . . . I don't think so."

Junebug sighed and picked up the ledger. "I figured not. It's an ordeal being a female, ain't it?" She put the book on her head. "Fine. I'll glide. But we better get to the good stuff soon."

She was surprisingly good at gliding. She had it down in two laps of the cabin. And then she started doing twirls and swoops, showing off.

"Do I got to keep this book on my head for the rest of my life?" she asked, once she'd grown bored.

"Just show me that you can sit down and keep it on there," Maddy suggested.

Junebug plonked herself on the stool, legs spread. The book teetered but stayed where it was. "I could be in the circus, don't you think?"

"You'd be the star," Maddy said dryly. Or get eaten by the lions. It was a toss-up. "Now let's practice sitting."

Junebug looked down at herself. "Well, look at that, I got this one mastered already."

"Put your legs together."

Junebug snapped them together. "That's us done for the day, right?"

Maddy gave in. She was suffering more than Junebug was.

It was a surreal time, shut up in the darkness with the McBrides. After a couple of days, she could put weight on her leg again, and Junebug told her she could make her own tea. Which Maddy was more than happy to do. She took to walking pained and clumsy circles around the cabin while the water boiled, trying to get her mobility back.

"You know what would help you get rid of that limp?" Junebug suggested.

Maddy had a feeling she knew what was coming.

"Put a big old book on your head."

Maddy turned her back so Junebug couldn't see her struggling not to laugh.

She felt like she was becoming part of the family. It gave her the strangest feeling, like she was where she was meant to be. She liked the lack of rules and schedules and formalities; she liked the comfort of the cabin; she liked the way Kit McBride darted looks at her, and the way he treated her, gently, as though she was something to be treasured. She got used to the rhythm of their life shut up in the cabin through the endless storm, although it pained her to watch how they fretted about Beau and Jonah as the days slipped by. The McBrides weren't enjoying it nearly as much as she was. For her, this was restful—she didn't have to cook or clean. But for them, it was a purgatory of waiting and fretting. Morgan worried quietly, grimly, while Kit and Junebug endlessly tried to reassure him.

"They'll be down in Bitterroot," Kit insisted, trying to keep his brother's spirits up. "Lolling around Abner's saloon, or Rigby's lounge, drinking too much and playing cards. Hell, Jonah's probably lost his hat. That kid has no poker face."

"I reckon they're at the Ella-Jean," Junebug disagreed, "and eating in that cookhouse they got there. Thunderhead Bill says the cook in that cookhouse is the best between here and Boise, Idaho. And he said he had the best beefsteak of his life in Boise, Idaho."

But as the days drew on, they found it harder and harder to keep their cheer up. It was the closeness of the cabin. The darkness. Their minds wandered to fearful thoughts.

"Beau's too stupid to know how to dig a proper snow cave," Junebug whispered to Maddy in the dead of night.

"I'm sure he's not," Maddy said, but how was she to know? She'd met Beau for all of ten minutes and she didn't remember him at all. Her memory of that time was nothing but blinding pain.

"What if they got lost in the blizzard? It's easy to get turned around in a whiteout," Kit sighed as Maddy rubbed the cold out of his hands. "I mean, I'm sure you never got stuck out in a whiteout, Mrs. Lascalles," he said, "but you could imagine . . ."

Maddy hated his calling her Mrs. Lascalles, but what could she say? *Call me Willabelle?* No, that was a thousand times worse.

The longer she was here, the worse she felt about letting them call her by Willabelle's name. It felt like a lie . . .

Jesus, Mary and Joseph, it *was* a lie. At first it had seemed so harmless, but now . . .

"We have fogs back in county Offaly that block out everything," she told Kit. "You can't even see the hand in front of your face." Her heart went out to him. He was so worried about his brothers. "Mrs. Egan said they were sent by the fairies to lure us into Mag Mell, the plain of joy."

"Fairies!" Junebug blurted. She was sitting by the fire, peeling potatoes. "Oh my *God*." Her huge, panicked eyes met Maddy's. "The *banshee*."

"The what?" Kit looked over, annoyed by her drama.

"The banshee, the banshee! We heard a banshee on the first night of the storm! What if it was for Beau or Jonah? Or for *both of them*?"

"We didn't hear a banshee," Maddy said calmly, even though her heart kicked up at the mention of it. "You didn't even know what a banshee was."

"But *you* did!"

"We heard the wind in the chimney and a tree fall in the woods." Maddy was firm. The girl didn't need encouragement.

"Morgan!" Junebug decided she didn't need encouragement either. She leapt up from the chair and went to rouse her brother, who was napping in his bunk. "You need to go find them! You have to find Beau and Jonah!"

Morgan wasn't happy about being woken, and he liked all the talk of banshees even less. "Sounds like a ghost to me," he complained, "and you know how I feel about ghosts."

"You don't like them."

"I don't believe in them enough to care about them either way." He scowled.

But Junebug wouldn't drop the talk of banshees wailing. She got everyone wound up. No one slept that night, listening to the banshee wailing of the wind in the chimney.

At the first clearing of the weather, Morgan and Kit resolved to go out after them.

"But what if *you* get lost?" Junebug fretted.

"I know my way through a snowstorm," Morgan said grimly. "On the trail we used to weather them, out in the open. I know how to survive, Bug."

Maddy's heart was in her throat as she watched them prepare. Her gaze lingered on Kit as he rubbed wax into his boots to further waterproof them.

"While we're gone, you ain't to leave the cabin, you hear?" Kit told Junebug firmly. "It ain't safe. We'll make sure you've got enough food laid away in the cabin and you can melt snow for water. You got no call to leave. I'll have Sour Eagle feed the animals."

"What if something happens?" Junebug demanded. "Like she faints?" She gave Maddy an ominous look.

"I won't faint," Maddy sighed. "I swear, I'm not a fainter."

"Three times," Junebug reminded her shortly.

"*Once*," Maddy snapped back. "Under duress."

"So, what if you get duressed and go fainting again?"

"What if *you* do?"

"Is it safe to leave them alone, bickering like this?" Morgan asked Kit.

"We ain't bickering," Junebug protested. "I'm speaking the truth; she's just being prideful."

"Junebug has a point, Kit," Morgan admitted.

Junebug mimed falling off her chair. "Morgan thinks I'm right about something!"

"I don't love the idea of the two of them here alone, defenseless."

"You could give me a gun?" Junebug suggested.

They ignored her.

"You should stay in the cabin with them," Morgan said to his brother. "One of us needs to stay here."

Kit didn't look happy.

"I can take Sour Eagle with me. He's useful in a pinch, unlike those other two."

Kit considered Maddy.

"And what about Junebug?" Morgan said quietly, leaning close to him.

Junebug's ears pricked up at her name.

"If something happens to me, you need to look after her."

"Nothing's going to happen to you. You better not let it," Kit told him.

Maddy's leg was still too weak for her to go outside, but the other two clambered up the snow tunnel to watch Morgan set off. They left the door open, and a pale wash of light fell down the shaft and into the room. The day outside was eerily quiet now that the weather had cleared. Maddy could hear the soft murmur of their voices, muffled by the snow, and the crunch of boots on virgin snow crust.

It was only after he'd gone, and Junebug and Kit were back down in the cabin, that it occurred to Junebug that the banshee might have been wailing for *Morgan*.

Eighteen

Kit came in from the cold with a bundle held close against his chest.

Books.

It was the only thing he knew guaranteed to take a person's mind off their troubles. Within two hours of Morgan departing, the storm had whipped itself into a frenzy again, and Junebug was at her wit's end.

"Go after him," she'd raged at Kit.

"He'll be safe and sound in Bitterroot by now." He'd done his best to calm her, but she wasn't of a mind to be calmed.

Mrs. Lascalles had told stories of Ireland until she was hoarse, trying to distract Junebug, and when she was out of Irish stories, she told tales of New York and St. Louis. Eventually, she'd trailed off, aware that Junebug was barely listening.

Morgan was more important to Junebug than all the rest of them put together, Kit thought with a sigh. He was her parent. Her rock. She clung to his craggy implacable sturdiness. He was the one who comforted her every night after their ma died and their pa ran off, when Kit was too distraught about Charlie to be much good to anyone . . .

He didn't want to sit here cooped up, thinking black thoughts about missing people. So he fetched his books.

"Which one do you want, Bug?" He'd got all her favorites, including the dictionary. He noticed Mrs. Lascalles was eyeing his armful curiously. Kit spread them out on the bench so they could see them. "*Frankenstein? The Woman in White? Ivanhoe?*"

"None of them," Junebug said glumly. She was flopped on the bottom bunk, where Morgan had been sleeping. "I don't want to hear about stupid Victor fainting all over the place, or dumb old Ivanhoe picking the wrong girl."

"He didn't pick the wrong girl," Kit sighed, although he privately felt exactly the same way. "There was no way he could be with the other one, remember?"

"I would have found a way, if it were me. If I were Rebecca, I wouldn't go giving my blessing to Rowena like that. I would have fought for him."

She was in a mood and would pick holes in whatever he read her.

"I've got a new one we haven't read yet," he said, picking it up. It was enormous, just about the size of his anvil. That should keep them distracted until the storm blew itself out, or Morgan returned with the boys. "It's called *Vanity Fair.*"

"It's sounds dumb," she muttered.

"Might be." He opened it. "But maybe not. There's a war in it, a big one."

"What war?"

"The Napoleonic Wars."

"Where was that, out in Mexico or something?"

"Europe."

Kit was aware of Mrs. Lascalles getting up to make tea for them. They'd all got a taste for it, thanks to her. He'd have to make her a proper teapot sometime; the saucepan just wasn't the same, she deserved a proper teapot . . . He realized he was thinking like she was staying . . . He tried to focus on Junebug. "A man named Napoleon conquered the nations of Europe . . . until the winters of Russia defeated him."

"Ugh. Winter. I don't want to hear about winter."

"I'd like to hear it," Mrs. Lascalles ventured, glancing at Junebug. She was trying to help.

"Read it to her, then, Kit." Junebug rolled over. "I don't care about your dumb book."

Mrs. Lascalles poured out the tea, leaving Junebug's on the floor near the bunk, where she could reach it if she chose. Kit stoked the fire and then took a seat in the rocking chair, under the lamp. He opened the book and carefully pressed the page down with his hand. There was an illustration of the author on the flyleaf: he was a square-headed fellow with a bouffant of hair. In the illustration he was peering at a book. Beneath it were the dates of his birth and death. He'd died when Kit was two years old.

"*Vanity Fair: A Novel without a Hero*," he read.

"Who wants a novel without a hero!" Junebug exclaimed, disgusted by the very idea.

"I thought you weren't listening."

"I wasn't! And I'm certainly not now!"

Kit scanned the introduction and decided that, with Junebug in her current frame of mind, he'd be better served jumping straight into the first chapter. He took a sip of tea and began: "While the present century was in its teens, and on one sunshiny morning in June, there drove up to the great iron gate of Miss Pinkerton's academy for young ladies . . ."

Maddy was enchanted. No one had ever read aloud to her before, except for Bible readings, and letters. She was entranced by the story of Amelia Sedley and Becky Sharp, by the candlelit days of a world gone by, a world of balls held on the eve of battle, of heartbreak and deception, loyalty and honor. And Kit read so well; his baritone was warm and heartfelt, conjuring the emotions of the characters.

Eventually even Junebug sat up in the bunk, pulled into the story. Now and then she interjected, displeased by Amelia's wetness, but even more so by Amelia's husband's rank disloyalty. She didn't know what to make at all of Becky Sharp.

Maddy loved Becky from the outset. Poor ignored Becky, treated worse than the kitchen servants because she was *nobody*, while everyone fawned over sweet, obedient, *rich* Amelia. Maddy could have cheered when Becky threw the book out of the carriage window. She didn't care if the narrator didn't like Becky, she did. Enormously. Even if Becky did do some nasty deeds . . .

Maddy was sore disappointed when they stopped the book for supper, and when Junebug declared she was done with it for today.

"You can read ahead if you want," Kit offered, holding out the book. As usual, he could read her mind. Only . . . she couldn't read ahead, because she couldn't read. But how was she to tell him that, when he thought she was Willabelle Lascalles, who'd written all those letters?

"I'll wait for Junebug," she said, but she couldn't keep the disappointment out of her voice.

He smiled at her.

Heavens, he was beautiful. He'd shaved again, removing the blue-black stubble that shadowed his jaw within a day. He looked like a pirate before he shaved; afterward, like . . . Maddy didn't know, but whatever it was, it was glorious.

"I'll cook tonight, Bug," Kit said, putting the book down. "We could all use a break from your cooking."

Junebug didn't seem to know whether to be happy or irked by that comment. "Can I read the dictionary?" she asked, hovering over his stack of books.

"If you're careful with it."

She snagged it from the pile and crept back to the lower bunk, where she and Merle nested in the quilt together to keep warm. Maddy was glad the dog had taken a shine to Junebug, because Maddy didn't fancy taking him home to Ireland with her. What could a maid do with a dog?

"What shall we cook?" Kit mused. "We have potatoes, salt beef, more potatoes . . . and beans."

"Your sister seems to be fixated on pie . . ." Maddy laughed. "Maybe you can make a potpie?"

Kit cocked his head. "You got any idea how to make one?"

"Not in the slightest."

"Guess we'll make it up, then. Fancy peeling some potatoes for me?"

Maddy did fancy it. She fancied doing anything with Kit McBride.

They fell into a companionable silence as they worked. Maddy stole glances at him. He wore another of Junebug's knits. It was a deep pine green, full of dropped stitches and odd patterns that petered out a few lines in. It pulled across his shoulders and rose up unevenly at the back of the hem. But he looked good, even in that. Kit McBride would look good in anything at all, Maddy thought with a sigh.

"Aha!" Junebug sat upright in bed, triumphant. "Inquisitioned! *An official investigation, political or religious.* I *told* you it was a word!"

Kit rolled his eyes.

Vindicated, Junebug fell back, absorbed in reading the definition.

"I assume this pie is supposed to have pastry on top," Kit said, looking at the beef and vegetable mixture bubbling away in the pot. "You reckon we can put potatoes on top instead?"

"I'm Irish," Maddy laughed. "You're asking the wrong person."

Once supper was organized and cooking, Kit gave Maddy an impish look. "Fancy a nip? I pulled up a bottle of Morgan's good whiskey. I didn't want to offer a lady our moonshine, but the whiskey is another thing altogether."

Maddy nodded. His smile was infectious.

Kit poured them each a dose in a mug and then sat next to her on the bed and clinked tins. "Cheers," he said, taking a sip. "Oh, that's good."

It was. A good peaty whiskey. It sent a bolt of welcome heat through Maddy's chest.

"Did you know *inveigle* means to entice, lure, or snare? That's a good word." Junebug didn't look up from her book. She didn't seem to expect a response.

Maddy felt perfectly happy, perhaps for the first time in her entire life.

Kit cleared his throat nervously. "I was wondering if you were feeling a little cabin feverish in here . . . I mean, I was thinking . . . if you wanted to . . ." He met her gaze shyly. "If you wanted to, I could take you to the forge tomorrow. Now that you're walking again. You could have a change of scene. I don't mind the company while I'm working . . ."

Was he blushing?

Maddy felt a blaze of something unnamable. Somehow, she didn't know how, there was something more than perfect happiness. Something named Kit McBride.

"I'd love to," Maddy breathed, feeling like she was saying yes to more than just a visit to the forge.

Kit felt absurdly anxious. Exposed. He wished he'd cleaned up, he thought as he dug the snow away from the door of the forge. The place was probably a mess. And cold. Damn it, he should have thought ahead and come out here and prepared. He could have shoveled the snow and lit the fire and cleaned up. Maybe he should have shoveled a path from the cabin to the forge while he was at it . . .

The snowshoes had been a trial for her, as her leg was still tender, and he'd felt responsible when he heard her breath growing labored. But she wouldn't hear of him apologizing.

"I love being out!" she laughed breathlessly. "Please stop begging for forgiveness."

"How's your leg holding up?" he asked, roughly a million times.

"Fine," she laughed, every time.

The winds had dropped, and the snow was falling in gentle swirls, the fatness of the flakes testifying to the cold. The drifts were so deep that it was impossible to walk without the clumsy snowshoes. They would have sunk waist deep. She had some grit, that was for sure, and she was surprisingly strong.

"It's so beautiful," she marveled as she waited for him to clear snow from the entrance to the forge. She was gazing rapt at the snow-laden fir trees and the iced-over creek. "You must waste hours just staring at the place."

He looked up, startled. He did. He just didn't know anyone else who did.

"We don't have to rush," he said slowly, straightening up from his task. He joined her, taking in the forest fringing Buck's Creek. The snow muffled everything. It felt like they were the only two people in the world.

"It looks so different to the day I came," she murmured.

"And in spring it'll look different again," he told her, remembering the way the first warm breezes felt after a long winter. The itchy feeling that set in. The smell of things growing. "You should see the wildflowers. It's a sea of color." He could picture them growing. "The buttercups in March," he sighed wistfully. "They come first, and then the milk vetch and yellow bells and phlox in

April . . . and by May it's ablaze with wallflowers and kittentails and larkspur and iris. And harebells." His voice caught on that. What he wouldn't give to pick her harebells the color of her eyes.

But she wouldn't be here in spring . . .

"I'd love to see it," she said, smiling. "We have wildflowers back home too. No harebells—I'm not sure what they are—but we have bog rosemary, which sounds awful but is really very pretty. Little pink and white bells on a lovely-smelling bush. And we have gentian and hawkweed. And then of course there are the formal gardens at the house. All the bulbs burst up in spring."

Formal gardens. He'd read about things like that but never seen them. Not for the first time he wondered what had brought her here. "You sound like you miss it," he said, feeling his heart pinch.

"Sort of." She gave him a sideways glance.

"Why did you leave?"

"I suppose I was running away." She bit her lip.

He blanched. Damn it. He forgot; she'd lost a husband. He couldn't imagine how hard that had been. He felt a stab of jealousy, even though the unlucky man was dead and gone.

She shivered and he felt a fool for keeping her in the cold for so long. Especially since her bad leg was probably paining her by now. He'd get the sled to take her back to the cabin.

"Come in," he invited, managing to open the door to the forge. It was dim and icy cold inside. Frost rimed the oilcloth at the windows, making the light milky and indistinct. Their breath plumed in the air. Kit unstrapped his snowshoes and hurried to find her a chair. He bumped into the bench in the dark. He found the lantern and got it lit. Then he helped her into the chair and knelt to unstrap her shoes.

She was wearing a pair of Junebug's overalls, which were a little too small and too tight, and his big flannel shirt buttoned up over the top for decency. Junebug had layered her up with Beau's old cardigan, then Morgan's much bigger one, and then Jonah's coat. She was heavy with clothing, but still shivering.

"Let me get the fire going. It'll be hot in here in no time." Kit got to work. The familiarity of the forge took the edge off his nerves.

"You built this place?" Mrs. Lascalles asked him curiously.

"Yeah," he grunted as he worked the bellows. "Well, my brothers helped, I didn't do it all by myself."

"Brothers must come in handy." She settled back to watch him work.

"Do you have brothers?"

"I did. I mean, I do . . . somewhere."

Startled, Kit stopped fanning the flames.

"I mean . . . I haven't seen them since I was thirteen. We were separated." She was playing with the buttons on Jonah's coat. "After my mam died, we were all farmed out. I've been alone ever since."

Kit felt like he'd been poleaxed. She'd lost her brothers? "Me too," he blurted.

She frowned, bewildered. "You too? But you're not alone."

Kit flushed. He was. He'd been alone ever since Charlie left. Since he'd *made* Charlie leave. Kit clenched his jaw and turned back to the bellows. Thinking about Charlie still hurt like hell. It had been years since he'd lost his twin brother, and he still felt guilty. It had been his idea for one of them to go after their father. Their pa needed to come home and face his responsibilities; Kit didn't think it was right for Morgan to get stuck raising everyone. They'd flipped a coin to see who'd go, and Charlie had won—or lost, depending on how you thought of it. He'd lit out after Pa, and Kit had never heard from him again.

His mind had conjured horrors in the long sleepless nights since: Charlie with his neck broken at the bottom of a ravine; Charlie washed away in a flooded river and drowned; Charlie bit by a snake; Charlie shot and killed. Charlie had died a thousand times in Kit's imagination, and each time Kit grieved as though it had really happened.

And now Morgan and Beau and Jonah were gone, too, out there in the snow . . . He knew they were all capable woodsmen, but still, he worried.

"You have your brothers," she said tentatively, "and Junebug. I don't see how . . ."

He turned his back. He shouldn't have said anything.

"I don't understand—"

"I thought I'd make cookware." He cut her off, his heart pounding. He didn't talk about Charlie. It had been a mistake to tell her anything. "Fritz sells everything faster than I can make it."

She'd gone very still. He felt like he'd revealed too much, and he didn't like it.

Heat shimmered as the forge heated. He peeled off his outer layers and gathered his tools. He took his place at the anvil. Gradually, the thought of work eased him, as it always did. In here he was in control.

The forge grew steamy with heat. He rolled up his sleeves. Normally he'd strip down as he worked, as it was sweaty labor, but he couldn't with Mrs. Lascalles in here. He felt his shirt sticking to his back.

"It's like July in here," she said nervously, shucking off Jonah's coat. She settled in to watch him.

He grunted as he hammered the hot steel, drawing and bending it into shape.

He didn't have any real experience with women, and he guessed it showed. He should have asked her more about her brothers instead of blurting out his own problems. He should have shown her more concern. Hell, he knew how it felt to lose people; he shouldn't have been so insensitive.

He got distracted when she stood up and started looking

around his forge. She was limping, he noticed. Damn it. He'd hurt her by making her walk out here. It had been stupid. The whole idea had been stupid. Kit plunged the finished work into the slack tub and it hissed, releasing a cloud of steam.

He wiped his face down. He was drenched with sweat. He probably stank, too, he thought glumly. This had been beyond stupid. He didn't know why it had felt important to bring her here. He'd had some idea about wanting her to see the place he was happiest . . .

Stupid.

"This is where you keep your books?" she asked. She was peering into the trunk where he kept his library. He must have left the trunk open when he'd come out for the books the day before. His collection was stacked in tight rows inside, alphabetically ordered. "You read a lot," she observed.

"I do." Kit felt increasingly awkward now that he wasn't working at the anvil.

She ran her fingers over the spines.

"Do you like to read?" he asked.

She didn't answer. She pulled a book from the trunk and opened it gently. "I liked that book you read yesterday," she said eventually as she turned the pages. God, she was pretty. "Could we read some more again later?" She met his gaze, her blue, blue eyes sweet as a spring sky. "Please? I want to know what happens to Becky Sharp."

"I'm sorry," he blurted.

"Because of Becky Sharp? Why? What happens?"

"No, I mean, I'm sorry . . ."

She half smiled. "I was joking. What are you sorry for this time?"

"Your brothers." He was making a botch of this. "I'm sorry about your brothers . . . and your sisters. I didn't mean to dismiss you." He took his creation, which had cooled, and crossed the room to her. "I made you a teapot," he said, clumsily holding it out.

"A teapot?" She gave a startled laugh.

"You like tea," he said lamely. "And it didn't seem right, you brewing it in a cook pot."

She gently took the teapot from him and examined it. "You made this, just now? For me?"

He nodded. He felt big and hulking beside her. Uncomfortable in his body.

"No one's ever made anything for me before," she admitted.

"It's nothing fancy. I guess you're used to fine china."

"No, not really." She touched his arm. "It's beautiful. Thank you."

"You're beautiful," he blurted. He was making a habit of letting his mouth run away with him, it seemed.

She went glowingly pink.

If he'd been a braver man, he would have kissed her then. But he wasn't, and he didn't. But he sure thought about it—then, and for the rest of the day.

Nineteen

"I'm going to eat up in my loft," Junebug announced, snapping her dictionary closed when Kit told them dinner was ready. Somehow, Maddy observed, Junebug had wriggled out of cooking and Kit was doing it. Again.

"I'm sick to death of people," Junebug said. "I'll take Beast up there with me though. He ain't people." Merle and Junebug had become near inseparable.

"He can't climb the ladder," Maddy pointed out, her heart leaping at the thought of having supper alone with Kit. There had been a moment in the forge when she'd thought he might kiss her . . .

Oh, who was she kidding? There was a moment—more than a moment, dozens of them—when she'd *wanted* him to. When *she'd* almost kissed *him*.

"I'll carry him up. Kit can hand me my plate once I'm up there." Junebug took the dog and the dictionary and climbed the ladder to her loft room.

"Can he now?" Kit rolled his eyes but passed Junebug her bowl of stew as requested. Once he'd ladled their serves into bowls, he and Maddy sat side by side on Maddy's bed, watching the flames in the hearth as they ate. The wind had died down outside, and for once the crackle of the fire was the loudest sound in the room.

"This is good," Maddy said happily as she ate. "You're a much better cook than your sister."

"I know." His dark eyes twinkled. "She never got the hang of it."

"Beau's the best at it." Junebug's voice came down from above. She didn't seem the least bit offended. "But he won't never do it."

"It ain't his job," Kit called up.

"What *is* his job? Other than looking real pretty."

Maddy laughed. She had no memory of Beau, but she'd heard an awful lot about his vanity from Junebug.

"I'll do the dishes," Maddy said after they'd each had two helpings of his stew.

He shook his head. "No, you sit. You walked too far on that leg today—I saw you limping."

Her leg *did* hurt. It was much better, but she had overdone it. The snowshoes were clumsy, and the forge was uphill; it had been exhausting, even though it wasn't a terribly long way from the cabin.

But it had been worth it . . .

She'd loved every minute of it, from the first frosty breath of fresh air. The cabin was warm but close, and the air had grown stale—it was bliss to drink in the wintry drafts outside. And the world was a white wonderland; the firs bending under the weight of snow, the stream a line of lacy ice through the powdery meadow. As she clumped through the powder, Maddy felt her energy rise. She'd sat on her rear for too long; she was used to working, and hard. She'd always envied Willabelle and other ladies their leisure, but now she wasn't so sure. As the kinks loosened in her muscles, she was glad to be moving.

Kit had been endearingly nervous as he showed off his forge. It was bigger than she'd imagined, certainly compared to the smithies she'd seen back home, orderly and well-kept. It smelled of him, she noticed. A pleasant smoky smell. She remembered the strength of him as he worked the steel, his hammer flowing through the air with muscular grace. After he'd made her lovely teapot, he'd wanted to take her back to the cabin on the sled, but she wasn't ready to leave. She encouraged him to work, and to forget she was there. He had no idea how much she enjoyed watching him work . . . He made it look easy, but she could tell it was brutal labor by the sweat that streamed from him. His skin shone bronze in the firelight, and his expression was intense. She imagined that intensity turned on her, and shivered.

He was quite a man. Strong, but . . . sensitive. He was powerfully built and capable, but he was also nervous and shy, gentle, thoughtful. Dreamy.

She loved the way he hoarded books like treasure. The way he was bashful about it. It sent slow rivers of warmth through her.

"Would you read from that book again?" Maddy asked hesitantly, after they'd finished eating and had done the dishes. "The one about Becky Sharp?" She'd been waiting all day to find out what had happened to Becky . . .

"Oh, yes please!" Junebug's voice drifted down from up in the loft. "Read loud, so I can hear it too!"

Kit radiated pleasure. He fetched the book and then pulled the whiskey bottle down from the shelf and poured himself and Maddy a slug. Maddy felt a low buzz of anticipation as he joined her sitting on the bed. She took the whiskey and settled in.

He picked up where they left off, and they sank into a world long gone, a world on the eve of battle. Maddy wasn't sure if the warmth spreading through her was from the whiskey, the romance of the story or Kit's presence beside her. As he read, his hand inched across the blanket between them until it touched hers. Maddy held her breath. He'd been so reticent; she was surprised. He covered her hand with his own and she felt her heart stumble. He paused for a moment, as though waiting to see if she'd take her hand away. She didn't. She was fizzing inside at the touch of his hand and fearful that if she so much as moved he'd be scared off. She remembered his awkwardness at the forge, the sweet gracelessness of his gift of the teapot. Kit McBride was out of his depth when it came to women, and Maddy couldn't believe how seductive it was to have a man unable to keep his composure or equilibrium. He made her feel beautiful, desirable and powerful.

He darted a glance at her.

She swallowed hard. That thickening feeling was in the air again; the sense of intimacy; a cocooning of the two of them together in a slow-moving moment. Arrested.

As he read, his thumb stroked the back of her hand and she felt it . . . everywhere.

Lord, who knew a thumb could cause so much havoc. It ran a slow magical path along her fingers, steady and strong, sending sparks through her. Maddy's limbs felt heavy. Slow pulsing desire uncurled, starting in her belly and tendriling through every last inch of her. She closed her eyes and struggled to breathe.

"Stop now!" Junebug ordered from up in the loft. They jerked apart, staring at one another guiltily.

"I'm sleepy," Junebug yawned, "and I don't want to miss any of the ball. Close the book."

Oh, the book. Maddy took a shaky breath. She noticed Kit's hands were none too steady as he did as Junebug instructed and closed the book.

"I hope there's a good battle after this ball," Junebug muttered. Merle barked. And then there was the sound of the quilt rustling as the two of them settled in for the night.

Maddy and Kit sat frozen until they heard her breathing deepen.

"Another whiskey?" he suggested eventually.

Maddy nodded gratefully. Her nerves needed it.

The air felt charged, like a lightning storm was gathering. Maddy could feel every inch of her body.

"You know what you said that night?" Kit said, his voice slow and thick. There was the sound of whiskey splashing into their mugs. "About me being . . . beautiful . . ." He sounded embarrassed. He gave a startled laugh and resumed. "You got no idea what you do to me," he said. "You're the most beautiful thing I've ever seen in my life."

"Me?" She didn't believe it. She was just Maddy Mooney. Once she'd believed Tom Ormond's compliments, but she wasn't that silly girl anymore. She wasn't beautiful, and she wasn't a goddess. She wasn't ugly either. But she was just Maddy, nothing more, nothing less.

But Kit McBride was staring at her, utterly sincere.

Which was mad, because *he* really was beautiful. One of the world's special people, as Mrs. Egan would say. He was made for someone like Willabelle, someone who looked like a perfect china doll. Not for the likes of her.

Maddy knew this couldn't last. Her leg was healing, and she'd get on that train, back to her life as a maid.

But now, tonight, she was here in this snowed-in cabin in the wilds, being stared at by a man who thought she was a beautiful, fancy lady. For now, she was answering to a name that wasn't hers. So why not enjoy the stolen magic? Let the mists lure her to the plain of joy . . .

"Kit," she said, feeling the shimmering magic tinge with melancholy. Everything was embedded with the loss to come.

He cocked his head, confused by her urgency.

"Kit." She reached out and took the sleeve of his pine-needle-green sweater between her fingers. "Kiss me?"

He was stunned. Frozen.

"Please . . ." She pulled on his sleeve.

The wait was painfully long, even though it took barely a heartbeat. Kit fell toward her, a soft breath escaping him. He took her face in his hands and stared at her, his expression torn between so many emotions that she couldn't read him.

"You're sure?" he breathed.

"Oh God, hurry up." She grabbed a fistful of his sweater and pulled him to her. Forget waiting for him to kiss her; she'd kiss him.

His hands slid into her hair as she kissed him; his lips were soft under hers. He was inexpert; inexperienced. Enthusiastic. Maddy pressed against him, opening her mouth, deepening the kiss. He groaned. Maddy felt a thrill of power as she realized she was the one in control. She slid her tongue along his inner lip. His hands tightened in her hair.

Jesus, Mary and Joseph, what was happening? Maddy lost herself in his kiss. His lips were firm, seeking. She melted into him.

"Oh God. Willabelle . . ."

The name splashed over Maddy like icy water. She jerked away, breaking the kiss. Oh, she was such an eejit.

Twenty

They woke to silence. Total muffled silence. The cabin was pitch-black, but they could tell something had changed.

"The storm's blown itself out!" Junebug flung herself down the ladder of her loft, all but exploding with joy. She'd spent the night up there, sleeping in her own bed.

Maddy and Kit had fallen asleep together, on Maddy's narrow bed. Eejit that she was, Maddy had succumbed to the pleasure of kissing Kit and had let him call her Willabelle, even though it cut her to the quick every time he said it. At some point, Kit had turned the lamp out, and the night had passed in the slow ecstasy of kissing, tongues sliding, the warmth of their bodies pressed together in the darkness. Ever cautious of her healing leg, he'd sprawled alongside her, on her good side, his hand playing with her hair as he kissed her.

He was clearly new to kissing, but he was a quick study, and keen. He drove Maddy wild, but never progressed beyond kissing. She knew he was aroused; she could feel the press of him against her, but his hands never wandered. She would have let them, if they had. But he seemed to revel in the languid sensation of simply kissing. All. Night. Long.

It was a delirium. She felt ravished, even though he'd kept his hands to himself.

When Junebug woke them, they were still pressed together, having slid into sleep only an hour or so before. She didn't blink an eye at the fact that they were in the same bed; she was too excited that the storm had abated.

"Sunshine!" Junebug threw open the door, revealing a flood of sparkling white light. She laughed. "We're free!" She pulled her boots on and scampered out.

"Good morning," Kit whispered to Maddy. His lips were pressed to her neck. He kissed her gently, trailing up to her ear. Maddy shivered. Oh Lord, that felt good.

He claimed her mouth again, his tongue slipping into her.

Merle set to barking up in the loft, and Kit groaned. "Really?" He looked up. "She couldn't have taken the dog with her?"

"Kit! It's a blue-sky day!" Junebug tumbled back in. "Come on, let's go see how Thunderhead Bill and Roy are holding up!"

"What about Willabelle?" Kit asked, sitting up. He gave Maddy a rueful look, and Maddy felt a wave of disappointment as the spell broke.

She hated hearing that name come out of his mouth.

"Bring her!" Junebug raced up to get Merle and to get properly dressed for the cold. "We can cart her about on the sled if her leg don't hold up."

Kit lifted Maddy's hand to his mouth and pressed a kiss to her palm. "I'll go dig us out," he said. His dark eyes shone. "Don't go anywhere."

Maddy considered all her borrowed clothes and then looked at the turquoise dress, still hanging from the peg, as she listened to the cut and scrape of Kit's and Junebug's shovels in the snow.

Junebug chattered away a mile a minute as they cleared the snow from the porch and the windows. Maddy felt an absurd urge to pretty herself up. She pulled the stained, but well and truly dry, turquoise dress over her long underwear. She left Kit's buttery-soft flannel shirt on the bed but wore the giant cardigan. She found a pair of thick wool socks in the trunk to pull over her bare feet, and a wool hat to keep her head warm. Her black boots were in her carpetbag. The swelling had gone down on her leg, so she fit into her boots again.

When she was done, she sat patiently on the bed, waiting for Kit to come back for her. Her lips were swollen from all the kissing, and she had stubble rash on her cheeks from his day-old beard. If he took to kissing that well, imagine what he'd be like at the rest of it . . .

Shame she'd never get to find out.

But she wouldn't think of that now. She'd enjoy herself while she could.

When Kit came back, he was red cheeked and smiling. "It's a beautiful day out there," he told her, scooping her up off the bed.

"I can walk!" she protested.

"I'll get you past the icy bit," he said. "Junebug'll salt the porch so you don't slip. The last thing we want is you spraining your leg again."

Although, if she did, she could stay longer, Maddy thought longingly. She never would have thought she'd like it out here in the wilds, but she did. She couldn't think of anywhere else she'd rather be. Maddy nuzzled into him, wrapping her arms around his neck.

He laughed. "Careful or I won't be able to resist staying in."

Maddy was tempted to test that. But then Junebug called out to them. That kid wouldn't give them a minute's peace now that she was up and bouncing around.

Maddy squinted as Kit carried her out to the porch and climbed the steps he'd cut into the snow. They emerged into the daylight. Bright splashing sunshine caught the crystals in the thick crust of snow, glittering and glistening. Icicles speared from the firs in the forest and flashed, their hearts as clear as glass. The sky was a pure blue dome above them, and everything shone as though it had been spit polished.

Maddy laughed. "I almost forgot what sunshine looked like!"

"Hey!" Junebug called. Kit turned, and Maddy caught a snowball in the face. She squealed and Junebug howled with glee.

Merle tried to run toward them and tumbled into a deep snowdrift. Junebug fished him out as he yapped up a storm.

The snowy meadow was filled with birdsong. The creek was iced over but making a wet rushing noise as the ice cracked and melted.

"There's so much snow you can barely see the trading post," Maddy observed as she brushed snow off her face. Her breath plumed white as frost in the air in front of her.

"Let's make sure Bill and Roy haven't suffocated under there and turned into ghosts!" Junebug plowed through the snow, hip deep in powder.

"Wear the snowshoes!" Kit called after her, but she didn't listen. "She's going to be soaked through," he sighed. "I'd best go after her with them, or she'll end up buried."

"I can sit up here and wait for you," Maddy said.

"Sit where?"

Oh. That was the question. "Maybe you could bring the porch chair out here into the sun?" she suggested sweetly.

"Only if you ask nicely." He grinned.

"That wasn't nice?"

"I reckon you could ask nicer . . ."

She laughed. "Please?"

"Maybe."

"Maybe?"

"I'll do it for a kiss."

She laughed at the cheeky glint in his eye. "Only one?" She

pulled him down to her and kissed him. He sucked at her lower lip and she quivered.

After a fair bit more kissing, he set her up on the chair in the sun and went wading through the powdery snow after Junebug. The chair sank down into the snow, leaving Maddy's leg even with the surface. It was handy. She merely had to stretch her leg out in front of her, and the snow cradled her stiff leg.

Oh, the sunshine felt good. She'd practically turned into a mushroom, locked down there in the dark for all those days. But for all that, Maddy mused, they might have been the happiest days of her life . . .

Laughing with Morgan and Junebug as Kit snored; brushing Junebug's hair; listening to Kit read *Vanity Fair*; kissing . . .

Across the meadow, she could see Kit emerge from the trading post with a shovel. He waved to her and she waved back. She watched as he set to digging the trading post out from the mountain of snow. He worked solidly, strong as an ox, clearing off the porch and digging out the windows.

She could hear the cows lowing in the barn and the whicker of the horses. She guessed he'd be going there next. Maddy wished she were completely healed so she could lend him a hand. She was almost as strong as an ox herself, after years of labor. She bet she could wield a pretty mean shovel. Maybe in the next couple of days she could be of more use . . .

The crust of snow softened under the sun, and Maddy felt her chair sinking more as the day burned on. Junebug and Merle followed Kit to the barn, disappearing under the snow a few times as they thrashed through the deep drifts. Thunderhead Bill and Roy emerged onto the porch down at the trading post. They waved; Maddy waved back.

It was late morning when Maddy thought she heard the jingle of bells. She strained to hear. Definitely bells. A steady, musical jingling.

It was a sleigh!

She saw it glide from the tree line at the far side of the meadow, the high-stepping horses navigating the snow with elegance. It was disconcerting to see people after all this time secluded up here.

"Someone's coming," she called in the direction of the barn, hoping her voice would carry through the clear air.

She squinted, trying to see the sleigh better. It was large, and full of people. There was a brilliant flash of red, the color of a robin's breast.

Maddy felt like the chair had slid out from under her.

No. Surely not. Surely, surely not.

But of course it was. Because, like her mam had always said, she was born under unlucky stars.

There, in the front seat of the sleigh, brilliant in a robin's-breast-red coat and a fur hat, was Willabelle Lascalles. And next to her, driving the sleigh and scowling something fierce, was Morgan. Behind them, Sour Eagle was squashed in between two more McBride-looking men. That could only be Beau and Jonah, although there was no sign of the doctor they'd been sent to fetch.

Well, the banshee hadn't claimed them, at least. That would relieve Junebug.

It didn't relieve Maddy. She had a sinking feeling the banshee might have been wailing for *her*.

Maddy wasn't going to wait to be humiliated. She was going to bite the bullet and own up to the mess. Her heart was stumbling and staggering at the sight of Willabelle. She couldn't abide that woman.

"Kit," she called as she watched the sleigh slide across the far meadow, headed for the trading post.

Kit and Junebug had poked out of the barn when she'd called the first time. Curious, they were fighting through the snow to get to the top of the rise to see who was riding in. Junebug's elbows were flapping like a duck landing on a pond. Maddy could see how charged up she was. And no wonder, she'd been beside herself waiting for news of Morgan, Beau and Jonah. Swallowing hard and screwing up her courage, Maddy gestured for Kit to come and join her. She couldn't risk him speaking to Willabelle before she could tell him. She could only imagine the horror . . .

"Who's that?" Junebug hollered. "Is it them?"

"Yes!" Maddy yelled over, trying to sound bright. "Why don't you go down and meet them?" She didn't need Junebug here while she told him. It was going to be hard enough as it was.

Junebug didn't need telling twice. She and Merle went galloping through the snow at full tilt.

Kit slogged uphill to Maddy. "He found Beau and Jonah, huh?" He was grinning from ear to ear.

Maddy's stomach curdled. The bright and glittering day now seemed overbright and blinding. She wished she could run away and hide.

But she liked Kit too much for that.

"Kit," she said, bunching the turquoise skirt of Willabelle's dress in her fists. Her palms had broken out in a cold sweat. Down the meadow, she could see the merry red of Willabelle's coat approaching.

"There's something I have to tell you," she said thickly.

He stuck the shovel in the snow and leaned on it. "Oh yeah?" He was staring at the sleigh too. The grin was slowly replaced by a furrowed brow. "Who's that they got with them?"

"That's what I want to talk to you about." Do it fast, she told herself. Quick, before you lose your nerve. "That's Willabelle Lascalles."

"Huh?" He frowned.

"That. Down there, in the sleigh, next to Morgan. In the red coat . . ." She swallowed hard. "That's Willabelle Lascalles."

There was an interminable pause, and then he shook his head. "I don't understand."

Maddy nodded toward the sleigh, which was pulling up in front of the trading post. Junebug was skidding down the hill toward it. "That's the woman who answered Junebug's ad."

He put his hands on his hips and stared. Straight at the woman in red sitting in the sleigh. Then at Maddy. He was frowning hard. Lord, it made him seem fierce. "But *you're* Willabelle Lascalles."

She shook her head miserably. She should never have let Junebug talk her into going along with this. It hadn't been as simple as answering to Willabelle's name . . . Not least because Maddy had gone and tumbled headlong in love with the man. The man *Willabelle* was supposed to marry. "I'm not Willabelle Lascalles," she said quietly.

"You're not Willabelle Lascalles," he repeated, still frowning. He shook his head. "But you *are*."

She took a deep breath. Oh, she hated this. "No. I'm Maddy Mooney," she said. She felt the hot prickle of tears rising. The look on his face. It made her feel sick about herself.

"Maddy . . . ?"

"Mooney. Maddy Mooney from Crinkle, in county Offaly in Ireland. Not Willabelle Lascalles from St. Louis. That's Willabelle down there, in the red." Maddy was trembling. She might as well admit to everything. "I'm her maid," she said numbly. "*Was* her maid." She bit her lip. "Do you remember that day at the hotel, when you knocked me into the mud?"

He was silent.

"I was fetching water for her laundry. That's what I do, I do laundry, and draw baths, and clean, and black fireplaces."

"You weren't fetching water, you were crying," he corrected her.

Yes. She had been. Because being Willabelle's maid was a torment. Oh, how to explain it! She glanced down at the trading post. Willabelle was standing up in the sleigh, her coat bright as holly berries, pointing up at the cabin, at Maddy. They were all looking up at her. Maddy met Kit's gaze. She felt wretched.

"I brought you flowers," he said, all consternated. "That day I knocked you into the puddle. I went and picked roses and wall-flowers and gave them to Alice Champion to give to you. I didn't know your name, I just told Alice to give them to the girl with eyes like harebells." He rubbed his face, scratching at his blue-black stubble. "I don't rightly understand what's happening here." He seemed to be struggling to put a feeling into words.

Maddy was stunned. The flowers had been for her? Oh. *Oh.* That was the day she'd thought Thunderhead Bill had been a Mc-Bride. Mrs. Champion had told her the flowers had been from Kit McBride . . .

This Kit McBride, not Thunderhead Bill . . .

And they'd been for *Maddy.*

He hadn't even known Willabelle Lascalles existed then.

He'd *still* never met her . . .

Well, he was about to, she thought miserably. And if he was like any other man on earth, he was about to lose his wits.

"I . . . I didn't mean to lie to you," she stammered. "Everything just got so messy."

He was still frowning. "You're not Willabelle, you're Maddy Mooney, the maid," he said slowly. "So, you never answered the ad? To be my wife?"

"No." Maddy felt time slipping away from them. Willabelle was sitting back down in the sleigh as Morgan took up the reins. They were coming up here. "I didn't answer the ad. *She* did."

Kit turned to watch the sleigh approach. "Does she know it was Junebug, not me?"

"I doubt it," Maddy said honestly.

"So . . . she thinks she's here to marry me."

"I guess so." Maddy felt a surge of despair. She wondered what had happened with Garrett, and why Willabelle had changed her mind. Knowing Willabelle, it had something to do with money.

"And you're her maid," Kit said tightly.

She nodded, unable to meet his eye.

"Goddamn it." He threw the shovel. It went flopping into the snow, sending clumps of powder skittering down the hill.

Maddy felt about an inch tall.

Kit swore. "You're her *maid?*"

She flushed and her chin went up. She wasn't going to be shamed for having to work. She earned a good honest living. Well, she would have earned a good honest living if Willabelle had *paid* her. "I work hard," she told him stiffly.

Kit rubbed his face. "Who's she, then? This Willabelle Lascalles? She a widow, or was all that a lie too? Like everything else."

Like everything else.

"Not everything was a lie." Maddy felt her throat grow tight.

"No," he said flatly. "Just the important stuff."

Maddy flushed. No. Just her name. And the mail-order bride bit. Everything else between them was real—and important.

"I ain't marrying her," Kit snapped.

"I should hope not!" That came out without her thinking about it. Maddy turned bright red as he shot her a look.

"You lied to me." He sounded grim.

She had. And it had ruined everything. He'd given flowers to *her*, Maddy Mooney. If she hadn't been so scared of Morgan, if she hadn't put her foot down that rabbit hole, if she'd been able to talk sensibly and introduced herself from the start, who knew what would have happened . . . because the lightning storm that kicked up between them whenever they touched suggested things would have ignited no matter what. But it would have been clean, and honest, and not a horrid nasty mess.

The sleigh came jingling up the slope, approaching like doom.

"Kit," she said, a touch desperately, hoping to hold off the inevitable.

"You let me call you by her name," he said, horrified. "You let me make a complete fool of myself."

"Not a fool . . ."

The bells jangled louder.

Kit glanced at the sleigh, and she could see the ruddy shame creeping up his neck. There would be witnesses to his foolishness, that's what he was thinking. She knew him well enough to know that. Sour Eagle and the boys had stayed down at the trading post, at least. Three fewer people to witness his sense of humiliation. Maddy could see Junebug standing behind Willabelle, pulling panicked faces.

"Did *Junebug* know?" Kit's horror was profound.

It was pretty clear that Junebug knew enough. She was miming strangling Willabelle behind her back.

Kit's anger turned to suppressed white fury. "She did, didn't she? The two of you have been laughing at me all along."

Maddy would have argued, only now Junebug was giving Maddy mimed instructions to push Willabelle under the runners of the sleigh.

There was no point having this conversation now, Maddy thought dully. He was too upset, and Willabelle was almost upon them. She resigned herself to the unpleasantness. After all, she couldn't feel worse than she did at this moment.

Or so she thought.

Willabelle was on the attack from the first. She exploded from the sleigh in a swirl of scarlet. "Madeleine Moore!"

The silly parrot didn't get *any* of her names right this time. "Maddy," Maddy corrected, feeling exhausted before it even began. "Maddy *Mooney*."

"This woman is my maid!" Willabelle declared, thrusting an accusing finger in Maddy's face. She was relishing the drama.

Maddy flushed, painfully aware of the audience.

Junebug swore, and not quietly; Morgan was stone-faced; and Kit . . . Kit was her judge and jury, she thought miserably. And he knew she was guilty.

"She's a deceivious woman," Willabelle cried. "An imposter!"

"*Deceivious* ain't a word," Junebug told her, dropping down from the sleigh. She moved to stand next to Maddy. Maddy found her presence strangely comforting, even though she was only a little bit of a thing.

Willabelle met Maddy's gaze. Her china-blue eyes were twinkling. She was actually *enjoying* this.

"I thought you found greener pastures," Maddy said quietly so Morgan and Kit couldn't hear.

Willabelle's eyebrow arched. "It didn't work out," she murmured. Then she pivoted to consider Kit, who was watching them like they were a nest full of snakes. Her entire demeanor shifted as she approached him. Maddy felt a grim satisfaction in the way she sank into the snow. She surely wouldn't be cleaning the hem of that coat.

"You're Kit McBride?" Willabelle breathed as she took him in. "The blacksmith?"

Maddy felt her stomach sink to her toes as she saw what Willabelle was seeing: the shoulders, the jawline so sharply defined it seemed outlined in ink, the sheer powerful masculinity . . . those liquid dark eyes. Her stomach scrunched as she saw him examine her in return. She heard Junebug swear under her breath.

"I want to apologize to you, Mr. McBride," Willabelle said in that same breathy voice. She put a hand on his arm.

Get your hands off him, Maddy thought furiously.

Kit was still seething. He shot Maddy a dark look.

"Your brother explained the fix to me as we rode up from Bitterroot," Willabelle sighed, sounding deeply regretful. "It's all such a muddle, isn't it?" She swayed closer.

"Bet you'd like to push her into a snowdrift," Junebug whispered.

"Why don't we sit down over a hot cup of coffee and work out what we do from here?" Willabelle suggested, her fingers stroking his arm.

Yes, Maddy wished very much she could push her into a snowdrift. Hard.

"That seems wise," Morgan chipped in from the sleigh. "Let's all go down to the trading post and work out what's what. I'm sure Beau and Jonah have brewed up a pot by now."

"Shall we?" Willabelle asked Kit.

Maddy went hot and cold as he met her eye. He didn't say a word, but he took his place in the sleigh.

"Not you," Willabelle told Maddy softly as she passed. "You've done enough, don't you think?"

The outrage was so keen Maddy was speechless. The nerve of the woman! Maddy was only here *because* of Willabelle. The stupid parrot had *gifted* him to Maddy! Like he was hers to give—which he most certainly wasn't.

"Come on, Bug," Morgan called as they all settled in.

"It'll be a cold day in hell before I go anywhere with that woman," Junebug hissed. Scowling, she clomped toward the cabin, muttering about goshawks and blockheads.

Maddy found herself left on the hill, shivering, as the sleigh slid over the glittering meadow to the trading post. Kit never once looked back.

"Well, that was bad," Junebug said. She was sitting bent over her ledger, scrawling a long complaint to Kit.

Maddy couldn't seem to stop crying. By the time she'd navigated her way inside, almost killing herself on the porch, which Junebug had never got around to salting, she was frozen through and completely miserable. She crawled under the quilt and tried to pull herself together. It wasn't working. She kept seeing the look in Kit's eyes: the flatness, the humiliation. The hurt.

They were alone in the cabin. The windows were thrown wide to air the place out, and Maddy blew dragon clouds as she cried. The cabin had lost its magic. It smelled of old potatoes and cooked beef, wood ash and musty bodies. And dog. Through the porch window, Maddy had a clear view across the meadow to the trading post, which had been dug out of its snowdrift. She could see them all sitting out on the trading post porch, gathered around Willabelle in her red coat.

Except for Kit. He was a hulking shadow at the far edge of the group. Even from here she could tell he was brooding.

"Look at Roy and Thunderhead Bill getting in on the fawning," Junebug complained, following Maddy's gaze out the window. "It's a sorry state of affairs, that's for sure. They're like moths to a flame. Don't none of them ever pay attention to what happens to moths when they get ahold of the flame?"

"I should never have let them think I was her," Maddy said flatly. She'd known it was wrong, and it only got more wrong as she and Kit . . . got tangled up.

"It was definitely the wrong move." Junebug turned back to her complaints book. "How do you spell *ignoramus?*"

"Wrong move!" Maddy reared up. "It was *your* idea!"

"Well, how was I to know that you'd go and get Kit all in love with you! If I'da known *that*, I would have given him your real name!"

"*You're* the one who wanted me to get one of them in love with me," Maddy raged. "Don't act all innocent. 'Which one?' That's what you kept saying. *Which one?* You bet that I wouldn't be getting on that train," she reminded Junebug.

"I think we can agree," Junebug said, striving for calm, "that we're both to blame here."

"How am *I* to blame? I turned up here and hurt my leg. It was all you mad McBrides who went around thinking I was *her*. I never said I was her! In fact, I told you I wasn't!"

Junebug slammed the ledger closed. "You answered to the name," she said sharply. "And you know it. So, you can stop blaming me and start owning up to it. So, things didn't work out the way we planned—"

"The way *we* planned! *I* didn't plan anything, except to get on a train out of here!"

"Maddy Mooney!" Junebug was outraged. "You cain't still be thinking of trains!"

Maddy blinked, surprised. "Of course I am! You promised me a ticket . . ."

Junebug looked to be considering throwing the ledger at her. "You cain't leave now!"

"And why not? I did what you wanted, didn't I? I answered to her name. That's my part of the deal done."

Junebug gaped at her. "But you *cain't*!"

"You keep saying that, but you haven't said why I *cain't*."

"Because you love him, you big blockhead!" Junebug glared at Maddy. "You're kicked-in-the-head, stupid in love with my brother! And he's kicked-in-the-head, stupid in love with you."

Maddy stared at her. Then she glowered. "That's not how love works!"

"Clearly it is. You two are so daft for each other you don't even see how sickeningly lovey-dovey you are. Rubbing his feet like that." Junebug mimed Maddy sappily rubbing Kit's feet.

"Because he had frostnip!"

"Did he have frostnip on his lips too? Is that why you spent all night smooching him?"

Maddy's mouth opened and closed like a bull trout.

"Now, maybe in Ireland, they give up on love easily," Junebug railed, "but that ain't how we do it in Montana. At least not here in Buck's Creek, anyway."

"You get a lot of love around here, do you?" Maddy goaded her.

"You and Kit are the first," Junebug admitted. "But that means you got a responsibility to set the standard. You better not set some giving-up kind of standard, Maddy the Maid."

"Don't call me that," Maddy snapped. "I'm no one's maid."

"That's the spirit!" Junebug jumped to her feet. "Let's fix you up and go barge in on that high tea down there."

"Junebug," Maddy groaned. "I don't want to go through it again." She didn't want to see that look in Kit's eyes. Just the thought of it made her feel sick.

"Oh. *Pffft*. It won't happen again. It's already done with." Junebug cocked her head. "Now fix yourself up. We need you to be able to compete with the goshawk."

"I can't compete with Willabelle Lascalles. Have you seen her?"

"I've seen her dresses," Junebug said slyly. "The trunks are still piled up in the sleigh—I could go get you some clothes. Don't she owe you money?"

"Well, yes."

"How much did she owe you?" Junebug asked.

"Twenty-eight dollars."

"I figure some appropriate undergarments should be thrown in, then, too."

"I can't!"

"Maddy!" Junebug stomped her foot. "I hate that goshawk and I won't have her join my family, you hear? *You*, on the other hand, I want to keep." She threw herself onto the bed and took Maddy by the shoulders. "Kit is my favorite brother, and he loves you. You don't fulfill any of my requirements: you cain't bake, you cain't complain in written form, you cain't use your wiles to save your life. But that blockhead loves you. So, you're going to let me lace you into a corset and cram you into one of that goshawk's fancy dresses. Then you're going to let me drag you down to that trading post on my sled, and you're going to give that goshawk some stiff competition."

Maddy took a deep breath. Then she nodded. Something had sparked inside her at Junebug's words. This wasn't Ormond House. She wasn't Maddy the Maid. She was Maddy Mooney, the woman Kit McBride loved. Even if he was too naive to know it yet.

She watched from the window, breathless, as Junebug took a winding route around the meadow, keeping out of sight, thrashing through the slushy snow toward the sleigh, which Morgan had pulled up behind the trading post. Maddy kept an eye on the porch, making sure no one made a move to the sleigh, and prepared to whistle if they did. A buzz of excitement was building in her belly at the thought of taking control of the situation instead of being victim to it. By the time Junebug came back, arms loaded, Maddy was feeling ready for the fight. So to speak.

Junebug dumped her haul on the bed next to Maddy. "Let's see your shoulders," she said.

"What?" Maddy was discombobulated by the change of tack.

"Your shoulders," Junebug insisted. "It's high time you learned how to use your wiles. And this dress is asking for some wily shoulders."

Twenty-One

Kit was gobsmacked by the woman Junebug had chosen to be his wife. It was as though she'd picked every trait he disliked in a person and put them in a single body.

Willabelle Lascalles was vain, showy, manipulative and self-focused. She flirted indiscriminately and she had cold eyes.

His brothers didn't seem to share his distaste. Beau and Jonah were tripping over each other to get her attention. The two of them were dressed up like eastern city folk, their hair pomaded and their pale faces mostly bare, except for some ridiculous attempts at sculpted mustaches and muttonchops. They'd clearly spent some time in Bitterroot making themselves pretty. All while Kit and Morgan had been fretting over their safety, Kit thought in disgust. Morgan himself hung back, tongue-tied and awkward, uncomfortable with the woman's sly sideways looks and bright charm.

Willabelle's bright charm, he corrected.

The clouds were gathering again, shredding the sunlight. Kit glanced up at the cabin, where Maddy was. She'd been white as a ghost when they left.

It had been a nasty scene. Willabelle had humiliated her. Mercilessly. All while playing the victim, Kit thought with distaste. And
once they'd got back to the porch, she'd told a convoluted and
hard-to-follow narrative about how Maddy had gone and be-
trayed her.

Maddy wasn't a liar. He remembered her bluntness as they
watched the sleigh come up the hill. She'd admitted it all. And Kit
knew his little sister—he was sure as hell Junebug had something
to do with this whole mess.

He remembered Junebug miming strangling Willabelle. And
then he remembered Junebug nervy at the hotel about meeting
"the fancy lady." Junebug *definitely* had a lot to do with this. And
the minute he got her alone, Kit was going to find out what she
was up to.

Maddy had looked practiced at being railed at, Kit thought as
he stared up at the cabin. That was the thing that bothered him
most. She'd been resigned. And there was a contained dignity to
the way she stood there, like she could withstand whatever nasti-
ness people threw at her, without so much as a flicker of emotion.

Goddamn, he thought. He didn't have the slightest idea about
her. Who she was. Where she came from.

Except that her mother's hands smelled of potato starch and
milk, he remembered. And she'd had brothers and sisters once, but
no more. And she'd come all the way from Ireland across the At-
lantic Ocean on a ship bound for New York. He remembered her
stories of New York and St. Louis as she'd tried to distract Junebug
from her worries about the banshee. That had been real enough.

Then there were her stories of that big house she lived in . . . the
formal gardens and big rooms, the festive dinners and tea parties . . .

She'd been *a maid* there. But she'd still been there.

Abruptly, Kit realized that he knew a lot about her.

Like the fact that she was calm and careful; that she watched
people, following their movements with her beautiful blue eyes;

that she was kind; that she loved a good cup of tea; that her hair was like silk and her lips were like strawberries. That when she laughed it was like the sun coming out from behind a cloud on a wretched day.

He remembered her bent over that water pump in Bitterroot, weeping fit to burst.

What had made her cry like that? This woman? This Willabelle Lascalles? Or something else?

"You not joining the rest of them?" Thunderhead Bill asked, pulling Kit out of his reverie. Bill was reclining on the porch rocker, chewing tobacco. He was the only one still on the porch, Kit realized in shock. Kit had been so deep in thought that he hadn't noticed the rest of them going inside.

"I'm getting as much outside time as I can, while I can," Bill confided, putting his feet up on the railing and taking a deep breath of alpine air. "Storm'll be back tonight. See the birds? They know." His jaw worked at the tobacco. Kit knew he'd pulled it from the jar inside. He'd probably written his name in the accounts book, too, but Kit didn't believe they'd ever see a dime for the chew of tobacco. Or any of the things Bill had his name down for in that book.

He was probably right about the storm, Kit thought. There were thunderheads building down the valley. He frowned. How the hell were they going to manage the sleeping arrangements? There were enough people here to fill a dance hall.

He'd best talk to Morgan.

"Kit?" Thunderhead Bill stopped him on the way in. "You're a young buck. And young bucks can be bullheaded." His bushy eyebrows drew together, and he fixed Kit with a paternal gaze. "Take some advice from one of the bachelor group: sparks don't come along every day."

Sparks? What in hell was the old coot talking about?

"When you're young, you think there's limitless beguilement

to be had," Bill sighed, his great shaggy head shaking sadly. "You squander those sparks, when you should hoard them."

"You been at the moonshine, Bill?"

"Moonshine!" Thunderhead Bill was outraged. "Listen up, you idiot, this is wise advice. I wish I'd had someone giving me advice like this when I was your age. Don't waste time squabbling over who went by what name. Just take those sparks and enjoy the hell out of them."

"Right." Kit managed not to roll his eyes. "Enjoy the sparks. Good advice."

"You're welcome." Bill sat back in his chair and turned to the sunlit mountains.

Honestly, it was time these crazy old trappers moved on. They were supposed to be out of here last summer, Kit sighed as he left Bill to chomping on his tobacco.

Inside the trading post it was a veritable cotillion. Willabelle Lascalles was seated by the stove, with them all gathered around her. She'd removed her red coat and fur hat and had arranged herself to full advantage. She was wearing a dress the color of sunset. It had a very low square neckline, and her large white breasts were straining at the beribboned collar. Her pile of blond curls was tumbled from the hat, giving her a blowsy, just-crawled-out-of-bed look.

Roy was hovering behind her, peering over her shoulder at her bosom. Every other man in the room was politely trying to avoid staring as crassly as Roy was, and failing miserably. Mrs. Lascalles was wittering on about silver mining, but no one was listening. They all seemed dazed, like someone had whacked them over the head with a shovel.

"You seen the clouds building down the valley toward Bitterroot?" Kit asked Morgan. "Bill reckons we're in for another blow."

Morgan frowned, only just managing to tear his gaze away from Mrs. Lascalles's breasts. "Not another one."

"Looks like it."

Morgan swore. "Rigby said he heard the storm wiped out Harry Eckhardt's entire herd. I reckon he wouldn't be the only one."

"Where the hell are we going to keep everyone?" Kit asked.

"The maid," Morgan blurted.

"Exactly." Kit rubbed his face, feeling tired. Maddy was exactly who he was thinking of. Where were they going to put Maddy, and Willabelle? He didn't fancy locking them in together in the cabin . . .

"No," Morgan said dumbly. "*The maid.*" He nodded at the doorway.

Kit turned and his whole body grew heavy as lead.

Maddy was in the doorway. And, hell, if she wasn't the best-looking woman he'd ever seen. He'd thought she looked good in his old flannel shirt, and in that shiny dress . . . damnation, he'd even thought she was a picture covered in mud in that ugly black dress back in Bitterroot . . . but *this* . . .

She was startling. Vivid. Her skin was pale against the dramatic blue of the dress and the sooty darkness of her hair, which was braided and wound around her head like a crown. Junebug had braided it, Kit guessed, because it was missing bits, just like her knitting. Maddy's eyes blazed like the bright bluebird day, and her elegant neck led down to shoulders that looked like they'd been sculpted from marble. The neckline of her dress draped like bunting across the swell of her chest.

"That's my dress!" Willabelle Lascalles was outraged, rustling angrily in her chair.

"Not anymore," Maddy said calmly. She met Kit's gaze. "It's only what I'm owed."

"This one isn't yours anymore either; I'm owed too." Junebug came gliding into the room, slipping past Maddy, resplendent in a crimson dress trimmed in black fur. She was grinning from ear to ear.

"Junebug!" Morgan was confounded.

"*Junebug?*" Kit wouldn't have recognized his little sister. Hell, she wasn't so little! She was cinched into a corset and buttoned into a dress so grown-up that she looked eighteen or more. She'd scrubbed her face until it glowed, and tied a fancy bonnet over her shorn hair.

"Take that off, this instant!" Willabelle Lascalles ordered. "That dress is *Parisian*."

"Well, *ooh la la*," Junebug said. She did a twirl, showing off her figure in the tightly cinched dress. And then she glided toward the knot of people by the stove, as graceful as a swallow in flight. "Do you know, Miss Mooney," she said, her voice musical and cultured as all hell, "I believe it's teatime, don't you?"

"Why yes, Miss McBride, I believe it is."

Kit was transfixed as Maddy unfurled a white lace fan and gave it a gentle flutter. It drew his attention to the sweet swell of her breasts over the neckline of her gown.

"Don't get up," Junebug cooed to Beau and Jonah, both of whom were thunderstruck. "I'll make the tea."

"What have you done to yourself?" Jonah scowled. "And since when do we have tea?"

"Forget the tea," Beau snapped. "What's all this?" He gestured at her getup.

Junebug fluttered her eyelashes at him. "I've been having lessons."

"Damn lady lessons," Kit growled at Morgan. "What in hell were you thinking?"

"I don't know, but whatever it was, it was dumb." Morgan had gone as white as bleached flour.

"Beauregard, where are your manners?" Junebug chided her older brother, tapping him on the shoulder. "There's a lady here without a chair."

"Just 'cause you're wearing a dress don't make you a lady," Beau said, disgruntled.

But it did. Somehow Junebug was completely transformed. She gave a tinkling laugh. "Not me, silly. Miss Mooney."

Miss Mooney. Kit felt his heart squeeze as he watched her glide across the room and sink gracefully into Beau's swiftly vacated seat. Not just his heart was squeezing. All the rest of him was getting in on the act too.

He felt like he'd had a lick of moonshine. The world was wobbly and out of whack.

It only got wobblier as he watched Junebug sit daintily with the other ladies, holding one of their beat-up old mugs like it was fine china, her little finger crooked in the air.

Willabelle Lascalles was fuming, Kit could see, but she didn't know how to combat Junebug and Maddy now that they were wielding fine manners at her.

"Hasn't the weather been simply ghastly?" Junebug observed mildly.

There was a long silence.

Kit swore he saw the flicker of a smile on Maddy's strawberry lips. She lowered her head to sip the tea. Which was a very good brew, Kit had to admit. It might have been the best-tasting thing Junebug had ever made.

"Indeed. Simply ghastly," Kit said dryly.

Maddy Mooney darted a glance at him. Her eyes were bluer than ever, their color magnified by the shade of the dress. God, she was beautiful.

"I do so *abhor* a storm," Junebug simpered.

"I don't like this," Morgan whispered to Kit. "It ain't natural."

"No," Kit agreed, feeling his heart thundering like it was fit to burst right out of his chest. He could see Maddy's pulse leaping in the hollow of her throat. He had a vision of kissing her there, and feeling the leap against his lips.

"We're in trouble," Morgan said grimly. "We could barely manage her the way she was. How in the hell are we going to manage *now*?"

"I don't know," Kit said. He didn't know much of anything anymore.

———

"How *dare* you!" Willabelle raged, the minute the three of them were alone in the cabin. "How dare both of you! Get those gowns off this minute."

"No." Junebug did an ostentatious glide across the room. "It was such a living hell to get laced into this bear trap, I ain't getting out until I've had my fill." She dug her fingers down inside the bodice. "Though that might not be long. This thing hurts like a bitch. How do y'all wear corsets all the time? I'da thrown it in the fire the first time I took it off."

Maddy had no intention of removing her gown either.

"You're nothing but thieves," Willabelle complained.

"I didn't take it, you ninny. I only borrowed it." Junebug rolled her eyes.

Willabelle huffed. "You've gone and dirtied the hem."

"So have you. You can't take a step around here without dirtying a hem. That's why I wear overalls." Junebug paused. "Well, that and the fact that I don't own a dress . . ."

"Why are you here, Willabelle?" Maddy asked. She felt as cold and sharp as an icicle. The dress helped. Junebug was right. Putting it on had restored something of Maddy's fight. And her dignity.

"To get married," she said innocently. "Lord, Madeleine, your mind is like a sieve. Don't you remember we came here for the purpose of matrimony?"

Jesus, Mary and Joseph, the woman was a trial.

"What happened with Garrett?" Maddy refused to play along.

Willabelle pouted. "Do you have any idea what it's like at a silver mine?"

"Muddy, I'm guessing, by the state of some of those dresses in your trunk," Junebug mused.

"Like a pig wallow." Willabelle turned on Junebug. "I wouldn't have had to know anything about the horrid place, if it hadn't been for you. You told me that old tramp was Kit McBride!"

"No, I didn't," Junebug said serenely. "I merely didn't correct your assumption." She shrugged. "He's practically part of the family, so it ain't a lie."

"It's a *complete* lie!" Willabelle disagreed, folding her arms.

Junebug dug at the corset, which was cutting off her circulation. "You're one to talk of lies. You said you were coming up to be my wife and then you go chasing after that old silver miner." She thrust herself in front of Maddy. "Can you get me out of this thing before it kills me dead?" She still had the bonnet on and was enjoying the way the feather bounced when she spoke.

"*Your* wife?"

"Junebug was the one who wrote the ads," Maddy told her shortly as she unknotted the laces of the corset. "Kit didn't know you were coming."

"Well, that explains that, then."

"What?"

"His complete lack of interest in me! I swear, I've never met a ruder man in all my life."

Maddy's heart skipped.

"Kit ain't rude," Junebug defended him hotly. "He's just discerning! Not like the rest of them idiots." She glared at Willabelle. "And you're to keep your goshawk talons off them too. I don't want you for a sister. I'd rather live with a wolverine than live with you."

Maddy managed to suppress a giggle. Willabelle looked outraged.

"As if I'd want to live in this hick town anyway," Willabelle snapped. "It's not even a proper town! Can you imagine *me*, living here?"

"No," Maddy and Junebug said at once.

Merle whined, peering out from under the bed.

"Even her dog don't like her," Junebug said to Maddy as she leaned down to peer at Merle.

"I can hear you, you know," Willabelle sniffed. "I'm right here."

"Not for long, I hope."

"Only for so long as it takes to find the train fare out," Willabelle said tightly.

"I'll give you the damn money," Junebug said brightly. "How far away can you go? I ain't stingy."

As she listened to them bicker, all Maddy's fears, all those doom-laden thoughts that had her crying all afternoon, evaporated.

"I know we've had our differences, Madeleine," Willabelle said, "but I still need a housekeeper. My offer stands. You're welcome to come with me."

Maddy couldn't believe the nerve of the woman. She hadn't paid Maddy a red cent.

"I ain't paying for *her*!" Junebug disagreed. "I want to keep her."

Maddy looked Willabelle square in the eye. "You're serious?"

Willabelle's china-blue eyes were guileless. "You were always a very good maid."

"Willabelle," Maddy said sweetly. "Go to hell."

Twenty-Two

Kit had no desire to be cooped up in the trading post with all those bodies for the duration of the next storm. He took himself off to his forge. He'd work through the next blow. It would save him from his thoughts.

Sparks. As he stoked up the forge, he noticed the embers, sparkling red and orange in the darkness. What nonsense had Bill been talking back on the porch?

Don't waste the sparks.

The wind was shuddering the rough planking of his forge. It was cold in here but wouldn't be for long. He stripped his shirt off and got to work. Kit felt himself settle as he worked. He never felt lonely in the forge. The shimmering heat, the clang of struck iron, the roar of the flames. It was the closest he felt to whole.

Except when he was kissing Maddy . . .

He'd not felt whole since Charlie left, he thought, grunting as he hammered. He still remembered the sickness in his gut when his twin had gone, haring after their no-account father, who'd left them all up here alone. They'd not heard from Charlie again. Kit had no idea if he was alive or dead. And the not knowing was a constant hole through the middle of him.

A hole that Maddy Mooney had slipped right into.

He pounded the iron on the anvil. He didn't hear the doors opening. He only noticed someone had come in when he felt the blast of frigid air.

"There you are." It was Morgan.

Kit paused to catch his breath. He plunged the worked iron into the cask of water. It steamed.

"I can't believe you left me there," Morgan complained, closing the doors behind him.

"Not snowing yet?"

"Nope. Just blowing. Inside and out. Hell, those trappers are a pack of windbags." Morgan took a seat and fussed in the pocket of his oilcloth slicker. "I found something," he said.

Kit wiped the sweat off his face.

"You remember that day Mrs. Lascalles . . . uh, I mean Maddy . . . hurt her leg? Remember I found that stack of letters in the pocket of that dress she was wearing?"

Of course he remembered. Kit remembered everything about Maddy. Every tiny detail. And who could forget finding a bunch of letters from a bride you didn't even know you had?

"Well, I missed one."

Kit froze. He wasn't sure he wanted to hear what Morgan had to say. He was sick to death of surprises.

Morgan was holding a letter. "It's addressed to you," he said. "I didn't open it."

"I don't want to read more of that Willabelle woman's drivel," Kit sighed.

"It ain't from her." Morgan turned the letter over and showed Kit the name scrawled on the back. "It's from Alice Champion."

Well, that wasn't at all what Kit expected. Gingerly, he took the letter off him. "Why would Alice be writing to me?"

Morgan shrugged. "I don't know, but she's the one who brought Maddy up here that day." He scowled at the memory, still pricked by the fact his solitude had been ruined. His life hadn't been calm since.

Not that it was before.

Kit opened the letter. He frowned as he read it.

"What's it say?" Morgan demanded, never one to be patient.

"She's vouching for her character," Kit said slowly. "She says she's a good girl, who's been poorly treated." He swore. "She really doesn't like Willabelle Lascalles. She said the woman hasn't paid Maddy since she arrived from Ireland. Has kept her impoverished and trapped."

"It's like something out of one of your books," Morgan said, once Kit had finished reading and had handed the letter over to him. "Ah hell, she was supposed to give us this when she got here." He swore a blue streak. "If she hadn't hurt her leg . . ."

Yes. If she hadn't hurt her leg . . .

Kit hated to think what would have happened if she hadn't gone down that rabbit hole. He might have lost her, before he ever found her.

"I charge twenty-five cents a page, and I require payment up front," Junebug said firmly.

"I don't have any money," Maddy admitted. She considered her options. "I'll do the laundry for you."

"Every week?"

"No, not every week."

"For two weeks?"

"Fine. For two weeks."

"Brilliant." Junebug laid out her ink and paper on the bench. Merle skidded over to join her on the floor.

"What's happening?" Willabelle poked her head down from the loft, where she'd taken up residence for the duration of the storm.

"I'm letter writing," Junebug told her.

"I don't want a letter," Maddy disagreed. Although, maybe later she'd get Junebug to write one to Mrs. Egan. But there was so much to tell. Maddy hated to think how much laundry *that* letter was going to cost her. "I want an advertisement."

"An advertisement!" Willabelle's curiosity was good and pricked now. "Are you looking for employment? Because I keep telling you I need a housekeeper!"

"No, I'm not looking for employment, and you can take your job and . . ."

Merle barked.

"You know it costs money to place an advertisement over forty words," Junebug told Maddy, "and you don't have any money."

"I'll take that under advisement," Maddy said dryly. "Now, do you want me to do that laundry, or not?"

"One advertisement, coming straight up." Junebug dipped her pen in the ink as Merle crawled into her lap. "Do you need help with the wording?"

No, she didn't. Maddy had it memorized by heart.

WANTED

Blacksmith, for an ex-housemaid looking to be a wife.
Must come with spirited younger sister, own town,
a pack of brothers and a couple of random trappers.
Must own a copy of *Vanity Fair*
and be able to make a good cup of tea.

"That seems a very specific advertisement," Junebug said, grinning.

"I'm quite particular," Maddy agreed.

"Where are you planning to send this? You know the *Matrimonial News* don't get delivered to Buck's Creek?"

"I thought I might deliver it myself," Maddy said.

Junebug nodded sagely.

"How?" Willabelle demanded, as usual a splash of cold water on things. "It's blowing a gale."

"Oh, shut up, you yappy old goshawk," Junebug said, wriggling with glee at the thought of an adventure. "As long as that old banshee don't get us, I reckon we can get to the forge without too much danger!"

"You can't leave me here alone!" Willabelle protested.

"You ain't alone, you got the Beast!"

But it turned out Merle didn't want to stay with her either; he scampered out after them as Maddy limped resolutely toward Kit's forge. The wind was tossing the trees, cracking branches and sending ice and snow gusting through the gray air. She had the advertisement tucked in her bodice, out of the weather.

Maddy was shuddering with cold by the time they reached the forge. Junebug struggled to get the doors open. When she did, the fierce orange firelight and heat blasted them.

"You could help me," Junebug scolded her brothers.

Morgan and Kit were gobsmacked to see them in the doorway. Kit was stripped half-naked, Maddy saw, shocked. He was slick with sweat, his muscles shining in the firelight. Black hair curled on his enormous chest, and down his stomach, which was ridged into a washboard of muscles. Jesus, Mary and Joseph, *look at him.*

And here she was, bedraggled from the wind and cold, her nose dripping and her teeth chattering.

"Maddy's got something to talk to you about." Junebug took up roost, ready for the show.

"Oh no you don't." Morgan wrapped an arm around her waist and lifted her bodily off the ground. "Let's give them some privacy."

"She needs a chaperone!" Junebug protested.

"No," Maddy blurted. "I don't. I'm fine on my own."

Junebug looked crestfallen as Morgan took her out into the cold and closed the doors behind them.

Maddy tried to collect herself. Surreptitiously she wiped her nose and tried to neaten her hair. Kit stood there, hands on his razor-sharp hip bones, staring at her.

He had every right to be mad, she reminded herself. Junebug and Maddy and Willabelle had careered through his peaceful life. He hadn't asked for any of this.

But she remembered his kindness after he'd knocked her into the mud puddle, the admiration in his eyes, the flowers he'd asked Mrs. Champion to deliver, the slow heaven of his kisses . . .

Oh hell. Do it fast, just like last time you had to tell him something.

"I wrote an advertisement," she blurted. His gaze followed her hand as she rummaged in her bodice for a scrap of paper.

"You wrote an advertisement?" he echoed. He was nonplussed.

He should try being here, where she was, looking at all that shining male flesh. That would show him what nonplussed felt like.

"Well, Junebug wrote it, but it's my ad," she said, freeing it from her cleavage. "I can't read it to you," she said bluntly, "because I can't read."

His black eyebrows shot up.

She flushed. "Not a word. I'm completely illiterate. The best I can do is sign a cross for my name, if I'm pushed to." She held the advertisement out. "But I've memorized it."

As he took it from her, she began reciting it.

There was silence after she finished. Her heart was pounding fit to break out of her rib cage and bounce around the forge. "Well?" she demanded.

"*Vanity Fair?*" he asked. Was that a twinkle? Oh goodness, please let that be a twinkle.

"I need to know how it ends," she said primly.

"And you can't read it yourself, because you can't read?"

"That's right." She drew a deep breath. "There's more you need to know. I've never been married," she told him, her nerves making her sound more aggressive than she meant to. "But I'm also not a virgin." She lifted her chin. "It's a long story, but one I'm happy to tell you." She paused. "Or really not that long. I got seduced by a man. He never meant me to be anything but a bit of sport. Not even serious sport, just something to pass the time. I was young, and stupid. No, not stupid. Just young." She pressed her lips together. "I don't feel shame about it, not anymore. If that bothers you, then I guess that's your problem." And hers, because she really wanted him. But she wasn't going to lie anymore.

Kit McBride stared at her for a good long moment. And then he pulled a piece of paper out of his pocket and handed it to her.

"What's this?"

"An advertisement," he said.

Maddy unfurled it and looked at the ink scratches on the page.

"Morgan helped me word it," he said nervously.

"I can't read it," she reminded him.

"That's all right. I know mine by heart too." He licked his lips and cleared his throat.

WANTED

Maddy Mooney, for the purposes of matrimony.
No other woman will do.
No other need apply.

Maddy couldn't decide if she was about to laugh or cry. Maybe both. Maybe a lot of both.

"You wrote an advertisement!" she laughed as the stupid tears started to tumble.

"I did." He took the page from her and folded it in half, his advertisement bent double over hers. "Do you think I'll get many takers?"

"Maybe."

"Maybe?" Kit stepped toward her.

"Probably."

"Probably?" He brushed her hair back from her face.

"At least one," Maddy sighed.

"But is it the right one?" He leaned close, until his forehead was touching hers.

"She has the right name. That's a start, right?"

"A good start," he agreed, tilting his head and kissing her.

Oh, kissing Kit McBride was better than a good start. It was the best start.

Maddy kissed him back, with every last bit of herself.

"I love you," he whispered against her lips.

"You forgot to put that in the advertisement."

"I'll put in a postscript."

Maddy laughed. "Don't bother, the idiot woman can't even read. You'll just have to keep telling her."

"Every day, for the rest of my life."

Maddy sighed. That sounded like a fine idea to her.

Twenty-Three

Junebug dipped her fountain pen in the inkpot and stared thoughtfully at her three unmarried brothers. Morgan was in chipper spirits, and not just because he'd overindulged at the wedding that afternoon. He was buoyant and had been for days. The idiot saw Kit's marriage as his ticket to freedom.

Junebug had overheard him talking to the others.

"Maddy's good for her; she'll be the sister Junebug never had. A mother almost."

Junebug knew Morgan; she knew *exactly* what he was thinking. He'd been itching to get out of Buck's Creek for years. He'd always said he was only waiting until Junebug was grown and then he'd be off . . .

Well, maybe now that Maddy was here, Morgan thought he could get out *before* Junebug was grown.

She tapped her pen against the page in front of her, making little black splotches.

Morgan, Beau and Jonah were sprawled in front of the trading post stove, all of them slightly liquored up. It had been a nice wedding. Nothing fancy, just the bunch of them and the new priest from Bitterroot, the one who was planning to build a church with colored-glass windows. They did it out on the trading post porch. Maddy the Not-a-Maid-Anymore had worn the forget-me-not-blue dress and the wonky old cardigan. It was too cold not to wear something over the dress, and she said she liked the cardigan, wonky holes and dropped stitches and all. There weren't any flowers in the depths of winter, so the bride held a bunch of dried herbs that Junebug had rustled up from inside the trading post. The bouquet was mostly crackly old bay leaves, but there were some spikes of rosemary mixed in.

Willabelle Lascalles had been one of the witnesses, dressed to high heaven, like she was at the wedding of the queen of England. She'd insisted Junebug wash Merle the Beast for the occasion, and he'd puffed up into a right little fur ball. Willabelle held him—she said he accessorized her dress well—and he spent the whole ceremony chewing on her fur muffler.

Morgan had stood by Kit's side through the ceremony, and Junebug had stood by Maddy's, holding the herbs when it was Maddy's turn to wriggle the ring onto Kit's finger. They'd got the rings from Fritz's mercantile; they were plain bands, nothing fancy.

Junebug had been thrilled about the whole day, at least until she'd overheard Morgan talking to the boys.

He was going to leave. She knew he was.

He was going to run off the way their pa had, the way Charlie had.

Junebug had watched Kit carry Maddy up to the cabin after the wedding, the two of them grinning like loons. Well, at least Kit wasn't going anywhere.

What she needed to do was to give Morgan more reasons to stay. To find a way to make him happy here in Buck's Creek, and to stop him from dreaming of happiness elsewhere . . .

Oh, it hurt her to the core to think *she* wasn't reason enough for him to stay. But she was a pragmatist. She could acknowledge the truth when she saw it. Morgan hated Buck's Creek and was marking time until the day he could ride out of here.

She needed him to stay, so she needed to give him a *reason* to stay. Something long term. She tapped the fountain pen against the page, thinking. Ordering Kit a wife had worked wonders for him, but Morgan wasn't Kit, obviously. He wasn't going to be quite as easy to get loved up. But if she found the right woman . . . if he fell in love, the way Kit had fallen for Maddy . . . well, then he'd be happy, wouldn't he? He'd *want* to stay. She just needed to find a woman who wanted to stay, too, here in Buck's Creek, surrounded by McBrides.

Resolved, Junebug put pen to paper.

WANTED

Wife for a bullheaded backwoodsman
with a surfeit of family.

Surfeit was a good word.

Junebug refreshed her ink. She had an awful lot to say about Morgan McBride. She only hoped she could afford an advertisement long enough to say it all.

ACKNOWLEDGMENTS

I would like to acknowledge the Blackfeet, Crow and Bitterroot Salish peoples of Montana and to pay my respects to their elders, past, present and emerging, and to recognize their spiritual connection to the country I write about in this book. I would also like to acknowledge that I write on the lands of the Kaurna people, lands never ceded, and to recognize that this Country is a place of powerful storytelling and knowledge. I pay my respects to elders, past, present and future. These lands are steeped in ways of storying and knowing that I recognize and respect—and I give thanks.

This is a book about brothers and sisters, and so who better to dedicate it to than my brother, G. I love you. You were my first friend—and the only person I know who laughs in their sleep. Also, the only person to fill a room with a foam Cloud City, and to pretend to be Jabba the Hutt on Saturday mornings . . . May the force be with you, bro.

I wrote this book in 2020 and 2021, during the age of COVID, and I would like to thank everyone in my life for their love and support. I am deeply grateful for my family, friends and community and I owe them more than they will ever know. Writing is a strange and lonely task, particularly so when you're a binge writer, as I am, and especially so when you're doing it during lockdowns. My family has always supported me in doing what I do, and I love them to the moon and back. Thank you, Jonny, for the million different ways you keep the ship afloat and going full steam ahead when I'm living in other worlds. And thank you, Kirby and Isla, for the shoulder rubs and coffees and kindnesses. Thanks to my parents for wisdom, architecture, landscaping and black humor at the necessary moments.

Thank you to Lynn Ward, Bronwyn Stuart and Victoria Purman for whisking me away to a writing retreat at Encounter Bay in the fortuitous window between COVID outbreaks, so I could redraft the book. Wine, beach walks, too much Haig's and cheese and more than a few laughs were the antidote to many ills.

Thanks also to Sean Williams and Alex Vickery-Howe, my fellow Word Docs. If you get a chance to listen to our podcast (available on Apple, Stitcher, Spotify and wherever you get your podcasts) you'll hear two very sweet guys entertain, challenge, tease and buoy me as I wrote this book.

As always, thanks to my postgrads, students and colleagues at Flinders University. Special shout-outs to the Creative Writing crew (Sean, Lisa and Alex the honorary); the Creative Arts peeps (Nat, Ali and the Unbound Collective, who are sublime; Julia, Nicholas, Tom and the Screen staff; the people past and present from Drama and Digi Media); Tully, Garry, Penny and the posse at the Assemblage Centre for Creative Arts; Stephen and Sandro and the Posthumanities Reading Group; and my postgrad Theory Reading Group. I love working with postgrads and students (there are too many of you to name) and I can't begin to tell you all how much you inspire me. I leave all supervision meetings, lectures and classes feeling energized and optimistic—thank you.

Thank you to the divine Ms. Sarah E. Younger. I am having *so much fun* working with you. You're a priceless sounding board, a tireless cheerleader, a whip when I need it, a calming presence when I'm hyper. I can't wait to see what we do next. And thank you to Clare Forster for taking me west in the first place. I will always be thankful.

Kristine, Mary and everyone at Berkley: it's been a blast, as always. I'm a freak for a good edit, and your edits are all good. Thanks for bringing Junebug and the boys to the world in style.

And lastly, to you, reader. The story doesn't even begin without you—thank you.

Keep reading for a special preview of
Amy Barry's next novel

MARRYING OFF MORGAN McBRIDE

Coming soon!

WANTED

Wife for a bullheaded backwoodsman
with a surfeit of family.
A secretly gumptious woman with a mind of her own and a
bit of backbone is required for wifely duties. Must be able to
soothe a fractious temper and not expect cosseting.
But he will mend your boots and give you unwanted advice.
And he has it in him to make you laugh—
mostly not on purpose.
Bad cooks need not apply.

Buck's Creek, Montana, 1887

Junebug drummed her fingers against the trading post counter.
She was perched up on the stool, watching the store while her
brothers were over in the meadow, building Kit and his new wife
a house. Junebug had been banned from the building site, which
was just plumb unfair. It wasn't her fault the doorframe got split.

Beau should never have left her in charge of it in the first place. He was nothing but a lazy no-good shirker. Still, Junebug didn't want to be out there in the soggy old meadow nohow, sweating up a stink while they all growled at each other. She was quite happy here, with her pot of coffee and her complaints book. She'd filled up two whole pages with complaints—*It makes me sick the way Beau flops out of work like a boneless rabbit; they got no right keeping me prisoner up here and not letting me off down to Bitterroot on my own—why, some gals are married by now and spitting out kids of their own, and I can't even go for a walk by my ownsome; if I have to do laundry when I don't want to, I don't see why Maddy gets out of it, just because Kit's all kicked in the head over her . . .*

Last year, Junebug had got the bright idea of ordering up a mail-order bride to help her with the chores. Hell, she had four enormous hungry men to look after up here—she needed help. And she *had* found a wife, after some trial and error . . .

Junebug remembered the first woman she'd hooked with her advertisement with no small measure of horror. Willabelle Lascalles had been the wrongest kind of woman possible for a Mc-Bride. Especially for Kit, Junebug's great big hulking blacksmith of a brother. Willabelle Lascalles had been like a china doll, all frilled and fancy, with pale pink kidskin boots not at all fit for the muddy mountain meadows of Buck's Creek. Worse, she was a *mean* china doll. The kind that wanted coddling. Or else.

Thank goodness Junebug had been able to head *that* off. She didn't need a china doll. She needed a cook. And someone who could deal with the caterpillars who kept infesting the vegetable patch. And maybe someone to do the laundry too . . .

She'd thought she'd found her answer in Willabelle's maid. A maid was *perfect*. And Kit had been good enough to fall in love with her and everything. It should have solved all her problems. Junebug scowled at the ink-scratched pages of her complaints book. But, in actual fact, things were worse than ever. It turned out Maddy the Maid could only cook colcannon mash and pandy—and Junebug was sick to death of potatoes in all their mash, as were her brothers. Which meant Junebug was stuck back in the cookhouse, cooking for them all. And she *hated* cooking. Almost as much as she hated laundry. Which she still had to do, because Kit had declared that he and Maddy were setting up house and Maddy was only responsible for the two of them. Ugh. Which left three whole brothers Junebug had to launder for.

And then there was the problem of Morgan . . .

Damn Morgan. The blockiest, bullheadedest brother of all. No one beat Morgan for stubbornness, or bossiness, or flat-out infuriating contrariness. He acted like he owned the world. Or at least this patch of it. Junebug bet he even bossed her around in his dreams.

But as irritating as he was, she loved him. And he was making noises about leaving again, which gave Junebug an awful feeling in her stomach. A swampy feeling, like things were crawling away down there. Lately he'd been poring over catalogs again, dog-earing the pages that advertised new saddles and tack. She knew Morgan pined for his days as a cowhand, for the time before he got burdened with his orphaned siblings. When he told stories about being a cowboy, his voice got a dreamy tone that was so out of character that it sent chills down her spine. Since when did *Morgan* talk that way about an orange sunset, and the way it cut through trails of dust, glittering with gold? Or the way the mountains rose blue and violet on the horizon, like a dream of what was coming? This was *Morgan*. Who had as much poetry in him as a cook pot.

But now that Kit was hitched, and there was a woman on the scene to mother Junebug, Morgan was getting all poetic. And he seemed to think he could saddle up and head back out running cattle, leaving Junebug behind to cook for everyone and to launder Beau's and Jonah's pestiferous underthings. Junebug didn't like it. Not one bit.

It didn't matter how many times Junebug hid or destroyed the catalogs, he always seemed to get his hands on more. It made Junebug sick how much he pined to leave her. They had a good life here in Buck's Creek. Look at the place! It was goddamn *picturesque.*

Through the open door of the trading post, Junebug could see the creek (which was really more of a river) tumbling by, silvery in the sunshine. The thick meadow grasses were spring green and feathered with larkspur and balsamroot, and the chokecherry was waving wands of white blossoms. The blue, blue mountain sky was fluffed with clouds so white they looked like new snow and the air was pine fresh and carrying the smell of sap and bloom. What more goddamn poetry could he want?

And aside from all the bucolic waxing on about the mountains, wasn't *she* enough?

Morgan had been a parent to her—a bossy, griping, captious parent, to be sure, but he had been *there.* He was constant, as solid as the ancient gray rock of the mountains, predictable and sure. Morgan just *was*, and Junebug felt something very like raw panic at the thought of him leaving. Hell, she'd lost a mother and a father, her brother Charlie and a bunch of sisters—did she have to lose Morgan too?

He seemed to think she didn't need him anymore. Which was just plain wrongheaded. But so much of Morgan was wrongheaded. It was in his nature.

Junebug was scrawling angrily in her complaints book about that exact topic—*Why in hell won't Morgan let me take the train to Butte? Thunderhead Bill says they got a saloon with dancing girls, on a real stage and everything. Morgan says dancing girls ain't no sight for a kid like me, which is the dumbest thing I ever heard; surely the whole point of a dancing girl is to be looked at?*—when Purdy Joe came by with the mail.

Purdy Joe was new to these parts. He was a broad-faced Midwesterner from somewhere down on the plains; he had wheat-colored bangs and a big gap between his two front teeth. His name was Jensen or Hanson, or something along those lines, but all anyone ever called him was Purdy Joe. He was up in the Elkhorns prospecting for silver and he was bright with expectation, like a kid on the hunt for candy. Beau and Jonah were prone to button-holing him to ask about the prospecting—those two idiots had a mind to go looking for silver themselves. Purdy Joe had got familiar enough with them that he volunteered to run the mail up from Bitterroot to Buck's Creek whenever he was passing through, to save the McBrides a trip.

Bitterroot was four hours down the mountain and was shaping up to be a proper town. It had the post office, the rail spur, a mercantile, a hotel, a saloon, a cathouse and now a butcher shop (well, it was a tent more than a shop), run by a man named Hicks, who had arrived on the train and decided that the miners would probably spend their coins on beefsteak. He wasn't wrong. As far as Junebug could see, miners liked spending their money on pretty much everything.

Up here in Buck's Creek, in the high mountain meadows, there wasn't any butcher, tented or otherwise; there was only the trading post and Kit's forge. Junebug didn't see that it was ever going to be much of a town—it certainly wasn't getting the railway, not up a mountain this steep. Junebug thought it would be fine to have a railway station on your doorstep. Why, just think. You could hop aboard and go just about anywhere. Butte, for starters. But there was also Billings, Miles City, Bismarck . . . and places she'd only read about in past-date newspapers. Places like Iron County, Missouri, or Wichita, Kansas. There was a whole world down that mountain.

But mostly Junebug would settle for heading down the hill to Bitterroot, the biggest town she'd yet seen. So Junebug was of two minds about Purdy Joe's kindness in bringing the mail up from

Bitterroot. She *liked* going down to get the mail. It was a whole day away from the sound of pounding hammers and grumpy brothers. And she could go visiting, gathering up town gossip and letting people ply her with coffee and (if she was lucky) cake. Purdy Joe was depriving her of all that, keeping her stuck in the trading post or the cookhouse, where there wasn't any cake, unless she made it herself. And she hated baking with a passion. Especially since she'd blown up the last cookhouse.

She also wasn't keen on Purdy Joe handling their mail. It was too risky. What if he found out about her secret mail-order bride business? She'd got in enough trouble over it last time. And this time would be worse, because this time she was bride hunting for Morgan. Who, let's face it, was the front-runner in the grumpy-brother stakes.

Still. Even if she was conflicted about him bringing the mail, at least Purdy Joe was company. Might as well look on the bright side.

"Mail for you, Junebug!" Purdy Joe stuck his head in the door and held out the pitiful handful of mail. It was only a single letter and one of Morgan's cursed catalogs.

Junebug slid off her stool. Purdy Joe knew not to go in the trading post while Junebug was there alone, so he didn't take so much as a step beyond the porch. It was annoying. Junebug's brothers were big, and they could get mean if anyone got too close to her. Which was dumb as a bag of hammers, since they kept leaving her to mind the trading post. How in hell was anyone supposed to trade if they couldn't come inside when she was here? Spit, her brothers were blockheads.

Purdy Joe grinned as she took the catalog and the tattered splat of an envelope from him. "Who you been writing to, Junebug? You got a suitor?" He wasn't in the slightest bit serious. People always underestimated her that way. It was 'cause she looked like a mite of a thing in these old overalls. But she could get a suitor if she wanted to, she was sure of it. She could do anything.

So long as her brothers kept out of the way.

"Ha. Sure," Junebug played along, glad of the conversation. "The only way I'm getting courted is from a great distance." Junebug liked the prospector. He was young and cheery, and he minded his own business. The suitor line was just a throwaway comment. He had no desire to stick his beak into her letter. Not like Thunderhead Bill or old Roy—if they'd brought the mail up, they would have pestered her mercilessly, until her brothers got wind of what she was up to. She was glad they were off with Sour Eagle on one of their long hunts, so she could get on with finding a wife without them meddling. Even if she did miss them a little . . .

"You want some coffee, Purd?" Junebug offered. She'd not spoken to anyone but her kin in days and Purdy Joe was a novelty. If she couldn't go visiting in Bitterroot, at the very least she could play host to Purdy. She bet he was full of good stories.

"Best not," Purdy Joe said, backing away from her once she'd taken the crumpled envelope from his hand. He gave her a rueful smile and jerked his chin in the direction of the din in the meadow. "I got no mind to tangle with Morgan." He just about tipped his hat as he said goodbye, straining to be as polite and proper as could be.

Spit. Her brothers ruined everything. Now she couldn't even talk to a damn prospector without him turning tail and running for the hills. She scowled as she watched Purdy Joe head across the meadow to the raw timber frame, which was starting to resemble a house. Seriously? He'd visit with *them* but not with her? It just wasn't fair.

She needed a new wife *now*. There were too many men up here by half. Once she'd watered them down with a couple more women, things were bound to improve . . . *surely?*

Junebug looked down at the catalog and the envelope.

And if she got Morgan the *right kind* of wife, one he could get all kicked in the head over, the way Kit was over Maddy, then he would stop this talk of leaving, wouldn't he? And he'd stop ordering these stupid catalogs.

Junebug rolled up the catalog and tucked it under her arm. She'd burn the damn thing before she'd ever give it to him. She considered the letter. Lucky she'd been here when Purdy Joe came by; somehow, she'd managed to keep her bride hunting a secret the whole season long. She had an excuse prepared, should her brothers ever get suspicious about the mail she received (because who the hell ever wrote to Junebug): she was going to tell them it was all part of her letter-writing business. They'd ask questions, because they liked to inquisition her, but she had a handful of decent answers up her sleeve, so she wasn't too afeared. But she might also just tell them to get their beaks out of her business.

Sometimes she whiled away a good couple of hours having imaginary shouting matches with Morgan over these letters. She sighed. It was a crying shame to waste all that good material.

This letter wasn't making a great first impression, she mused as she turned the envelope over. Postmarked Nebraska, it was a travel-stained splat of a thing. She didn't have much hope as she opened it. She'd advertised for a mail-order bride for her brother Morgan months ago, and none of the responses had yielded the right kind of wife. It wasn't that there weren't takers; there were. There were passels of women looking for men, and in particular men with a patch of land to work. There were widows and spinsters, women of means and women of none, tall women, short women, stout women, thin women, women who wrote with charm and others who could barely write at all. They promised fidelity and loyalty, labor and love, honesty and hardiness. But they were all just too . . . well, *girly*.

While she needed a woman with wiles, and a measure of feminine charm (to achieve the kicked-in-the-head bewitchment), she also needed a worker, and one with a stern backbone. Junebug didn't like the simpering some of these brides were prone to in their epistolary endeavors. Simpering never got you anywhere with a McBride man. You needed the capacity for combat.

The letter itself was hefty, Junebug noted as she pulled it from its sleeve. The woman had covered both sides of more than a few pages. She was the wordy sort, that was for sure. Junebug counted that in her favor. She was starved for conversation up here. Her brothers were prone to doing little more than grunting at her. When they weren't bossing or complaining, that was.

To whom it may concern, the letter began, all formal and stiff-like. *I never pictured myself the type to be answering an advertisement like this . . .*

They all said that. Why, Junebug didn't know. Hell, she wanted them to answer the ad, didn't she? Or she wouldn't have placed it. So why did they all act like answering an ad was a bad thing?

At least this one was more direct than most when she finally got past the "I'm not the type" coyness. *You've done the courtesy of being honest in your advertisement, which my Granny Colefax says is an admirable quality, as most men are arrant liars.*

Arrant. That was a good word. Junebug would look that up in the dictionary next time she stole it from Kit's trunk of books. Still reading, she wandered back inside to collect a fresh cup of coffee. Then she settled in on the porch of the trading post to ponder this woman.

Since we're founding this correspondence on the promise of honesty—

Junebug pulled a face. Well, sort of. The ad in the *Matrimonial News* had been honest enough about Morgan, it just wasn't honest about who had placed it. The words *surfeit of family* were the only suggestion of Junebug's existence.

I shall tell you my qualities plain, Miss Nebraska promised.

Junebug rolled her eyes. This was where they waxed lyrical about their charms or the contents of their glory boxes. Most of which were completely useless to Junebug. What did she need with a good soprano voice or a wholecloth quilt? Let's hope Miss Nebraska included pies and cakes in her list of qualities . . .

I'm a tall woman, and strong. No one has ever labeled me beautiful, but I'm not homely neither. I always wished I looked like my sister Naomi, who is pretty as a picture, but my mother says it's not right to wish for what we don't have and that at least I don't have to fight the sin of vanity, like Naomi does. So, I'll tell you that I'm well-formed and not vain, and grateful for both.

This Naomi sounded like she might be a woman in Willabelle's vein. Junebug felt a stab of sympathy for Miss Nebraska, and then she flicked to the end of the sheaf of pages, looking for her name. *Miss Epiphany Hopgood.*

Epiphany. Hell, that was a name and a half. Junebug had a vague memory of the word. It was akin to getting hit on the head hard with an idea, she thought.

Promising.

I'm hardy and not prone to illness and, forgive the bluntness, according to Granny Colefax I'm built for bearing children.

Children. Let's not rush things. Junebug felt an irrational flare of jealousy. Of course marriage led to children, but not yet . . . she wasn't ready for Morgan to be parenting anyone but her.

I've all the necessary skills of housekeeping, including cooking, which I note is one of your necessary requirements.

This was getting good. Junebug sat up straighter.

My specialties . . .

Lord, she had specialties! That's what Junebug needed.

. . . include corn fritters, cornbread, sweet and salty roast corn . . .

They must have a lot of corn in Nebraska.

. . . pork chops, ham steaks, fried chicken—regular and southern style . . .

Junebug had no idea what Southerners did to chicken, but she was willing to give it a try.

. . . also southern fried catfish, and fish pie, although I do believe nothing beats throwing a bass or a walleye straight from the stream into a skillet of butter and frying it nice and simple.

Junebug wouldn't complain about simple fried fish, so long as she wasn't the one doing the frying.

I will confess to a sweet tooth and so also make more than my share of desserts. I'm not sure if you consider this an asset or a failing of character (my mother declares it the latter, as she is not one for self-indulgence and she says I am profligate with sugar).

Definitely an asset, Junebug thought fervently. This woman was the answer to her prayers! Her mouth watered as she read the list of sweets, which Miss Epiphany Hopgood couldn't seem to stop herself from adding (even though her mother would disapprove).

Fried apples with fine sugar, gooseberry pie, honey cake, molasses pie, milk pudding and of course the usual range of cakes.

The usual range of cakes! Like cakes were *usual!*

Junebug's heart was skipping a jig in her chest. She'd found her wife!

I can keep a thriving kitchen garden and own my own cow and half a dozen chickens. These were left to me by my Granny Hopgood, who hoped a milk cow and some brooders might help my marriage chances.

Junebug could care less about another cow—she had her own to milk. And as for chickens, she had enough of those too. But *cakes!*

Lord, she'd done it. She'd found the needle in the haystack here. She'd best gather up the chokecherries this season, so the woman could bake up a pie as soon as she got here.

Junebug headed back to the desk and reached for her writing paper. It was only as she pulled her inkpot toward her that she remembered she had a problem.

Morgan.

Two problems.

Telling Morgan. And then introducing him to the woman—and not having her turn straight back around and run home.

He just wasn't an easy man to off-load. Listen to him out there, cursing a blue streak through the mellow afternoon. The man was too fractious by half. Junebug took note of some new words, planning to look them up in the dictionary, when she looked up *arrant*.

She'd been as honest as she could be in the ad, because she sure didn't want to sell some poor unsuspecting woman a false bill of goods. These potential brides needed to know he was an ornery old cuss, stubborn as hell and not prone to niceties.

I think patience is the best virtue, don't you? Miss Epiphany Hopgood wrote, a little shyly, Junebug thought. Shyness wasn't ideal. *It's hard-won, but really the only thing that keeps harmony. I confess I have to wrestle hard with myself to practice it, but I win more often than not; I have trained myself to be a patient person.*

Well, that was good, wasn't it? Morgan would try the patience of a saint, so the woman would need a dose of patience. And the notion of wrestling was also helpful. It implied a warrior spirit, as Sour Eagle would say.

Over yonder, there was a great crashing and a bellow loud enough to shake the oilcloth over the trading post windows. Then a whole bunch of new words. Absently, Junebug scrawled them down, so she wouldn't forget to look up what they meant.

I will caution you, Mr. McBride, I am not always an easy woman. But I will endeavor to do everything in my power to make you a house you'll be happy to come home to.

Junebug chewed on the tip of her fountain pen as she stared at the catalog, which she'd dropped on the counter. Forget happy to come home to, she wanted him to *stay put*.

Not an easy woman, huh?

Junebug listened to the invectives Morgan was shouting out in the meadow. You know, that might be just the thing. He wasn't an easy man, so why would he need an easy woman? A difficult woman with a dose of patience and a steady output of cakes might be just the thing.

For all of them.

Dear Miss Hopgood, Junebug wrote, coming to a firm decision. *I'm glad you answered my advertisement. Your letter was a breath of fresh air after the mail I've received from of a slew of ninnyhammers. I appreciate your honest talk . . .*

Especially about the desserts . . .

. . . and I hope you took my plain speaking serious. I am about as difficult a man as you could find, so your patience will come in mighty handy.

Junebug found herself whistling as she filled two pages with Morgan's honest faults. And then another two with praises for her talk of pies.

This time she was sure the mail-order bride thing would work perfectly.

Outside, there was mayhem as the roof came down. But in here, everything was just dandy.